This intelligent debut novel, drawing its inspirat
Land, is a confessional tale of love, loss, fragme
it is skilfully interwoven with enough sardonic wit and popular culture to make it a most engaging read with a powerful philosophical punch.

Julian Fellowes, creator of Downton Abbey

The intensity of misplaced love, bad timing, the devastation of loss, and then understanding – which comes, alas, too late – all of these will strike a chord with many people. For all its serious themes, there is a lot of wry observational humour in this moving literary novel.

Richard Morrison, Chief Culture Writer, The Times

Few female writers can pull off a convincing male narrator; Janet Taylor does it in spades. A paean to the power of memory and lost love.

Sophia Myles, actress

The Unpredictability Of Frogs

Janet Taylor

Amazon Kindle Direct Publishing
© Janet Taylor 2020
All rights reserved.

This book is dedicated to my husband, Paul and our three lovely sons,
Joe, Matt and Ben.
They are truly the best family anyone could wish for.
It is also for my dear parents, Jean and Stan and my sister, Jackie.
And for the many friends who hold a special place in my life.

Janet Taylor read English at Sheffield University and later trained as a copywriter at Watford Art College. However, most of her working life was spent as a teaching assistant and learning mentor in primary, middle and secondary schools working with some wonderful pupils.

She is married to Paul, a retired Archdeacon, and they have three grown-up sons. They have lived in London and Dorset and currently live in the Midlands.

She has enjoyed writing all her life and has written lyrics for school plays and an unpublished situation comedy. The Unpredictability of Frogs is her first novel.

Introduction
'The Unpredictability of Frogs' is primarily the story of one man's relationships. It focuses on a passionate affair that begins in the 1980s and traces the lasting impact of life choices and the way experiences resonate through the years. It explores how the past is always in the present and how apparently fragmented experiences actually form a whole.

Alistair narrates the story of his romance with Anna, a young student. As the novel progresses, his wild infatuation is challenged and as a consequence both Alistair and Anna experience great loss. He begins to write his story, believing he is writing about the past, but as he writes, his present life intrudes and the narrative of the past becomes inextricably intertwined with the present. Although often heart-rending, this story of finding love and losing it again also abounds with observational humour and a host of well-drawn characters, particularly strong female roles.

Thematically the novel draws on T S Eliot's, The Waste Land, reimagining and echoing some of its themes, particularly those of: dislocation; sterility; various aspects of sexuality; the experiences and roles of women; religious uncertainty; the impact of high and low culture; and the overall confusion of trying to make sense of the world and our fragmented experience. The novel incorporates short extracts, quotes, and references from literary works, reflecting Eliot's own use of classical texts and modern culture; it also speaks of Alistair's love of literature and its resonance in his life.

The chapter titles are drawn from The Waste Land, seeking to reimagine the themes of the poem through fiction. The epigraph, 'And I Tiresias have foresuffered all/Enacted on this same divan or bed', is taken directly from the poem. Eliot uses, Tiresias, a blind prophet of Apollo in Thebes, famous for clairvoyance and for being transformed into a woman for seven years, as a character who understands the emotional and sexual suffering of both men and women. This reflects one of the novel's aims to explore a range of male and female sexual experience from the spiritual, to the empty, to the ridiculous.

The novel can be read and enjoyed without any knowledge of The Waste Land. However, reading The Waste Land and exploring some of the other texts quoted or referenced may add to your enjoyment.

There is a list of quoted and referenced works at the back of this book, which you might find helpful.

Contents

Prologue: October 1981: The Burial of the Dead 10
Chapter One: September 1980: spring rain 12
Chapter Two: October 1981: a handful of dust 19
Chapter Three: October 1980: a game of chess 24
Chapter Four: October 1980: The Hanged Man 33
Chapter Five: October 1980: when lovely woman stoops to folly... 37
Chapter Six: 'good night, sweet ladies' 46
Chapter Seven: the human engine waits 55
Chapter Eight: a straight look 65
Chapter Nine: waiting for a knock upon the door 71
Chapter Ten: a record on the gramophone 74
Chapter Eleven: the expected guest 86
Chapter Twelve: cigarette ends 91
Chapter Thirteen: If you don't like it you can get on with it 99
Chapter Fourteen: Elizabeth and Leicester 103
Chapter Fifteen: the brown fog 109
Chapter Sixteen: indifference 115
Chapter Seventeen: the marble 126
Chapter Eighteen: You *are* a proper fool 131
Chapter Nineteen: I sat down and wept 138
Chapter Twenty: the lowest of the dead 143
Chapter Twenty one: her hair spread out in fiery points 144
Chapter Twenty-two: It's them pills I took 157
Chapter Twenty-three: We who were living are now dying 166
Chapter Twenty-four: HURRY UP PLEASE IT'S TIME 173
Chapter Twenty-five: While I was fishing in the dull canal 180
Chapter Twenty-six: April is the cruellest month 192

Chapter Twenty-seven: The nymphs are departed 195
Chapter Twenty-eight: My nerves are bad tonight 199
Chapter Twenty-nine: a pocket full of currants 210
Chapter Thirty: What you get married for if you don't want children? 222
Chapter Thirty-one: The time is now propitious 226
Chapter Thirty-two: a burnished throne 234
Chapter Thirty-three: Speak to me 253
Chapter Thirty-four: Wo weilest du? 258
Chapter Thirty-five: Summer surprised us 264
Chapter Thirty-six: And I Tiresias have foresuffered all 283
Chapter Thirty-seven: The shouting and the crying 288
Chapter Thirty-eight: After the agony 296
Chapter Thirty-nine: bats with baby faces 305
Chapter Forty: Entering the whirlpool 321
Chapter Forty-one: under the shadow of this red rock 331
Chapter Forty-two: each in his prison 335
Chapter Forty-three: yet there the nightingale 339
Chapter Forty-four: September 1983: "a new start" 348
Chapter Forty-five: the wisest woman in Europe 349
Chapter Forty-six: among the mountains 351
Chapter Forty-seven: The sea was calm 353
Chapter Forty-eight: Shantih shantih shantih 357

> **And I Tiresias have foresuffered all**
> **Enacted on this same divan or bed...**
> *The Waste Land* T.S. Eliot

Prologue: October 1981: The Burial of the Dead

At some moment in my past, I had simply gone to sleep and ceased to live. When I finally awoke, I was surprised to find myself gazing through the bewildered eyes of a middle-aged man.

The world I once knew had changed... colours were muted almost to shades of grey, sound blanketed to a distant rumble, and my body numb to all feeling... but emptiness.

Life had become an aching disappointment. The promising overture of my youth, my much-anticipated grand opera, had rapidly lost its way, drowned by a mumbling cacophony. And here I was, spiralling helplessly towards the final groove in this dull recording at a relentless $33\frac{1}{3}$ rpm. All that remained was the waiting: the anticipation of the soft click, click, click of the needle in perpetual orbit, a fading heartbeat...the last noise ever heard. Then, there would be nothing, but pure unadulterated oblivion: a silent shrieking in an empty waste.

You could perhaps say I was mildly depressed.

This profound insight had been arrived at some eighteen months ago while in the pub, when I'd overheard a student quizzing his companions with the most pertinent of questions:

'If your life was a drink,' he had burbled loudly, 'what sort of drink would it be?' His fellow drinkers' answers varied from the good, 'a vintage Dom Pérignon', to the bad, 'Pineapple Cresta', to the ugly, 'a pint of lukewarm goblin's piss'. Although it was a stupid game, having been posed the query, I felt compelled to answer silently in my head. My life. My life as a drink? At first, the only image that came to mind was tepid tap water: colourless, tasteless, odourless...drank without pleasure, purely perfunctory; something to be got through out of necessity. No, no, too awful. I allowed myself a second chance...only this time, the real spectre appeared – an empty glass – an absent life, leaving me with a thirst which would never be slaked by the flow of arid air and powdery dust poured continuously down my throat. I acknowledged I had not really lived my life. It was as if I was never really quite there, so much of it just a confusing montage, peered at through a vast, cloudy dust storm. Something was missing…but what? Indeed, my life had all the charm of a rather disappointing holiday, initially embarked upon with giddy expectation, and now, to my regret, I realised I had spent my entire fortnight sat in my hotel room, futilely dialling for a room service that did not exist. Somewhere, just beyond the view from my hotel room window, I am vaguely aware of the sound of laughter, the splashing of a fountain, church bells clanging through the still, warm air - somewhere, a life of intense colour. I know it's there somewhere, but how to find it? In desperation, I pick up the phone and dial rapidly. As usual, no one answers. Soon it will be time to return home. Perhaps I shouldn't have left that 'Do Not Disturb: Sleeping' sign on my door.

In fact, there were endless metaphors, but only one conclusion: *I was much further out than you thought / And not waving but drowning.* Yes, I see it now. I was indeed *'Not Waving but Drowning.'* Drowning. Drowning in my own dust. And nobody heard me.
But all of this was before...

This is the story of how I smashed through my second-hand existence, and lived with an intensity of such brilliance that it both opened my eyes and blinded me in an instant. So now, let us return to the beginning, to the past, where everything that has happened was set in motion, where all the dice were rolled. There will be no surprises for me along the way – only a past which is set, mistakes already made – a life already lived. For in a strange way, only the past is real to me, all other times seem illusory. The only reality is the eternally present moment of past time.

Before we go any further, let us stop for a moment... look down and see beneath our feet, the path we trod...the path we tread. All I have laid before you: *'I have spread my dreams under your feet; Tread softly because you tread on my dreams.'* Tread softly…yes…very softly. For these dreams are shattered and broken. Though they dazzle the eyes with an array of glittering fiery shafts of light, remember, you are walking on shards and slivers, and the crunching, cracking sound can fracture the heart. So, tread softly – you may not know it yet, but our feet are bare, and these fragments, believe me, can pierce the flesh to the bone.

Chapter One: **September 1980: spring rain**

It is said that grief is the price we pay for love. And I suppose on more than one occasion I believed myself to be 'in love' even with Marion, my wife, 'once upon a time.' Every element necessary seemed in perfect alignment: our mutual admiration; occasional laughter; I'd felt relaxed, happy, even elated – once. But, never vulnerable; never had her existence upon this earth mattered more to me than my own. Surely, with 'real' love, all those joys are present, but in addition, one has to live with a sort of dread, a fear...a dark swirling mass of emotion – the terror of losing the one you love. It is then, and only then, the terrible deal has been struck. And the price, the debt, is waiting to be paid: grief, hunched solemnly in the shadows with barbed arms outstretched, patiently marking time... aching to embrace you.

Anna. Anna. The worst of it is, it was all my fault really. She played her part of course, but in truth I was to blame. I shaped our destinies with stupid, clumsy hands. I would imagine, for the time being, her view was that ours was a relationship that could be chalked up as one of the many 'also rans' of her love life, which I can safely presume will be rich and varied. Yes, grief is the price we pay for love. And the pain is truly visceral.

So, let us return to the beginning.... My work as an English lecturer bored me; one of my closest friends and colleagues had died horribly of a particularly ferocious cancer, which had swept through his body like a bushfire; and the only reason Marion and I stayed together was that neither of us could be bothered to move house. Actually, each of us felt the onus on moving out lay with the other, and so we were locked in an inert stalemate. (And, yes, I do mean to tautologise and say the same thing twice.) We were indeed each other's 'stale-mate'. Living quite separate lives, even with our own bedrooms, but we'd meet at various points in the week to exchange a few musty 'unpleasantries' with one another. To quote my wife during one moment of drunken inspiration, we were like: 'two shits that pass in the night'. Marion has a rather lovely way with words, don't you think? What a skill she is blessed with, always able to elevate things to the next level. Funny to think of our home as a fetid sewer in which we bobbed around lost and generally indifferent ...each harbouring a deep foulness within our souls.

And then, just as it was all becoming too unbearable, and I began to understand why those who suffer often embrace death with such alarming ease – she arrived. It was on the very first morning of the autumn term, and even before I had laid eyes upon her, some sixth sense must have been at work. Having decided to walk to the University via the park, unusually for me, my spirits were lifted by the weary late September sunshine filtering through the organza mist. Dew transformed the grass into a dazzling swathe of tiny crystals, while beaded cobwebs, like discarded diamond necklaces, trembled in the bushes. Several ducks, waddling in an ungainly manner, descended the bank and plopped into the lake; its greenish brown surface rippled in a maze of concentric circles around a half-sunken shopping trolley. The strange, extraordinary beauty of everything seemed to fill my body with a wonder forgotten for months, even years. Approaching the department, this strange sense of happiness, this unfamiliar feeling of being more at one with the world, grew. Now, looking back, I must have subconsciously anticipated my life was about to change forever, that my whole being was being prepared for an epiphany.

I attempted to come through the double doors, just as a girl from one of my old tutorial groups was coming out. Backing to let her through, she beamed her fat smile. 'Tamsin! Gosh, you do look well. How was your summer?' Unfortunately, she suffered from quite a severe lisp, although I have to say, this never seemed to undermine her confidence, which was more than ample, as indeed was her figure. 'Bellissimo! Bellissimo!' She enthused in a silly giddy voice. 'Ah, yes, you went to Florence if I remember rightly. It is truly breathtaking, isn't it?'

'Well, it certainly was for me.' A little shimmy trembled through her entire body. She grinned broadly, resembling a benign and somewhat cheerful salamander. Leaning forward, her breath pink and fruity from bubble-gum, she whispered, 'Italian men are simply divine, and they adore English roses!' She framed her face with her pudgy fingers.

Giving an exaggerated shrug, I said, 'What's a girl to do?' – a ripple of flesh and laughter. A few moments later, I asked what she'd thought of the Uffizi Gallery and Santa Maria del Fiore. She rolled her eyes heavenward and explained she just simply hadn't had time – 'Old churches aren't really my thing. Maybe next time.' She bounced eagerly down the steps off to her next adventure. Oh, the joy of youth. Finally, through the doorway, I allowed myself

a wry smile – when without warning – the moment when it all began – began. And I was: *'Looking into the heart of the light...'*
A group of three girls were scanning the notice board. It seems so extraordinary, but I 'knew' even before she turned around. Something in her posture, the cascade of dark hair falling down her back, the shape of her body beneath her jeans...it was like standing behind someone you'd always known, and usually you'd just say their name and they'd turn and smile. But I didn't know her name. She was a stranger to me. It was such a bizarre sensation; I was almost trembling. I needed to see her face, to fathom out why I felt so drawn to her. When I spoke, my voice sounded thin, lacking in confidence. 'Can I help any of you?' As they turned, I swear it is no exaggeration to say, I caught my breath, and my heart tumbled in my chest. Time ceased to exist. Her eyes held mine. It was the same feeling as if you had just come face to face with yourself. Not that she looked anything like me at all, but it was the same feeling of shock – recognising someone you had known all your life, but never actually met. And here she was.

An abrupt Yorkshire accent woke me up. 'Not unless you're Dr Iris Sate,' said the shortest and widest girl, looking me up and down. 'That's who I've got to see.' Barely losing eye contact with the beautiful girl, I witnessed now, for the first time, something which would always stir me, her eyes shone – dancing, radiating pleasure, amusement, a sexiness such as I had never seen before. We exchanged the briefest moment of understanding, and with my heart on fire, I turned to the diminutive Yorkshire lass, and surprisingly managed to speak.

'Well, I hope I'm clearly not – her office is upstairs, third on the right – but she won't be in yet. First day?'

'No, I've been here a week already, for 'Freshers.' But first day 'proper', I s'pose.'   With a wild hope in my heart, I asked who they were and if they were all studying English this year. 'Well, I'm Jane Waterhouse – duel wi' Ancient History,' beamed Nora Batty's understudy.

'Lorna, straight English,' croaked the thinnest of the three, almost performing a nervous curtsy, while trying to quietly and unsuccessfully clear her throat. 'And you?' In rapture, I held my breath, waiting for her to speak, to hear her voice, to know her name.

'Just English... and I'm Anna.' Her name, her voice, slid around my mind in spirals...around and around, dropping deeper and deeper into my consciousness. All eyes turned expectantly towards me. 'Oh, I'm sorry, I haven't introduced myself yet. I'm Alistair Johnson, on the staff here, English lecturer.' They continued to stare at me. 'Didn't I see any of you at interviews?' They shook their heads. Undeterred, I stumbled on crassly. 'Well, obviously I couldn't have done,'- a nervous laugh - 'because certainly I'd have remembered you three charming young ladies if I had.' Waterhouse almost winced with disbelief at my inept bumbling. I squirmed internally. Anna's eyes still laughed. (She knew, even then, she knew.) 'Well, I can say for a fact I've never clapped eyes on you before,' Waterhouse said forcefully. 'It were a woman interviewed me. Now what were 'er name?'

Anna spoke again.

'Was it, Ruth Collins? She interviewed me.'

(God, what a beautiful voice – say something else – please, say something else.)

'That were 'er! Ruth Collins. Tall woman wi' big glasses. Never thought I'd get a place mind. It were an awful interview. Didn't think she right took to me, like.'

'Oh, just testing your metal, I expect.' Smiling encouragingly, I diplomatically told them all that Ruth was an excellent tutor, and not anywhere nearly as fierce as she seemed in interviews. In a confiding tone, I shared that she was one of the best tutors to go to if they ever had any problems with student life. 'Can't cope with your work, your love life, your lack of love life,' – Lorna suddenly looked to the floor– 'or anything else for that matter,' I offered hastily. 'Anything, she'll sort you out.'

Jane Waterhouse snorted. 'Well, I for one weren't immediately struck by her overwhelming empathy. What is she then really, some kind of psychotherapist?'

Tempting as it was to say no, just a straightforward psycho, I managed to keep that thought at bay.

'More of a counsellor, apparently, she's very different in her tea and sympathy sessions. I guess it's all to do with techniques and skills one can be taught, I suppose. Interviewing and counselling, not exactly the same. Oh, no really, Ruth is surprisingly quite an expert with the tissue box. But let's hope none of you have to find out, eh?'

Everyone gave a polite laugh, although I experienced an unpleasant stirring of anxiety as I wondered if perhaps my comments had been less than professional. It was sometimes hard to conceal that Ruth and I had differing attitudes on many subjects close to my heart.

Making an exaggerated study of her watch, Lorna said, 'Gosh, it's quarter to ten already.' As much as I wanted to stay in Anna's presence, to marvel at her perfection, and enjoy the ecstatic thrill which gnawed through to the very marrow of my bones, I knew I had to get away, before I let my mask slip any further down my face. Increasingly agitated and nervy, my head was swimming with intoxicating emotion. Like a drunk, whose words and private thoughts slip and slide so easily off his tongue before he has the wherewithal to shut his mouth, I didn't trust my mouth not to actually say: 'My God, you're beautiful,' as the thought rushed at me again and again like the tide beating incessantly upon the shore. I needed time to gather myself, to think, to pause a moment.

'Goodness,' I exclaimed, 'quarter to ten. Well, I must get on. I hope I have the pleasure of having you sometime...um, in one of my tutorial groups or whatever.

They all grinned, although as I realised what I'd said, a blush threatened to expose me, and I caught that look in Anna's eyes once more. But still nobody moved as if gripped by a collective seizure. Lorna made one last successful effort to clear her throat; now vocally clear she thankfully rescued the embarrassing moment. 'Shall we lot go for a coffee?

'Yes, I'd love one,' said Anna, pushing her hair from her face– the most exquisite cheekbones, the soft skin of her neck– where already my mouth explored.

'There's a very nice coffee shop at the bottom of the hill, The Court Garden,' I said, trying to sound as casual as possible, as I backed down the corridor. 'It's just across the road, or there's a machine in the corner of that room to the left, although the coffee's pretty grim.'

'Ooo, I can't be doing with 'orrible coffee. As it's our first day, we'll treat ourselves t' coffee shop, shall we girls?' The Waterhouse strode towards the door. 'Ta'ra then, Mr Johnson!'

'We're not at school now," I laughed. "Please, feel free to call me Alistair.' However, my getaway was thwarted. Lorna slung a large duffel bag over her shoulder, pulling several notices off the notice board as she did so. Paper skated

16

in every direction, accompanied by a little pot of drawing pins, which had also been caught in the up thrust of Lorna's duffel, and after a brief flight, rained down upon the floor.

'Oh no!' she groaned, immediately flushing crimson.

'Don't worry,' Anna said kindly, bending down to pick them up. 'I'm always doing things like that.' (I bet you're not I thought, and my heart filled.) Immediately, I also began to enthusiastically gather scattered pins and strewn papers as if we were all engaged in some important team building exercise.

'Is that the lot?' I scanned the floor.

'Just this last one, I think,' said Anna, and dropped a red plastic drawing pin into my open hand. She didn't even touch me. But standing that close to her, my guts twisted with pleasure. For the first time since I'd laid eyes on her, I caught the scent of her. Every cell in my body expanded. My blood was rushing. Had she heard me catch my breath?

As they finally made it out of the door for their trip to the coffee shop, Anna turned and met my eyes. She knew I would be staring after her... holding on to every last second.

I hurried away, up the stairs to my study, where I sank into my chair totally dumbstruck. I had just fallen in love: the connection was palpable. And the sense of falling was literal, truly disorientating. I was in a chasm with unfathomable depths and still I fell; unable to ever climb out – to ever go back. I was free-falling. And I was frightened. But down I went ...the fear of it all the rush. Oh God, the thrill. Motionless in my chair, I held on tight. With the image of Anna in my mind, I fell and I fell. I am still falling now.

Yes, that was the start of it – a late September morning – when I slipped my skin, and a new life - a real life - began. Thinking back is the only way of feeling alive anymore. Now I exist, from day to day, remembering the sensation of living. Not dead, just recently extinguished; a dying fire, still glowing red, with white embers still hot, remembering what it was like to be ablaze. A gentle breeze, a soft breath of memory, is all it takes, and I glow in response. But I will never know the intensity and ferocity of real life again. That much I accept. Like the Anglo-Saxon's image of the sparrow flying through the mead hall, I had flown from the darkness of the night into the brightly lit hall, been dazzled by the brightness, and, all too soon, flown out through the open window at the opposite end into an eternal blackness.

Chapter Two: October 1981: a handful of dust

There was something distinctly colder and darker about the mornings and afternoons. Everything was closing in upon itself: the day closing in upon the night, the night closing in upon the day. Soon, so close... they'd be almost indistinguishable. Laid out in my bed in this morning twilight, sensing the chill of the air outside, only the need to go to the loo forced me to creep silently from bedroom to bathroom to watch in a trance my flow of urine... the initial vital surge declining to an unwilling dribble. In keeping with my usual routine, I showered for some time under a feeble flow dropping reluctantly from the shower head. The soap, a lump of useless slivers compressed into a scentless cake, depressed me further. On returning to my bedroom, I did not draw back the curtains, preferring dim to illuminated solitude, and silently dressed in some cords and a beige shirt I'd been wearing for far too many days.

The kettle boiled, I fed Thaddeus who swirled around my ankles, reminiscent of a plump ginger serpent, drank some tea, took a couple of painkillers and stared aimlessly out of the window. A net, yellow and ragged, once full of bird seeds, now blew like a flaccid windsock from a thin, bony branch. I watched its tethered flight for some time, before slipping my mug beneath the surface of the mud-coloured water in the washing-up bowl, to join the other drowned crockery.

Just gone eight, I left the house, a fine Victorian property, well-positioned, overlooking the park, and at last, glowing autumn days had ceased and the weather was damp and depressing. Soft, fine drizzle wafted along the street; the roads and pavements all a shade darker than yesterday. Reflected in the puddles, even the gloomy half-light of the sky seemed to sigh.

In the past, this darkness, this foggy oppressive dullness, was as familiar to me as breathing, but then she had come, and like a goddess plucked me from it into the sunshine above the low clouds. Trudging along, tormented about where and when it all went wrong, I returned, again and again to all that had happened; wondering was that the moment when this desolation began? Was that the moment, where I took a wrong turn, said the wrong words? When I forgot I was trying to hold water in my cupped hands? In my mind's eye, the moments drift in and out of focus... sometimes the autumn term, when the whole creature that we were had sprung into being, leading its charmed life throughout the idyllic spring and early summer. But mostly I see Italy, flickering hazy vignettes slowly rising and falling: a large stone villa in Tuscany, a terraced garden, a hot country. Now, a far-reaching mountain, which you stare at through half-closed blinds; upon the wall a green brown lizard flits. And once you caught a firefly and held it in your hands looking as if you had caught a tiny falling star, and I held my breath in wonder. And your face when the waiter brought you a ridiculously huge gelato sundae... when, for a moment, I glimpsed you as a child. And your eyes, filled with tears as we stood amongst the crowds in the heavy closeness of the church to see St Rocco revered. The candlelight on sweaty faces; the incense and the crowds seemed to suffocate you, make you queasy, so I walked you around the courtyard on my arm, led you out into the darkness. I suppose now, with hindsight, I understand. And some things I see over and over again...the red dress... flowers falling through the air... a face, pallid as bone ...lost.

And now this England, in the wet, damp mornings of late October. Mornings where I never switch on the light, do everything in slight darkness, always keep the bedroom curtains drawn. Funny, the habits I have now. How I wish you were with me in the early mornings. Strangely, I find it easier to go to sleep by myself than to wake up alone. Lately, I kick off the covers... my sleep disturbed by strange dreams. I wake up feeling cold. We loved to be naked in bed, didn't we? I wear pyjamas again now. You would say I look much older, possibly a little ridiculous.

If you were with me now, Anna, you'd be commenting on the changing colours of the leaves... so beautiful and yet so sad. I see it all so clearly now and feel overwhelmed with pity. They're on fire with their vanity. Little do they know it's all a sinister plot... that blazing colour, that glorious glow, as if they are burning with life, is ironically caused by being sapped of all their strength and vitality. Photosynthesis stops: their life is over. In a blaze of glory, they die. They won't know until it's too late, until their dry, crisp skeletons desiccate to dust beneath our feet.

Funny, just thinking about those leaves, the coppery reds, merging with burnished orangey bronzes, shot through with a bolt of sickly jaundiced chartreuse and suddenly I was in the pub with you, the very first time I touched you. It was the first breath of autumn... and leaves everywhere were unknowingly becoming their own multi-coloured shroud. Remember, I was next to you, someone else came and sat down, necessitating everyone to move up a little; for the first time ever my body touched yours, my thigh against your thigh. My entire body gave an involuntary jolt, as if a current of intense, tingling, but painless electricity had passed through it. For a split second, a shudder, imperceptible to anyone else but you, shivered through me. Looking straight ahead, a mirror in front of us reflected a strange look pass across your face. It was as if you had just seen a ghost, and realised with a sort of dread that it was your own. I never told you I observed that look, nor what I thought it meant. I don't suppose I ever shall now.

Of course, I had done my best to get seated next to you, and was already quite overcome by that, but nothing had prepared me for the sheer exquisite pain of touching you.

Not surprisingly, I was the first one in the department. I made a cup of strong black coffee, stirred in two sugars, lit a cigarette and gazed out of the window at the glistening, wet slate rooftops. I didn't really care if my teeth got stained now, fell out from decay, or if I died from lung cancer or heart disease. That's the trouble with health campaigners, they assume everybody cares whether they live or die. Now, I don't even care about my teeth.

When the weather is clear, it is possible to see right across the city – this darkly beautiful place. Even the motorway in the distance has a resplendent glory all of its own. At night, it's spectacular: a never-ending thread of bright stars or angels even, snaking into the grim, God-forsaken high-rise flats on the edge of town. Sometimes, I've studied it for hours; the glitteringly beautiful lights disappearing, momentarily, behind the tower blocks, only to emerge once more – coiling upward. The other night, it appeared more like a diamond necklace disappearing up someone's backside, and then appearing again through their gaping mouth. I never used to think like that: bad, cynical, 'ugly, unlovely thoughts,' as mother would say.

On these bookshelves are hundreds of books, containing some of the most cherished words in the English language; once I used to love them, revere them, now I can hardly bear to pick one up. It's become all so meaningless and empty. Well, that's not entirely true, but the things that are meaningful are too painful to bear. For instance, the other day while taking a tutorial on Hardy, 'At Castle Boterel' I was completely undone. My eyes and mouth filled with tears, and my voice became faltering, thick with emotion; overwhelmed by this sense of loss, of complete loss. If she had died still loving me, I could have died with her...my existence on earth now no more than a beautiful empty shell on the seashore, patiently waiting to be washed away with the tide. But like this I was a soul in perpetual purgatory –neither living nor dead, a strange half-life, moving in the shadows cast by gravestones; clutching at vaporous threads of hope. She'll come no more. But wait, her memory still mists this mirror…

'I look back and see it there, shrinking, shrinking,
I look back at it amid the rain
For the very last time; for my sand is sinking,
And I shall traverse old love's domain
Never again.'

From the top drawer of my desk, I took out a photograph, which was taken during a blissful week-end spent together in Wales. It was the very start of the Easter holidays, blustery and daffodil yellow, and Anna's spiralling long Pre-Raphaelite hair was wild and flaming. Even I looked fairly respectable in some 'wonderful' jumper Anna had insisted on buying for me the day before. In the photograph, which was taken by some passing walker, we are arm in arm by a gate in which a group of lambs are springing about. I remember being so happy, convincing myself that I would marry Anna: it was my destiny. Vowing, in a year or two, I would come back to this very spot and be photographed with Anna, my wife. I even allowed myself to visualize her heavily pregnant, with me standing behind her, my arms as far round her belly as they could reach; I can smell her hair; feel the warmth of her body – pure radiant joy. But hope does not shape destiny.

I suppressed my desire to propose there and then, and instead suggested an early pub lunch. There was leek and cockle pie on the menu, which, feeling adventurous, we both thought we'd try. Watching her eat was one of my great loves, although I recall this was not one of our successful meals out as Anna had never eaten cockles in any shape or form before, and thought they looked like baby birds, the sort that you find fallen out of nests when they're really tiny. As a child, I used to see them all the time; strangely, I haven't seen one in ages. Anyway, after Anna had pointed this out it was rather difficult to carry on eating it – fledgling sparrow never whetting my appetite. Plus, there was an unpleasant odour of ocean bottom emanating from somewhere, so we filled up on stodgy sponge pudding and custard instead.

Somewhere I remember reading that photographs are like a postcard we send to ourselves in the future, to say, 'Hey, look what a good time we're having!' Well, here is one such postcard. She used to come alive in my presence. Just look at her eyes.

Anna, I shall never forget the touch of your lips upon my cheek, your hand in mine. The way you used to kiss my fingers. And when you said, 'I love you,' it was like a prayer. You'd often say 'I love you. God, I love you,' and I really thought you had some awareness of how frail you'd be without me. When we were making love, I felt so at one with your body, the phrase, 'and they became one flesh' was more than symbolic. Like conjoined twins our bodies were one shared living organism, and separation would mean inevitable death – at least for one of us. Could I have been so deluded? How can anyone give to someone else, the way you gave to me, and then in a few short months be unable to stand the very sight of them?

Chapter Three: October 1980: a game of chess

A short time after the occasion in the pub when I first made physical contact with Anna, I was waiting in the same pub for Tom Gower who's been in the English department nearly as long as me. You wouldn't think he was an academic to talk to him, as he comes across as a man of limited sensibilities, but this bluff exterior belies his quiet and thoughtful centre. Old English is his interest really, and he's rather lost in the gloomy, dreary world of OE declensions. Whilst I loved all the images of Anglo-Saxon poetry, enjoyed our game of inventing Kennings to describe other members of staff – Ruth was 'ancient cave-bird'– loved to listen to him recite texts with his 'authentic' pronunciation, and I even liked the visual appearance of the language on the page, I found the study of formal grammar tedious: he loves it.

Tom is on his second marriage now, and happy, it seems. His first wife left him for another woman. Even in these so-called liberal academic circles that raised a few eyebrows, and Tom had to endure weeks of his colleagues' ponderings about whether Amanda, 'had always been that way inclined,' or was it that he'd been unable to fulfil her, both emotionally and sexually, that not only had he put her off him, but men altogether? At first, it seemed his bitterness and confusion would never subside, but mercifully, it did. I was genuinely taken aback at how thrown he was, after all, he and Amanda had hated one another for years.

But eventually Tom fought back from this surprising blow to his manhood, and married Eve, who always describes herself as a 'resting actress.' I don't know exactly what kind of 'parts' she's resting from, but I've a pretty good idea. She's never heard of Ibsen, used to drive a top of the range BMW and has most 'bosomiest bosoms' I've ever seen in all my born days. She doesn't care much for Anglo-Saxon declensions either. Intellectually they're a complete mismatch, but I think he'd had enough intellectual sparring with his first wife to last him a lifetime, and they're very compatible in other ways. They seem truly happy: in fact, they've had four children in nearly as many years.

Anyway, so there I was waiting for Tom. I'd already ordered lunch because I'd less than an hour to spare, and even a humble pasty can take forty minutes to meander from the oven to a plate and out of the kitchen.

Noisily, the doors of the pub swung open, almost everyone in the pub looked up, and in came a loud group of ten or so students, seemingly all trying to fit through the doorway at once. Amongst them, one face appeared, and as always when I saw her unexpectedly – a sudden intake of breath. This was immediately followed by the pleasurable sensation of blood pumping; the base of my spine contracting; desire tearing through my body. I grabbed my menu and pretended to scan it intently. When they'd settled in the corner of the pub, I risked glancing upwards. Anna was talking to her friend next to her, so I allowed myself as long a stare as I thought I would get away with. Sometimes out the corner of her eye she caught him staring at her. Without being entirely conscious of doing so she would become more animated. Her eyes opened wider, her mouth, lips, moved with a liquid exaggeration, and she laughed so delightfully, and with such pleasure – often at nothing at all.

Anna stood and left her seat, although I didn't think she'd seen me, so I continued to gaze at her as surreptitiously as I could, watching her weave a path across the pub. Her hips had a particular flow, which was intensely erotic. For one terrified moment I thought she was coming to see me, but she swept past as if I wasn't there. By this time, I was pretending to adjust my watch, but as she went by, she was so close that I inhaled the scent of her. It sounds ridiculous now, but I actually swooned, like in some Victorian melodrama – light headed, almost faint, my head swam, my limbs felt weak.

As I recovered myself, sipping at my beer, I nodded to Tom who'd just entered the pub, and was now at the bar doing the 'shall I get you another one?' gesture. A strange spine-tingling sensation made me aware Anna was hovering next to me. Like a small child looking up at his mother, I turned my head, gazing upward into her face. As I did so, I sensed some froth from my beer on my top lip, which I wiped self-consciously with the back of my hand. Her eyes danced. I tried to stand up to talk to her, but only ended up trapped in an awkward position between my chair and the immovable table.

'Hi, I hope you don't mind me interrupting your lunchtime,' she began, 'but I just spotted you, and I'm really struggling with The Waste Land essay and I... wondered if I could possibly see you before the next tutorial. I feel so confused by it, lost almost, could you possibly help me find a way through it all – a way through The Waste Land.' And she waved her hands about in a gesture that reminded me of someone walking into a spider's web.

Never, have I seen skin so pure; never heard such a voice, which so easily sends blood shaking tremors through my heart; never have I been turned inside out, in an instant, by the simple presence of another.

Out of nowhere, in a voice which sounded alien to me, I heard myself musing, 'Yes…a way through The Waste Land…' – then, creeping in, the slightest suggestion of a laugh –

'However, you make it sound like finding a way through a real, treacherous place, like finding, 'a way through the woods.'' I gave a more open laugh at my own rather elitist joke (an obscure reference to Dante's Inferno) which she obviously didn't get, and, somewhat embarrassed, continued. 'Mmm, it's sometimes difficult to find the key to open a text up. I'm afraid this requires a whole bunch of them.' My nerves were making me sound like a complete idiot, but still I stumbled on. 'I will gladly be your guide. The Waste Land – it's complex, but certainly not impenetrable.'

My cheeks reddened.

'When would be a good time, then?' She was almost unable to contain her amusement.

With my heart galumphing away in my chest, I answered hesitantly, 'Today, if you're free. Five, five-thirty, things are usually quieter then.'

Her eyes smiled provocatively as she backed away.

'Thanks. See you later then.'

Tom arrived with a pint in each hand, and a packet of crisps between his teeth which he dropped onto the table. 'You're in there.' He winked.

'Don't be ridiculous – I'm merely arranging a tutorial to help her find her way through the woods – The Waste Land, I mean.' Tom raised an eyebrow. 'Anyway,' I continued, 'I don't suppose I have to remind you of how I got my fingers burnt with that sort of caper in years gone by.'

'Oh, yeah, caught with your hand in the cookie jar that promptly ignited.' He went silent for a moment. 'Interesting though,' he said, glancing backwards at Anna's table of friends.

'Come on Alistair, I know you too well. I know that look…just what you need if you ask me.'

'Part of me says I need that kind of situation like a hole in the head, and part of me…'

'…. And we all know which part…'

I gave him a look of exasperation, 'and part of me,' I continued, 'screams out, why not? Life's too short not to. I mean, God, just look what happened to Ray.' For a brief moment, Tom and I made the kind of eye contact far too painful for sitting in a public place, as the memory of Ray rose like incense in our minds.

'Poor old Ray,' Tom mumbled, and shook his head, while making a study of the contents of his glass.

'But, to be realistic,' I continued, trying and failing miserably to lift the mood, 'I've probably got more chance of romantic success with your ex-wife, than a girl like that.'

'That was uncalled for.' Tom was hardly able to disguise his hurt expression.

'Sorry, it's just, well, you know how it is when someone is so obviously off limits. And I think even I've gone past the justifiable age for a mid-life crisis, let alone the age when I thought such things were within my –'

A plate was thrust unceremoniously between us.

'Who's for the Ploughman's gentlemen?'

Unexpectedly, Tom laughed heartily. 'O' I'll take the Ploughman; he'll have the Ploughman's gentleman!'

I raised my hand, and then a Farmhouse Fresh Ploughman's landed with a thump in front of me. The barmaid didn't smile.

I glanced again in Anna's direction; her crowd were all munching crisps from a pile of communal packets, downing pints, talking and laughing far too loudly. Now I wished I hadn't ordered any lunch. Struggling with this giant piece of cheddar, and chewy bit of bath loofah being passed off as French bread, I felt foolish. The whole plate was a minefield of social gaffs. The bread kept breaking off in impossible ungainly lumps, and there was no way I'd eat the pickles with the appointment I'd got lined up later on. Defeated, I pushed it to one side.

'Don't you want it?' said Tom hopefully. 'Lost your appetite, eh? Bad sign. You don't mind… if I?' he said, drawing the plate to his side of the table.

'Be my guest... and Tom, sorry for mentioning…ehm.'

'No, forget it. I'm over it. Really, it's ancient history.' Tom set to the problem lunch with gusto. He must have very sharp teeth or at the very least strong jaws, the ease with which he tore away at the loofah.

'I'm always hungry. I already had a butty from the cafe at eleven,' he explained through a mouthful of dough. 'Eve used to be great with the breakfast, wonderful, cooked breakfasts every day and all that, but she just doesn't seem interested these days, and I'm not really a Weetabix sort of bloke.'

'I shouldn't think Eve's got time, has she, what with all the children?'

'All the children!' he laughed, chasing a pickled onion around the plate with a fork. 'You're right of course; I suppose I am something of a Mr Quiverfull these days! O Sod this!' He picked up the onion in his fingers and crunched on it aggressively.

'And just how are dear Mrs Gower and all the little Gowers at the moment?'

'Eve's all right, just tired all the time, but she loves it, she does. It's what we'd always planned, to have them all, Bang! Bang! Bang!' He chopped the air with his hand, and then added with a snort, 'So to speak.'

I forced a grin. 'But it must be hard work for you both, with four of them?' All the while Tom regaled me with tales of his domestic life, my thoughts were on Anna, and what I imagined doing with her.

'You've no idea,' he continued. 'I watch them sometimes, particularly twin partners in crime, 'Ronnie and Reggie.'

'They must be two now, aren't they?' I interrupted, trying to show interest. (It was surprisingly easy to talk with my mouth mentally engaged elsewhere.)

'That's right, last week in fact. Anyway, this morning, I watch them eating, and shit, it's all over the place! Oat and apple porridge in every orifice. Ronnie even blew an oat and apple porridge bubble out of his nostril! Eve thought it was hysterical. Food's splattered and dropped all over the kitchen, and I think to myself, one day they'll be sat here, like us, adult men, having adult conversations…' He stifled a burp, 'Excuse me – onions. And I think that, that seems more of a miracle than life itself. Well, the whole of creation's got that, from the lowest amoeba to mankind. But becoming civilised, that's the bloody miracle. Well, it'll be a bloody miracle if it ever happens to those two.'

I gave a light laugh and nodded, but could think of nothing to say in reply and continued to repeatedly flip a damp beer mat, over and over.

'Alistair, you're not with it today, are you?'

'Sorry, I've got a lot on my mind.'

'Hey, no I'm sorry, probably boring you to death with tales from the home front. If you haven't got kids yourself, it's probably not of one io ta of interest.' I glanced up trying to muster sincerity. 'No, really, it fascinates me.'

'Yeah? Like hell it does! Mind you, I know something that might interest you. Remember a few years ago we went to my parents' house in Tuscany? You and Marion, myself and Dick. (I should explain that since Amanda's departure for her lover, Stella, Tom would only refer to her as 'ex-wife' or 'Dick'. A shortened version of the name he gave her at this time, 'Dick Van Dyke'. This nickname was inspired by Amanda's newly discovered liberated dress sense, which seemed to aggravate him. The striped jacket and bow tie combo she wore to their divorce hearing reminded him of Bert's outfit in Mary Poppins, worn while singing, 'Supercalifragilisticexpialidocious.' He insisted the name seemed fitting on so many levels. It seemed to make him feel better every time he referred to her as Dick and somehow the name stuck. Only once did his bravado slip. He'd been ranting on to me about how he thought this was just Dick's way of sticking two fingers up to him and the male sex in general, a women's lib gesture gone out of control, when I'd made the mistake of offering my own theory, which I thought seemed fairly obvious. 'Oh, no Tom,' I disagreed, quite unaware of the impact my words would have, 'I saw Amanda only two days ago, she looked like a different person, so happy. I think she just fell in love, pure and simple.' I think I had intended these words to make him feel better, less 'got-at'. However, alarmingly they had the reverse effect, and this fifteen stone, forty-year-old mountain of a man, crumbled.)

'How could I possibly forget our Tuscan idyll?' (My voice thick with sarcasm.) 'I don't think I've ever spent a more memorable two weeks.'

'Yeah, those were the days. Dick and I were like Elizabeth Taylor and Richard Burton in "Who's Afraid of Virginia Woolf?" you and Marion our understudies! God! When I look back! I can only be thankful we didn't have children together.' He drained the rest of his beer.

'Time for another?' I asked

'Just about. Oh, and a pack of nuts, if you don't mind please.'

While waiting at the bar, I glanced across at Anna's table, and realised they were already leaving. As I watched her disappear through the door, one of the young men in her group put his hand on her shoulder and whispered something to her. She mirrored him, leaning in to whisper her reply; he burst out laughing. An uncomfortable clash of emotions collided inside me, as plummeting disappointment met a rising fury. I'd hoped perhaps she would have turned to take one last glance at me, and the fact that she did not, seemed to put pay to everything I was pinning my hopes on. And the possibility that the joke they were sharing could have been about me produced a feeling of genuine nausea. I didn't think I'd been the least bit obvious in my intentions, but perhaps I'm giving too much away with my eyes.

When I returned with the beer, Tom was eager to resume his topic of conversation.

'Now, as you know I've been in the habit of spending as much of the summer as I possibly can down in Tuscany, but to be perfectly honest this year, well, and last year, were a bloody nightmare.'

'Even more of a nightmare than the year we came down?' I enquired with incredulity.

'It would be a close-run thing. But bloody hell, let me tell you, a three-year-old, twin toddlers, and a heavily pregnant wife don't travel well. At one point I could have cheerfully put them all out on the side of the road and hoped a passing gypsy would take a fancy to them.' He took a long draught of his beer, and gasped in a satisfied way.

'Anyway, my point is this. Eve is refusing to even entertain the idea of Tuscany next year, my parents are doing the States, and so the place is going to stand empty, unless we find friends, family to take it. So…' he paused to wrestle with the peanut packet. 'My first thought was you. Would you be interested?' He held the packet tightly between his clenched teeth and tugged at it aggressively. It ripped wildly spilling a good amount of its contents.

'Bugger!' He poured the remainder into his large open palm. 'No charge of course, but I'd be grateful if you could oversee some maintenance, quite a bit of building work needs doing.'

All the time he'd been talking, I could guess what he was leading up to. I tried to picture myself and Marion laid out on our loungers, reddened, roasting crisply by the pool; bristling in local restaurants, ingesting far too much; endlessly, incessantly, relentlessly, admiring art and architecture together…the two of us despising one another in the hot sun.

'Tom, I don't know what to say really. On the one hand, I'd love to take up your offer, but you know with Marion's work commitments and… well, quite frankly, just with Marion really…'

Now, there's something else I should explain. As much as most people, especially close friends were aware of the unhappy state of my marriage (although, none of them knew the detail) most also knew that I did not find it easy to admit to the sham of my life, and subsequently for all intents and purposes would still try to act as if Marion and I were a fully functioning unit, which to be honest, in some shape and form, we were.
He waved away my protestation with his hand, his mouth too full of peanut mush to speak.

'Mmm, I know, I know.' Tom ran his tongue around his teeth. 'Marion's a busy woman and all that. Don't give me a decision now; it's not till next year after all. Think about it for a week or two. Anyway, if Marion doesn't want to come…' He hesitated. 'Or you don't want to go with her…' He paused again testing my reaction. 'What's to stop you going on your own? Or, with someone else?'

I smiled weakly at his venture into the role of 'agent provocateur', and rose from my chair. Tom was sweeping up the spilt peanuts from the table into his hand, picking out the odd bit of fluff and detritus.

'And who have you got in mind? Auntie Joan?' (An old dear in the department, who should've been retired several decades ago.) 'Seriously though, Tom, it really is a very kind offer. I'll mention it to Marion on the phone tonight, but to be honest, I think she'll say she's got too much on. However, I must say I am tempted. Alone in Tuscany for the summer sounds a damn sight better than staying alone here.'

'Don't be such a pessimist, Alistair,' he said, throwing his head back in the direction where Anna had been seated. 'Why don't you go for it? The worst she could do is say, no.'
The phrase, 'that's what I'm afraid of' ran through my mind. But what I did was laugh and say in a coy way, 'I really don't know what you mean?'
Tom shrugged his shoulders, 'Well, either do something about it, Alistair or get rid of that dreamy 'hangdog' expression I catch on your face every time she's around. I know it's a minefield, but life is short. And as you know, you're a long time dead.'

'I'll drink to that!' I said, without a trace of irony, and raised my glass and took a final gulp. Tom grinned, his homemade peanut butter plugging the crevices between his teeth.

'Anyway, thanks for the offer, Tom. I must dash – running late. I'll let you know soon as possible.'

'Yeah, fine. It's just these builders, even out there they're hard to pin down. Take care, Tiger! Keep your pecker up!' Thankfully, for once, he didn't add his usual 'Up, down, or whatever angle suits you best' quip.

Chapter Four: October 1980: The Hanged Man

As I left the pub, I began to wish I'd eaten more of that damn lunch. Not only was I hungry, but my head felt light, and three pints on an empty stomach was never a good idea. An Eccles cake from the bakers swabbed up some of the beer sloshing in my guts. But it was far too sugary and had an unpleasant greasy texture. I hated being disappointed by food, but my mind was too full to dwell on the short-comings of pastry.

Fantasising about meeting Anna later that afternoon and indulging in the seemingly impossible dream that I would discover she felt the same way made my soul sing. But trawling through the worst-case scenarios were agony, imagining that she would give me every signal to back off, or even more worryingly, that I would make a complete fool of myself by attempting some kind of botched advance. Could I really dare to force the moment to an inevitable crisis – one way or the other?

My best plan of action, I considered, was to let the last tutorial group of the afternoon go early, which would give me time to sort myself out before Anna came. If only I had said a later time, I could've suggested we chat in the pub, which would relax the whole situation, for, to be honest, the thought of being alone in my room with her made me feel agitated beyond belief. The pub would be neutral territory; I could test the waters very subtly.

Back in my study I made a half-hearted attempt to tidy up a bit, opened the window for a blast of fresh air, that sort of thing. A heavy knock at the door signalled the arrival of my first tutorial group. Young Mr Greg Donavan strode into my room, sat on the edge of a chair with his legs wide apart and planted his large palms firmly on his powerful-looking thighs. He was Australian to the wishbone: huge, sporty, and confident. Moreover – I hate to say it – incredibly handsome, enhanced by that unusual combination of brown eyes and blond hair...he was clever too. I couldn't bear the sight of him. The longer I was in his presence that afternoon, the more my hope drained away. The sad truth is it doesn't matter how much you want someone; if they don't want you back 'you're on a hiding to nothing.' And it seemed almost laughable now that I could even have hoped for her to give me a second look while there were young men like him around.

There were only two others in this group: some poor lad whose acne was so bad it made you want to weep for him or throw up on him depending on how benevolent you felt that day, and a shy girl from Norfolk, who hardly ever spoke, unless forced to. Anyway, she often had her gaze fixed on Greg's groin, rather than the text, so maybe she was preoccupied. He seemed aware of this girl's interest, as every now and again he'd push his hips forward and then relax again. But he'd have never asked her out, ever. It was a torturous hour, what with Greg's groin and Philip's acne, which was particularly irascible today. When they all shuffled off at three o'clock, I felt more than a little relieved.

My next group were already loitering about in the hallway, with the inevitable 'hoo ha' as they exchanged banter with one another. This group was preferable to the last, consisting of two girls, both from the North East, who could be good fun; Thomas, who was a nice kid, but frankly dull; and Simon and Hugh, a very 'out of the closet' gay couple, who always chose the same options. Honestly, the freedoms young people enjoyed these days. In my youth this sort of thing was definitely swept under the carpet, firmly locked in the closet, certainly not perched – blatantly – on the sofa sharing of a pot of tea and a slice of Battenberg, thank you very much.

We'd been studying American poetry of the twentieth century recently, and Hugh had prepared a short introduction to the poetry of William Carlos Williams, which he read out to the group. "This is just to say," was intoned tenderly, with his Welsh sing-song caressing the words.
That's not true really... he did actually sound like he was reading a note stuck to the fridge apologising for having eaten someone's breakfast plums.

Nevertheless, the poem stunned me with its simplicity; I could not begin to explain how it worked nor did I want to. An unexpected rush of happiness, an almost uncontrollable sense of *joie de vivre* spilled through my veins. I loved that poem, and in less than two hours Anna would be there. Every bone, every muscle, every sinew and nerve ached for her, longed for her, with an almost exquisite pain. Anna, forgive me – but I could not help but want you – to consume you. Perhaps you were never mine for the taking. *Forgive me...*
Soon I would be sitting next to her, breathing in that scent that still makes me weak, that heady odour of subliminal delight exciting something in one's primitive brain, like the sensuous, lingering waft of warm chocolate. How intertwined is the food sensuality link - the fulfilment of appetite. The sheer complete beauty; one simply just had to consume it. I picture myself and Anna lying in a field of gold-spun barley, which gently whispers and ripples in the

breeze, the sky is intensely blue; the late afternoon sun still hot on our skin. We are sharing a bowl of strawberries, bright crimson and swollen with ripeness. Kiss her... the fragrant sticky sweetness of strawberries still on her lips.

'Excuse me, eh, that's it. That's the end.'
Abruptly, I became aware of Hugh's voice again, sounding very odd, in the way voices sound too loud and echoing just as you fall off to sleep.

'Are you all right?'
'Yes, yes, I'm sorry. I've a bit of a headache coming on, I think, that's all.' I smiled encouragingly and bade him to proceed with his thoughts. After a brief discussion, to which it must have been obvious I was not giving one hundred percent, I pointed everyone in the direction of Wallace Stephens for next week, with particular focus on 'The Emperor of Ice Cream.' Finally, I dismissed them all early on account of my headache. They all looked slightly bemused, but shuffled to their feet, gathering their many belongings, and had the usual difficulty of five students trying to get through one doorway, after which began the obligatory clomping down the stairs.

'Well, what a waste of effort that was!' said Hugh. 'Headache? He looked quite perky.'

'That's what I thought,' chirped Simon, 'positively glowing – but I suspect it's more to do with being overcome by the thought of sinking his teeth into all those ice-cold plums.'

'Cheeky!
One of the girls piped in with, 'I just thought he was pissed again.'

'Well, he's certainly on something.' There was a flutter of giggling.

'Titter ye not, it's wicked to mock the afflicted,' warned Simon, coming over all 'Frankie Howerd' (no doubt posing with hands on hips, pouting ludicrously at the others). 'No, really, no, missus, at his age you can overdo it on one too many Garibaldis, never mind plums. Yes, madam, plums! Oooh noo, please... I have eaten the Garibaldis that were in the biscuit tin, which you were probably saving for dunking...yes, dunking, missus.'

Laughing, they left the building, each having a go at the 'No! Missus! Please yourself!' routine. Then they were gone. Silence.

I did actually overhear that conversation, standing behind the door, peering through the crack, with impending terror that Anna would soon be ascending that staircase. It was almost impossible to cope with the rollercoaster ride of emotions I was experiencing, elation changing to fear, despair to hope, in a matter of seconds. No wonder I felt physically sick. Plus, a phrase, from next week's 'The Emperor of Ice Cream', had wormed its way into my ear and circled repeatedly: 'concupiscent curds' 'concupiscent curds' 'concupiscent curds'. It always unsettled me, causing a slight nausea – well, that and the 'horny feet'.

Chapter Five: October 1980: when lovely woman stoops to folly...

It was slow going in the library...one of those soporific afternoons, where the dull grey sky was so low and oppressive... it was as if the day was wrapped in greaseproof paper. As Anna stared at page after page of words that would not form coherent meaning in her mind, she vowed not to drink at lunchtime again. Well, maybe not to drink two pints quite so quickly, and without any food, at lunch time again. The A4 pad, on which she was supposed to be making copious notes, was a mass of doodles, and even quite a good biro drawn study of a female nude.

'Chris,' she whispered, 'do you want to go for a coffee?'

'We've only been here half an hour.'

Anna threw a glance towards Chris's blank notebook. 'Well, you're not getting on that well either,'

'I've been reading,' she whispered, picking up her bag and packing away the notebook. 'Come on then.'

They perched on the red plastic chairs in the revamped library coffee shop, which in spite of its new decor still served the same warm brown liquid in plastic cups. You could tell the difference between tea and coffee because coffee had slightly more light brown bubbles floating on the top.

Chris held out a pack of cigarettes. 'Anna?'

Anna reached out, but withdrew her hand. 'No, I won't, thanks, actually.'

A smirk lit Chris's face. 'Suit yourself. Keeping our breath fresh then, are we?' Her eyebrows shoot up and down knowingly.

'Meaning?'

'You tell me. Don't you have a little bit of 'one-to-one' tutorial coming up later on? I wasn't born yesterday you know.'

'Well, yes...' Anna answered trying to bury the smile that would betray her, 'but I still don't see what you're driving at.'

'You don't? Well, let me spell it out to you, then.' She leant forward and whispered, 'What the f.u.c.k. is going on between you and Johnson for God's sake? Not what it looks like to all the world, I hope?' Chris flicked a bloom of ash into a tinfoil ashtray and swung her feet up on the chair opposite and reposed, her angular features taking on all the ugly-beauty of a cubist portrait.

'With me and Johnson?' She made a face of non-comprehension.

'Lunchtime,' sang Chris. 'Oh, please sir, flutter, flutter, you're so clever sir, you couldn't possibly help a poor little girly like 'moi' with her homey-worky. I'll make it worth your while.'

'Ah. Is that what you thought?'

'Not just me, dear.' She wagged her finger at Anna and gave an exaggerated tut-tut. 'You just stopped short of waving your knickers round your head. It was obvious you were giving him the 'come-to-bed-eyes' even from the other side of the pub. I mean, I've thought he's had a thing about you for a while now but, come on; do you really have the hots for him? He's got to be fifty or something, if he's a day.'

'He's not fifty. Honestly, I was just trying to be nice because I was asking a favour. Anyway...' added Anna, valiantly attempting not to radiate her gratification, 'what makes you think he fancies me?'

'Got you!' exploded Chris with a laugh. 'I knew I was right. I'm an expert at spotting suppressed lust. It's so fucking sexy, I can even smell it!' and she drew a clenched fist to her nose as if to do just that. 'I mean, I suspected him a week or two back, but I wasn't so sure about you, until today.'

'So, let me get this straight. You think he fancies me, although you've said nothing, and that I am equally besotted?'

'In a nutshell, yes. Am I right? Come on you can tell me. There's something going on, about to be going on, or even has gone on.'

'Well, don't have an attack of the vapours; my virtue is still intact. Nothing's happened or happening. And even if he did, you know, fancy me, I'm not sure that I'd really want anything to come of it. Do you seriously think he fancies me?'

'I know he does. So, am I right though? Do you dear lady, return his affections?'

'You promise not to breathe a word to anyone.'

Making the three-finger scout salute, Chris declared solemnly, 'Guide's honour.'

'To be perfectly honest, I don't really understand what I feel. I do like him, well, it's more than that really, there's certainly that spark, that something extra in the air when I'm near him, but to proceed from that to...well, you know.' She smiled almost apologetically at Chris, took a sip of her coffee and proceeded to dig herself into a hole. 'Obviously he is way too old, and a tutor. But he's got that certain twinkle in his eye–'

'– So does Father Christmas.'

Anna laughed a little.

'I'm just, well, you know, having a bit of flirt… some fun. It's like, what's the right way to describe it?'

'I think 'prick-tease' is the phrase you're looking for.'

'No, nothing like that.'

Chris looked directly at Anna. 'Well, you should be sure of what you want before anything happens. He has quite a reputation, you know? A taste for young female flesh. A use 'em and lose 'em man.'

(Of course, this was the last thing that Anna wanted to hear, because although she wouldn't admit it to Chris, I think that deep down she already knew that she had fallen in love with me, and she knew that it was only a matter of time before one of us would make a move. Anyway, she said none of this to Chris, and instead maintained a light-hearted casualness.)

'Go on then. Dish the dirt. But I don't even know why I'm having this conversation. It's only flirting around after all.'

'Well,' said Chris leaning closer, 'it generally goes like this: lots of out-of-school hours' tutorials, you know the kind of thing, "Let's talk in the pub, it's so much more sociable," and then after plenty of free booze, he'll say: "Oh, I know just the book to help you with this essay, only it's in my study. Come on, we'll go and get it now, while we're thinking about it..." and I can guarantee, he's thinking about it.'

Chris slipped into a Vincent Price voice. 'But, by now my dear, darkness has fallen, the department is deserted, he even has to use his personal key to unlock all the doors.... You follow unsteadily up the stairs. You enter his study which is as dark as your bedroom in the middle of the night. The small desk lamp he flicks on emits a strange soft romantic glow; a half-formed thought in your brain wonders why a desk lamp has such a low wattage bulb. You're invited to relax on the shambolic sofa. After finding the book, he perches above you on the arm of the sofa, and guides you to the page; you notice he has surprisingly beautiful hands. As you try to focus on the words, you sense he's staring down at you. A brief glance upwards - his hand is already touching your hair, then… the kill!'

''Oh God,'' he sighs. ''You really are the most beautiful girl I have ever seen. I can't help myself any longer; I am deeply, deeply attracted to you," and with luck (he hopes) in the dim light and after five gin and tonics (which you don't usually drink, but it seemed sophisticated at the time) that you'll respond that you've always found him utterly desirable too. And then after lots of uncomfortable, embarrassing wriggling about on the armchair, you'll walk home with nasty wet undies.' Chris leaned forward and whispered, 'Because he'll presume you're on the pill; old guys always do, so it's a good job you are.'

Anna had sort of smiled all the way through Chris's performance, but inside she was filled with a gnawing inexplicable grief. Somehow, she maintained her composure and simply replied, 'And how come you're so knowledgeable? Don't tell me you fell for it last year?'

'Don't be ridiculous! But I know a girl who knew a girl who did.'

'And she told it to you, just like that.'

'Naw! I'm making most of it up. Hey come on, don't let it get to you. I mean, surely you wouldn't expect to be the first student he'd had a go at, would you?'

'It's irrelevant to me in any case,' Anna said without conviction. 'But tell me the rest of the gory details anyway. What happened then, with Johnson and this girl?'

Chris lit another cigarette and took a long drag before continuing. 'I suppose I shouldn't be making so light of it really; it was actually quite a tragic story for everyone concerned.'

'Tragic? Now you are trying to wind me up.'

'No, this bit is deadly serious, and as far as I know true. My cousin's girlfriend came here, left the year before I arrived, and as soon as I said where I was going, and that I was going to study English, she filled me in on a bit of the gossip about the staff here. Who'd had who, and whose lectures were any good, and whose were crap, that sort of thing.'

'And?' pressed Anna impatiently.

'She said the biggest scandal had been this tutor called Alistair Johnson and this student, whose name escapes me at the moment. It was um, no, I can't think, anyway, he'd been carrying on with this girl, who by all accounts was frankly a bit unstable and after they'd been together a few months she flipped - tried to commit suicide.'

She took a well-timed puff and blew a huge plume of smoke to accompany this revelation. 'Probably nothing to do with Johnson, she was just a depressive, you know, really clinically cuckoo. But of course, she left a suicide note blaming naughty old Humbert, sorry Johnson, for her actions, and although she was discovered in time, pumped out, and saved etc. her parents obviously found out all about her relationship with him and went absolutely ape shit. The whole thing became very public knowledge, and was deeply embarrassing for everyone concerned. I mean, she didn't 'beat about the bush' in her letter, (unlike Johnson, who I gather has beaten about quite a few bushes in his day!) I think the entire University knew it word for word. Johnson was this close to being chucked out; I think he took a, what-do-you-call-it, not a sabotage …'

'Sabbatical?'

'Yeah. It wouldn't have been so bad, but the reasons this girl cited as the cause of her distress, in her letter, were basically that Johnson had used her (and here Chris slid into her Jean Brodie voice) 'for all manner of sexual depravity not suitable for little girls' while also screwing around behind her back with even more students. She said that he'd promised her better grades and so on in return, but that was of course a complete lie. And she claimed to be pregnant - but she wasn't,' Chris added, 'just deluded. Anyway, this was some years ago, and really, the girl was bonkers. If it hadn't had been him and his philandering, it would have been something else - voices, demons, abducted by aliens.'

Chris drained her lukewarm coffee and shuddered. 'Bluh! To be honest, I was surprised to find he was still here.'

With some deliberation, Anna asked, 'Why didn't you tell me this before?'

'Don't know really. I suppose when I first came here, and realised it was him, the one and the same, it was in my mind, but he hasn't been one of my tutors since the first year. I was going to say something to you, when I realised you had him, but never sort of got round to it.'

'Never got round to it?'

'God, don't get shirty. I'm telling you now, aren't I? In any case, it was some time ago. And most of my sympathy is with him. No one should take men like him seriously. She was an idiot. What did she expect?'

For a moment Anna was silent, then said, 'You can't be the only one who knows, people don't forget that sort of thing that easily.'

'I don't suppose they do. It's probably part of the shared mythology of department these days. But all I'm saying is be warned, be on your guard, this may be one almighty can of worms. Have your older man experience if you must, but if I was you I'd wait and have it with some rich consumptive O.A.P. who'll expire on the job and leave you all his loot.'

'Was he married?'

'Oh, of course...they always are. That's why I think she was so naive; after all, to sleep with her he was already being unfaithful to his wife, wasn't he? Sexual depravity aside, did she really expect faithfulness to her? But his wife doesn't understand him you know, they haven't slept together for years, and blow me down, you feel so sorry for him; you just want to make him feel a complete man again. And God, the saints be praised, you did it! You shagged that man back into existence. Never, never, but never, join the mercy fuck mission.'

At this point Chris sucked dramatically on the little stubby bit of cigarette she had left, it glowed furiously, and then she squashed firmly into the pile of ashes in the tinfoil tray.

'I'm not naive Chris, and I'm not mentally unstable either.'

'Well, so long as you keep taking your medication, you should avoid the lobotomy. But if you've developed some 'thing' for him - and I think I can see that you have - just go carefully. Be sure it's not just some sticky residue left over from schoolgirl crushes. Be sure you want all that married middle age weighing down on you, sliding from you, cleaving to you, in some loathsome, lusty, damnable darkness.'

'Oh, Chris, for God's sake, all I did was give 'the eye' a bit at lunch time.'

'I know, I know.' She held up her hands in appeasement. 'But you are planning to see him this afternoon, aren't you? Hoping that he might endeavour to engage you in an exploration of more than the text in hand. He's been there before don't forget, and you haven't. How are you going to play it? Are you going to continue with the 'Here I am! I'm 'yours for the taking' routine? Or play it a bit cooler?'

With a grin, Chris pulled the tin-foil ashtray across the table, and made a great show of hovering her hands over it, in a series of mysterious circling movements. 'Let us consult the portents revealed in this burnt offering.' She blew lightly into the pile of grey-white ash in which nestled the broken split stumps of cigarettes; the once pure clean spongy filter tips now impregnated with the brownish-yellow fog of nicotine. Her hands flew to her chest, where she crossed her arms and held a theatrical pose, fingers fanned out over each shoulder. Chris's eyelids snapped shut for a few moments, then springing them open as if awakening from a trance she peered into the ashtray once more. 'Here, in this ancient carcinogenic dust, may we discover if all augurs well or not, for your venture, my little querent.'

Anna shuffled forward, mildly placated by this unexpected diversion. 'Ah, observe this portent here.' Chris pointed to a dog-end rising proudly from the ash.

'Mmm?' Anna's tone rising in anticipation.

'Reading the ash is neither as crude, nor as obvious,' reprimanded Chris. 'This... shall we say... 'ambitious' shaped object, my sweet, is in fact a plane - the sign of a...'

'Let me guess…a journey?'

'Do not mock. You too may unknowingly have the gift. But wait. See how it curves, there at the end. It could be 'the snake'.' She held her hand up in stop sign, forbidding the obvious interruption. 'The snake could signify... an enemy - or wisdom.' She sighed deeply. 'The ashes are unforgiving today, closeted...and ambiguous.'

Beginning to warm to the game, Anna asked encouragingly, 'What about this big blob, here?'

'Oh, that. Mmm. Not a good sign I'm afraid.' She turned the ashtray this way and that. 'Ah, 'the inverted mushroom' unfortunately.'

'So, that's bad?'

'It means frustration. How to interpret that is up to us I suppose. It could mean your heart's desire is impotent of course - very frustrating, or it could be a signal that you should frustrate him.'

She paused dramatically saying, 'Aha, I see…' as the truth of the ashes slowly dawned on her. 'You must frustrate him. Delay, delay! Build up the anticipation, the longing. That's the best way to get some real fireworks going. Today, you should just not turn up at all.' In her excitement, she drifted out of character, her clairvoyant's trappings vanishing in a wisp of smoke. 'You must take control of the game. It's the only way not to get totally shat on. Play a few little seduction games with him. We'll let him sweat it out a bit. Put some fire in his belly. He'll be so built up for what he's hoping to get at five, the disappointment will kill him. By the time he sees you again we'll positively see him crawling on all fours. He'll be putty in your hands, ready whenever you want to play with him. Like I said, suppressed passion so much sexier than expressed.'

'You're a hard-bitten bitch.'

'I know,' she said smiling proudly. 'Anyway, we girls need to put this kind of man in his place.'

'Oh, God,' Anna exclaimed with a start, 'doesn't this look like a skull - the portent of death?'

Chris shook her head with great gravity, 'Yep, worst omen of all.'

'But specifically, what does it mean? 'Anna seemed genuinely unnerved.

'It means,' Chris paused momentarily, 'that smoking kills you.' Their eyes met across the ash tray. 'I should give up,' she added gesturing at the grey dust between them, 'but who really believes in this shit?' They laughed.

By the time they'd walked back to the library, Anna was already locked into Chris's 'Fire in the Belly' game. She was going to miss going along today, and although they went through various elaborate stories, which could provide an excuse as to why, they settled on the tame one of saying Anna had had a migraine, which was more popular with Anna than Chris's suggestion of violent menstrual pains.

Back in the library, Anna felt awful, marking the minutes leading up to and away from five o'clock. She kept wishing Chris would go home so she could slip off and see him. In spite of everything Chris had said, she felt as if she was in some sense betraying Alistair, just by sitting here with Chris, playing these stupid games. Suddenly, it didn't seem like such a laugh to toy with his emotions. If he really were waiting, with any greater expectation than that of giving a tutorial, was it right to let him down? After all, she knew she said as much with her eyes at lunchtime. And she couldn't help but remember, that time, a week or two ago in the pub when she'd sat close to him and their legs had touched. It still rolled her insides over to think about that sensation. And apart from anything else he was a tutor, who'd given up his time to help her.

She began to feel annoyed with herself for allowing herself to be controlled by some agenda of Chris's. They'd met on Anna's first day at university, and although they had only known one another a few weeks, they'd had struck up quite a close friendship. Chris lived in the bedsit opposite Anna's in the house which they shared, so they saw quite a lot of each other. She was in her third year and had seemed to be good company, funny, 'over-the-top', but now Anna detected something in Chris she didn't like. It was becoming more apparent to her that Chris liked to be the superior voice of experience, 'the been-there-done-that' sage of university. Now she wondered perhaps if Chris just liked to have someone younger around her, so that she could feel more worldly wise. Maybe Chris was making the whole thing up, or at least exaggerating? She would have to take control of things herself. What she didn't need was a friend who acted like a parent or worse still like a cross between a fairground fortune-teller and bloody Jiminy Cricket.

She tried desperately to wade through the pile of books on T.S. Eliot; she couldn't concentrate on what the critics had to say so she read through The Waste Land again. It always made her feel so isolated, as if life was nothing but aimless uncertainty.

Chapter Six: 'good night, sweet ladies'

At four o'clock, I brushed my teeth, and combed my hair in the Men's loo. I always kept a little wash bag in my study, a habit left over from the days when I might return to work not having gone home the night before. I took off my tie and opened my shirt, to try to look a bit more casual, but after looking in the mirror, I put the tie back on and just loosened it a bit at the neck. I was trying to achieve the kind of look of Robert Redford or Dustin Hoffman in All the President's Men; you know, as if I was slightly dishevelled from overwork, sexy, but too preoccupied to be aware of it. Looking in the mirror, I smiled, then frowned, and then wished I had an altogether different face.

Hurriedly, I returned upstairs and perched on the swivel chair at my desk, drumming my fingers and tapping my feet in a state of nervous excitement. Every time the main door of the building slammed, my stomach began to contract and a little flock of humming birds took flight in my chest cavity. At quarter past five, I had a quick glass of whisky to calm my nerves. My hair must've looked all over the place by now, from having raked through it with my hand innumerable times. It was probably a bit on the long side for someone of my age, although not long like some sort of hippie, you understand, just bordering on the mad professor look, which was not the image I wanted to project at all.

It was darkening outside now, and raining steadily. Brollies fled past in the orange street light. The office staff were packing up and going home, and the cleaners begun clattering about with their buckets and Hoovers. Shrieks of high-pitched laughter shot up the stairs, but I couldn't quite make out what they were saying. Strangely, I began to hope that Anna wouldn't come, not now that they were here. I couldn't bear their knowing glances; their presumption of what they thought was going on. As I switched on the desk lamp, a warm, soft light filled the room, but I felt strangely cold. I should have given her a more specific time. I watched the hands of my watch creep towards 5.30pm and hope began to desert me. Pouring myself another whisky, this time a very large one, and lighting a cigarette, I tried to muster the energy to go home. However, at 6.15pm, I was still there, lighting up my third cigarette, when someone burst into the room. Startled, I swung round in the seat, in a state somewhere between despair and wild anticipation.

'Oh, sorry, Mr. Johnson, didn't think anyone was still here, shall I come back later?' said Dot, one of the cleaners, to whom I chatted occasionally.

'No, no. It's okay, really. I was just about to leave; just thought I'd see if the rain was going to ease off a bit.'

'It's terrible, isn't it? And there's more on its way if the forecast's to be believed.' She gave an exaggerated 'tut' and peered hopefully into the wastepaper basket, 'No bits today?' And then began to cough as the smoke caught her throat. I stubbed out the cigarette immediately.

'Sorry,' I apologised with a smile, 'it's a bit of a fog in here.' And I made a rather exaggerated show of fanning the remaining smoke towards the slightly open window.

'You can say that again!' She guffawed, but it only set her off on another bout of coughing. Apologising again, I put on my coat. Dot managed to stop barking enough to say, 'Honestly, what with your smoking, and drinking.' She pointed at the whisky bottle left on the desk, 'It's no wonder you don't look the picture of health. Still, just like my Frank, you won't be told.'

'We're all as bad as each other, Dot!' I laughed. 'Hopeless. Just hopeless!' and gave her my errant schoolboy look; though God knows why, I arrogantly refused to lump myself in the same hopeless pile of humanity as Dot's husband. Not wishing to be disrespectful to anyone in the cleaning profession, but most of those I've ever come across seem to have stumbled seamlessly from playing extras in some worthy BBC production of Dickens, straight into my office. And Frank, Dot's 'other half', well, I saw them together in town once, he definitely had a look of Magwitch about him - gnarled, marshy-grey and life-beaten.

I backed out of the room and padded slowly down the stairs, having to negotiate 'Irish' Mary, who was vigorously mopping the stairwell with a foul almond-scented disinfectant. This was no mean feat as she was an enormous bulk of woman, whose size and her ability to engage one in conversation thwarted any hope of a quick getaway. But she was a good-hearted sort in spite of her fairly disturbing appearance. (She was a sufferer of severe rosacea and always looked alarmingly as if she would expire any minute.)

'I think I'd better get the kettle on for Dot. Honestly, hark at her coughing!' I shrugged. 'My fault, I think,' I whispered confidentially, doing a mime of smoking. 'Terrible habit, ought to give up.'

'Well, 'snot easy is it?' She pushed the mop forcefully into the drainage basket of the bucket, her fleshy arms shuddering. 'I should know, me! T'irty years a smoker!' She gave me a look I could have mistaken for pride. 'But 'snot easy! Like me late husband used to say, I'll be needing a coffin with a little chimney on the top 'cos I'm as like to die with a fag in me cakehole!' She took the lead on another round of cackling, although the merriment of this image was lost on me. Five minutes later, and after two failed attempts to extricate myself, I finally turned the corner of the stairwell.

'Goodnight then, Mr Johnson. Mind how you go now,' Mary shouted over the banister.

'Goodnight, ladies,' I called back cheerily. 'Goodnight, sweet ladies,' I repeated into the night air as I walked down the hill.

I can remember that evening so well. I don't think I've ever felt so lonely, well, at least not until now. The house was dark and unwelcoming; the central heating seemed to have packed up and every radiator in the house was cold and dead. I looked at the boiler and tapped the timer and the thermostat hopefully, but haven't got a clue about things like that, so I concluded I'd have to suffer tonight and ring up someone tomorrow. As neither Marion nor I had thought to order any logs yet, there wasn't even the possibility of lighting a fire.

On the way home, I had bought one of those 'ready-to-eat' dinners for one. It was not enjoyable, and so pathetically small, it was a good job I didn't have much appetite anyway. Three, maybe four 'bits' of chicken, and here I use both 'bits' and 'chicken' reservedly, same number of carrots or swede cubes, and no less than six peas! It all resided in a gloopy effluence the colour of German mustard: nice. I'd eaten what there was of it, and drank a few beers, while watching some wildlife programme about Emperor Penguins - very apposite - poor sodding creatures living in a frozen, barren wasteland.

I couldn't believe it! Now, did you know, the male penguins incubate the egg, while the female goes off to feed? I didn't. These penguins had to stand on the ruddy ice in the middle of Antarctic for weeks and weeks, trying to keep an egg warm. Balancing it on their feet, they all jostled around in a huddle in some effort to maintain body heat - for weeks and weeks, standing in the darkness, or half-light, in winds of one hundred and twenty miles an hour and in temperatures dropping as low as minus 76 degrees - they cannot even eat. Their only distraction, the wonder of the ethereal wisps of unreal light above, but I doubt they even notice, let alone marvel at the beauty of the aurora borealis. What a life! Victims of biology, driven, to what must be one of the most wretched existences on Earth, by the sheer compulsion to breed: to pass on one's beautiful spiralling staircase of DNA. That most mysterious stairway to life.

God, I felt even more cold and depressed. But at least I'd had a revolting 'Country Chicken Casserole for One.' Moreover, I'd remembered Marion kept a small fan-heater in her room, so I'd brought that downstairs. Now, I had hot ankles to celebrate. Nature programmes!

I switched off the television and washed up my plate, then sat at the kitchen table in the stark fluorescent light, thinking and thinking. Had Anna simply forgotten to come? Although, that seemed unlikely as she had made the arrangements only a few hours before. And had she really been giving me a green light, or was that just wishful thinking? But even Tom had said, 'You're in there.' Therefore, it must have been obvious to him that she fancied me. However, even that phrase 'she fancied me,' made me squirm like a maggot on a hook. I did not feel I could apply it to myself; by any stretch of the imagination, I did not feel 'fanciable,' but I was hoping I suppose that she might be infatuated by me, or by some miracle have fallen in love with me; in the way that people sometimes do fall in love, flying in the face of all obvious external logic.

Suddenly, the phone rang. It made me jump, sounding twice its normal volume in this chilly, sterile air. It was Marion, and she was in a goddamn awful mood. She was trying to negotiate a deal for a series of books called, 'Be Your Own....' which she knew was going to be a sure-fire hit. The concept was infinitely 'campaignable', beginning with: 'Be Your Own Garden Centre', that she confidently predicted would be on the coffee table of nearly every home in the country. However, the powers that be did not agree with her, and Marion was spitting feathers.

'Can you believe it?' she seethed down the phone, 'Mike Smith even said at the meeting, in front of Joanna Murphy no less, that the formula was tired, hackneyed and already overworked. He then thought he'd be 'oh so terribly amusing,' and quipped, "Where will it all end, Marion? 'Be Your Own Heart Surgeon!' Ha! That better be the last in the series, eh?" Joanna thought that was sooo funny and smiled at Mike like a Cheshire Cat that had just got the cream

– humph – some truth in that, I suppose. God, I loathe colleagues engaged in carnal shenanigans with one another. It's pitiful, truly pitiful.'

She continued on in this vein, while I amused myself with compiling a list of 'Be your own' books which Marion might like to peruse, starting with, 'Be Your Own Gynaecologist'. Although I foresaw this particular tome might leave women wide open to all sorts of malpractice and self-abuse...

To increase her level of venom, the hotel room, in which she was staying, 'smelt distinctly peculiar.' (Marion was almost phobic about odd smells, especially unpleasant odours possibly emanating from other people.) Anyway, after she'd got that off her chest she wanted to know if I'd remembered to give Thaddeus his second dose of worming tablets, which were due this morning.

'Yes, I had,' I said, picking the packet of the shelf and laying it by his dish so as I would not forget later on.

It was probably totally the wrong time to ask, which is probably why I did: Would she be interested in the Gower's house in Tuscany next summer?

'What do you think?' came the curt reply.

'I'll take that for a no.'

'Correct. I've never heard such a ludicrous proposition. Honestly! After the fiasco we had last time! And that was just with you, me and Amanda in tow. Whatever possessed him? Surely he's got enough company with the delightful Eve and all their squawking offspring?'

'He wasn't inviting us to go with them – they're not going. It was just an offer to us.'

Even though we were on the phone, I realised Marion was spluttering on a swig of gin and tonic, that had caught her throat before being able to respond. That's how well I knew her

'To us? Good grief! Does that man walk around with his eyes shut?' She coughed noisily. 'It's out of the question, Alec. It wouldn't work; besides, I've got too much on. You have no conception of my workload. We don't all get the entire summer to ourselves, you know.' ...that old chestnut.

'Well, shall I tell Tom I'll take it on my own then?' There was a significant pause while Marion processed this information.

'On your own?' she repeated with incredulity.

'Well, yes, I know it's not till next year, but Tom needs to get it sorted. There's some building work to organise.' I waited for her to interrupt, but the phone line was silent. 'I've been quite down lately, Marion,' I went on, 'and this would give me something to look forward to… I thought I could try and rediscover my talent for writing poetry.'

Marion gave a dismissive snort. 'Talent? Alec, how can you *rediscover* something you've never discovered in the first place? Please no, there's enough doggerel in the world without you putting your two-penneth in. Anyway, let's cut the claptrap. Why are you even bothering to lie to me? You don't want me to come at all in any case. I know you too well Alec, the only talent you'll be rediscovering is the one of bedding those rancid leathery expat housewives, who hang around the bar, drinking that god-awful Grappa.'

I tried to interject, 'Mari...' but she was having none of it

'You go. Go on, I shall be glad of the break. The only thing that does bother me though, is who will look after Thaddeus? You know, if I have to go away on business, or something, now that poor Mrs Joyce isn't with us anymore?'

'What about putting him in a cattery?'

She put the phone down.

Well, I suppose at least that was something to be grateful for, Marion would not be coming to Tuscany at all next summer. She was right of course; we were one of only a handful of couples who could make a summer staying at a villa in Tuscany like a trip to the Underworld. The truth was Marion didn't really like holidays these days. She hated to be away from her work, from Thaddeus, and of course from 'Poor Edward'.

(Have I mentioned him yet - her long-term lover, Edward? It's all very amicable, and I quote, "Alec, your acceptance of the situation is the least you can do considering the kind of pathetic excuse of a husband you have been." So, I do the least I can do. I accept.)

Further objections to Tuscany were that Marion found the heat to be very disagreeable, and was picky with Italian food, as tomatoes in any form gave her chronic indigestion. Added to this she had this terrible 'been there, done that' attitude to all the notable architecture, art and landscape that Tuscany had to offer, and of course she had an overriding dislike of spending any more time with me than was necessary. I ought to face facts. It was time for one of us to do the right thing, and put this poor beast, that was once our marriage, out of its misery for good.

The more I thought about it, the more appealing the villa seemed. If things worked out with Anna, - IF…IF… It would be the most perfect summer of my life. On the other hand, if my obsession with Anna, were found to be only a painful unreciprocated love, then I would need to escape to the solitude I would find there.

Anticipation of my Italian summer prompted thoughts of a large glass of red wine, so I opened a bottle and took a glassful of Chianti into the study with me. Now in my study I was fatefully drawn to the stereo, and as was often my habit, selected an LP at random to listen to while I drank the wine and read through a few essays which needed marking.

How strange it should be Elgar's Cello Concerto, Jacqueline de Pré's version which, quite by coincidence, I had listened to on the evening of Ray's funeral. It was as unwise then as it was now. Poor Ray. He was just forty… just forty… when life begins. He had it all: a promising future as an academic; a beautiful wife who earned a fortune in marketing; two fantastic kids - and cancer. Not just any old cancer, no. Ray had a top drawer, a 'no-holds barred' variety. Ray's cancer didn't pull its punches. No, no, his cancer was the Titanic sort that took you under on its maiden voyage. His cancer didn't mess about. It knew its business in life and got on with it. Poor Ray.

From the outset, the prognosis was grim, but I have never seen anybody 'rage, rage against the dying of the light' as much as Ray. His spirit, his determination, his sheer guts, were something to behold. His mental and physical courage humbled everyone around him. And at first, we all applauded and chorused our own version of, 'Do not go gentle into that good night,' as he reeled from each almighty blow, and then with increasingly tottering steps stood to his feet again.

For a month or two, he clung to life, like a man dangling from the edge of a cliff, until his fingertips turned white and were bleeding; until all around were, with silent pleading hearts, secretly begging Ray to bugger off into that 'good night' albeit raging, screaming or singing 'Knees Up Mother Brown', but to just go. We could not bear his suffering. We hadn't the stomach for the fight.

I knew on the morning of the day he died that he would die. His demeanour had changed; the blaze in his unseeing eyes was out. By all accounts, he went into that good night like a lamb. And I was heartily glad. There's a time to fight and a time to be gracious in defeat, and I thank God that in those final hours,

Ray had the wisdom to know the difference. It made it less painful for all of us. I'm a coward you see, and I could not bear his courage, but I could identify with the passive acceptance of one's lot. When you can no longer battle against the current, it is better to relax, to lay back and let the water rush over you. To be swept along like so much debris.

At his funeral, the vicar spoke of 'Raymond's remarkable fortitude'... and then I watched appalled as they bore his coffin away with such ease, it may as well have been empty. It was all so unreal – each of us taking a handful of dry dusty earth, casting it upon the polished, wooden coffin lid – the cries of disbelief smothered in my throat - the prim neatness of the greengrocery grass layered carefully around the abyss; and his little three-year-old daughter, with bright eyes searching for the blackbird, singing so beautifully, somewhere, just out of sight. One of my favourite Beatles' songs drifted into my head, the guitar's gentle twang, the sound of fingers sliding between frets, and the culmination of the heart-breaking beauty of birdsong almost crushed me. Now in the everlasting dead of night, I wondered if his blind eyes had begun to see afresh, and if, at last, he was free from that moribund bony cage of a body that had taken him prisoner. 'We have but a short time to live. Like a flower we blossom and then wither; like a shadow we flee and never stay. In the midst of life, we are in death.'

Juvenile blackbirds practise singing all through the autumn and winter, a low song of jumbled notes. It is known as a sub-song, and apparently one can hear blackbirds in the hedges self-consciously singing softly to themselves, perfecting their voice for spring. I find that so remarkably touching; their achingly beautiful song always brings a lump to my throat.

And now, alone in this cold, cold house, listening to Jaqueline du Pré, whose rendition climbed up my soul with the aid of crampons, fingering every little painful nerve and making it glow. The essays remained unopened. The pictures and photographs on my study wall began to swim before my eyes, and in my mind's eye, clearly, not blinded with tears, I saw alternating images of Ray (strangely, it was memories of Ray alive and well, which broke my heart the most) and Anna. The cello strings wrapped around my heart like a cheese wire, and I wept long aching sobs. It was at this moment I knew that I had no choice in the matter any longer. Whatever embarrassment I risked, whatever humiliation lay in rejection, I must do everything I could to have her. Even if it cost me all that I had, I no longer had a choice. My mind swirled with images of me kissing her, touching her, making love to her. It felt like madness. Even after the record had finished, and it continued in a perpetual orbit of the final groove, I still sat there, my eyes closed, my breathing erratic. My desire for her gnawed hungrily at my innards; it was physically painful – I could not continue like this. However, my thoughts were finally penetrated by the sound of rhythmic scratching on the carpet at my feet - Thaddeus, back from his early evening sortie and ready for his supper. I ruffled his thick fur and smiled down at him, while he purred and pulled at the carpet again. We'd given up shouting at him not to scratch the carpet; he was impossible to control. Thaddeus believed that scratching carpets directly produced bowls of food and opened doors, just like pressing a button, and, at nine years old, nothing would persuade him otherwise.

To be honest, I was profoundly glad of his company, so I opened a tin of pilchards, and gave him the whole lot, even remembering his damn worming tablets, which I crushed into a fine powder between two spoons. He purred like a London cab, and after he'd finished, he spent a good half hour licking around his face, savouring every last fragrant trace of pilchard.

During the night he thanked me for the richness of his dinner by relieving himself in the corner of the kitchen, followed by skating round the lino on his bottom. 'Bloody cat!' I yelled at him, while mopping up the smears. Thaddeus took no notice and smiled in a pool of late autumn sunshine on the back step.

Chapter Seven: the human engine waits

I went into the department as usual, wondering if Anna would come and see me today with some plausible reason for not keeping our appointment yesterday. Then I could make light of my waiting for her for two hours, by which she would infer how desperate I'd been to see her. Perhaps I could then say more seriously I was very much looking forward to seeing her; that I was hoping to see her so much, because I…and at this point, the sentences wouldn't form.

However, I had to endure another day of not seeing her. She did not come and apologise; in fact, she was nowhere to be seen at all in the department, although she did send a message via a friend. The message being that Anna had developed a terrible migraine after lunch, had gone home to rest for an hour or so to see if she could shake it off, and then fallen asleep, and not woken up again until the late evening. She was very sorry about missing the tutorial, and would have come in today, but still felt so groggy. 'Oh, dear,' I said sympathetically, although a gush of happy relief was flooding through me. 'Is she OK now?'

'Well, like I said, a bit groggy, but she'll live.' The friend smiled, and turned and looked directly into my eyes.

'Do you have a message for her?'

I was slightly taken aback. 'A message?'

'Yes, about arranging another time or something, you know'

'Oh, yes,' I said gathering my composure, 'tell her I hope she's feeling better soon, and to pop by tomorrow afternoon, four o'clock onwards, if possible. Thank you, erh?' I struggled to remember her name even though she'd been in a tutorial group of mine before.

'Chris, Chris Bicknel'

'Thank you, Chris. Sorry, I'm hopeless with names. Very good of you to drop by,'

'It's no problem, Anna was very anxious to get a message to you; she felt awful letting you down.' She smiled at me in a way which should have spoken volumes, but my mind was already elsewhere. Swiftly, I shut my study door, and embraced myself. She really hadn't been able to come! I was not just forgotten, or being led on, she genuinely couldn't come, and had cared enough to send her friend to let me know.

I pictured her lying feebly in bed, in a darkened room, which was strange as usually I found the thought of people being ill distasteful. I had always felt guilty when Marion was ill, because I could hardly stand the sight of her, especially if she was down with flu, and ended up with this distorted, puffed up face and dry red flaky skin round her nose. But, in a weird way the thought of Anna being ill almost excited me, as I visualised myself stroking her hair, and running back and forth with drinks and paracetamol. Certainly, I didn't enjoy thinking of her in any kind of pain, but I was beginning to feel unseemingly aroused. I suppose it must come down to the thought of her in bed, and sort of passive, incapable of resistance. I expect you can guess down which path my thoughts were travelling.

After that particular fantasy, I loathed myself. I was supposed to love her, and feel sorry for her in her ill state, and here I was conjuring up some very perverse scenario, which did not strike me as real love at all. However hard I tried, all sorts of ideas would pop up in my mind at the most inappropriate of times. I must have thanked God on more than one occasion that my thoughts were not broadcast out loud, when standing in a queue at the bank, or wandering through the silent aisles at the library. The one idea, I must confess, I returned to frequently, was that of ...no, perhaps here I should draw a veil over my thoughts...anyway, I must admit during the entire time we were actually together I never dared asked if she'd like to do anything like that, but I wish I had now.

Now of course I can't ask her about anything. I can't ask or tell her anything at all. There was a time when I used to share almost everything with her, from my most serious thoughts on life, love and death, to my most trivial of notions; my opinion of a newly published novel; a funny comment someone made in a tutorial; the fact I got soaked on the way to work this morning. But now she doesn't want any of it. I can't even ask her the time. Superficial, or deep, public personae, private persona, she doesn't want to know me anymore. No, I can't even ask her the time.

Let me explain the significance of asking the time. It was a sort of private joke between us because most of the time we were together I'd often ask her, 'What time is it?' This was because my watch was at the menders, and although Anna didn't have a watch, she did have the uncanny ability to guess the correct time day or night, to within five minutes or so. It fascinated me; I'm lost without my watch. I've got it back now, keeps as good a time as it ever did, but you see part of the significance of asking her the time was because it was her fault it got broken.

Anna had this thing about baths, well, any water really. She was always taking baths, showers, swimming, paddling. I used to say it was like going out with a golden retriever, any puddle of water and she'd be in there. Anyway, not long after we'd first started our relationship, I took Anna down to London for the weekend; we were going to go to the theatre, look around the galleries, that sort of thing. We were staying at a very opulent hotel, (Marion would've killed me if she'd seen the bill) and we'd no sooner settled ourselves into the room, when I heard Anna running a bath and shouting to me to order some champagne from room service. The champagne arrived only a few minutes later – I was amazed at the speed of the service. When I took a glass in for Anna, she was already lying in a deep bath overflowing with slippery bubbles. I knelt by the side of the bath to give her, her champagne, which she took from me and after drinking it far too quickly, lifted her mouth for a kiss. As I leant over the edge of the bath, she grabbed me, pulling me into the bath on top of her. It was at times like this I had to remind myself that she was only nineteen; I was, you must understand, still fully dressed, apart from thankfully having removed my jacket and shoes when we'd arrived. Anna was laughing and purring obscenities in my ear. Now, with the uncomfortable feeling of the majority my clothes wet, warm and clinging against my skin, I did my best to make love to her in the bath, which I guessed had been her intention.

Making love in the bath, well, any ordinary-sized bath, is one of those things that only works in films. To be honest I just kept worrying that some irate hotel manager was going to appear at any moment complaining that we were flooding the room below, as great gollops of water kept flopping over the side of the bath.

Anna kept giggling because I just couldn't get it together, sliding about most unsatisfactorily, so in the end we swapped over, which seemed marginally more successful, if not impossibly acrobatic. Finally, the death throes of the drowning man ceased, and the water gently rocked itself to stillness.

Afterwards, we put on clean bath robes, and lay on the bed in a cosy post-coital closeness, lost in our love talk, and champagne. It was about an hour or so later when we were sat up in bed eating smoked salmon sandwiches, and drinking our second bottle of ridiculously priced room service champagne, watching a 'Carry On' film (Yes, we really were) that I suddenly thought about my watch. The leather was beginning to irritate my skin from where it had got wet and was now going dry and hard. It was a very old watch, a twenty-first birthday present, but of course, it wasn't waterproof.

It had stopped with what looked like a smile on its face at ten to two, which delighted Anna when she realised this. I was more concerned for the watch, but in many ways now I wish I hadn't got it mended, and had left time to stand still. However, the watch had been a twenty-first present from my mother, and I was torn between present infatuation and past sentiment. The sentiment won out and my watch spent many months at the jewellers in the high street, while I was too busy, too preoccupied to collect it.

It has a new leather strap now, and when I put it to my ear, I can still hear it whirling and ticking as beautifully as it did on my birthday all those years ago. And sometimes I see it, with that smile on its face at ten to two, and I think of Anna and me in the bath and sort of laugh to myself, imaging how ludicrous the scene must've looked. I think my performance owed more to Moby Dick than James Bond (and no, I am not alluding to part of my anatomy.) Don't get me wrong, it was very sexy, and slippery, and all of that, but at the same time so ridiculously comical. Jasmine – that was the smell – it's just come back to me, mounds and mounds of jasmine scented bubbles that were sweeping round her breasts, like foam rushing round sand castles as the tide comes in at the end of the day.

After Chris had been, I felt happier than I had felt for a long time. There was a certain edge to her attitude… no, more than that, a secret in her eyes – made me sense that something was going on. The more I recalled her face and the nuance of her speech, the more I became convinced that I was being sent an encoded message. Chris and Anna must be friends, because I'd often seen them walking around the university together. Perhaps Anna had confided in her, or then again, she could be helping Anna warn me off. But no, she'd kept emphasising how sorry Anna was not to have come, and that phrase: 'She felt awful letting you down,' sounds a little over the top really, and far too personal for the circumstances. I ruminated that conversation all day, and by the time, I went home I'd allowed myself to be drawn into the happy fantasy that Anna really did have feelings for me.

How different from last night when I had tortured myself with the Elgar. Tonight, I played the opening of Vivaldi's 'Gloria' over and over again, which made my spirit rush with giddy anticipation. Later, I opened a rather fine bottle of Cabernet Sauvignon, to accompany some re-heated left-over beef bourguignon, which I'd found in the bottom of the freezer; my evening was improving considerably. The bourguignon (or beef stew as I always refer to it – just to annoy Marion) was left over from some boring Sunday lunch 'do' she had laid on for her tedious relations, who were passing through on their way to Scotland. Marion has a limited culinary repertoire, but what she does, she does well, and her beef bourguignon was excellent. The other bonus to the evening was that Marion did not ring, and interrupt my imaginings. When I tired of the ecstatic 'Gloria', I ran through other uplifting favourites, and then settled to marking the essays I should have marked the previous night. Looking very much like a large tatty ginger sporran, Thaddeus, curled up on my lap, vibrating with pleasure. I had pardoned last night's misdemeanours, and with no one else available, he and I made the most of one another's company.

Sleep did not come easily that night; I was just too plain excited. There's no other word for it. Sheer childish excitement of being unable to wait for what tomorrow could bring. So, this is what it's like to be alive. I remembered this sensation from way, way back, when I was a child. The anticipation of Christmas, one's birthday morning, the eve of one's summer holiday. Children are truly alive. It seemed to me the longer we've lived; the more we lose the sensation of being alive. But this feeling of bursting anticipation, of longing, of ravenous craving for tomorrow, was blissful.

The next morning, I was up early, and decided to forgo my usual shower for a long soak in the bath. Rather than just letting my hair dry naturally as I usually do, I dried it with the hair dryer, hoping that, perhaps, if I could get it to stay swept back, I might look slightly less mad. However, I couldn't seem to achieve the look I wanted, and resolved that a much-hated trip to the barbers was necessary. All the time I was rehearsing in my mind hundreds of different ways of playing the scenes I thought life had in store for me that day. Should I be subtle and only hint and tease about how I felt? After all, I didn't want to frighten her off by coming straight out with the real strength of my feelings, or would a show of true emotion sweep her off her feet? Of course, when the time actually came, what actually happened hadn't even figured in my plans.

There was a light knock on my door at about ten in the morning. 'Come in,' I announced loudly, not even looking up from a letter I was reading. The door opened slowly, and when I finished the sentence, I swung my chair round, and there she was…strangely misty-looking, because I was still wearing my glasses, which are for reading only. It sounds corny, but my heart actually missed a beat, and began to bang audibly in my chest. As I took off my glasses, she came into sharp focus. I could hardly speak. 'Ah, Anna, feeling better, I trust.' She nodded. 'Good, good. Terrible things migraines; get them myself from time to time, all down this side.' I said this drawing my hand down the left-hand side of my face. (What the hell was I saying? This was not what I was supposed to be saying, so formal, so old fashioned!) Anna said something in reply, but I wasn't listening to a word; I just watched her mouth moving, and heard sounds, but I have no idea of what she was talking about. I smiled and nodded when she'd finished, which only made her look slightly puzzled, and she began to get a few books and pens out of her bag, and sat down at one end of the sofa. Somewhere in my mind, an autopilot switch must've kicked in, and led my turbulent inner self by the hand. Somehow, it told me to give a tutorial. I saw the words 'Waste Land' and it loaded the correct programme.

We actually sat side-by-side on the sofa, and I don't think I've ever played the straight no-nonsense tutor quite so well. I did nothing, but seriously consider the text. I didn't crack a joke, make any innuendo, casually touch her, or even look at her for longer than I should. I couldn't believe myself. I was petrified. 'This is a very complex work; I think one could study it for all one's life and still find some new meaning, reference, hidden in the layers and then find someone who disagrees, who interprets it differently. The major themes are, as one would imagine in any waste land, to do with a sense of emptiness, malaise and loss.'

Anna seemed tense too; she kept putting her hand to her head, and I must have asked her on more than one occasion if she felt all right. 'Yes, I'm fine,' she'd reply and half smile.
She was wearing blue jeans, with a very slight tear on the thigh, where she must've caught them on a nail or something. Just seeing that fraction of her skin through that tear was one of the most erotic things I have ever experienced, but I was paralysed. She was also wearing a baggy grey sweatshirt, and her hair was piled up in some kind of falling down bun. She looked stunning.

'...in the twentieth century, after the Great War, society had changed forever. Eliot, like many others felt this seismic shift, which had caused everything to crumble. The poem is, as it says in this line: '...a heap of broken images' which I believe Eliot is holding onto as an anchor: all the voices of a million mouths that passed, all the history and literature, all the human experience of past ages, which seem more noble than the present, are shattered and mixed with the awful moment of the present age and somehow they will hold it together. Here, right here towards the end: 'These fragments I have shored against my ruins' – perhaps the past must be in the present to anchor us as human beings.' I continued to stumble on, describing the major themes of loss of faith, of the images of sterility and death, of the symbolism of water, and, with a slight awkwardness, pointed out the repeated theme of heartless lust, or worse, indifference, resulting in desolation and sexual failing. I think I probably blushed ever so slightly when describing the Fisher King myth and his struggle with impotence. 'The poem,' I continued, 'with its innumerable references and allusions was considered so obscure by many that Eliot had to add notes at a later date. It may seem strange coming from me, but Susan Sontag's 'Against Interpretation' has an enlightened view, postulating that in many ways we can over analyse some works... lose the magic, by teasing it all apart.' A memory from childhood resurfaced in my mind. 'When I was a boy, I was amazed by my mother's sewing machine. One day, to see how it worked, I undid a couple of screws with a minute screw driver. All at once, about ten tiny springs exploded from within it – it was impossible to put back together. I never saw it in motion again.'

Anna smiled. 'I understand.'

The tutorial came to a natural conclusion, and I was desperately trying to think of some reason to extend it, but nothing would come to mind. I think because of my nerves I'd gone through The Waste Land at an impossibly cracking pace. I knew I'd talked far too much. I'd shot myself in the foot really. 'Thank you for your help,' she said very seriously.

'Anytime,' I smiled, placing my glasses gently on my desk. There was a definite pregnant pause, which I knew in my heart was a vacuum of space into which I was being invited to jump and fill with my declaration of love. But the leap - the leap of faith - terrified me...within seconds, the moment had passed – the portal was closed.

She had her hand on the door handle, and with a very quick, 'Thanks again, then,' was gone. 'Shit! Shit! Shit! You fool! You bloody fool!' I ranted to myself. I moved quickly over to the window, and moments later, from behind the curtain, watched her hurriedly crossing the courtyard, disappearing between the buildings.

'God!' exclaimed Chris, as Anna joined her in the library, 'didn't expect to see you here so soon, quick worker is he, then?' She looked at her watch, in mock disbelief. 'Chat up and foreplay, thirty minutes at the outside, plus around five for the main event, oh, hang on, older man probably should reckon on more control, let's say ten. After glow, quick ciggi, walk back here… an hour and ten minutes. Not bad for a fifty-year-old.'

'Oh, Chris, for God's sake, give it a rest!'

'Woo! Oh dear, that bad, was it? I did try to warn you.'

'Nothing happened, all right. Nothing at all. We went through 'The Waste Land' the entire time. He didn't so much as look at me. I just feel so embarrassed. I should never have listened when you said he fancied me. 'Leave him to smoulder for a day, I can smell suppressed desire'.' Chris opened her mouth to speak, but didn't get an opportunity. 'Well, my little bloodhound, I think you found a false scent this time. I feel like such an idiot. I mean, what's wrong with me? I thought you'd said he have a go at anyone, who was female with eyes, nose and mouth in the right order! And all that stupid ashtray stuff!'

'Hang about,' interrupted Chris at last, now assuming a phoney American chat show voice. 'What I'm getting here is anger, sexual frustration of the highest order. I think the bottom line is, (and we are talking '*bottom*' here folks!) is that deep down, in your inner most psyche, the feelings you want to share with me now, and our dear viewers, is that you're as pissed as hell he didn't screw the ass off you. Am I right?'

'Chris! Will you shut up!' said Anna exasperated. 'I know this is all one huge joke to you, but if you're any kind of friend at all you would take this seriously.'

'Seriously?'

'Yes. Seriously. I've been rejected. I hate being rejected. Rejected by some, some...' (She searched her mind for the most apposite invective, but couldn't retrieve it, and rather disappointingly settled for *'man'*) 'who's been coming on to me for weeks, and then cuts me dead just like that.' Anna put her head in her hands, then looking up peered through her fingers at Chris. 'I don't want you to breathe a word of this to anyone, but what I was saying the other day about just messing about isn't entirely true. I really think I do like him, you know, in *that* way.'

'You mean the rumpy-pumpy way?'

'Yes,' said Anna, in a resigned tone,' I mean the 'rumpy-pumpy' way, and more besides.'

'You mean there *IS* more than just rumpy-pumpy?'

'I said '*seriously*'.'

'Sorry.'

For a moment Anna looked on the verge of tears. 'Maybe I'm just embarrassed. I feel such a fool even talking about it. But I really thought he liked me.'

Chris's voice, whole demeanour softened, she drew closer to Anna, placing her arm around her shoulder. 'Let me tell you this for certain, Alistair Johnson fancies you rotten. I told you how he was yesterday, all pent up and flustered. If you ask me, I think his actions today prove something even I hadn't thought of.'

'What?'

'Well, my dear, I think you're twanging with more than the elastic on his Y-fronts.' She whispered in Anna's ear, 'I think I hear a little tune being played on his heart strings too. He's serious. He's in love, bless him. So 'in love,' he's afraid.' Anna pulled away to assess Chris's face for sincerity. 'Oh, sure, I should have known that all along, that's why he treated me like some pariah today.'

'And doesn't it work like that sometimes? What were you doing today? Were you all flirty, loading everything you said with a message of "Get your kit off, Big Boy, today's your lucky day?" No, I suspect, that when you finally found yourself alone with him, the air was so thick with unspoken desire, you were totally lost.' Anna shrugged her shoulders and poked at the crack between the tables with a plastic spoon. 'I don't know. I was trying to concentrate on The Waste Land.'

'No, you weren't! But for God's sake Anna, if this is the way things are going, do be careful. Remember, that there is a world of difference between five minutes fun, and falling in love, especially with men of a certain age.'

'Honestly, sometimes you sound like my mother. I'm not a child you know.'

'I know, but then again neither is he. And think about it, Anna, what would your mother really say if she knew you wanted to sleep with someone your father's age?'

An uncomfortable look passed across Anna's face. 'Don't say that. It's different, and you know it.'

Chris sighed, 'If it's what you really want, it'll happen. Believe me, it'll happen, and best of luck to you when it does.' Chris stood up, she looked tired and suddenly a lot older than twenty-one. 'I'm sorry about yesterday, and today. I haven't been a lot of help, have I?'

'Maybe not,' said Anna flatly. Chris began raking through her bag.

'Oh, cheer up Anna. You just have to be more direct. Just go for it, you've nothing to lose... but your virginity.'

'I wish!'

'Shit, I'm out of fags again. Gotta go. See ya!' Anna called after her, 'Chris! Wait!' But she was already lost behind a crowd pouring out of one of the lecture theatres.

Chapter Eight: a straight look

As soon as Anna had gone, it dawned on me that had she come around four as I had suggested, things would have been different. I'd have had a few drinks at lunchtime, been easier, more relaxed. The tutorial would have drifted on past five o'clock; my room would have become gradually darker and darker, until eventually, in the half shadows of twilight, I would have been brave enough to say something. I even believed that if I could have managed to tell her how I felt, she might have told me she felt the same. And then who knows what heaven would have awaited me. It suddenly came to my mind that there was another reason why I'd suggested four; it was because I was tied up all day with other things. So, what was I supposed to be doing at ten? Oh, hell! I was supposed to be seeing Ruth Collins about setting up a poetry workshop in December. Oh, God, why did I put myself in a position of having to eat humble crumble for her? I wondered why she hadn't come to knock for me, as her office was only just across the corridor from mine. I padded across the corridor expecting to be greeted by something like, 'Oh, I'm so terribly sorry Alistair. Would you believe it, for some insane reason I didn't enter it in my diary?' However, nothing had prepared me for the conversation, which followed.

'Ah, Alistair,' she said soberly, 'you'd better come in.'

Oh dear, I thought as I sat down heavily in one of the worn leather chairs, she sounds peeved.

'Ruth, I'm sorry about this morning's meeting, no excuses, I just clean forgot. I guess you did too as you didn't come and fetch me.'

'Well, no Alistair, I didn't forget. In fact, I'd just opened my door to come over and remind you, when I saw Anna Martin outside your room. Unobserved, I watched her for a few moments; she seemed to be gathering her courage, or something of that sort. After she'd gone into your room, I didn't like to interrupt.'

I was genuinely bewildered by what Ruth was saying. 'Oh, yes,' I began slowly, 'I was giving a tutorial. But it wasn't even scheduled; you could've come over and got me at any time. I should've remembered I was already booked with you.'

"Well, maybe I should have done, but it's just Anna looked so troubled, how can I put this – so preoccupied? I thought perhaps it was personal.'

'Personal?'

'Look, please don't make me have to spell this out to you. I don't want to pry into your private affairs, but memories are not as short as you may imagine, and things will get noticed.'

'I was giving a tutorial,' I repeated coldly.

'Well, fair enough. Just bear in mind taking advantage of students in your care is frowned upon with increasing gravity these days.'

'I've no idea what you mean,' I said, barely able to disguise my anger.

'You really want to make this difficult for me, don't you? You know full well what I'm talking about: taking advantage of your position here, with young women, who in any other circumstances wouldn't give you a second look. It is, in my opinion, always damaging, both to them personally and to the general atmosphere of the relationships between everyone else in the department.' The light caught the front of her enormous glasses making her look like a praying mantis. I could feel my blood running hot.

'I can't believe you've got the audacity to speak to me like this!' A nerve in my top lip began to tremble, 'About something which would not concern you even if your curtain-twitching suppositions were true.'

'You may not like it Alistair, but it does concern me. Students' welfare is what concerns me. The last thing we all need is another Fay Morgan situation.'

'Oh, for God's sake Ruth,' I exploded, leaping from my seat, 'that was a few years ago now. Talk about 'Give a dog a bad name!' Besides, you talk about these students as if they were thirteen-year olds in gymslips. Anna's nineteen for goodness sake. If I was having an affair with her, *which I'm not*, it would be none of your God-damn business.'

'You still don't get it, do you?'

Ruth also rose from her chair, and quietly walked across the room to me. She was quite a formidable lady, fortyish, unmarried, with dun-coloured hair, cut into a shoulder length bob, that never seemed any shorter or longer, and her eyes were alternately concealed or magnified by her absurdly oversized glasses. Now, close enough that I could smell what I can only guess was her antiperspirant activated by her simmering fury, she used her marginally taller height to her advantage. Tilting her head ever so slightly downward, she spoke in a very quiet, controlled way, going into her bloody fucking therapist mode, which angered me even more.

'May I suggest you seem very tense and defensive, Alistair.' My mouth opened to speak; she raised her hand to silence me. 'Just listen. Anna attends my drama sessions, and from what I observe, she is a very interesting girl: intelligent, artistic, obviously physically desirable... but she's also very vulnerable.' (At this point, I began to wonder if my long-held suspicions were true and she was actually a repressed lesbian who desired Anna for herself.) 'And it's patently clear to me that she has developed some sort of crush on you, which I am afraid you will be tempted to exploit.'
'A crush?'
'Yes, a crush, such as young girls are prone to suffering from.'
My dumbfounded expression obviously annoyed her.

Oh, come on Alistair, don't play the innocent - all the usual signs. Main symptom being 'mentionitus'; drops your name into conversations, quotes your ideas, has the unnatural glow of someone in the grips of an infatuation, watches you when she thinks no one is looking, that kind of thing... Now I know,' she continued, pushing at her eyelids beneath her glasses as if her eyes ached, 'at one level, you're probably right, it is none of my business, but I should hate to see such a promising girl come to grief in any way.' She removed her glasses and looked at the lenses irritably. 'And believe it or not I do care about seeing you take a fall, as always seems inevitable in these situations.'

I was completely off balance, I can tell you. My words stumbled angrily from my mouth. 'Well, let me assure you, although...although, why I should even be having this conversation God knows, nothing, let me repeat, nothing, inappropriate has taken place between myself and Anna Martin.'

'Yet.'

We exchanged a look of contempt, her eyes looking cruel and small without magnification. 'I've said my piece,' she said haughtily, 'perhaps only to try and save you from yourself, or to assuage my own guilt when it all blows up in your face again.' She rubbed the lenses of her glasses on the corner of her long flimsy cardigan.

'Your sense of duty is entirely misplaced. I am not your responsibility, and apart from a very superficial responsibility to Anna as student welfare officer, her private life is none of your concern either.' She went very silent for a few moments, and then replacing her glasses looked directly at me, 'grasshopper' once more.

'You nearly cost Fay Morgan her life, Alistair. Doesn't that ever make you think?' I shot her a look that could have cost her, *her* life, and paced quickly towards the door.

'You have strayed seriously out of your territory, Ruth. I don't know by what authority you think you can speak to me like this. Under the circumstances, you'd best sort this workshop out with someone else.'

'This isn't about 'authority', or 'territory' Alistair, but simply about what I consider to be right. Pursuing such involvements compromises teaching, compromises assessments and affects other students adversely too. My concern is ultimately for the well-being of all our students and of the department.'

'How very noble,' I said sarcastically, as I swung open the door, 'really, your altruism knows no bounds.'

****

I stood outside in the hallway; my internal organs contracted into one tight ball. I felt cold fingers of fear running up and down my back, and I drew my shoulders up as if in pain.

Such a cocktail of emotions stirring round inside me: absolute indignation at Ruth daring to poke her nose in, and on such circumspect evidence; to be so judgmental on something which hadn't even happened. I was also racked with guilt, on being reminded, yet again, about that deluded girl Fay Morgan. An image of her fiery hair against the pale, almost translucent skin of her face hovered momentarily in my mind. I banished it. That had been then, way back, when I was an altogether different person. And besides, what people do seem to forget easily is that she had a history of psychological problems, from anorexia through to xenophobia. There was no way anything like that could happen now. There was no comparison.

But the over-riding emotion, which writhed amongst all this molten fury like a giant serpent, the gut twisting elation, that someone else thought that Anna loved me.

I hurried back to the safety of my room, whereupon I saw the gods had smiled on me. There on the floor, poking out from under the sofa was a small brightly coloured textile bag, decorated with embroidery and mirrors. I knew immediately it was Anna's. Picking it up eagerly, I put it to my nose. I swear I could smell her. Then I did something quite out of character; I opened it. Inside a zipped-up pocket were the usual assortment of loose change, a tatty five-pound note, and a screwed-up shopping list, which I read with as much interest as if it were a newly discovered Shakespeare sonnet. Another section revealed mascara, a lip salve, and two tampons of varying sizes. Feeling almost thrilled with my audacity, I kissed them and brushed them against my cheek, before carefully putting them back in the purse. There was also a collection of cheque cards, library cards, Union cards; the latter bearing some photos of her now sealed in acetate. Behind these, I found another photograph, which caused such an instant pain in my chest. I thought for a moment I was having some kind of heart attack. (I suppose in a way I was.)

My mouth went dry as I stared at this image of this boy in his twenties, filling a cement mixer of all things. He's only wearing jeans. There's hardly a hair on his chest, smooth light brown skin, biceps flexed, brown tousled hair. He's so exceptionally good-looking he could be a model. The smile on his face tells me Anna is taking the photograph. Nothing is written on the back. I slipped the photo back into the purse, and put the purse on my desk. I sat motionless, staring at the purse. What now?

The rest of the day passed by with my thoughts totally preoccupied by the question of who the boy in the photograph was, and whether or not Anna would come by to recover her purse. Not daring to leave my study all day in case she returned, it was a happy coincidence that a lecture I was due to give was cancelled, due to a flood in the lecture theatre. The only food I had in my room was a stale packet of crisps and my bottle of whisky. Not a very healthy lunch, but it got me through the last seminar of the day.

I was so confused: one minute I was devastated, thinking of him in the photograph, whom I felt I could safely assume was her boyfriend, and the next I was elated, almost unable not to smile at the thought of Anna mentioning my name, and apparently, even gazing at me when she thought no one else was looking. After the seminar group had gone, I lay back on the sofa with my eyes closed, and gave my mind over to my desires.

I wanted to kiss her mouth. I wanted to touch her face, her hair. I wanted to hold her fiercely to me, to gently lay my head on her breast and hear her heart beating. I wanted her to press herself to me and beg me to make love to her. I wanted someone to *want* me, to need me, to desire me, to the point of death – before I died. Was that so wrong? Clamouring to experience the extremities of life's emotions. Grasping at the intensity. Crying out to say, 'God, I'm alive!

This is living!' as each cell effervesces and pops, in her presence. And if just sitting near her was so ecstatic, what if? Oh! My stomach turned over. It would be bliss. Bliss. I knew it would.

I expect you're thinking the next thing I'm going to say is that she turned up for her purse, while I was still half drunk and so desperate to consummate my feelings that I finally seduced her right there and then on the carpet. But no, what happened next is this.

Chapter Nine: waiting for a knock upon the door

I left for home quite early at about four o'clock, taking the bag with me. I had found out Anna's address weeks ago, and was formulating a plan of returning it to her personally later on that evening. It seemed like a gift really; a genuine excuse to see her. I knew exactly where her house was, because I'd driven past it on several occasions. However, when I got home my courage evaporated as quickly as spilt water on a sun-baked paving stone, and all I could do was wait the night out and take the bag back into work the next day.

It was most likely she'd be at the ten o'clock lecture I was due to give that morning, so I took the bag with me in my briefcase. She was there all right, standing in the corner of the lecture theatre, chatting away to a couple of friends. As soon as she saw me, I heard her say, 'Here's hoping!' and she sort of bounded over in the way that young girls do. 'I was just wondering if I had possibly left...' but before she'd finished her sentence, I had pulled the bag triumphantly from my briefcase with great aplomb, as if I had just performed a conjuring trick.

'Thank goodness for that!' she cried, smiling with genuine relief. 'You were my last hope. I'd searched everywhere else I thought it could've been left. I was just saying to Emma, if it wasn't with you then I'd have probably said goodbye to it for good. And you know what a hassle it is trying to replace cards and passes and all that junk.' She smiled again with eyes that dazzled me, and all I could do was shrug my shoulders and say 'Problem solved,' which I suppose was better than saying, 'Make merry and be glad, for this bag was lost, and now is found,' which was also running round in my mind and looking for airtime. I sometimes wondered if I was losing my mind.

I pretended to peruse my lecture notes, but every so often scanned the room to glimpse her. She was sitting to the left-hand side of the lecture theatre, towards the front. Once I saw her checking through the contents of her bag, and I broke out in a sweat, wondering if she thought I'd done the same.

Thankfully, the lecture was one I'd given many times before – standard stuff on Marvell. I knew I was good at delivering this lecture; the students were with me all the way. I don't think I lost one to attending to its manicure, filing through its social diary, passing notes, or wind for the hell of it. Once, ever so briefly, I caught Anna's eyes, and I do believe she looked proud of me, as if she thought I was wonderful, and for a moment, I felt it. Perhaps, 'To My Coy

Mistress' was a little too painfully apposite, but nothing could contain my love of this work. The sheer mirth I felt as I shared this poem with them. Not one of them would forget the phrase *carpe diem* for the rest of their lives, and I hoped they would take it, as their life's motto, as I, unfortunately, had not... until now that is.

During that lecture, the whole picture became clear. Rejection would feel no worse than the way I felt now. 'Had we but world enough, and time....' It was not coyness, which held me back, but fear. Fear of rejection, humiliation, fear of things going wrong, even a fear of things going right –a fear of the loss of hope.

The danger is to delay, and delay, until the moment is past. And of course, as we all know, it's not the things we have done we usually regret, but the things we have left undone. With the rush of winds from 'Time's winged chariot' cooling the back of my neck, I decided there and then to act, to take my destiny into my own hands, 'to shape the still unshapen.' To seize life with a great big YES, rather than a hesitant maybe.

As the lecture theatre emptied, I realised Anna was hanging back, so I made a pretence of busying myself, getting out a little diary and writing one or two notes in it. Eventually, the room was empty and we were alone. With an ever-frantic heart, I heard her footsteps approaching, and looked up in feigned surprise at seeing her there. She was standing very close, closer than one normally would in such circumstances. She was wearing a jumper, made of very soft wool, which one could only describe as ethnic; I'd hazard a guess at South America. In my peripheral vision, I could just see the gentle swell of her breasts beneath. She swept her hair back with her hand. 'I just wanted to say thank you again for finding my bag. It was a present – so it has sentimental value too.'

'It was just under the sofa in my study, must've toppled from your bigger bag, during our chat. I'm sorry I wasn't able to return it to you sooner.'

'Not to worry, Chris lent me some money. I did come by your study though, at about five-thirty, in the hope of catching you before you left. I'd been back to everywhere else I'd been that day. You were my last hope!'

Nervously, I struggled to close the zip on my brief case. 'Oh, really? What a pity. If I'd known that I'd have waited for you.'

'Would you?' she said with an unnatural gravity.

'Well, yes, I would've. I would have liked to have seen you in any case,' I replied with equal seriousness.

'What? About The Waste Land, again?' (She was treading so carefully; it was like a slow dance to and fro, around a pool of quick sand.)

'No. Not about work.'

'What, then?' Her question hovered in the air, which seemed thick and dreamlike. Breathing very deeply, as if I couldn't get enough oxygen from each breath, I sensed that we were very close to breaking through that glass wall, which surrounds us all. The pause was interminable. I was searching for the next phrase, which could shatter the wall into a thousand invisible fragments. We were looking directly into one another's eyes. Searching. Perhaps she saw the words she was waiting to hear in my eyes. Because it was Anna who surprised me. She disintegrated our glass wall, not with words, but with a touch. Her hand was suddenly upon my arm; I looked down at her hand, and then back into her eyes. And at that moment, I knew. Her eyes lit up, teasing me. 'I wanted to see you too.' And then she added with emphasis, 'But not about work.' Then, as if this moment of recognition had been enough, she withdrew her hand and turned away to pick up her bag. She began to walk slowly towards the door. 'Time's winged chariot' hit me full force in the back of the neck and shoved me forward. 'Anna,' I called out. She turned and smiled, a smile, which was so arousing, I felt like a gauche teenage boy.

'Anna. Would you like to, um, you know, come for a drink then? With me, sometime?'

'You know I would. What about tonight? The Stag, at about eight?'

'Yes, great,' I replied, although I was hoping to suggest somewhere quieter myself.

'Bye, then,' she said breezily, and was gone.

I stood motionless for a few moments. It had been so easy when the moment had finally come. I had not read the signals incorrectly; she had met me more than half way. I had my chance now. God help me that I don't mess it up.

Chapter Ten: a record on the gramophone

Can you imagine how I spent the rest of that day? There was no room in my mind for anything other than Anna. Everyone I passed in the street, everyone I spoke to, did not know I was hiding within myself a great secret. You don't know what I am thinking. You don't know where I am going. You don't know what I'll be doing soon, very soon. You don't know I am a man standing on brimstone. You just don't know. My ordinary mask gives nothing away. Only a smile playing around my lips, a light burning in my eyes betrays me.

At seven o'clock I was ready, standing in front of the wardrobe mirror, dressed in casual trousers, a white shirt, jumper, and an olive coloured cord jacket, which I think suits me. Sadly, I don't have much idea about clothes, so dressing is always something of a trial for me. Marion says I have all the fashion sense of a man who's dressed himself at a jumble sale during a blackout. That's probably somewhat of an exaggeration, but I'd have to admit 'stylish' is not an adjective that will ever be attached to my character description.

I turn this way and that in front of the mirror. How puzzling it is to confront the reflected image of oneself. In my mind's eye, I am quite different. Although this probably sounds vain, but when I visualize myself, I am kinder, more generous, to myself than, a camera, or a mirror can be. Whenever I see a photograph of myself, I find it extraordinarily unsettling. Is that really me? Set in some moment of my past. All the days of my life, I have spent in this face, this body, (albeit in its many guises) and still I have no idea how I appear to the world. I wonder if any of us really feel the inside and the outside are a perfect match. The answer to the question of who we really are isn't always obvious. *'Mind the gap. Mind the gap. Mind the gap.'*

As I left the house, I was shaking with cold as well as nerves. The autumn was relinquishing to the winter, and every now and then, out of the corner of my eye I'd see a leaf bowling along at speed in the gutter and think for a moment it was a rat. It was really chilly actually, and already I regretted not wearing my winter coat. Hurrying along the railings of the park, one could see a thin film of frost already bedding down for the night, turning the grass a ghastly shade of lime; each blade stiffening, as tiny spiky shards of ice formed upon their shafts.

At 7.45pm I arrived at the pub, so as to establish myself in the corner before she appeared, but to my surprise she was already standing at the bar, drink in hand, chatting in a very animated fashion to two young lads. I, who was supposed to be older, more confident, hesitated, transfixed. A strange fear overwhelmed me and I was almost about to withdraw quietly back through the door, when one of them spoke and nodded towards me. Anna suddenly spun around and lit up with such radiant sexuality that I was eaten up, from inside out. Pretending to have just seen her, I smiled and started to move across the pub towards her, my nerves jumping like sand fleas. As we met, half way, she touched my hand ever so briefly. (Ah, God, there goes my breath.)

'You're early,' she said brightly. 'Why don't you go and sit over there, and I'll get you a drink. What would you like?' Her confidence amazed me. She walked back from the bar carrying two pints of beer, while I just sat watching.

'Aren't your friends joining us?'

'Friends?' She laughed, looking mystified.

'Yes,' I nodded towards the bar, 'those two.'

'Oh, you mean those blokes! No, I've only just met them, but I'm sure they'll join us if you'd like them too.'

'Eh, no,' I sighed, smiling with relief.

We talked very easily, just ordinary conversation really, the weather, the pub, why she'd chosen to do the English course here, and that she liked beer, by the pint. It was almost as if she was deliberately avoiding the fact that perhaps the two of us sat here, like this, was the only real topic of conversation. All I wanted to talk about was how I felt, and to determine to what extent my feelings found even the slightest echo in her heart. She'd obviously already had a few drinks, making her surprisingly relaxed and flirtatious. There was something different about her eyes... darker, larger, even more compelling, and she was dressed in a midnight blue shirt, which was undone just enough to see the top curve of her breast, whenever she bent forward to pick up her bag or whatever.

'I'm really hungry,' she announced putting her hand on my thigh. 'Have you eaten yet?'

'No,' I replied, with my heart pulsating so rapidly I could hardly speak.

Well, shall we go and eat somewhere, or just stay here and make do with a pack of pork scratchings and some mixed nuts?'

'Tempted as I am by the pork scratchings, I think I know somewhere that can offer us even greater culinary delights,' I said finding some form at last, although I wished I hadn't attempted the word culinary. 'I know just the place. Come on.'

As if I had been doing it all my life, I helped her into her enormous long black coat. 'Now, nobody's done that before,' she commented, and I was slightly confused as to whether or not this old-fashioned gesture had gone down well.

We were walking swiftly down the street now, me already half frozen with my hands thrust in my pockets, she head high, hair blowing wildly, like a defiant mermaid bursting through oceans.

I gazed appreciatively at her. She saw me.

'Fantastic coat,' I said with an expansive sweep of my hand.

'Thanks.' She buttoned up the high collar. 'I got it from a charity shop actually. I think it makes me look like Russian spy, don't you?'

'Yes, I guess you do a bit.' (The mermaid slipped beneath the waves.)

'You like it then? My espionage look.'

I smiled. 'I love it.'

'Good. Then next time we go out you must do me the compliment of dressing in black tie, and doing your best Sean Connery impression all evening.'

'I'm afraid I'm unable to oblige with that, Miss Moneypenny,' I said in an uncannily perfect impression (what luck! This just so happened to be my party piece) but I can do a great Roger Moore eyebrow if that will suffice.'

She turned to me looking absolutely stunned, 'That's brilliant! Can you do anyone else?'

'You'll have to wait and see,' I teased, 'but that's probably my best.'

'That's incredible! Connery has such a sexy voice. God, that's amazing. Say something else.'

I can tell you I was more than delighted with the effect of my party piece.

'Later, later,' I intoned in my best 'Auld Reekie' accent, 'All in good time, agent Annaslovski. At the moment my top priority is an urgent appointment with dinner.'

'That is so good! My friend Chris is good with voices too. She wants to be an actress, practises her accents and voices all the time. Did you ever act?'

'Me? No, I'm far too shy.'

'You're joking?'

No, really,' I said earnestly, 'I'm a very quiet, private sort of person. I just do voices. "You mightn't think it, but Sloppy is a beautiful reader of a newspaper. He do the Police in different voices.''

She grinned. 'Our Mutual Friend?'

'Well spotted.' I was truly impressed. 'But honestly, I am... very quiet, very shy.' She just looked at me and sort of laughed in disbelief. 'Why don't you believe me?'

'I never said I didn't.'

An unexpected sharp blast of wind bit into our faces. 'Gosh, isn't it freezing!' Anna sounded almost thrilled, and slipped her arm into mine, as if to huddle up for warmth. With her body so close to mine for the first time I was thrown into a complete inner turmoil. An intense surge of energy flooded through me, with every step I took I wanted to throw her up against a wall, and almost crush her with the passion raging within me. To burst my mouth onto hers, push my hands under her clothes; hold her to me as if my life depended on it. Thankfully, I controlled myself, and strolled along trying not to tremble too much from the cold. As we approached 'The Amalfi', she exclaimed, 'God! Here?'

'Don't you like Italian?' I asked, trying not to sound too disappointed.

'No, it's not that; it's just this is a bit pricey, you know.'

'Oh, come on.' I grabbed her hand and pulled her gently towards the door. 'You bought the beer; I'll buy the dinner.' I suppose alarm bells should have gone off, because as we entered the restaurant, which I knew she could not afford, a magnanimous glow radiated through me. My sense of power grew as we sat the table and a waiter, I'd met there several times before greeted me by name. 'Order whatever you like,' I encouraged. The phrase 'Sugar Daddy' never once entered my head.

As I have mentioned before, I loved to watch her eat. And tonight, was the beginning of that love affair. We both had antipasto. 'Mmm! Black olives,' she murmured, and with a real sensual pleasure popped the shiny nugget into her mouth, rotated them with her tongue, until torn of all its flesh, only the stone emerged, which she then pulled through her teeth with her finger and thumb. I was fascinated. (Marion had such an aversion to finger food that I've even seen her cut grapes in half to scrape out the pips with a teaspoon.) The spaghetti was an equal delight, leaving a glistening trace of olive oil upon her lips. I finished up with a lamb dish, which was sweet and fragrant, while Anna plumped for a Chicken Veneto.

We both drank rather a lot of Chianti, and although Anna showed no embarrassingly obvious signs of getting drunk, she was touching my leg with hers under the table. When our eyes met, hers were wild. I was paralyzed. My mind was racing, all I had wanted was now so tantalisingly close, but how to get from sitting at a quiet table in 'The Amalfi' to her bed, to any bed even, without breaking the atmosphere, seemed impossible. Everything was moving so fast, even by my standards. I had imagined she'd be quite reserved, but God was I wrong. We declined desert, coffee, and liquors; the waiter backed away with a gracious knowing air. I blushed ever so slightly when I requested a taxi.

As we fell into the taxi, she said that she doubted very much I would want to go on to a nightclub, so should she just give the driver her address. I was unsure as to why she had reservation about my ability to 'boogie on down', but at another level, I felt relieved. I wondered if she would invite me in after all now. Perhaps I was jumping the gun earlier on? This was our first date as it were, and although she seemed to have been fizzing with sexual desire over dinner, I didn't want to presume anything. Quite casually, I put my arm around her and she sank against my chest. Turning towards her, my lips touched her hair, so fresh, so soft, so clean.

For the rest of the journey home, she went very quiet, and I worried that I'd overdone it with the red wine, because it seemed to me, she had gone to sleep. However, as the cab pulled up, the engine, throbbing, waiting, she came to. Jumping out quickly and then swaying ever so slightly, she held on to the cab door, and stared down at me. 'Aren't you going to walk me to my door?' 'Of course, I'm sorry,' I apologized and turning to the cab driver said, 'Stay here a moment, please.' She must've over heard, because the next thing she did was stick her head in the cab window, wink at the driver and say, 'Oo, I don't think that'll be necessary.'

I'd just managed to give him five pounds, before Anna had grabbed my other hand and led me up the flight of steps to her front door. The taxi drove away at high speed; I could tell he was over-revving like mad. Jealous as hell, I bet. Still, he had got a good tip out of it. Anna lived in one of those huge four-storey Victorian houses converted into a warren of bedsits. The hallway was cold, with a lingering damp odour, and the light from the single light bulb was cruel and harsh.

'Up, I'm afraid.' She started up a flight of stairs covered in a swamp coloured carpet. 'Attic rooms are the best, don't you think? Just such a bugger to get to.'

'You don't share with anyone, do you?' I asked anxiously, as a vision of myself, Anna, and a flatmate bedecked in their dressing gown, all drinking cocoa together, rose uneasily in my mind. 'No,' she grinned, reading my thoughts. 'Well, not officially anyway. Chris lives opposite, that's how I know her. You know Chris Bicknell; she said you were her tutor in the first year.'

'Oh, yes,' I paused to catch my breath. 'Just for a term I think - short course. She came the other day…with your message.' She gave a rather nervous laugh. 'Oh, yeah, she's away in Liverpool at the moment...gone home for a long weekend.' Three flights of stairs, the spaghetti and the fragrant lamb, were beginning to take their toll. 'For God's sake, stop panting!' Anna said turning round to me. 'What will the neighbours think?' I tried desperately to control my breathing, as the last thing I wanted was to appear as unfit, flaccid, and susceptible to dying in flagrante. Finally, we were outside of her room, she turned the key, and I entered into her space.

I cannot tell you how rapidly I tried to absorb every bit of information divulged to me by the contents of her room. The scent, well yes, there was that wonderful smell of Anna (which only now I discover was Pears soap of all things! So ordinary, and yet so evocative); also present was a layer of joss sticks, and one of oranges too. I scanned the room, and noticed one half-eaten orange on a plate on the window ledge. Underneath the ledge a few items of underwear hung from a little rail in front of a radiator; there was a bamboo blind, half rolled down; bright cotton striped rugs covered bare wooden boards; an eclectic mixture of posters, prints, and photographs, and a giant Chinese kite upon the walls. Small Indian bells hung around the room, and mobiles made from slithers of shell twirled in aimless circles from invisible threads. There were plants curling their brown-tinged leaves around bookcases; and papers, books, and pens scattered everywhere. And in the corner of the room a double mattress on the floor, spread with an Indian print quilt.

'I'm sorry, I've got nothing better.' Anna waved a bottle of wine in the air. 'It's nowhere as good as what we had tonight, but at least it's red, and look, even Italian too.'

'It's fine. I love your room.'

'Do you?' she said with genuine surprise.' Well, I did tidy it up bit, just in case you came back.'

'Well, it's lovely,' I enthused, but where the tidy bit came in was lost on me. She handed me a glass of wine and then knelt to light the gas fire, immediately transporting me back to my student days as the smell of burning dust and gas filled the room. Taking another long match, she lit various candles and tea lights that were dotted about the room, and turned the central light out. Through the softly lit air she gazed at me. 'Doesn't that make it look even better?'

I watched her look around the room with a satisfied pleasure and then she asked me what kind of music I liked, to which I replied that I usually listened to classical music, mostly baroque, but not wishing to seem too staid added that I was also partial to the odd bit of pop. A smile flickered across her face.

'But put on whatever you like. I'd love to know what 'rings your bell'.' Smiling quietly to myself, I gently blew on the slivers of shell, which span before my eyes. Bach's prelude in C Major began a graceful meander about the room, 'I love this,' I whispered, 'it's beautiful.'

'Yes, it's lovely, isn't it? I'm glad you approve. It's my grown-up mood music.' For a fleeting second, she looked slightly bashful, and then the light was in her eyes again.

'It's a bit of a mixture really, all sorts of bits and pieces I've taped myself. I'm a Philistine at heart you know. I only like pieces I can hum.'

'So, we won't be hearing John Cage's 4'33 then?' I quipped.

'Well, as I've never even heard of him, I guess not.'

Rather disappointed my joke had fallen on deaf ears, and feeling it would only be awkward to explain it, I pushed the conversation hurriedly on. 'You obviously like music though,' I encouraged, indicating towards a pile of LPs, which were slumped up against the bookcase, 'and all these tapes!'

'Ah, well, one of my hobbies is compiling tapes for all occasions.' She crouched down in front of the cassette rack. 'I hope one day to make a million out of this idea.' She pulled out several cassettes and handed them to me. The cardboard inserts had been customised with a stylised pen and ink drawing, a pastiche of Beardsley, but with a very modern twist, each one very different in content, but consistent in style. I read aloud from the little pile in my hand: 'Music to Induce Outrageous Happiness', 'Music to Accompany Mild Intoxication', 'Music to Accompany *Extreme* Intoxication.'

I raised a questioning eyebrow.

'Yes, these are just wonderful,' she enthused. 'I've been drunk to this one so often now, I'm like Pavlov's dog; I only have to hear the music to experience that intense pleasure of crossing the line between my usual screwed-up inhibited self to the fun-loving sex goddess I am when drunk.'

'Powerful stuff!' I quickly scanned the selection, trying to commit the contents to memory.

'Oh, this is also one of my favourites! She handed me a cassette with 'Music to be Thoroughly Depressed to.'

'Interesting,' I mused reading the list on the back.

'Mmm' she said with a faraway look in her eyes, 'Part two is 'Music to Commit Suicide to.'

'You're kidding?'

She laughed.

'I just can't make up my mind what should be in it. I mean you'd think it should be sad, but then perhaps some people who commit suicide *really* want to die, and it's not just a mistake, a cry for help when things go wrong. So, it should perhaps be music of joyful release. To take control over the one event in our life over which we have no control.'

I doubted very much that death was the *only* event over which we had no control – most of life seemed like that to me – a runaway train we'd boarded by accident. More importantly, I didn't like the turn the conversation was taking, so I said: 'I don't think anyone *really* wants to die.' Surely, I thought, ultimately, it would always be considered regrettable, not least because even if successful in the attempt, one could not celebrate one's success. And that would be real a party-pooper. Anyway, I couldn't imagine anyone wanting to leave a world with Anna in it. Anna looked thoughtful for a moment. 'Sybil does.'

'Sybil?'

'Sybil, in *The Waste Land* – you told me yourself the other day. The boys asked her: 'What do you want, Sybil?' She answered, 'I want to die.'

'Mythology is not real life though, is it? And she was tortured by incessant questions. And goodness, who would want to live forever as a wizened life in a jam jar?'

'She lived in a jam jar?'

'Well, not quite a jam jar, but in the end, she was nothing more than a voice.'

'Really? But there is something so romantic about despair, don't you think?' (Only to those who've never known it, I thought)

'This man has not yet seen his last evening; But, through his madness, was so close to it, That there was hardly time to turn about'

'Perhaps,' I smiled, nodding thoughtfully as if giving her last comment consideration. 'And the title of the collection playing at the moment?'

'That's for you to decide.' She looked deeply into my eyes, 'It remains, as yet, untitled,' – almost challenging me. 'Back in a minute,' she said, leaving me alone in her room for the first time. I sipped my wine; the harsh tannins drying my mouth. Now feeling no doubt that her intention was the same as mine: wine, candles, music. It sounds like such a romantic cliché, but believe me it did not feel that way. The room was possessed of a strange atmosphere, hushed, private and full of mystery, as if one were kneeling in front of a votive stand full of thin tapering candles, in an otherwise unlit cathedral. I could scarcely believe I was here.

    I felt so unsure of myself. Let me confess that I had always put myself in the role of the seducer, but here I was, feeling she was seducing me. And an unfamiliar sense of vulnerability shivered through my body. Having only just got used to the idea that the feelings I had for her were mutual, or at least to the point that she would accept me as... as what? Her lover? I felt so much was expected of me. Other times I don't think I'd even given it a thought, but now, I wanted everything to be so perfect. If she was prepared to give herself to me, could I even make it worth her while? Would I be able to love her in the way I dreamed I could? I had wanted her with such pain; I don't know how I'd ever endured it. And now, here I was, the man standing on brimstone: living a dangerous life, almost ecstatic with the thrill of the risk – a man on fire. Here I stood, ready to fulfil my dream. Not just a dream I had had since I first fell in love with Anna, but a dream I realised now that I had held all my life, only not remembered until this moment. It was a dream of perfect love, complete and utter. That I could say, once in my life I loved someone truly more than I loved myself. That I knew I would lay down my life for them, without so much as a second's hesitation. In Anna, I saw that person, and I thought I saw that dream could be fulfilled, at last.

Anna came back into the room; possibly she'd been to the bathroom or something. Somehow, I was afraid to even meet her eyes. 'I love an untidy desk!' I exclaimed, moving rapidly across the room to admire the dishevelled piles of books, old coffee cups, scattered biros, postcards, folders, lists, photographs, and my God, it was him again, the handsome cement mixer, only this time he'd got a child riding on his shoulders. Surely if he was her boyfriend, she would not be here with me, like this? But then, I suppose, I was still married.

I turned my attention to the window, peering beneath the gap in the broken blind. 'Quite a view from up here,' I murmured, trying to see beyond my own soft reflection and the room in which I was standing, to the pattern of lights below extending far into the distance. A doner kebab takeaway sign in the street below flashed on and off, on and off... I became mesmerised. From the items of underwear drying on a little rail in front of the radiator arose the perfumed scent of damp laundry. And then, without a word she was there: her hands around my waist, pressing herself against my back...her breasts pushing against my body. Her hands rose up to caress my chest then travelled down my sides to rest on my hips. Her face nestled against the back of my neck, her breath gently blew into my hair, kissing softly my neck, her lips soft and open. The base of my spine seemed to rise to meet my rib cage. My blood rushed. I heard my breath snag upon a wire. Then she turned me round, held my face in her hands, and pulled my mouth to hers.

The sensation of being touched by her, kissed by her, made me want to fall to my knees, as if every ounce of strength were drained from me. Somehow, I stood my ground, half swaying as in a drunken dream.

I cannot remember the last time someone undressed me. It is one of the most erotic steps of foreplay, and yet so often lost within weeks of starting a relationship. But here, tonight, as we kissed with such intensity, I was acutely aware of the sensation of Anna slowly taking off my clothes. Undressing me. Her hands undoing the buttons of my shirt, slipping it off my shoulders. Caressing my skin. Painlessly, peeling the layers of me, until I would be left raw and exposed before her. Often my eyes would close, as if lost in sleep, but my sightless eyes saw everything.

Finally, we were totally naked. We sort of half fell, half lay upon the Indian quilt, our bodies seeming to coil around one another as closely as two intertwining serpents. The smoothness of her skin was breath-taking. She felt unreal under my hand. Her nakedness was even more beautiful than I could have ever imagined. She was perfect, and I, yes me, I was permitted to gaze upon her, to touch her, to place my body next to her, onto her, and even into her. Utterly new sensations, never experienced before, swept around my body jangling every nerve ending. Being with her thrilled me to the marrow. That's where I felt it, in my bones. So close, against her, seeing her, holding her, my marrow contracts, expands, contracts, expands. It was a unique sensation. I was Lazarus being raised from the dead. ...that dry, dead unfeeling form now coursing with life. (Sometimes I can almost recreate the sensation. For a second, I almost have it, but then it is gone.)

'You're trembling,' she whispered. 'What's the matter?' Already she could read my thoughts through haunted eyes, 'It's OK, really.' She stroked my hair, kissed my mouth, and then, slid her hand down my back, across my backside, round my hip. Then, the moment was upon us. She took hold of me, guided me into her, and a glimpse of eternity was mine. I swear, in that brief moment when I first entered her, the world rushed away from me, so completely focused on the moment, the sensation, the feeling. I was a pure distillation of my being. Buried in the soul of another. She must have felt it too. Neither of us barely moved, and I heard my voice saying over and over, 'God, oh God.' And I remember feeling her legs and arms around me, as if she would never let me go. We barely moved, that was the strangest thing. We just seemed to hold one another closer and closer; I felt I was disappearing, dissolving even... melting. From the very depths of my being I heard a strange noise, like an animal crying out in fear or pain, and with a final torsion of my body, it was over. A moment's surrender.

For a while I lay so still, were it not for the pounding of my heart, she might have presumed I had died. I was not making a sound, but I knew I was crying. Eventually, she gently pushed me from her and we lay side by side, very quietly. Her head lay against my chest, listening to the rhythm of my still frantic heart. I think we had terrified each other...like two teenagers, who had tampered with a Ouija board, and tapped into forces they did not really believe existed.

Both of us knew there was something to be said, but neither of us seemed to be able to find the right words.

I was grateful for the music, which filled the silence and calmed me from my state of extremity. Eventually Anna drifted off to sleep, but I lay awake for what must have been hours, just listening to her breathing, trying to understand how she had made me feel something that I had never felt in my life before. I realised that before tonight, I had been sub-consciously afraid that the first time we made love may not be all I had hoped it would be. After all I had thought of nothing else for weeks. However, now I could safely say, I was no longer afraid. I was truly petrified.

Chapter Eleven: the expected guest

At last, I too must have slipped into a very deep sleep, as I didn't wake up at all during the night as I usually do. I was woken by a loud clunk resounding in the sink every time a tap was turned off somewhere else in the building and sounds of water rushing through piping. A pale, thin shaft of sunlight fell across the bed.

To awake feeling utterly overjoyed was indeed a new sensation. I turned on my stomach to look at her sleeping. Yesterday morning all I had of her was the briefest of touches, her leg against mine, her hand on my arm. Now she was mine. Intimacy gives one the sense of possessing. She was mine, always mine. She could not take away the imprint in my mind of last night, nor eradicate the moment I lived now, studying her sleeping face, and knowing in my heart, she was mine forever.

I lay my head down on the pillow, with my face only inches from hers, examining every feature in the way that is only possible with the sleeping or the dead. Even her eyebrows had a natural line of beauty, arching and tapering perfectly to frame her sleeping eyes. Eyelashes, were not terribly long, but were thick and curved upwards at the edges. She has an incredibly straight nose, and such a wonderfully big mouth; full, full lips, white teeth, and when she talks or laughs, she could bite a chunk out the moon, if she put her mind to it. I follow every little crack, and crevice of her soft lips, and notice the downy hair on her top lip, and realise there are tiny fair hairs all over her skin. You see, I'm that close. Normally you would not see them at all. Perhaps that is what is meant by having skin like a peach, this soft almost imperceptible down, covering the surface, like invisible suede. Suddenly she turned over, and her face all but disappeared under a mass of long Pre-Raphaelite ringlets.

With a sudden urgency, I became aware that I needed the loo, so I slipped out of bed, very quietly, so as not to disturb her. I was not happy at the prospect of using the communal bathroom, but 'needs must'. Fortunately, no one was about, so I nipped into the bathroom sharpish, went to the loo, and took the opportunity to freshen up a bit. As I came back out onto the landing, I was utterly thrown to see Chris squatting on the landing madly scrabbling about in her bag. For a split second, I didn't know whether to dash back into the bathroom, or make a break for Anna's room. But of course, she glanced round before I had an opportunity of doing either. She did a double-take, almost cartoon style, raised her eyebrows into two exaggerated rainbows, cocked her head on one side, and barely concealing her gleeful sarcasm, greeted me with, 'Good morning! Fancy seeing you here!'

I was at a complete loss for words, so with one hand trying to hold my open shirt together, and the other stretched out, I shook her hand in a rather ridiculously formal way. 'You've come back early from Liverpool?'

'Apparently,' she smirked, and began rummaging in her bag again.

'Actually, I'd only been home for a matter of hours when...' she retrieved her keys from the bottom of her bag, 'Ah, thank goodness! When, I had this fucking awful row with my dad. Sorry, I suppose I shouldn't swear in front of you, should I? But then I guess this is different. Anyway, I thought well sod it, I haven't come all this way just to be yelled at and I walked out. It's taken me all the bloody night to hitch-hike back here.'

'You hitched! At night? Good grief, that's living a bit dangerously.'

'Yes, it is living dangerously.' And then with her eyes laughing added, 'But then, we all like to live dangerously from time to time, even if we know it's stupid, don't we?' She knew she'd unnerved me, and as she turned the key in her door she swung round saying with a certain amount of satisfaction, 'Tell Anna I'm back, won't you? But I'll speak to her later - gonna catch up on some sleep now.'

Chris disappeared into her room and shut the door firmly behind her. It was obvious from that encounter that she had been aware of the impending situation between Anna and me. I began to feel uneasy, who else had Anna discussed her feelings with? How discreet was Chris? She seemed like trouble to me. The ghost of Fay Morgan leapt on my back, and squatted there like a giant toad. All I wanted was to be held in the safety of Anna's arms again. I tried the door of her room, only to discover the damn thing had locked me out. I had to tap, and then tap again louder. Eventually she came to the door, and as she smiled, Fay Morgan flopped silently from my back. Once inside her room again, Anna flung her arms about my neck and kissed me happily.

'For a minute, I thought you'd upped and gone,' she said, going over to the kitchenette to make some tea.

'I wouldn't do that. No, I just went to the loo, and eh,' I hesitated, 'I'm sorry, but as I came out, your friend, Chris was on the landing.'

'Chris?'

87

'She seemed to know why I might have been here. Well, I suppose at this time in the morning that's obvious, but let's say she didn't seem that surprised. I guess you've talked to her about... about, me.'

'I wonder why she's back?' Anna mused, ignoring my question and dipping a tea bag in and out of two mugs of hot water.

'She told me she'd had a row with her father.'

'Oh, what's new?' She grinned like a bashful schoolgirl. 'So, you had quite a conversation then?'

'Well, not really. I was so embarrassed. I mean, talk about being caught with your trousers down.'

'Idiomatically, I hope?'

'Of course – but my shirt was undone,' I admitted guiltily.

'Oh, Alistair,' she giggled, obviously highly titivated by the whole episode, 'for God's sake. Chris's glimpsed a man's hairy chest before, and a lot more besides.'

'But, not mine.' I gratefully embraced the mug of tea she was offering me. 'And in any case,' I added nervously, 'I think a relationship, such as ours would benefit from being more private, secret even. I mean, this friend Chris, she's not going to gossip, is she?'

She walked over to the window, and stared out of it.

'You are funny,' she began, 'what are you so worried about? I am over sixteen, and forgive me if I'm wrong, but I think I'm safe in presuming you are too.'

'It's just, you know, with you being a student, and me your tutor. It's frowned upon really.'

'By whom?' She asked. She was looking directly at me now, although I could not see her face, because the morning sun had framed her into a silhouette.

'Everyone, I guess. I mean who would applaud it? Anyway, here, it's definitely not encouraged. We have a code of conduct.' I paused, struggling somewhat. 'But as you can imagine, it isn't always adhered to that strictly.'

'And you? Have you always played according to these rules, up until now of course?'

I struggled with my internal demons. If I told her everything now, we could begin with no skeletons in the cupboard, but if in confessing.... The truth is, I was ashamed. And shame, my friends, is a very powerful emotion.

'Can I assume you're exercising 'the accused's right to remain silent?'
I stood up and walked over to her. As I got nearer, I began to see her features again. She didn't look cross actually; she almost looked as if she was mocking me. Always one step ahead in the game. I held her face in my hands. 'Do you mind if we have this conversation some other time?' She must've seen the imploring look of pain in my eyes, because she softened immediately, 'I'm only teasing you,' she said affectionately. 'Anyway, how much longer do you think I'm going to resist you, stood here with your shirt open in that rakish manner? Either make yourself decent, or do the honourable thing.'

I smiled a self-depreciating smile, and she began to kiss me again, running her fingers up and down my back beneath my shirt. She slid it from my body and threw it into a corner of the room.

'Sorry. Too late to make yourself decent now.' And she led me by the hand to her bed. 'Lay down.' I did as I was told. Slowly, she began unzipping my trousers, and gently tunnelled her hand under the soft material of my underwear. Then, she whispered, 'Code of conduct. What bollocks!'

'Well Gee, Thank you Ma'am!' I grinned, and she rolled on top of me laughing. She continued to caress me, saying, 'and another thing...you like etymology and all that origins stuff, don't you? So, just where does the phrase, 'iron fist in a velvet glove' come from? Because I think I might have just found the answer.'

Once again, under the exotic complexity of the Indian print quilt, the mood changed again. The playful banter taken over by this strange, charged atmosphere. The feeling one might get if a storm were brewing. I, for one, had never known a more heightened sense of fearful excitement and yet ironically also felt safer and more content than I had ever experienced before in my life. It was bliss being with her. She both thrilled me and calmed me in an instance. For me the most perfect internal equilibrium. I stretched her arms up above her head and kissed down her neck and breasts.

We'd been together less than twenty-four hours, and yet the trust, the intimacy that existed between us, not just physically, was as if we'd known each other all our lives. The peace I felt, surely, we were two old souls, reunited. As I entered her, the same emotional feeling swept through me, only this time I began to understand, as if an inexplicable dream were given meaning. That strange rush, as the world hurtled away from me, and my entire being focused into hers, like two droplets of rain breaking through each other's surface tension to become one conjoined droplet. I began to see what was happening. I can only believe, this was, for the first time in my life the experience of soul communion. You may laugh, think me pretentious, gushing, but this is what it felt like. It was almost holy. My soul had joined with another soul. There seemed no other reasonable explanation to me. No amount of sexual chemistry could take me to this heaven. It was more than mysterious to me. She was my soul mate. I had been lost and wandering all my life, but now had come home.

This time, our lovemaking was more conventional, for want of a better phrase; almost as if I'd got over the initial immobilising shock, I'd experienced the night before. After all, I reassured myself, it's not every day a man loses his soul.

Chapter Twelve: cigarette ends

I have wondered about this so often since that day. How did she do it? How could someone so young, relatively inexperienced, call a man's soul from him with such apparent ease? Do you recall that line in Dr Faustus: *Her lips suck forth my soul: see where it flies*? I do.

At one level there is obviously no comparison: one woman being a devil in the guise of Helen, helping Faustus on his way to Hell, the other being Anna, an extraordinary, but yet ordinary young woman, helping me on my way to a kind of heaven. I don't want to even suggest some supernatural goings on, but do you see my point? I'd lost my soul to her. And surely it follows, if I wasn't with her, I was a man without a soul.

Now I see the profound paradox more acutely than ever before: so little and yet so much, in a single absurd act, so brief, yet so timeless, so together and yet so alone, the oneness and the oneness.

'Why are you crying? Do you always cry after sex?'

'No. I didn't realise that I was.' I wiped my damp face.

She propped herself up on one elbow. 'You know,' she whispered, with a big lazy smile spreading across her face, 'you are such a good fuck!'

An expansive sense of pleasure, pride, contentment, swelled and swelled within me, until I was consumed. No one had ever called me that before. Well, apart from this rather irate puce-coloured man in the car park at Sainsbury once, when I'd backed my car into him and his trolley. However, he'd employed an altogether different adjective and called me a 'stupid fuck!' Anna's use of the word I must confess was more accurate – and certainly made me feel…well, wonderful!

'And another thing, I just love this line of hair that goes all the way from here... to here.' And she traced her finger down the line of hair that began at my belly button.

Truly, this was one of the happiest days of my life. Quite early on, I rang the department from a payphone in the hallway and lied convincingly about having a migraine, which I did suffer from occasionally, so it wouldn't seem too suspicious. However, Anna insisted on doing highly inappropriate things to me, while I was on the telephone, but well, as you know from my Connery impressions, I'm a consummate character actor, and my performance was flawless. We stayed in her bedroom all day. It's ironic really, I mean, she was so young, and yet what I felt with her wasn't, as many might imagine, pure undiluted lust, but the warmest sense of security I had ever experienced in my life. How boring and pedestrian that sounds, but it wasn't. I was whole with her, so at one. All the emptiness, anguish, the sense of dangling in a disconnected universe were pushed out and replaced with the fullness of her being. She was totally intoxicating, like red wine running through my veins; she warmed me, relaxed me, made me lose myself, my mind, to her, the Yin to my Yang. I became a perfect being.

Some would say this is absurd, having only been with her twenty-four hours. But I knew all this from the start, which makes it only the more painful that I let her escape from me with so little fight.

Well, what did we do during this day of wonderment? I recall we had cheese on toast for lunch, and drank quite a lot of tea. We talked and talked, the conversation switching from the sublime to the ridiculous, as if someone were randomly turning the dial through various radio stations. She would always mock me if she thought I was becoming too earnest, or too serious. But her sincerity was more evasive. It was like a game to her. Sometimes she would tell me details and memories from her life with great gravitas and just as I was pouring forth my most empathetic response, she'd laugh and say, 'You didn't really believe me, did you?'

It was almost as if she were testing the boundaries of my sense of reality... deliberately elusive.

The journey of discovering her would be intriguing. She was actually far more unconventional than I had at first presumed. Well, they say it's always the quiet ones.

The rest of the day, we made love, slept, and watched television in bed. The latter was something, which I hadn't done before, and to be honest still strikes me as dissolute, but it felt enjoyably rebellious at the time. Marion still struggled to overcome the belief instilled in her by her father, that ITV was the work of the devil, and would have certainly been uncomfortable with a screen in the bedroom. A comedy film was on, that I'd seen previously, but I don't think I've ever laughed so much. There was no light in the room, save for the flickering black and white. It felt quite decadent, and yet also in a sense everything seemed completely beautiful, good and pure. That was the strange thing: Anna created a sort of nuclear fusion of emotions in me. Feelings I had

always kept in polarity now clashed and violently embraced one another. Eventually, at about six o'clock, Anna became restless, and left the bed. 'God, I'm so hungry! Aren't you?' she asked opening and shutting the kitchen cupboards. 'Tin of tuna, half a packet of noodles... ...small tin of chickpeas...erghh, doesn't look very promising. Shall we go out?'
'Yes, of course. If you want,' I replied, almost afraid of breaking whatever spell hung in this room.

Anna went to take a shower. For a while I lay in bed, just savouring the fact I was here. Eventually, I dressed myself, recalling how her fingers had undone every button that I now fastened. The fabric of my shirt felt soft and pleasing to the touch. Running my hands across my chest, I wondered how my body beneath it had felt to her. Next, I turned off the TV and the bedside light, and stood silently in the darkened room, lit now only by the street lamps outside. Picking my way through the debris on the floor, I stood at the window staring out at the view. The city lights twinkled with more vitality than the night before, the sky clearer, the stars more defined, the kebab sign pulsated with a renewed vigour. I was a different man from the one who'd stood here last night. DNA may be the building blocks of life, but experience is the building blocks of the soul, and mine had been demolished and rebuilt overnight, with Anna as architect, builder and interior designer.

Anna flicked on the light. Blinking, I turned to face her. 'That was a *quick* shower? You've been gone nearly half an hour.'

'Missed me?' she suggested casually, while rubbing her hair dry with a towel. 'Actually, I popped in to say hello to Chris.' A naughty smile spread across her face. 'She wanted me to give her the low-down of course.'
I covered my eyes with my hands. 'You didn't, did you?'

Anna came over to me, her eyes on fire. She kissed me, then slid her mouth round to my ear and whispered, 'I said you were a beast, an insatiable love-machine, and that I hardly knew how to walk straight after the night I've spent with you.'

Pushing her away at arm's length, I searched her face, certain I was being wound up.

'No,' she said, looking crest-fallen. 'You're right. I didn't say that at all, but you should have seen her face when I told her you were tragically impotent, with a winky the size of an acorn!'

I was still begging her to tell me what she'd really said, half an hour later when we were putting on our coats. All she'd do is keep smiling at my anxiety, and finally said, in a rather exasperated way, 'Perhaps we didn't even discuss you. Have you thought of that yet?'

We descended the stairs in silence, for my own part so as not to draw attention to ourselves. The stairwell smelt of curry and drains, all wrapped up in a chilly dampness. Our flushed faces were illuminated starkly by the light from the bare 100-watt bulbs, which seemed blinding after the warm, dark, belly of her room.

Anna insisted on treating me to dinner as I'd bought dinner the night before. Well, nothing too expensive then, I'd protested...

We ate fish and chips from the paper sitting in the tiny public park at the end of her road. It's a sensation I'd always enjoyed, eating hot food, while sitting outside in the cold. When I was very small, I remember endless holidays in Wales, stood on street corners, or huddled together on a sheltered bench on the prom, eating chips, soaked in so much vinegar it made my nose burn, and sipping piping hot, weak tomato soup, from a paper cup.

We kissed with greasy, salted lips.

The last thing I wanted to do was go home, but eating the fish had reminded me of Thaddeus, whom I had not seen since yesterday morning. 'I ought to go back to my house tonight, Anna.'

'What makes you think I was going to let you bed down at mine again?' And she threw me a teasing glance.

'Well, as much as I'd like to convince you to give my 'acorn winky' another chance, I really must go back, and at least sort the cat out, get a change of clothes...'

'You have a cat?' She seemed incredulous.

'Yes, a ginger tom, called Thaddeus. He's a big bruiser of a cat, more like a feline bulldog really. Why are you so surprised?'

'Oh, I don't know,' she said screwing the fish and chip paper into a ball and chucking it in the bin. 'Well, I suppose, I never thought of you having a domestic life. If I'm honest, I almost forgot you have a life outside of your study, the lecture halls, the pub. It seems unreal the thought of you in a cosy domestic situation. You know, feeding the cat, weeding the garden, painting the window frames in the spring....' She paused; her eyes fixed into mine. 'You're not still married, are you?'

I pulled up my jacket collar around the back of my neck against the cold. 'It depends what you mean by married?'

'Oh, come on, for God's sake! I presumed you were divorced. I mean married means married, doesn't it? As in: not single, not separated, not divorced, but living with a wife. You are, aren't you – still married?'

'Well, on paper, yes, although, we don't have a relationship as such. There are so many different degrees of marriage; it's too simplistic just to say are you married, yes or no?'

'Don't patronise me!'

'I'm not. I just don't want you to think there's more to my marriage than there is– or isn't.'

My voice trailed into nothingness. Fumbling about in my pocket, I found a pack of cigarettes, and lit one nervously. In silence, she took the packet from my hand, withdrew a cigarette, and lit it with the sharp fizz of a match. Anna never looked right smoking somehow. (Subsequently, I discovered that she wasn't really a dedicated smoker and in fact ended up persuading me to give up – which I managed briefly – but that's another story.) After the first puff, she quizzed me further. 'Do you still live together?'

I wanted to protest that these questions should have been raised last night if these things bothered her so much, but knew that would not work in my favour. Instead, I remained calm and reasonable; acting as if none of these issues were of that great importance to me. I tried to explain that Marion worked a lot in London and that we basically just shared the house when she worked from home. 'It's like this,' I said, 'some friends become lovers, we were lovers who became friends, well, not even friends actually, really more just co-dependants.'

'So, you don't still sleep with her?'

'Sleep with her?'

'Sleep with her! As in *'fuck'* her. Do you?'

At least I could answer that one truthfully.

(I can even pinpoint the very evening our sex life fell downward, spinning its final spiralling descent to earth: the night of The Eurovision Song Contest. Sometimes the TV remains on in spite of every intelligent thought in your head telling you to switch the damn thing off – this was one such night. It is a truth universally acknowledged that there's only so much soporific banality and 'Bing Tiddle Tiddle Bong' you can take before you lose the will to live. And it is at such moments I think 'a primitive survival instinct kicks in'– and your thoughts turn to sex. In fact, I wonder how many of us actually owe our existence to a sexual union which provided a diversion from some tedious moment in time. Anyway, Marion must've been equally stupefied because she relented fairly easily for once. (Perhaps it was also the effect of the Chablis we'd consumed earlier to accompany a roast chicken dinner; the smell of chicken fat now clung unpleasantly to her clothes and hair.) However, it was not our habit to make love in the light, and if ever we did in the past, I had noticed that Marion kept her eyes firmly clamped shut – I'd always presumed this was to concentrate on her own private moment of ecstasy. Unfortunately, on this occasion I suppose she was distracted by the results coming in for the British entry, and couldn't resist glancing up from the sofa towards the TV. As her eyes returned from the screen, she suddenly produced an odd guttural noise in her throat, like someone throttling a hyena in full cackle.

'What?' I said, pausing momentarily.

'I'd just forgotten about the off-putting face!'

She then went on to explain – in her usual sensitive manner –that whenever I performed, especially while on the home straight, I always looked like the runner-up in a gurning contest. Hence why she always kept her eyes closed. Never once for us our *'eye-beams'* twisting through the night.

With a cold shrinking sensation, I replied, 'Only the 'runner-up' Marion? I can't win at anything for you, can I?'

By the time the next year's contest came round, we'd been sleeping in separate rooms for at least ten months.)

'No, not for a long time, years probably. She has a...' I tried desperately not to let a trace of jealousy show in my voice, 'a serious lover, a boyfriend, you'd call him, I suppose. She's been seeing him for a long time. Ironically,' and here I sort of laughed, as if even I found it amusing, 'she won't be unfaithful to him! They'll not get married or anything, he's already married, with a daughter. He won't leave his wife, because of his child. So, Marion, that's *my* so-called 'wife,' she stays with me, for the time being. So, you see,' I said taking hold of Anna's hand, in the mistaken belief I had allayed any worries she had, 'that's

96

all my marriage amounts to, a hollow sham, a way of sharing the rent if you like.'

She pulled her hand away from me. 'And so, this is where I come in is it? A bit of casual sex, another easily laid student, just to keep the works oiled.'

'Of course not!'

'I refuse to be anyone's bit on the side, Alistair. It may sound egocentric, but I have to be all or nothing to someone. Do you understand?'

How in a few short moves had I travelled from the bliss of being wrapped up in her, in her bedroom, to this? Her anger was almost palpable. I could feel it, like the rush of wind preceding the arrival of an underground train.

'Anna,' I implored, 'it isn't like that at all. I don't pick up students....' I touched her arm; it felt hard and unyielding

'Ah, I'm the first then, am I?' A challenging sarcastic sneer invaded her face.

'Well...I...' The words wouldn't come.

'Oh, forget it!' She threw the cigarette to the ground, where it exploded like a tiny bomb and began walking away.

'Anna!' I ran after her, grabbing her by both arms, locked her face into mine and forcibly held her still. For a moment I thought she was going to spit on me, really, that's how wild she looked.

'For God's sake, Anna, I'm forty-eight. I've had a lonely, loveless marriage for years; there were bound to be occasions, when if the opportunity presented itself, I wasn't going to say no, but this is so different, Anna.' I had her totally in my gaze now. 'I've been watching you, wanting you for weeks, driven out of my mind with my need for you. Too afraid to make a move, in case I destroyed the hope I held within my heart.' The strength of my emotion rose up inside me like turbulent magma. 'You cannot imagine what being with you has meant to me. What I have shared with you in the last day or so, I have never known before, ever, with anyone. Don't cheapen it with meaningless comparisons. Wasn't it extraordinary for you to? Please, Anna, can't you see what you mean to me?'

Inside I was already thanking God, that my petition had been heard, for I could see the tension and anger visibly draining from her. The thundering train became no more than a rumble down the tracks, well on its way to the next station. She began to accept my arms around her, and as I drew her close to my body, I realised she had placed the palm of her hand against my chest, almost as if she enjoyed feeling the violent beating of my heart. I kissed her gently on the forehead.

'Alistair,' she said slowly, without looking at me...

'Yes?'

'If I ever suspect what you have just told me is a lie, I'll kill you.' And she meant it. The irony of that threat is not lost on me now.

'Come on,' I said, holding her cold hand in mine. 'I'll walk you home.'

As we walked in silence, I was strangely overtaken by an appalling sadness. We turned up the hill to go to the corner shop. The air was still and chilled. My breath hung before me like a vaporous ghost. Softly, the footfalls of Fay Morgan fell in behind me. I didn't look round.

'What we need is a bottle or two and a slab of Dairy Milk,' said Anna confidently, which I knew was her peace offering. The wine selection was dismal. However, the potentially migraine-inducing cocktail of comfort foods did the trick, as an hour later I was warm, blissful and whole once more.

Needless to say, Thaddeus went hungry a second night, but what else could I do?

Chapter Thirteen: If you don't like it you can get on with it

When I arrived home the next morning I fully expected to be savaged by Thaddeus on the doorstep, but he was not in evidence. I turned the key and waited for him to rush up and immediately bite my ankles in remonstration; a guilty fear ran through me. Oh God, what if he'd been run over while I was with Anna. What if he'd lain in the road for hours in agony, waiting for me, and I'd never come to rescue him, to comfort him? 'Thaddeus? Thaddeus?' I called out hopefully.

'He's in here,' came a firm voice from the kitchen: Marion. She walked briskly into the hallway.

'For goodness sake, Alec! It's like leaving a child in charge of the household. I go away on business,' (God, how she loved that phrase) 'for a matter of days, come back to find you haven't even been here to feed the cat. If I hadn't have come back unexpectedly last night, I don't know what could have happened. He could have wandered off in search of food, got run over, been taken by vivisectionists! I don't know what!'

I thought, I wish you'd been taken by vivisectionists. But I said nothing.

Thaddeus sauntered in, purring the fattest purr he could muster, and wrapped himself around Marion's legs. 'My precious one,' she crooned, lifting him up and placing over her shoulder, as if to burp him after a feed.

'Honestly, just look at you. I don't give a toss as to which sad old tart's duvet you've just disentangled yourself from, but I do bloody care that you've neglected to feed Thaddeus. Putting down a bowl of cat food, twice a day is hardly the most arduous of responsibilities, is it? And you can't even manage that!' She swept past me, and marched upstairs, with Thaddeus smirking over her left shoulder. 'Come on, sweetheart.' I watched in silence as her buttocks took it in turns to rise and fall in the tight seat of her trousers.

At that moment, I wanted to murder her, let alone divorce her. Every time I climbed out of my trench Marion was there to shoot me down. Every moment of joy, happiness, my hopes, my dreams, all my achievements, such as they were, had been crushed, destroyed, annihilated by that woman. She hated everything I was. And to think, how her eating away at my confidence, had caused me the inertia, which prevented me from leaving her, and had nearly cost me Anna. She would not control me anymore.

Continuing down the hallway, I picked up the few letters which were on the hall table. As I glanced up, I caught sight of myself in the mirror, and for the first time in two days I saw myself as I really was: every greying hair, every wrinkle, those dark sagging shadows beneath my eyes, those eyes with no light in them. Hands that less than an hour ago had lovingly caressed the most perfect face on God's earth, now looked alien to me, with veins like a myriad of grey liquorice tributaries coursing down them. All the vibrant energy, life force I had felt, was gone. I looked weary, exhausted....old

But then I had to admit I was so tired; I could've lain down in the hallway and slept quite peacefully. The physical and emotional heights of the last few days were all new to me, and I suppose, to be frank, I'm just not used to having that much sex. It's been years since I'd had that much uninspired mechanical sex, let alone the soul wrenching kind Anna created. As I climbed the stairs weak and trembling, I began to feel almost anaesthetized; I needed to lie down.

'Huh! Completely spent then?' barked Marion as she bustled round the room, collecting dirty laundry. 'Demanding, was she?' I lay perfectly still, and said nothing. 'Swallowed your tongue, has she?'

I opened one eye.' How was your trip?'

'How was my trip? How was my trip?' she repeated as if she'd just got the punch line to a joke. 'Answer *my* question before you ask any of your own bloody daft questions.'

'It's not daft. Why didn't you stay down there and spend the week-end with Edward, like you were going to?'

'If you must know, because he had to look after his daughter; she's unwell with a high temperature. His wife's Aunt is having a fiftieth wedding celebration in Dorset - in a village called 'Piddle-… something' would you believe, to which they were all supposed to be going – cosy family do and all that. Edward was the one who was *supposed* to be 'taken ill' and not be able to go.' I was watching her now, rummaging through the cast-off clothes I'd left piled on the chair, her mouth suddenly did a little sour downturn. 'Do you know what he said to me? That he was afraid this was God's way of punishing him. Telling him that what he was doing is wrong. I thought don't be *so* bloody pious and ridiculous. Hattie'll get over it; it's only a virus for goodness sake. But what could I say? …Go and talk to a priest? 'She huffed theatrically. 'Not a thought for me and my ruined week-end.'

All I said was, 'Ah, I see…' and she threw the armful of dirty clothes all over me.

'Do your own wretched laundry!' She stomped out of the room. Then I heard a slight stumble, and Thaddeus let out one of his blood curdling yowls. 'Now look what you've made me do!' Marion yelled from the landing.

Purposefully, I picked the items of clothing off the bed and tossed them on the floor; slid down under duvet, and stared into the darkness. Now, I knew for certain that my marriage with Marion was over. It should have been dead and buried years ago, but perhaps through weakness, sentimentality, or just plain old apathy, we'd let it exist for too long on a metaphorical life support machine. Surely, it would be the best thing for everyone concerned to switch it off, and let it rest in peace. It had no part to play in the world any longer. Her heart was somewhere else, and now mine was too. I could see our marriage was a charade that had no meaning. We could carry on acting it out for the rest of our lives, and at the end of the day neither of us would be any the wiser as to what it, or even life itself, had all been about.

From the bottom stair, Marion began shouting up to me.

'Right, I've put *my* washing on, and now I'm going to get some groceries, seeing as you've done no shopping all week. I suppose you've been spending a fortune on takeaways and pub lunches.'

The front door slammed, followed by the sound of the house being instantly filled with a beautiful sense of peace. Smiling the smile of a self-satisfied man, I emerged from under the duvet, and lay on my back with my hands behind my head.

A deep, deep, contented peace flooded through me. I retraced and retraced every moment of the time I'd spent with Anna, particularly from when I first felt her body pressing against my back. I could still feel her there now:

> Her touch was like a footprint on the moon
> It would never go away
> No breath of wind erase it
> No onward march of time
> Would fade it.
> I can still feel her there now.
> Her touch was like a footprint on the moon...

The man, who stood on brimstone, did a little celebratory dance, and did not even feel his feet burning. Eventually, he curled up into a tight ball as if hugging himself, and slept deeply.

Chapter Fourteen: Elizabeth and Leicester

When I awoke, it was already nearly dark. Guessing it was about five o'clock, I lay for some time, just enjoying that relaxed feeling of being between sleeping and waking. Even before I woke up, Anna was in my mind; I must've been dreaming about her. Drowsily, I began to have this bizarre fantasy, which I think dissolved into a semi-conscious dream, in fact I definitely slipped back to sleep. Anna and I had been abducted by aliens, (not original I know, but true nevertheless) and were being kept in a sort of observation chamber. We were totally naked. The walls of the observation chamber were made entirely of mirrored glass, but I knew our every move was being watched by alien eyes. Anna whispered,' What do you think will happen to us?'

'Goodess knows,' said a bored voice. I span round in astonishment. There, also utterly nude, was Marion, although she was sat in such a way, that nothing of any consequence was revealed.

But before I could react or reply, a voice boomed out: 'We wish to observe the manner in which you humans procreate. Demonstrate this procedure and you will be set free – unharmed.' I rose to my feet, and as I did so I heard the aliens shuffle forward, pressing themselves closer to the glass. Anna stared at me, horrified.

'Anna, I'm sorry, but I don't think we have a choice,' I said gently, while she closed her eyes, as the dreadfulness of our ordeal swam in her mind. Hearing an 'eye-rolling' huff, I swung round to plead with Marion. Only *this* time it was Mother sat there! Heavens! Also stripped bare, but mercifully reading *The Telegraph* at close quarters. 'Six across, Alistair,' she said without looking up, 'Great Scott! Gladstone's wife mangled then dismembered by velocipede's spokes! (4,5)'

'Gosh! I haven't the foggiest, Mother.'

The deafening voice echoed round the chamber again; at first the words would not make sense, partly because I was also being physically shaken by an invisible force. I thought it said, 'I've brought you a cup of tea.' I made a face of non-comprehension at Anna.

'Alec! I've bought you some tea.' I opened my eyes; Marion hovered over me, like some fearful Matron, bringing a patient round after an operation.

'Erh, uhm, what time is it?'

She switched on the bedside light.

'It's five, well, nearly five. Have I woken you from a dream? You were very twitchy when I came in.' Half sitting up, I sipped the tea, 'Not that I was aware of.' All the clothes I'd dumped on the floor by the bed, I noticed were gone. Marion perched on the end of the bed, well actually, on my foot initially.

'Sorry,' she said, raising her right cheek so I could move it. 'I've been thinking, Alec…'

For some reason I thought, Oh God, here it comes, she wants a divorce. This is really it. I realized my body had stiffened, braced for the news.

'While I was shopping, I gave it a lot of thought, and well, I really think I owe you an apology.' I opened my mouth to speak, but she raised her hand up to stop me. 'Let me say my piece. Not about the cat, that still stands, but what I said about your…' here she searched for the right phrase, but failing tried several, 'your liaisons; your women friends; your private life; you know. It was unfair and uncalled for. You've always been so understanding about my relationship with Edward. You know, as well as I do that if things were different, I would be with Edward, but as they are, and have been for some years, I've had to make do with being with him when I can. And you, my poor Alec,' and here she stroked my head quite affectionately, 'stay with me. Both of us supporting one another through this no-man's land, of... this no man's land of...' (and it was at this moment I realised she was the worse for drink) 'of lost love. You and I, Alec, staggering back and forth between the trenches, from one to the other and back again. Not really belonging anywhere. If you've got some woman, you like, if someone makes you feel just a fraction of the happiness I feel when I'm with Edward, then I should be happy for you, shouldn't I? I know it's been some time since you've, you know...' Her voice trailed off, half-choked with emotion.

Glassy tears brimmed in her eyes. She was drunk and maudlin, but in spite of that, and all the animosity that existed between us, I could not help but to gather her to me and hold her while she wept onto my shoulder. Sometimes the sense of pain, bitterness and loss, the groaning ache of failure, over-whelmed her. I let her cry on me; I knew only too well, such feelings.

She felt larger and heavier than I remembered, although the familiar scent of her hairspray was strangely comforting. When she finally rose to blow her nose, she said, 'It's someone special, isn't it?' I suppose my silence answered her question. 'I had a feeling you were building up to one of your assignations.' (From the tone of her voice, I knew she had recovered herself.) 'You've had that stupid, vacant look for weeks now. To be perfectly honest, I wasn't that surprised to find Thaddeus by himself, just annoyed really. What took you so long to divide and conquer? I know you're a bit out of practice, but it's taken a few weeks hasn't it? Is she already married or something?' She gave her nose one last fulsome blow, sniffed haughtily, and said, 'I won't mind, really I won't,' and began blotting her eyes as she checked herself in the dressing table mirror. 'After all, how could I, when I have Edward?'

'I'd rather not talk about it; you know it only makes you cross.' Immediately, she found my gaze in the mirror, and fixedly addressed my reflection. She said tersely, 'I've said I won't mind, haven't I?' A sigh of weariness escaped from me. 'But you do have some one new, who you like, don't you?' Marion persisted.

I suppose, at the irony of this understatement, a boyish smile passed across my face. Marion's eyes narrowed. She spun round to face me, tottered slightly and held on to the bedpost for support. 'She's not a student, is she? You promised, no, you vowed, swore, whatever, didn't you? Never again!'
I shook my head vigorously in denial. 'Whatever made you say that? No, she's not even anything to do with the university. She's divorced.'
Marion's eyes rolled in their sockets and she declared sarcastically that there were no doubt hordes of screaming kids for me to finance. Marion's two big 'no-nos': one, no students, and two, no divorcees looking for me to play daddy to their kids. This, as you can imagine, somewhat narrowed the field of lovers my wife would find acceptable. (How had my life come to this?)
'Ehm, just one, but nearly grown up, lives with his father, in Newcastle.'

Finding herself too unsteady on her feet, Marion plonked back down on the end of the bed. 'What does she do then, this woman friend...this lover of my husband. I don't even know her name!'

'What does it matter? I thought you didn't care anyway?'

'I don't. But you know all about Edward. Why should you have a secret life? I only want to know her name and what she does. That's not too much to ask, is it?'

My eyes scanned down one the pile of books balanced on the dressing table, Gerard Manley Hopkins, Aldous Huxley, Charles Dickens, ah, 'Virginia,' I said confidently. Marion's head seemed to wobble precariously on her neck, looking as if it might roll into her lap at any moment.

'Virginia?' she repeated, her eyebrows knitting up. 'Well, I've never met anyone called Virginia. What kind of a name is that? Virginia Wade, Virginia Woolf? I can't think of any others. Oh, that 'born-free' one of course. What does that mean then? Virgin? How delightfully ironic. Ha! 'And she began to shake with laughter.

I suppose in an attempt to calm her down I said, 'I call her Ginny, actually.'

She threw her head back and let out a scream of hilarity. 'Oh please, Alec!' I watched, with an embarrassed smile, as she almost sobbed with mirth.

'What's so funny?' I enquired. Putting her hand over her mouth, she took a deep breath. 'I'm sorry, Alec, I shouldn't laugh, really I shouldn't. But it's just the thought of you saying, 'Oh, Virginia! Virginia!' and then her saying, in some dreadful Geordie accent, 'Eh, Alec pet, you can call us Ginny if you like, man.' I could see she was biting her bottom lip, and her face was contorted with the strain of not bursting out again. 'I don't know why,' she said wiping the tears from her eyes, 'The thought of you, manfully pumping away at some middle-aged divorcee, Ginny the Geordie, just makes me...' and the rest of her sentence was lost in her final guffaw as she tottered – uncertainly – from the room. I shouted after her, 'I said, the son lived in Newcastle with his father. That doesn't make her a Geordie. Anyway, I like regional accents.' I sat up in bed and finished the tea. I wish Marion wouldn't drink. At least when she was sober, she didn't laugh very much, if at all. Now you can see how I've suffered with Marion. She even found my infidelity derisory.

As I wandered down the landing, I was glad to see Marion had crashed out on her bed. Honestly, sometimes we were like some sort of drunken tag team. However, knowing she would not stir until two in the morning, in search of orange juice and paracetamol, I thought it best to leave her, covered her with a couple of blankets. So, I left her – dead to the world.

Marion was a private drunk: only at home, never in company. She presented such a together front to the world, and yet.... Maybe this was one of the privileges of marriage: these moments of intimacy, where we revealed our true selves to one another, and one another only, in the private confines of our marital home. Perhaps I should treasure such moments.

Spending that evening without Anna was something of an endurance test for me. Desperate as I was to see her, she'd said, quite firmly, that she had to get on with some work and had already promised to go to a party with Chris. My heart had sunk at the thought of her at a party. But what could I say?

'You wouldn't, you know, go off with anyone, would you?' She looked quite insulted. 'I've told you, haven't I? I have to be everything to someone or nothing at all. How could I be everything to someone I've just met at a party, who's looking for a quick shag, a bit of fun? That's why I don't sleep around. I never have and I never will.' Anna stood up and walked across to where I was sitting at her desk.

'I slept with you because... how can I put this? Because I saw a need in you, a need for me, which was greater than just lust, something beyond desire. That's why the sex is so amazing – I knew it would be.' Then placing her hands on my shoulders, she whispered, 'Now don't you worry,' and softly kissed the top of my head as if I was an anxious child being left with a new babysitter. 'I'm going to have a drink, dance, have a laugh. I'll even call you later if you like. What's your number?'

'Something greater than lust?... Something beyond desire?' Did she not know true love when she saw it?

'Hello?'

'Hi, it's me.'

'Anna! It's one o'clock in the morning. Where are you?'

'I'm at home. I said I'd ring, didn't I? You sound surprised. Were you in bed?'

'Well, no. But my wife's back, what if she had answered the phone?'

'Oh, she did. Earlier on at about three-thirty, I was missing you so much, I...'

'Did you speak to her for God's sake?'

'No. I was so surprised to hear a woman's voice, I just put the phone down quickly. But then I rang again a few minutes later, because I thought perhaps I'd dialled the wrong number, but she answered again. She sounds a bit scary to me. She kept saying, 'Who is this? Hello? Who is this?' You're not annoyed, are you?'

'No, it's just when I said call me, I was thinking she'd still be away.'

Marion's drunken binge and strange behaviour fell into place. She really didn't love me at all, but still she could not bear for anyone else to have me. She tried to rationalise it to herself of course, but always the old vestige of jealousy seeped through, like fetid poison weeping from a wound.

'Well, it certainly surprised me,' Anna continued, 'I thought if she answers the phone now, she'll probably start thinking I'm some sort of heavy breather. Anyway, are you missing me?'

'Oh God, of course I am. I've thought about you every waking moment, and sleeping one too... so, you went to the party then?'

'Yeah, it was all right, but this hairball of a guy kept trying to chat me up, so I left early. Thought I'd come home early and ring you instead.' A real stab of pain shot through my stomach.

'When can I see you again, Anna?'

'Tomorrow, if you like, any time after midday. Gotta sleep sometime! I'll be waiting for you.' And she hung up.

Chapter Fifteen: the brown fog

'How sweet,' Marion intoned, studying me as I descended the stairs at noon the next day. 'Ginny's invited you for a Sunday roast. Am I right? Mmm! I can smell the beef sizzling and see the Yorkshire pudding rising from here.'

'Marion, please. You said you didn't care.'

'True, I don't, Alec, but to see you all spruced up, and setting off for your sumptuous Sunday dinner washed down with some 'Newcastle Brown', and no doubt followed by some, 'Eh pet, I feel that sleepy mun, I think I'll tek a nap like.' Marion nudged me sharply, and winked manically. 'Ah! It does my heart good.'

'I'm glad to be the cause of so much felicity. Now if you'll excuse me,' I said trying to reach past Marion, who was stood smiling like a dog with two tails, in front of the coat stand.

'Very becoming, quite debonair, *'reet champion!'*' Marion commented, as I put on my long black cashmere coat. 'But won't it look a bit incongruous with your flat cap?'

'I don't know when I'll be back.'

'Well, my darling, don't think for a minute I shall be anxiously awaiting your return. I've plenty to be getting on with. I'll give your mother a ring later, see how she is, shall I?'

'Yes do,' I answered, determined not to rise to the bait. I walked briskly down the path to the tune of Marion whistling, *'When the Boat Comes In.'* I turned and gave her a withering look.

'Sorry, couldn't help myself.' She grimaced, and turned to go indoors...still whistling. I decided to take the car, partly because I couldn't be bothered to walk, but moreover so as Marion wouldn't have any real idea as to whether my 'new woman' was local or not. I thought I'd park in the street adjacent to Anna's, in case anyone recognized the car.

As I descended the hill into the city centre, the fog, which had been quite thin and distant by my house, became close and thick. I suppose it had sunk into the valley bottom and found a soul mate with the exhaust fumes. Tentatively, I shuffled forward to the edge of my seat, and peered through the windscreen of the Morris. Cars and buses appeared like sinister apparitions. Everything moved as if in slow motion, cautiously, almost serenely, the outlines softened, the world subdued. In places it was so thick it was almost opaque. I put my headlights on to full beam, but it only made it worse. Eventually, I found myself trundling down Anna's road, so I took the next left, and parked behind her house, quite near to the fish and chip shop. Ever since childhood, being in a fog has always reminded me of death. From where you are in the fog, no other reality exists, and yet, as you walk forward, a new reality emerges and the one you have left behind disappears. When you are here, there cannot be seen: and when you are there, here cannot be seen.

As I hurried down the street, Anna's house, like some smoke and mirrors phantasm, slowly emerged, a cloudy haze veiled her bedroom window; the broken blind a drowsy half-closed eyelid.

I crept softly through the vegetation sprouting up through the cracked stone steps to the door, where I realised with anxiety were a whole host of doorbells relating to individual flats. I knew Anna's doorbell would be one of the top flats, but which one was going to be an educated guess. The last thing I wanted to do was to conjure up Chris. I pressed number eight… Above me in the clouds, a wooden sash rumbled open and as I looked up, the soft-focus face of Anna appeared. 'I've only just got up. Can you catch the keys?'

I nodded. The keys narrowly missed my head and landed on my foot. Wincing, I bent down, picked them up. There were quite a bunch and I had to try several before I heard the key turn in the door. Having successfully negotiated the door, I shut it behind me quietly, though goodness knows why I bothered as there was such loud rock music of some sorts blaring out from one of the downstairs flats, no one could've heard if I'd come in by blasting the door with dynamite. The bass pulsated in my stomach as I walked up the first flight of stairs, only to be exchanged for a different more frantic beat as I ascended the second staircase. It hadn't been this noisy the other night.

With some urgency, I knocked quite loudly on Anna's door. The door swung open; she was still wearing her old man's stripy pyjamas and as my eyes fell upon her, I felt my whole body cave-in as if I was being crushed and compacted. I could scarcely breathe. 'Come on in then,' she said, dragging me by the hand through the doorway, kicking the door shut with a thud. While I stood motionless, she slipped her hands inside my coat, holding me seamlessly against her. To be so close to her again, to feel her body embrace mine, to breathe in the scent of her, my lips against her skin. The intensity overwhelmed me. I was becoming denser, more concentrated by the each passing second.

'Oh, Anna, Anna.' My words expelled from me like a dying breath...her eyes looked into mine, bewildered, concerned.

I pulled away from her suddenly, covering my face with my hands, and after a few staggering steps, sank down onto the sofa. 'What is it for God's sake? Are you ill?'

She had her arm around me now; I turned and buried my face into her body. (Oh, God, the warm balmy perfume of her. It was intoxicating) She held me quietly for a few moments. Gradually, I felt myself growing calmer, and at last was able to lift my head and meet her eyes.

'I'm sorry, Anna, really. I don't know what came over me. It's just nobody has ever moved me in the way you do. The emotion rising up in me – it damn near kills me.'

'Really?'

'I'm so scared, Anna. We've known each other such a short time, but in you I know I've found something I will never find again.'

'Honestly?'

I looked at her with the eyes of a condemned man, and I saw a slight shock of realisation in hers.

'You're so young,' I continued, 'I'm terrified. Can you understand that? It won't last. Not forever. One day you'll go off with someone else, and then what will I do? I don't think I could bear not having you in my life anymore.'

'I don't know what to say. We've only spent a couple of days together.' Anna had released herself from my grasp and began pacing round the room. I knew I'd unnerved her; she had that look of one who realizes too late that they have bitten off far more than they had wished to chew.

'Where's this all come from? You're talking as if we've been part of one another's lives for years. Look, none of us knows what the future holds, do we? This is what I want now, and as far as anyone could tell it's what I'll want tomorrow, and the next day. You worry too much.' Now, clutching a cushion she'd picked up off the floor she continued, 'I mean, what kind of person do you take me for? You still don't get it, do you? I don't spend every other week of my life falling into bed with someone different.'

'Well, of course not, but that isn't the issue here. For me this is more than 'just falling into bed' as you put it. It's the real thing. Well, it is for me.'

'You think you have such a monopoly on genuine emotion, don't you?' Anna had gone to the kitchenette, and began agitatedly making some coffee, while I continued to lay my heart on the line.

'No, I don't mean that. But be realistic, Anna. I know I'll be the one to get my heart broken, as surely as night follows day. This is my problem. I'm sorry, I know I should just enjoy the time I am privileged to have with you, and then face the consequences, pay the price whatever. Maybe in the long term my pain would be less if I walked out of here now and never saw you like this again. If I could finish with you here and now, like I ought to, I would.'

'You would?'

'If I could, yes.'

'Just like that?' As she placed two mugs on the grubby coffee table, she added, with a challenging stare, 'Is this some kind of over-dramatized brush off?'

'You know not. I'm already at the point where I would endure anything, whatever pain or suffering comes my way – I can't help it – I have to be... I have to be with you.' An almost imperceptible smile flickered behind her eyes; she curled up next to me on the sofa, leaning her body into mine; her breasts pressing against me. Gently, she lifted my hand and began to kiss each finger in turn, almost as if to taste them.

'I want you to be with me,' she whispered, her breath warm against my neck. My whole body trembled...if only I could be sure.

'I'm in love with you, Anna. I mean *really* in love with you. I know this is all too much, too soon. Can you cope with it? 'She held my face in her hands and in between gently kissing me, she said quietly, 'I've already told you, I'm a very serious person. I don't mess around. I like total devotion. In fact, I insist on it.'

She slid down my body and knelt at my feet. Slowly, her hands felt their way beneath my clothes. I should have resisted. I should have got up and left. I should have vowed to never see her again like this. But self-preservation sometimes has a very tiny voice, and mine whispered to me from the other side of the world. Besides, the blood rushing in my veins drowned out every other noise. I should've left. In spite of everything that was to follow, I am eternally grateful that I did not.

(Even now I don't know if I was some pawn in an elaborate game of let's pretend, or if her feelings were genuine at the time. Now, sometimes I think that what started out as a game for her, led her unexpectedly into a harsh land of grown-up reality. Obviously, it was a case of 'mea culpa'. That rush of power she must have felt, as I quite literally expired in front of her very eyes, with the very agony of wanting her. It was my fault she felt immortal. The only thing that still troubles my mind is: is it still true love if it's not utterly reciprocal? Have I ever known true love at all?)

Now, I'm not into drugs, apart from a ten-or-so a day cigarettes habit, and a sincere love of booze, but I disapprove strongly of real addictive drugs. But from the first evening I spent alone with Anna, I understood drug addiction in a whole new light.

Let me confess: I was afraid of being with Anna, knowing from the start that she was a forbidden fruit... but I was fatefully drawn. She promised an escape, an irresistible chance to feel a completely new ecstatic sensation. Surely this was right, though? A 'Drink Me' moment of faith in the unknown.

After the very first time we made love, I knew I was hooked for life – addicted to the mysterious high; captivated by my 'otherworldly' experience. I became obsessed with my habit. My whole life revolved around thinking about her, how and when I would have her again, and then in having her, experiencing a relief, a surrender, an ecstasy. Deep within my soul, these sensations of being started whispering to me from the moment I descended the stairs: never satisfied. When I couldn't see her, a malaise crept over me... a longing that felt like sickness. And as with most drugs, this dependency would eventually lead to my destruction.

I'm still very anti-drugs, but I think I'm a little less condemnatory of those who fall prey to them now. Self-destruction can come in so many seductive disguises.

I realise it sounds like this addiction revolved around sex. It didn't. I just loved her, truly loved her. I would have happily spent eternity sat in a cardboard box with her, fully clothed, and still been in a state of perpetual bliss.

So that was how I spent the autumn, gradually becoming accustomed to the sensation of being 'head-over-heels in love'. As the weeks passed, I relaxed, beginning to trust, little by little, that Anna was not about to slide from my grasp into the fumbling hands of some young, inexperienced boy. She deserved better than that. (But what in God's name gave me the audacity to think that that 'better' was me I'll never know.)

It even turned out that the boy in the photograph in her bag and on her desk was her older brother, James. What a relief! Anna was very amused by my belief that he was her boyfriend. Now, looking at him again, I could see the family resemblance. Strangely enough, I didn't know anything about her former boyfriends at all, but then apart from asking about who James was, I deliberately avoided the subject so that I could eschew a similar inquiry.

Chapter Sixteen: indifference

We were very discreet in our relationship. After that first night out with Anna, I was very careful never to be seen with her locally again. Especially as I had told Marion a direct lie about whom I was seeing. Marion had quite a few friends (surprisingly) who would have been only too delighted to drop me in it if they'd seen me out with anyone, especially anyone under the age of thirty. They, like Marion, couldn't bear the injustice that a middle-aged man could still bed girls half his age, while they had to make do with someone else's reject; philandering husbands, who were neither rich enough, successful enough, or attractive enough to hook the younger end of the market; the middle-aged divorcee, (looking for unbridled sex, plus additional childcare at weekends); or some merry widower (looking for meaningful relationship, country walks, plus light domestic duties). I suppose it was true. Mind you, the thought of Marion or any of her cronies bedding some nineteen-year-old lad seemed utterly obscene.

I don't know why it's different for men, but it is. And God, doesn't the female race hate us for it?

Now, I suppose at this point you may be wondering about Edward – Marion's long-term lover. Obviously, he's married, but is he too old, fat, bald and unsuccessful to get anyone else for his mistress except for my middle-aged wife. Well, apparently not. Edward, you see, is on his third marriage already. First wife, college romance: both too young, lasted three years, one child, a daughter, who went to live with her mother somewhere abroad. Second marriage, lasted longer, nearly ten years. Now, this wife was a television presenter, would you believe! I've seen her on television frequently. I worked out who she was quite easily, because every time she came on the screen, Marion would start to criticise her. At first it was mild: 'What a ghastly blouse!' or, 'I think it's ridiculous, a woman her age wearing her hair in pigtails.' It didn't really register initially, because Marion made quite a hobby of criticising people who could not mount their own defence. But gradually, it became an attack of such vehemence it aroused my suspicions. 'That awful talentless harpy. Look at her! She's got all the political acumen of a... of a... bloody pickled gherkin, and yet they reel her on to discuss issues with top politicians as if she were frigging Robin Day in drag!'

'Now *there's* a thought!'

'I was using frigging as an a*djective,* not verb, Alistair,' she explained acidly.

I smiled secretly to myself, as the penny dropped.

'She isn't Edward's second wife by any chance?' I ventured hesitantly.

'Whatever gave you that idea?' She sounded quite affronted.

'Well, you had mentioned his second wife was in television, and although you never wanted to let me know who she was precisely, I just sort of guessed.'

'As a matter of fact, it is Edward's ex,' and then she added,' but that isn't why I think she's an absolute travesty of a presenter. Just look! She's straining to read the auto-cue. They could put anything they like on that and she'd say it. All looks and no brain. She slept her way to the top you know.'

'Oh, come on,' I protested, 'I find that hard to believe in this day and age. I've always thought 'Our Miranda in the studio' to be rather personable and quite astute really.'

'Astute? Do you actually know the meaning of the word? And why must you always be so perverse? Always taking up the opposing line.' Marion stood irritably, hands on hips. 'Well, believe what you bloody well like! I know it for a fact. And don't sit their thinking she's got fantastic breasts, because she hasn't.' There was a little pause, while she tried to resist divulging her reasoning, but unable to she whispered confidentially, 'Totally inverted nipples - has to wear some sort of nipple prosthesis.' And she made a 'put that in your pipe and smoke it' face.

'Is that so?' I mused, staring intently at the screen, turning my head this way and that. 'You'd never guess, would you?'

'Oh, shut up, Alec.'

Anyway, to cut a long story short, Edward's marriage to Miranda was over apparently because of her excessively long hours spent on the casting couch, and not because of the nipples. Edward consequently moved onto the stage in life of proving he was still young and attractive by bedding lots of young girls, and finally in his early forties married eighteen-year-old Lizzie, because she was pregnant.

Their marriage was into its increasingly itchy seventh year. (Although Edward had suffered from bouts of personal and embarrassing irritation since taking up with Marion four years ago. How Lizzie never found out is beyond me.) Perhaps it was because Lizzie's most significant other was their daughter

Hattie, with whom she got on like a house on fire, because (according to Edward) they were so similar in mental age. So perhaps now you are beginning to anticipate where Marion fits in the scheme of Edward's life: tired of trying to pretend he's a teenager; tired of being mistaken for Lizzie's father, and Hattie's grandfather; tired of coming home to find his wife spinning round the room with Hattie to the latest chart topper, and tired of plastic-encased frozen pizza; he fell with narcoleptic gratitude into Marion's untoned arms. I expect Marion revived and dazzled him with lashings of her Boeuf Bourguignon. And what a bonus: a real woman, with no children to get in the way of her mothering of him.

I suppose I was a thorn in his side for a while, but somehow it all slotted into place like a cheap self-assembly occasional table. He had the best of both worlds (albeit in reverse to what most people would expect) a young firm trophy wife in Lizzie, and in Marion, the comfortable safe haven of a squashy bosom. Marion loved to mother and love him with as much vigour as she hated to mother and love me. That's what I resented most of all: the way she cared for him.

In fact, Marion loved him so much she put up with him staying in his marriage. It was for Hattie's sake. She was after all only two or so, when their affair, sorry, *'relationship'* began.

Marion even accepted that having two marriages behind him already, he really ought to try and keep this one together. And I suppose Marion must've have made mature sympathetic noises of understanding from under the duvet. If it were at all possible for me to be objective, Marion could still be perceived as being attractive, in that older woman way. But was almost unrecognisable from the girl I had met in our youth. Now, she was, 'well presented'... what would be the right term? I think 'well-groomed' is probably more accurate. Like an overgrown version of a 'best in show' Pomeranian at Crufts', Marion strutted busily about on ridiculous high heels with her hair unnaturally coiffured, looking this way and that for admiring glances. She exuded the whiff of a successful career woman: a vision of a mature lady, all tailored trouser suits, jewellery worthy of a woman of her age and standing, and not forgetting her studied business-lunch laugh, so light and mannered. Oh, yes... she wore her age very well. She was a complete anathema to me now, but something of her womanly charms attracted Edward. At least it made me feel less guilty, and I could carry on my sexual conquests, knowing confidently there were never going to be any shattered dreams at home.

I think I've been off at a tangent for a while there, haven't I? I was supposed to be telling you why I didn't want Marion to know about Anna. The reason I lied to her wasn't just because of her loathing the injustice of young women being attracted to older men, but also because of the pretty unfortunate incident with me and that rather self-absorbed, mentally unsound, Fay Morgan. This albatross was not entirely of my making, whatever others may believe.

About a year after Marion had taken up with Edward, I carried on my usual pattern of seducing as many of my students who would acquiesce. (To be honest I think there was only a handful, if I don't include the groping, or should I say the hoping!) During this period of my life the only person who wasn't a one-night stand was a second year, called Fay, who had the most amazing auburn hair, cut into an elfin crop; green, cat-like eyes, and pale white skin, lightly dusted with freckles. Not the type I usually go for - she was like some sort of porcelain ceramic figurine escaped from the small ads featured in the back pages of *Woman's Weekly* magazine: 'Fairies and Nymphs for you to treasure.'

Unfortunately, I did not treasure my *'so life-like'* fairy companion well enough. (In fact, to tell the truth, I didn't treasure her at all, but she turned out to have formed a rather serious attachment to me.) Oh, but goodness, was she tiny! Barely, five foot. I felt quite tall stood next to her. Irish dancing, of all things, was her main interest, and she was so fit and trim, she really did resemble a little sprite. But nevertheless, she seemed fragile. Things never felt quite right between us. In the back of my mind, I always felt like I was brutalising her in some way. I felt like some big coarse hairy satyr, stealing a wood nymph's virtue. And she was always so silent. Honestly, I never knew what was going on in that perfectly-formed little head of hers.

However, I didn't see her total passivity as a problem; I just thought it was partly to do with her personality, and partly just her ethereal fairy way of enjoying herself. Although it sounds really unkind, almost abusive really, she didn't seem to mind being used - *exploring hands encounter no defence.* She made no demands on my time, made no requests of me emotionally, financially, or sexually. I saw her when it was convenient to me, and had her in whatever way suited me. I welcomed her *indifference*. Neither of us mentioned love. It didn't even figure in my mind.

I don't know why I carried on seeing her, but I did. Eventually, another opportunity presented itself. Funnily enough, a voluminous girl - theatre type - who called herself Jessie, although that wasn't her real name. She had breasts that brought to mind milking parlours at dawn, 'Miss Piggy' hair (and come to think of it, thighs like a couple of Christmas hams), and blue nail varnish! And she was never silent. God, What a screamer! (Frightened me half to death to be perfectly honest, what with the constant snorting and whooping, compounded by the fear of suffocation.) But it was some light relief (or fairly weighty relief) from the rather introverted Fay. I had no intention of starting anything like a relationship with farmyard lookie-likey Jessie, but our brief and somewhat overwhelming coupling had made me realise that I was in fact bored rigid with Fay.

I'd be mortified if someone thought I was boring, so I obviously had the good grace not to mention tedium in my goodbye speech. However, it was only when I tried to cool things off with Fay that the reality of her hidden emotional intensity came to the fore. I'd done my usual spiel of it's been fun while it lasted, but...and she started to weep right in front of me, weeping without moving, without making a sound...just slow tears, falling onto her dress in two darkening circles. Honestly, I had no idea she was so fond of me. I tried to comfort her, really, I did. But eventually, becoming so frustrated because she wouldn't speak to me, I left her alone to cry it out. It seems so callous now, but at the time how was I to know what she was capable of?

The next evening, I was at home marking some essays, while Marion was brushing Thaddeus, taking great satisfaction in the gathering ball of ginger fur she was extracting from him.

'Look!' she exclaimed. 'I could make a jumper out of this!'

Visualising Marion in her moulted cat hair jumper, I laughed inwardly.

'Well, I guess the only thing that's stopping you is the fact you've mislaid your spinning wheel again.'

'Oh, very droll.'

'No, seriously, Marion, it could be the hobby you've been looking for. Hey, come to think of it, once I saw a picture of a woman who'd crocheted her *own* hair into a hat. So, anything's possible.'

'Really Alec, you have a mind full of the most puerile nonsense. Unfortunately, I don't share your infantile enthusiasm for the 'strange, but true!''

'Pity,' I said half-smiling, as the image of the proud hirsute-milliner, Mrs E.E. Smith of Dallas, Texas hovered in my mind.

'But to be honest, perhaps if you brushed him more often, the hair wouldn't build up so much. He'll get hair balls you know.' And I made the noise of a cat coughing up a particularly awkward hair ball. She looked disdainfully at me, but otherwise ignored what I thought was a very realistic imitation.

'Well, I wasn't here most of this week, was I? I notice you never trouble yourself with the cat brush.'

The phone began to ring.

Not wishing to struggle from my chair, I asked, 'Is it likely to be for you?'

'How the hell should I know?' she snarled, pacing towards the phone, furiously pulling cat hairs from the brush. 'But I'll save you the bother of getting up, shall I?'

'It's Ruth.' She paused, holding the receiver out towards me, 'For you.'

She was alive – only just. Several other students in her hall had found her. It was the usual cocktail: pills and drink. The students had found a note still in her hand. My name was there, intimate details...very intimate. Her parents were already on their way. Things did not look good.

A nightmare with my name on it had just broken through the gates of hell, and still screaming and dripping now enveloped me like a second skin.

Realising that the conversation I was having was serious, Marion was now right by me mouthing, 'What's happened?' and furrowing her eyebrows. When I put the phone down, she said, 'Well?'

'It's one of my students,' I replied blankly. Shock had drained all emotion from my voice. 'She's tried to take her own life.'

'Oh, good God!' Her hands flew up to her face in a somewhat melodramatic fashion. 'How awful, but the way you went so white, for a moment I thought it was bad news about someone you knew well.'

'It was.' (I'm sure I didn't say that out loud, only thought it.)

I just looked up. I don't even know what kind of face I was making or what was said in my eyes, but Marion saw.

'Oh, no Alec,' she said backing away from me, 'not one of *YOUR* students. Oh, my God! You bloody stupid fool! What have you done? What the hell have you been playing at?'

I don't know why she asked, because she then went on to catalogue, for the next half an hour or so, my ridiculous immaturity; my preying upon young emotionally vulnerable girls; my lack of professionalism; this whole sorry episode somehow being related to my inability to father a child; my sad male menopausal state, which would be laughable were it not for its tragic consequences; the reputation of the other teaching staff besmirched by my activities; the reputation of the university (no less!); the embarrassment for her; my selfishness; my self-centred personality... the list was endless.

I listened, saying nothing in my defence. Perhaps I was all of those things, and more besides.

Eventually, Marion began to tire of taking the prosecution stand. In fact, I think she began to tire of the sight of me.

'Oh, Alec - just take a long hard look at yourself. You are pathetic. What little respect I had for you has gone. The scales have fallen from my eyes. I see you for what you are, and it disgusts me.' She poured herself a large glass of whiskey and drank it down in one draught.

'Have you nothing to say to me?' There was an edge of desperation in her voice. I could only shrug. Then she refreshed her glass and walked toward the kitchen. As she strode away, she announced, without looking round, 'I'm going to ring Edward. I think it's about time some decisions were made for all of us.'

She was an awfully long time on the phone.

However, life regurgitated itself onto our plates, looking very much as it had before. Marion and I continued to live in domestic disharmony; Lizzie and Hattie spun round the room in blissful ignorance; and Edward continued to have his cake (although in Marion's case I imagine it was like his 'Hardtack biscuit') and eat it. The only person who made any changes was me. I stopped trying to make it with my students. Full stop.

What did I do about Fay? Well, my first reaction, once I'd got over the initial shock, was that I should rush up to the hospital and see her. Say I'd made a dreadful mistake, and that yes, I really did love her, and hope that all would be forgiven, but I knew that that was the coward in me reacting. And to be perfectly honest, I didn't love her...that was the awful truth. But what does one do in such circumstances? Send flowers, a box of Dairy Milk, and a get well soon card? If I went to the hospital at all, how would her father react? He would be about my age, possibly even younger. He'd hardly shake my hand and say, 'Oh dear, my daughter seems to have rather overreacted to your calling it a day.' I haven't got a daughter, but if I did, in such circumstances I imagine I would want to half-kill someone like me.

In the end I did nothing. I just stayed away from everything. The doctor put me on sick leave for a week or two: stress. Fortunately for me, the initial reports of the incident had been grossly over exaggerated and she was successfully pumped out, and made a full recovery. There wasn't even any significant liver damage, (which is more than you can say for me, because I think I took ten years off the life of my liver with the amount I drank during those desperate months which followed.)

Thank God she'd had some Irish Dance Jamboree coming up the following weekend, which is why the other dancing leprechauns had come prancing round for her when she hadn't turned up for jig practice or whatever they did. If they hadn't turned up that evening, by the morning, the whole sorry episode would have had a very different and more final ending. I suppose you could say I was lucky.

It also came to light that she had had severe problems with anorexia and depression as a teenager, so I wasn't entirely to blame. She was obviously unstable. Quite honestly, I felt the aggrieved party in many ways; I mean, imagine putting that sort of private detail in a suicide note, which she obviously knew would be found. But then I suppose being so introverted, and self-obsessed, she was incapable of empathising with anyone else's feelings but her own.

Now please don't think me terribly uncharitable, but in the long term it could be said that Fay Morgan recovered from her suicide attempt far more quickly than I did. My life was in tatters. By all accounts she returned home, and took some sort of business course in East Anglia. But there was no easy fresh start for me. Over the next few months, I don't think I've ever met so many people with such strained looking faces. You could watch the thoughts running round in their minds: me seducing the poor innocent girl; me being an unfaithful husband; me being a shallow philanderer... a sexual opportunist of the worst sort. Let me tell you, what she said in her letter made me out to be the most lascivious descendent of Priapus ever to have strutted his ghastly form across the earth. I mean, for goodness sake! Even Marion allowed herself a hollow laugh at my reported sexual athleticism. Fay also claimed to be pregnant. She wasn't of course. (I must admit to gaining a secret pleasure from that rumour though).

In tutorials I could sense in my peripheral vision eyes upon me, wondering. Some girls flirted with me more, a reaction I found hard to comprehend. The other staff were either silently condemnatory, or given to, 'there but for the grace of God, mate,' innuendo. It was exhausting.

I didn't know how to be myself any longer, or how to relate to the students anymore. My usual manner had always been friendly and relaxed, jokey, and there was always a little buzz of flirtation in the air. Now every time I smiled at one of the girls, found I'd inadvertently touched someone, or just made contact with their hand as I took a paper from them, I'd feel myself colour, and my heart would begin to flutter, but not in a pleasant way. It felt more like a panic attack. Eventually, I could not meet people's eyes in case it looked like I was hungering after them in some way. I became very withdrawn.

After a few weeks, I requested a sabbatical, and it was very quickly agreed to. Shortly after, we had that holiday in Italy with Tom Gower and Amanda. Marion came too, as you know, in spite of things being still pretty dire at home. But Edward had taken the 'kids' (Marion's phrase) to Disney so they 'Could meet Mickey Mouse in the flesh,' (Lizzie's phrase), which naturally met with heaps of derision from Marion. And so, she decided to come with me, as a sort of tit-for-tat.

It was the last thing I needed. Here we were, two couples whose marriages were both ravaged by prolonged death throws, trying to make the pretence of having a good time. Every day everyone drank too much, and said too much. Some days Amanda and Tom were so verbally spiteful to one another I couldn't bear to stay in the same house, and retreated alone up to the bar. Marion, on the other hand, liked to lie under a large flowery parasol on her lounger, pretending to be asleep, beneath an enormous pair of sunglasses. Other people's misery fascinated her even more than her own, and I think she secretly admired Amanda's lively and inventive insults. I think she was probably storing them up in the hope of getting an opportunity to use them against me one day. Indeed, one could say Schadenfreude was one of Marion's favourite hobbies, and although disappointingly, knitting was not another, she shared many other notable similarities with Madame Defarge.

Up at the bar I met a very accommodating lady, called Maggie. Maggie was then at least mid-sixties, if she was a day. She was marvellously easy to talk to, and we hit it off from the first time that we met one another. It transpired that she and her husband had come to live in Italy when he retired some five years ago. He had then promptly died of a heart attack, but undaunted by his inconsiderate departure, Maggie had stayed on alone in Tuscany, where there was 'plenty to paint, and plenty to drink.'

If there is one thing that comes to mind when thinking of Maggie, it's fruit, particularly apples. To look at she was like a Bramley windfall that one would find forgotten under an ancient apple tree in December; her skin of burnt umber, slightly blemished with age spots, collapsed and wrinkled in some places, while in others still imbued with a swollen, glossy sheen, like a well-polished saddle. Tiny eyes, screwed up against the sun, like two nut brown, shiny apple pips, smiled out at the world. At heart, Maggie was an entire bowl of over-ripe fruit left out in the sun – colourful, luscious, warm, soft, and ever so slightly mushy in places. Moreover, if you got too close, she always smelt far, far, too sweet, like an intoxicating liqueur, (I think it was the combination of the heady scent of suntan oil, in which she was always basted and the underlying aroma of alcohol in which she was always pickled.) She made me wonder if she were not just one large well-oiled barrel of fermentation. Even her voice was fruity, rich, slightly vibrating, very upper class. She called me, 'My dear boy,' or 'My dear Alistaaiiir' and we drank rough local Grappa together, or sipped the crimson bitterness of an ice-cold Campari and soda. As the days rolled by, I spent more and more time up at the bar. Maggie always seemed to be there. I found myself telling her about Fay and about the situation with Marion, and Edward. She was an excellent listener: 'My dear boy, what a simply dreadful time you have had.'

Later, as the night descended, she told me of some of the traumas she'd been through, and how she'd learned to 'let it go.' 'I put it all on an imaginary raft, say a sad goodbye, then I shove it out to sea until I can no longer see the tiniest speck... and then I turn, and walk away. Just let it go. We cannot change the past, Alistair my dear, only the influence it has on our present.'

It all sounded well and good, but didn't really explain why having put all those rafts to sea she was still here every day lost in an ocean of alcohol. Perhaps the fatal flaw in her argument was that these rudderless boats had a habit of being washed up on the same shore, many months - even years – later, basically the same, just a little more battered, a little more festooned in seaweed and barnacles: home once more.

However, it was not all shared misery; Maggie had a wonderful relaxed easy-going attitude to life, and loved nothing more than to laugh. And she could laugh too. She made me feel incredibly witty; always fell about at my jokes. She'd laugh, in such a fulsome manner, her whole body would undulate, and her mouth fell open like a snake trying to eat an egg. I was captivated by the fact all her remaining bottom molars were golden.

Oh God, and all that flesh that moved – glistening, gleaming with oil, her upper arms were always bare, as was her cleavage, which was so fat and squashed, that her breast looked just like one big bottom heaving in a pair of ill-fitting knickers. When she finished laughing, she always made a little descending dying sound, like a vacuum cleaner being switched off. I really loved her. Her physical person fascinated me, and her company was most congenial, but we would never be more than friends.

Maggie, Maggie? How did I get on to Maggie? Oh, yes, I was trying to explain why I didn't want Marion, and the rest of the world for that matter, to know about Anna and me. Yes, it was Fay I was explaining about, and then I got diverted onto Maggie. I'll leave Maggie there, for the time being, with the sun turning her the colour of a Christmas date, and her laugh expiring in my ears.

So that was, in truth, the real reason why I lied to Marion, and why I wanted to keep my affair with Anna as private as possible. I had a reputation, which I did not want to live up too.

Chapter Seventeen: the marble

It was thus that Anna and I only met in her bed-sit. It became our private world, and in spite of my initial reservations about Chris she proved to be quite a confidant. Of course, there was gossip and rumours, after all I only had to be in the same room as Anna and my whole being began to glow. I couldn't help it. And our eyes could not meet one another's gaze without revealing an inner fire. But that was all they had to go on.

I have to admit, I found it intensely erotic to be in a formal situation, such as a lecture, and have Anna in the room. My heart would race as pictures of our nakedness pumped through my brain. I was so afraid that my thoughts would pour out of my mouth, instead of the lecture notes I was supposed to be delivering. Although sometimes I couldn't resist dropping a little encoded message into my lecture, which I knew only Anna would pick up on. A private word, a double-entendre only we two would understand. It was so childish, wasn't it? There were, no doubt, many people in that room engaged in some sort of groping of one another's bodies in their private lives, so why did I feel mine was so uniquely exhilarating? The answer is partly, I believed then, and still believe it now, that I had something which went beyond what most of them hadn't even dreamt of – even wet dreamt of. I was in the most complete love of my life, and it thrilled me to the very core of my being. And of course, my love was, akin to the love that dare not speak its name – a secret; a love that few would approve of. And all of this fanned my flames.

During this period, Anna and I had that wonderful trip down to London; the one when my watch was ruined. In spite of spending most of the afternoon in bed together, we did manage to get ourselves out to the theatre in the evening. We went to see *Lear*, at the National, a bit heavy for a romantic weekend away, I know, but Anna had chosen that above anything else. However, it was only once we were there that I realised it was more than a love of Shakespeare that had drawn her to it. She had a bit of a thing about one of the lead actors, and was visibly transfixed by him all evening.

'He's too old for you,' I whispered in a light-hearted way without really thinking.

'He's three years younger than you, actually. And considerably richer.'

I wanted to say, 'But nowhere near as sexy,' just to keep up with the light-hearted banter, but instead I made no reply, and just sank back into my chair seething. Her, admiring him, probably even now fantasizing about him, made me want to jump up on the stage and push him off it. What is it about actors? You see them being someone else and you fall in love with them. How absurd. Would you really feel the same if rather than pretending to be the local postman or whatever, he really was your local postman? Of course not! It is the distance. It is the money. It is the sheer sex appeal of fame. They belong to a charmed circle – you do not. They are the gods: we the mortals. To be chosen by such a god, to be thought worthy of the god's attention, one would drown in reflected glory. Ah, the magic of the unobtainable. I should know… I'm living it.

My goddess beside me sat engrossed, ignoring me. It was more than I deserved. When we got back to the hotel, she teased me mercilessly, and even went so far as to say that she often imagined that I was him when we were having sex, especially if she was finding it difficult to climax.

'You are joking, aren't you?' I asked.

'Well, don't you ever think about anyone else when we're doing it?'

'No, never,' I answered truthfully. Although occasionally Marion had figured uncomfortably in my thoughts, but she didn't really count.

'Anyway, what do you mean, 'finding it difficult to come'? You don't, do you? And besides, I thought our love making was always, well, wonderful. '

'Love making?' She began to laugh. 'Nobody says, 'our love-making' anymore Alistair; you sound like you've just read a book entitled, 'The 1930s newlyweds' guide to married love' or something.'

'What term do you prefer then? Shag? Copulation? 'Bit of how's your father?'

Almost wearily she explained: 'Sex is fine, even a simple 'fucking' is better than 'our love making' And look, if it makes you feel any better, yes, I'm joking. I promise, no other image ever enters my mind but you. It's just you're so easy to wind up. And that hurt expression of yours,' and here she made a face like a dejected spaniel, 'when you look as if your world has just fallen apart, it's so appealing. I can't stop myself from teasing you from time to time.' And with that, she switched off the light.

Was that the truth?

Ten minutes of 'joyous coupling' later, I still couldn't help but wonder. Although, as I held her close to me, she did make me laugh by quoting from one of her favourite novels, *The Prime of Miss Jean Brodie*, complete with a clipped Edinburgh accent: "Allow me, to congratulate you warmly upon your sexual intercourse, as well as your singing."

I gave forth a rousing burst of, 'Hey Jonny Cope', which unfortunately led her to modifying her effusiveness about my ability to serenade, but I hope the former praise still held.

On the Sunday morning, we went to the V&A. It was a particularly cold morning for a stroll through London. The sun was almost white, bleaching the stone of the buildings we passed, and the air was so brittle, it felt as if our faces were breaking through a thin film of ice with every step. But we didn't want to get a taxi; it was so exhilarating just to walk along arm in arm, knowing the chance of meeting anyone was remote.

While we were in the Cast Court, it suddenly struck me. 'Isn't it bizarre,' I began, gesturing at the assembled stony company, 'so many of the world's most notable statues and architectural landmarks, all thrown together, none of them in their natural place, a hotchpotch of images.'

We were now standing before the statue of David; he towered above us, his colossal form quite overwhelming. My admiration was touched by sadness as I looked up at the beautiful figure, now positioned incongruously in a South Kensington museum; a lesser copy of his glorious former Italian incarnation. His intense puzzled gaze strangely focused on the exit, as if wondering where on earth he was, and if he ought to leave.

Somewhat pompously I declared, 'Isn't it incredible that one man could create such perfection, carved from a single piece of marble; it's just stunning.'

'Or in this case to have made such a good cast, with no air bubbles. Hey, look. I've never really noticed before but hasn't he got a little 'doo dah.' Just compare the size of his hand to his willy. Look! Even his some of his toes are bigger!'

'Anna!' I whispered, conscious that her voice was carrying around the gallery. 'Let me explain. It's not that his thingy is so small; it's that his hands are so big. They're expressive distortions,' I went on, knowledgably quoting something I read in a guide book years ago, 'symbols of power, showing that the hands rule. His feet are disproportionately large as well to show that they bear the weight of a hero.'

'Ah, *now* I understand. So, some blokes haven't got little todgers, it's just an optical illusion due to their disproportionately large hands and feet?' She picked up my hands and examined them, 'So according to *your* theory; big hands, small willy: small hands, big willy? Is that right? '

'Really Anna! To be fair, it isn't *that* much of small genitalia. Although, maybe you've been rather spoilt,' I added playfully. 'Believe it or not,' I continued, regaining a teacherly air of authority to my voice, 'It took a half a metre-high fig leaf to cover it, so as to spare the blushes of delicate Victorian ladies.'

'Are you talking about yourself in your younger days now, or the statue?' Smirking, she strolled with a jocular swing towards 'The Dying Slave'.

'Ah, but what about him then? I mean gosh, he is beautiful, in a kind of homoerotic way. Is that intentional do you think? But *quel dommage!* even he's got a little one, and little hands too. Bang goes the theory!'

'Anna,' I said, grabbing her arm and steering her towards the exit. 'Honestly! Here we are, confronted by the some of the world's sculptural masterpieces and all you're focused on is how they measure up. Is that all you think about?'

'Of course not. Anyway, if you weren't trying to be so damned cultured, I bet you'd admit to the thought passing through your mind too. And I suspect the same is true of everyone else, only they're all too polite and high-minded to say so. And stop wheeling me along!'

'Sorry.' I let go of her, and smiled sheepishly. 'You're probably right...only next time, can you keep your voice down; I was so embarrassed.'

'What about? My Philistine attitude or my mentioning penis size, and small penis size at that, in a public place?'

'You are incorrigible!'

We linked arms again and made our way down the corridor towards the shop.

'My trouble is this Alistair. When in the presence of something as wonderful as those sculptures I am deeply moved; so moved in fact that I cannot express what I feel. I can't stomach standing around and making facile meaningless comments, trotting out words like 'beautiful',' incredible', when they all fall short of what I really want to say. For me there are no words I know which can adequately describe the response such things evoke in me. So, I'd prefer to say nothing or just make a joke of it. Do you understand?'

I must admit I was somewhat stunned by this slightly pretentious speech. For one, I was not expecting it, and for two, I suddenly had the most uncomfortable feeling that I hardly knew Anna at all. What was real? What did she really think? We walked in silence for a moment or two, the atmosphere between us hazy. Then she gave my hand a playful squeeze and with lightness in her voice, whispered, 'In the summer, when we go and see the real thing in Florence, I promise you there will be no mention of penises in the gallery. Cross my heart. But really Alistair, I had no idea that you were such a prude.'

We went into the shop, and bought a few postcards, including one of the statue of David. No wonder he has such an intense expression. Such an exposed and powerful representation of manhood in all ways, but one. I felt slightly sorry for him. He might have been happier with his fig leaf of dignity after all.

I hope she's kept the postcard.

Chapter Eighteen: You *are* a proper fool

Well, that was it. Apart from that trip to London, most of our early relationship was conducted within the four walls of her bed-sit, with me coming and going as discreetly as I could. The other students in the house were all reading either science or engineering, so none of them had a clue about me. Chris, I can safely say, never breathed a word to anyone, although she did always look at me with a slight glint in her eye, as if wryly amused by the situation. Anna and I locked ourselves away inside our own private world, and lost ourselves in one another. Some nights we ate together, on others we talked, listened to music, watched her little black and white portable or simply sat working; she at her desk: me with my feet up on the sofa. Nearly always, we made love (and yes, I still use the phrase unreservedly.) Sometimes in a great rush of passion when I'd first arrive - once still wearing my coat - and at other times the moment was delayed for hours, so as to enjoy the anticipation, the rising swell of desire (if you'll pardon the pun). But when I look back now, it was always Anna who controlled this game of 'when and how'; I was so desperate for her, she'd only to say jump, and I'd eagerly asked 'how high?'

But of course, like all clandestine relationships, our days of secrecy were numbered. Everything had gone quite smoothly, up until just before Christmas. By having successfully thrown Marion off the scent with such a complicated web of lies that I almost began to believe them myself, I thought we were safe. Ginny was forty-two. Originally, I was going to make her thirty-seven, but I knew that pushing her over forty would please Marion no end. Ginny's ex-husband ran his own business, and she worked as a secretary.

'A secretary?' Marion repeated with incredulity. 'As in: "Miss Moneypenny, I'd like to give you some dictation," secretary?'

'Yes. And?'

'Nothing. I just can't imagine you with a secretary.'

'You're such a snob, Marion. There's nothing wrong with being a secretary.'

'I never said there was,' she said making a wide-eyed 'who-me?' face.

'Ginny has a very high level of responsibility,' I added.

'I wouldn't doubt that for a minute, Alec,' she assured me, insincerity trickling from the corners of her mouth.

Nevertheless, I was pleased I'd achieved my purpose, allowing her the secret thrill, the glow of triumph, that my new woman wasn't her intellectual or social equal. Their son, Jonathan, was at catering college near Newcastle. Although as much as I tried to convince Marion that Ginny wasn't a Geordie, she still persisted with having her little joke about it. Whenever I returned from having seen Anna, Marion would be ready with an, 'Eh, but pet, the smell o' that Newcassel broon on your breath is reet champion.' Or her favourite,' Is that eh bottle of Newkie Broon in yer pocket pet or ar' yoo jest pleased t' see me?'

I even invented a black cat, called Mr Tibbs. Tibbs for short, so that Marion could enquire about the cat when she grew tired of quizzing me about Ginny.

But there were times when I had to think fast, and inevitably, there came a time when I did not think quite as rapidly as I needed to. Marion picked up my coat, which I'd thrown over the back of a chair, and was about to hang it up when she noticed one or two long dark wavy hairs, which she then proudly laid on the papers I was marking.

'One of Ginny's short blond hairs - I think not! She is 'bottle' blond, isn't she? Fairly short, or so you said.'

'Ah,' I said, pausing for just a second, 'Must you really pry. Is it really any of your business?'

'It is if I find out you've been lying to me.'

An idea came to me.... 'It's just, it's rather personal.'

'Yes?'

'It's the hair from a wig if you must know.'

'*You* have been wearing a long dark wig?'

'No! Of course not! Ginny did the other day.'

'Go on. I'm all ears.'

'Well, if you must know, it was just for fun. Ginny was a French maid and I was a ma...'

'Enough!' Marion cried abruptly, 'You were right, it's none of my business. Honestly, you surprise me, Alec. Even I wouldn't have thought you'd be quite so horribly clichéd in your choice of sexual role play. And deary me, how bored you must both be, to have reached *this* stage of experimenting with the 'How to spice up your flagging sex life tips' from some woman's monthly magazine, quite so early on in your *'relationship.'* I don't know whether to laugh, cry or just feel sorry for you.'

She scooped up Thaddeus into her arms, and shut herself in the kitchen with him, as if to protect him from my pitiful perversity. I chuckled to myself at my ingenuity. Marion hated anything that smacked of kinkiness, plus she now misguidedly assumed my love-life was in the doldrums already, so I felt a double triumph in knowing that my answer had not only avoided detection on this occasion, but would slow down any future paths of enquiry somewhat. (How lost I had become in my own deluded sense of reality. Little did I know that at that moment I had already shot myself in the foot.)

I could hear her talking quietly on the phone in the kitchen. Then she raised her voice haughtily, 'Well, I'm sorry, Edward, it didn't make me laugh.'

Sniggering silently to myself, I stood behind the door, so I could enjoy what else she had to say. But the conversation was taking a turn I had not expected.

'I'm sure he does it just to annoy me...Well, why else would he possibly want to make such things up, when things are as they are.... Do you really think so? But after all the trouble that was caused last time.'

The smile disappeared from my face.

'Well, I suppose I wouldn't put it past him, he's unbearably self-satisfied these days... But nobody's said anything to me, and I'm sure someone would have rung me by now if he were...Now I think about it, it would all add up. That bloody smugness he exudes like a cheap aftershave... If he is, that will be it! Although there's obviously nothing between myself and Alec anymore, I just feel it's so humiliating to be lied to. Maybe I should just confront him directly.' Silence, while Edward speaks. 'I've been taken for a fool, haven't I? I think the game's up ...'

She paused for a moment. I heard my heart pulse.

'Well, that's the thing, lots of people do still presume Alec and I are still together of sorts.' There was an agonizing few minutes while Edward spoke at length and she just remarked in a nasally way, 'Oh, I know,' at intervals like some watered-down version of Sybil Fawlty. 'Oh, I know,' she intoned for the fifth time '...Well, you've hit the nail on the head there, unethical! That's the word! At least we agree on something...'

One phrase circled my mind like a mantra, 'The game's up.' I'd sort of lost concentration at this point, and the next sentence, which really penetrated my consciousness was Marion cooing reassuringly, 'Edward, however this turns out, you know I'll always wait, until you feel the time is right for you...and Hattie...of course I'm not forgetting Hattie.'

Oh, God. I'd overdone it. I felt a horrible jostling of nerves in my stomach. I should have just said nothing. I got carried away. It had seemed like a fairly harmless tall story. Now I knew Marion seriously doubted that I was telling the truth. She smelt a rat...a big, filthy, slimy sewer rat.

She really didn't care about me seeing Ginny; she could cope with that. But if she knew about my relationship with Anna, she'd do everything she could to destroy it. She'd find out. I knew she would. It was only a matter of time. (Although even I did not realise quite how little time I had.)

Quickly, I sat back down in the chair as if I'd been working there all the time. The door from the kitchen sprang open. Marion appeared, framed in the doorway, her jaw slightly clenched, glass in hand... *'Alright Mr DeMille, I'm ready for my close-up.'*

'It's a lie, isn't it, Alec?' she said in a resigned monotone.
Pretending to have been drawn from the depths of concentration, I replied, 'What is?' She rolled her eyes with theatrical weariness.
'Oh, you mean the wig thing,' I said snapping my fingers as if I'd just fallen in. 'Yes, of course. I was joking. The French maid thing, just a joke. I was just teasing you, Marion. To tell the truth, it was Jonathan's girlfriend's actually, her hair. She was down for the week-end and left her coat on the coach, so I lent her mine when they went out to the pub.'

'Really?'
'It was freezing. Sunday night, flurries of snow and all that. You remember?'

'Yes, I do now you come to mention it. I have a very good memory - remember? But you, Alec, apparently, have not.' Marion span round to face me, with a somewhat dramatic flair; I swear she missed her vocation at the bar. I shrugged.

'For example,' she continued, 'do you remember that I've seen you dig yourself into a hole before? That I've seen you lie before, make a complete... *arse*... (Now that word doesn't fall naturally from Marion's lips - she must have been really mad) of yourself before, screwed up people's lives before?'
She had started off quite calmly, but was rapidly building up to an angry crescendo.

'Where's all this come from?' I asked, trying my best to look bewildered and dumbfounded.

'The lies!' she shouted. 'The lies, Alec, were becoming just a little too fabulous, just a little too much fantasy and too little reality. I was beginning to feel I was living with Baron Munchausen. It's all lies, isn't? There is no Ginny, Geordie or otherwise, is there? There is no Jonathan, there is no fucking feline called Tibbs.' (In my mind a voice said, *'They call me Mr. Tibbs'*)

Tiny beads of sweat were pricking through the pores of my skin; my mind began to race with the thoughts of what to do. I had expected my undoing to come slowly, like a death from a prolonged illness, but this was like watching an accident. It was all happening too quickly. Panic. I would leave my job. Anna could leave the university. We could leave this city. Marion could not really destroy anything. No law had been broken. For us, no vows broken. But she terrified me nevertheless.

Pleased by my stunned silence, Marion's tone became deeply patronizing.

'What I cannot help but wonder Alec, is that if all these lovely people were just a figment of your sordid imagination, a human smokescreen of not just one imaginary person, but an entire family no less! Who are they shielding, I wonder? No doubt in a week or so's time they would have been joined by dear delightful old Granny Postlethwaite down from Newcastle to celebrate the season of goodwill with her dear daughter Ginny. Or perhaps you'd have told amusing anecdotes of how Mr Tibbs pulled over the artificial Christmas tree on Boxing Day. It would be artificial, wouldn't it, because Ginny can't stand the mess of all those needles, Am I right?'

'What are you saying? I don't understand?'

'Ha!' she exclaimed. 'Spare me, Alec, please! Oh, you do understand, you understand only too well, don't you? It's all a pack of lies, isn't it? You're at it again, aren't you? There's only one reason for these lies and you know, and I know what it is.'

I must have looked like a rabbit caught in the headlights.

She sensed victory and rushed in for the kill.

'What is she? Eighteen? Nineteen? Flattered by the attentions of her tutor? Makes you feel the big man, does she? My goodness, I bet you can't believe your luck? Last chance to run your trembling little hands over a firm bosom, before they retire you and you're just another pensioner, without a hope in hell to do anything more than gawp and remember.'

There was no point trying to conceal the truth any longer. I knew the cat, if not entirely out of the bag, was fighting, spitting and scratching and would shoot out any moment, but in spite of being awash with fear, I suddenly found a calm strength within me to face her.

'Marion, you have no right to pass judgement. You're not exactly a paragon of virtue yourself, carrying on for years with someone else's husband. Your comments are cruel and unwarranted.'

I stood up so as not to be disadvantaged by being lower than her. 'Yes, you are right,' I continued, 'I have lied to you.' (I'm afraid I was sounding a bit like a politician making his resignation speech after an indiscretion.) 'Everyone you've mentioned, Mr Tibbs included, a tissue of fabrications. But Marion, just look at your reaction, just listen to your venom. Faced with such vitriol, what person wouldn't lie?'

'A decent one,' she replied curtly, 'an honest one; a grown-up one.'

'It isn't like you think, Marion. This time is very different. Couldn't be more different than anything I've known before.'

'Don't kid yourself!'

'I'm not,' I said defensively.

'Humph! So, I'm right then? You don't deny you're having some ridiculous carry on with a young student.'

I shrugged my shoulders in acknowledgement.

'Stop doing that! That stupid thing with your shoulders…you never learn, do you?' Marion's voice began to falter a little. 'And don't you ever try to compare your petty gropings to my relationship with Edward ever again. Edward loves me and I love him. We're two mature adults. Our relationship is grounded. You've no idea, have you, Alec? These girls, I don't know what you see in them. Well… I do. But that's nothing. Not in the long term. I hope for your sake and hers she's not another nutcase.'

'She's anything but,' I remonstrated. 'She's beautiful, fun, intelligent, creative, very loving, and very sane actually.'

'Actually!' repeated Marion. 'God, the next thing you'll be telling me is that you're madly in love with this divine creature!'

In silence a smile spread across my face, my eyes shone with the thought of her, my body radiated the bliss she made me feel. A queer look came over

Marion's face: astonishment, mixed with distaste, as if she had just discovered something very unpleasant crawling about amongst her salad leaves.

'Good grief! You really think you are, don't you? In love? Really *'in love.'*'

I looked at her with the eyes of man on fire.

'Yes. Yes, I am... totally and utterly. And if you do anything to try and destroy what I have, God help me, Marion, I'll... I'll...'

'You'll what?' Her eyebrows raised into two mocking arches. 'Well...?' She harrumphed right in my face. 'No, no, no, no. You're quite right of course. This is different. This is the real thing at last!' Then, clutching her hands in front of her bosoms, she began to sway back and forth singing out that great Italian celebration of love, 'That's Amore'. I had no idea she knew the words so accurately. She even accompanied the line about pizza pie with a humorous little mime as if she were in some Girl Guide Gang Show.

'Shut up Marion!' I yelled, quite forcefully for me, but ignoring me she continued lustily, swinging an imaginary skirt around her legs in a provocative fashion.

'*...that's amore!*'

'For God's sake, Marion! Have you taken leave of your senses?'

'Alec, Alec.' She said soothingly, rounding on me. 'You're so excitable. Calm yourself, dear. Ooo, I can see your dander is really up this time. What kind of a woman do you take me for? I wouldn't come between you and your *grande passion*. Trust me, my darling. Your secret is safe with me. My lips are sealed.' And she performed an annoying little pursing gesture with her fingers to her mouth.

She turned away from me, and walked towards the hallway, but years of experience taught me that she had not quite finished. I was right. She got to the doorway, and turned on her heels, as if an afterthought had just struck her.

'Just one thing Alec darling, please do ask me to be matron-of-honour at you and your lovely child bride's wedding. It would be such an...honour.' She said the last word with a sense of delighted surprise, as if by accident she had stumbled across the very word to express her sentiment, when gosh, it was there, in the title of the role, all the time. With that she tottered up the stairs, still singing *Amore* under her breath. Of all the reactions I might have expected, this performance certainly wasn't one of them.

Chapter Nineteen: I sat down and wept

I couldn't understand why Marion was being so apparently reasonable. It wasn't like her at all. I thought she'd have been straight away back on the phone to Edward or Ruth, or round at Tom Gower's, grilling his testicles over an open fire. Maybe I'd underestimated how far Marion and I had grown apart now. Maybe she didn't feel responsible for me, and my actions anymore. Maybe she saw this as the push she needed to sort out her own life with Edward.

Anyway, whatever the reason, we didn't speak about things again that evening, because she'd shut herself in her room, and was listening to her Barbara Streisand album, a sure sign to steer clear. For a few moments I stood outside the door wondering whether to knock and see if she was all right, but I wasn't sure if I could hear her crying. To be honest I knew she was; the vitriolic sarcasm so convincingly performed downstairs was her natural defence mechanism. But I didn't want her to lose face, so I crept away again, leaving her rheumy eyed, and lost in the esoteric lyrics of '*You don't bring me flowers.*' The strange thing was that the thought of me actually being in love with someone else would really get to Marion.

I took myself for a very long walk. Inevitably, I was drawn towards Anna's house. Obviously, I needed to talk to her about the evening's revelations and to warn her of any impeding repercussions from Marion, or elsewhere. By the time I got there, it was beginning to snow. It wasn't the nice sort of snow, with large soft flakes, but the pinhead oatmeal sort, sharp and wet. Watching the beads of snow land on my coat, and sink into the fabric, I stood patiently on the doorstep and rang the bell. There was no reply. I pushed it again; still no reply. Carefully, I came back down the steps, which were already slippery with icy slush, and crossed the road, so that I could see more clearly if there was even the slightest sign of life in her room. The room was in total darkness.

A young couple were pacing up the road with their heads down against the snow, and as they drew nearer, I asked if they had the time. As they looked up, I realised with surprise that the chap was Greg Donavan; *(*Remember him? The gorgeous one in my tutorial group?) and with an even greater sense of shock *(*which I think I barely managed to conceal) I saw that the girl he was walking with was Anna.

'Oh, hello there!' said Donavan, the grinning bastard. 'Fancy bumping into you down here at this time of night.'

'Yes. What a coincidence.' I said flatly, throwing a split-second accusatory glance to Anna.

'We're just on our way back from the union, me and Anna here,' he offered. 'You live round here too, I guess?'

'No, just walking.'

'In this weather? Still, it's good for you though, exercise. Keeps a man fit!' And he gave a mock, 'Get you buddy' kind of punch to my arm - the cheek of this boy.

'Actually, do either of you have the time?' I said rather pointedly.

'The time's about ten-thirty,' Anna told me smiling, as if nothing were amiss at all.

'Aw, that's just a guess, Anna. I'll have a look at the old timepiece, here. Time is....' he pushed up the sleeve of his fake World War II leather bomber jacket, 'ten thirty-five. Wow! Not a bad guess at all, Anna!' (I wished he'd stop using her name so often).

'Anyway, if you don't mind, we'll leave you to your evening stroll, and go and get ourselves warmed up a bit.' He flashed his big, broad, perfectly-formed smile at Anna. 'It's a rotten night, isn't it? I'd chug off home too if I were you, sir. You're soaked through as it is.'

He took hold of Anna's hand. He actually touched her hand with his. He held his skin, his flesh and bones against hers. I watched them walk across the road, together. Their two sets of footprints side by side in the thin film of snow. Anna glanced round only once, but her hair blew in her face and I couldn't make out what she was trying to convey to me.

How I managed to walk home I will never know. My legs were paralysed as ice cold muscle fought with a cocktail of hot blood laced with adrenaline. I moved like a glacier over an unforgiving terrain. Grinding. Grit between each joint. Something else? Moving like a parasite between the imperceptible layer between muscle and bone. I felt them there. Writhing, slowly swelling like leeches.

Pain, real physical pain wracked every part of my body. My chest heaved every time I tried to take a breath. I was in a vacuum. I could hardly expand my chest. Pressure crushed me from all sides. She'd given me no warning; there had been absolutely no indication that her feelings had changed. I made my slow progress towards home; the eerie silence of the snow pressing down on me.

The pain in my chest was so intense, that I did wonder if I was actually having a heart attack, and half hoped I would die out here alone in the cold dark streets, not to be found until the next day with my lips drained of colour, and ice matting my hair and eyebrows. The sound of Anna's front door being slammed, banged again and again in my head. And I saw her lighting the candles, putting on the music, turning on the gas fire. I saw him checking his looks in the mirror; then lolling about on the sofa with his legs wide apart, as if he owned the place.

They'd open some wine, (wine, which no doubt I had bought) and then it would begin. I wondered if I would subconsciously know the moment when my life had come to an end. If, at the moment he took her, I would know, as if struck by an invisible bolt of lightning.

For some time, I stood motionless in the park gazing at the ice which had formed across the darkness of the lake, petrified by an almost irresistible urge to walk out across its mysteriously hard flat surface, and listen for the creaking groans of ice under pressure. To stand in the centre of the lake and see the stress patterns radiate about me like a web, and know there was no escape. Only seconds left, to still breathe the air, to shout and hear my voice, to know or feel anything, other than the sinking, icy cold, dark green silence.

Voices from my past haunted me:

*Is not short paine well borne, that brings long ease,
And layes the soule to sleepe in quiet grave?
I do not find
The Hanged Man.
Fear death by water.'
'Vex not his ghost: O! Let him pass; he hates him
That would upon the rack of this tough world
Stretch him out longer.'*

I saw my face bloated, mottled, greeny-black, distorted - pressing up from beneath the thick layer of ice - unnoticed for days perhaps. Then a sudden burst of unexpected winter sunshine, and the ice melts around me and I emerge wet and slimy like a new-born, floating in the middle of the pond. How ashamed I am, at the unforgettable horror I have brought into the life of the little girl who is first to spot me.

Could I have stopped it happening? Should I have said something? I could not think fast enough. I had wondered whether to stay and wait until he'd left, but I couldn't bear to be so close. And what if I had to wait until morning? What man could endure standing on a street corner, powerless to stop another man, silently, and without laying a finger on him, kill him?

By the time I got home, it was well past midnight.

After struggling out of my wet shoes and heavily sodden coat, I padded quietly down the hallway, in my damp socks. Marion, I was surprised to hear, was still up, and chatting on the phone. I had no intention of listening to her, being as all I wanted to do was go to bed and die. But as I began to climb the stairs, I couldn't help but overhear the tail end of her conversation.

'Yes, he actually used the word 'love'. Isn't it priceless?' She laughed in her 'fishwife-at-Hull-docks' way, at the reply. I froze, rigid with indignation and agony. 'Well, of course it will! I won't have to lift a finger to see him have his comeuppance. I'll just sit back and watch him building his own gallows...Oh yes, a master craftsman!' (I could tell from her manner that she'd been drinking heavily again. Oh Marion, how did we both become so lost?)

She sighed.

'My poor Alec. He's his own worst enemy. Do you think I should feel the teensiest bit sorry for him?' The raucous explosion led me to conclude the answer was no.

'Yes, yes, you're right. He's made his bed, as they say...oh yes, no longer my problem, dear!'

I felt as if someone had injected iced water into my spinal column, such a hideous chill ran down my spine.

Had it all been a delusion? A few hours ago, Marion's words of ridicule would have been water off a duck's back. Now her mockery held some truth. That phrase she had used,' Watch him build his own gallows' was already hideously pertinent. It was like a real-life game of hangman. If my conclusions about tonight are founded, then the game could already be over.

I wondered to whom she was betraying me. It wouldn't have been Edward, because, as far as I could make out, she never showed him this side of herself. When she spoke to him, she used a slightly softer, more refined voice, kept her forked tongue well in the back of her throat. She used her silly pigeon laugh with him, kept her true donkey-self well concealed. I could only guess it would be one of her women friends, the evil Caroline, or the inappropriately named Joy Goode.

Now I could add public humiliation to my woes.

My bed contained no warmth for me.

I glimpsed Marion pass by my bedroom door with her face buried in Thaddeus's fur. She didn't even check to see if I was back. I heard her cooing and clucking at the cat, and heard her say in those dulcet tones reserved only for Edward and Thaddeus, 'You *are* a naughtiness, kitten boy, aren't you? No, outside the bed for pussycats. Thaddeus you are incorrigible!' Marion giggled, (which is a contradiction in terms) 'I said *no*. And purring like a train won't help either. What did Mummy say?' A moment or so after she had turned off her light, I heard her whisper, 'All right then Thaddy, just this once.'

I wondered if that's how she spoke to Edward, if he liked all this 'mummy' business. Thaddeus certainly did. He'd be in there, doing that 'pawing thing' under the duvet, until his ecstasy reached drooling point.

Chapter Twenty: the lowest of the dead

Did I sleep that night? I really couldn't say. *I was neither Living nor dead, and I knew nothing.* I remember vaguely hearing cars pass by; a strangulated catfight; the odd bird chirruping too soon for the dawn chorus. I saw headlights trace around the room; the green specks of luminosity on the bedside clock taunting me. The monochrome world of the new day emerged from the blackness of night. I felt the coldness of my skin shroud me, through the endless hours. The pain in my heart, not metaphorical, but real and all consuming, mesmerised me. I examined it from every angle, saw it calcify, gradually, throughout the night, until by dawn there was hardly the slightest tremor to be seen. I waited to hear the constant tone of the monitor. 'I'm sorry we've lost him. There was nothing else we could do.'

What other images ran through my mind? Surely, you know? Or are you '*men of stones*'?'

Chapter Twenty-one: her hair spread out in fiery points

'Don't you think it's time you got up?' demanded Marion, forcefully drawing back the curtains. 'You're going to be late.' Had she not noticed that I was dead? With little anticipation of success, I attempted to open my eyes. The daylight hit my retina like a punch.

'I thought you went off to your little paramour last night. Didn't hear you come back. Well, what did the poor thing have to say when you told her your liaison was no longer secret?' She stared down at me with distaste. 'I mean what nineteen-year-old is seriously going to want to publicly admit they're going to bed with you?' Realising too late just how unkind she was being, she added, 'Well, you're forty-eight, Alec,' as if that qualified everything.

She sat on the end of the bed and sighed. 'I'm sorry, shouldn't have spoken to you like that - force of habit. Oh dear, makes it all the more difficult. You know what I'm going to say, don't you?' She put her hand to her mouth as if in hope of preventing the words escaping, but it didn't work. I think Marion's mouth could've still worked from under five layers of duct tape.

'I had a long conversation with Edward last night, after you'd gone out. Both he and I agree that you are behaving in a completely irresponsible manner again. For once Edward can see the unbearable strain you put me under. He refuses to let me suffer any more humiliation at your hands.' She swallowed hard and sniffed; I swear there were tears in her eyes.

'He's ready to commit to me, Alec. You've won you see. You've finally pushed me away.' She scanned my face intently looking for a reaction. When none came, she continued, painstakingly explaining the situation to me.

'This next disaster will be yours and yours alone, Alec. You see, Edward is planning to tell Lizzie he wants a divorce. Then he and I will set up home together in London. Your life can crash and burn in whichever way you choose, but without me there to pick up the pieces.'

Disturbed by my lack of response she rose from the bed and stood at the window, nervously tracing a line in the condensation.

'I thought you'd be pleased. You'll be free. There's no point in us delaying the inevitable any longer.' She faltered, gave a little cough. 'Now, now that you think you love someone else. There's nothing in this marriage for either of us, is there?' she asked despondently. My mouth stayed closed. 'Oh, for goodness sake, say something, Alec!' Her tone was almost pleading.

'What can I say? You've said it all.'

'Have I? I'm telling you our marriage is over and you have nothing to say?'

'It was over a long, long time ago, Marion,' I said flatly. Marion seemed to ponder this as if it really was the first time such a thought had struck her. She looked surprisingly sad. Surely after all the years of spleen she'd vented all over me she couldn't have imagined that ours was a relationship that could be categorised as a marriage? Then I remembered my conversation with Anna, when I had given her the degrees of marriage speech and thought that perhaps I too had deluded myself from time to time.

'What will you do?' she muttered. '... This '*thing*' with this girl... when it's over. Will you be all right?' She turned back to face me, looking vulnerable for the first time in years. As I said nothing, she anxiously filled the silence.

'I should apologise, you know, last night after talking to Edward, I was so overwhelmed, I had rather too much to drink. I've waited so long for him. And the effort, and the struggle I've put up with here. For some time after, all I could do was cry, and drink. I rang Joy in the end - I had to tell someone. I'm afraid I told her about you too. I didn't want it to seem *all* my fault. I really had had too much to drink. I was a bit unkind,' she said weakly, looking strangely ashamed. 'I shouldn't have told her, should I?'

'No,' was all I could say.

'Are you going to go into work?'

'I don't think so.'

I didn't either. I got Marion to ring up and say I was sick.

Somehow being able to tell me about Edward, knowing that her passage out of here was booked and all she had to do was wait for the boat, she seemed quite different. There was a calmness about her. It was the acceptance of one who has agreed that it's time to turn off the life support machine. All we waited for now, was the moment of our final goodbyes. The last breath...

Most of the morning, I drifted in and out of sleep, exhausted by the long, disturbed night. After assurances that I was not suicidal about the demise of our marriage, Marion declared she was going down to London for a day or two. A few Christmas works gatherings called, as did some Christmas shopping, and naturally she would need to see Edward too.

'I'm surprised how nonplussed you are, Alec. Surely you and your little friend should be only too pleased with this outcome.'

She must've left while I was asleep. At about midday, I rose, hardly knowing how to breathe or to move. Even lying in the bath until the water went cold did nothing to revive me. Near-death experiences certainly sap your strength. I couldn't eat anything, but I managed to drink some coffee consciously swallowing, gulp by gulp. Oh Anna, Anna, your timing is unbelievable. What a moment for you to see me for who I am. What a time to return to your own kind, and leave me here alone. Oh Anna…

Through the kitchen window, I watched a squirrel and a crow squabbling over a crust on the lawn. The squirrel was making a horrible nasally chattering noise and flicking its tail wildly up and down, while the crow stalked to and fro squawking dementedly. Last night's snow was patchy, watery and unattractive. In the corner of the kitchen, Thaddeus stretched out fully on the arm of the chair where he slept, and promptly fell off. Life persisted, in all its absurd struggle. Indignantly, Thaddeus shook his head, giving me an accusatory glance. 'I guess you'll leave me too, won't you?' He licked his paws, wiped behind his ears, held his tail erect and headed off for the cat flap. 'You won't like it out there either.' He went anyway.

The doorbell rang. I hated the doorbell more than the telephone, I really did. If Marion were at home, I'd never answer the door. It was the whole business of being summoned to connect yourself to the outside world, to face the invisible barrier, where the two worlds of one's private, interior home life buffeted against the outside world of others. I could have happily been a recluse. Furtively, I stayed in the kitchen, out of sight. It rang again - probably the blasted postman, delivering something from Marion's aunt for Christmas. Last year she sent garden quoits! Can you really see Marion and me spending our summer evenings blithely competing at quoits with one another? I hoped it wasn't another joint present. Who would have it? Marion, I guess, as it was her aunt. Besides, what use are presents to a dead man? Any minute now the postman would leave one of those notes to collect it from the post office. I just had to hold my nerve. The bell rang again more persistently. Perhaps it was the Christmas box he was after? He had already sent that 'Bob your postman wishes you a happy Christmas' card, meaning Bob wants a couple of quid or else your mail gets dropped in a puddle. Steeling myself for the opening of the front door, I walked purposefully down the hallway. So convinced was I that it was the postman that I didn't even look through the spy hole.

'Anna!'

'Is she in?'

'Marion? No.'

'That's a relief,' she said grinning, 'but I had come prepared if she was.' And she waved a bundle of flyers for a Christmas carol extravaganza in my face. 'Picked these up from the church porch down the road, just in case.'

She peered beyond me into the hallway and did a little dance from foot to foot.

'Aren't you going to invite me in then?' Adding conspiratorially, 'I didn't really come here delivering church leaflets, you know?'

'Sorry, yes of course,' I said waving her past me. 'I'm just a bit shocked to see you.'

'Well, well, well, so I get to see your place at last!' she said looking excitedly about her. 'She's not coming back soon, is she? I don't want to be caught here, but your phone has been engaged or off the hook, since last night, and you weren't at the department, and I thought we needed to talk…' Her voice trailed off. I told her quite matter-of-factly that Marion had left for London a few hours ago.

Without saying any more, I led her into the kitchen and proceeded to fill the kettle. Anna sat incongruously at our kitchen table, chatting away as if life couldn't be more normal. I began to wonder if the last twenty-four hours had been some sort of hideous dream.

'This isn't at all how I imagined your house,' she commented, while regarding the décor of our home. As her eyes traced the history of our lives together here, I felt uncomfortably self-conscious. How our possessions expose us. I felt particularly embarrassed by a tea cloth of 'amusing' *'Rules of Ye Kitchen'*, which Marion had seen fit to stick in the alcove above the boiler.

'We haven't done anything for years,' I said, disowning my life.

Anna bit her bottom lip nervously. 'Alistair, are you mad at me for coming here?'

'Me? No.'

'I thought you'd want to see me.' She lowered her eyes. 'You haven't even kissed me yet.'

I shrugged my shoulders.

'Oh, for God's sake!' she almost shouted, her face still flushed from the bitter outside air. 'Why don't you just come out with it? You think I'm sleeping with Greg, don't you?'

A hot coal hissed as it dropped into my stomach. My back teeth clenched together with such force I'm surprised they didn't shatter and fill my mouth with fragments. My breathing rate became laboured and erratic. Robotic like, without looking at Anna, I picked up the coffee cups and dropped them into the sink. Awakening suddenly, the leeches, which had been sleeping, swarmed up and down my bones in a frenzy, ripping through muscle fibre, pushing their way to the surface, pressing, pressing under my skin. The calcified heart burst from its shell and quivered, then ballooned and shrank, ballooned and shrank.

'Thought as much. Do you want me to explain what happened last night?' The trees outside shuddered in the wind, and silhouetted in the highest branches, the crow lowered his sleek black head and cawed ominously. Thaddeus' plump body was doing its best to stalk up to the bird table.

I lost sight of the garden; the shapes blurred and dissolved; I heard the kitchen chair scrape on the vinyl; I felt Anna's body against my back, just in the same way she had ever first held me. I gripped onto the edge of the sink for support. How had she led me to this place?

'I know what you're thinking, Alistair. But when will you trust me? When will you believe? It's you I want.'

My whole body shook with heaving sobs. Was it true? Had last night's pain been the viciously sharp teeth of jealousy gnawing my cold flesh and nothing else?

"O, beware, my lord, of jealousy;
It is the green-ey'd monster, which doth mock
The meat it feeds on"

'But, last night -' I gagged, choking on my own words, 'you were hand in hand; he went into your house.'

'He grabbed my hand; he's just friendly like that. It was icy; he didn't want me to slip. He came in for a coffee, and spent most of the time telling me how much he misses his girlfriend who's at Cardiff. I presume I am allowed visitors?' She had her hands on my shoulders, and now turned me around to look at her. I searched her face like a mad man.

'So, he didn't try to…?'

'No! I don't fancy him anyway. He's such a big kid. So full of himself.'
'So, you didn't...?' (I just couldn't say the words)
'No.'
(At that moment in time I think I truly believed her.)

'I can't tell you what I went through last night. I thought I'd lost you.' My voice quavered, 'Oh, God and all this followed Marion finding out about you, and now she's leaving me. Marion and I... finally going our separate ways.'

How instantly I felt the sands shifting. Now it was her turn to look uncertain, almost afraid. Both these disclosures could not help but have a bearing on her.

'I never expected to feel guilty,' she said baffled, plonking herself down in Thaddeus chair, before I could warn her about the hair.

'How on earth did she find out? Did you tell her?'

Reluctantly, I unfolded the story of last night's revelations. When I got to the bit about the wig, she remarked that no sane person would have fallen for such a ludicrous lie. I felt exposed, knowing I had revealed one of those private moments of my life that was just too foolish for public airing. But the rest of the time she sat quietly listening. There was the painful telling of Fay Morgan to come out. As I recounted the details out loud to someone I loved so dearly, I felt a sense of deep shame creep over me. It seemed as if for the first time I connected myself with the events. When Anna told me that Chris had told her a version of the tale before I'd begun to see her, I felt even more contemptible.

'You knew?' I moaned with disbelief, 'All the time, and you said nothing?'

'I gave you several opportunities to tell me. Maybe, I was hoping it wasn't true at one level, and besides what can either of us do about it now?' She brushed cat hair off the sleeve of her sweatshirt.

'You should have told me though.' Anna rose from Thaddeus's armchair and sat opposite me again.

'I just didn't know how,' I mumbled wearily. 'I was afraid you'd think, you know, that I made a habit of...' Feeling desperate for a diversion, I went over to the sink and re-boiled the kettle, aware of Anna's eyes watching me from behind.

'Some coffee?'

'Yeah, Thanks.' There was an awkward silence, while I tried to frame my next sentence, but suddenly it blurted out, ill-prepared.

'But Chris, this so-called 'friend' of yours, where could she have possibly...surely people aren't still gossiping? I mean who would know...to tell her? What did she say exactly?'

'If you'd care to calm down a little, I'll tell you what she said word for word.' And she isn't a 'so-called friend'. Considering what she knows, and has kept quiet about, I think she's been a very good friend.' Suitably admonished, I acknowledged Chris's true and noble friendship, but when I heard what followed, privately I wouldn't trust her as far as I could throw her.

We talked for the rest of the afternoon, just sat in the kitchen, in the gathering gloom of that mid-December afternoon. Anna wanted reassurance that my marriage was over before she came on the scene, that *she* wasn't really the cause of Marion leaving me. She reminded me that even when we first began our relationship, my being married had bothered her greatly. I repeated what I'd told her then. 'You have to understand,' I added, 'it takes a lot of energy to pull out of a destructive relationship. It's like being in a whirlpool; it seems to take all your effort just to keep your head above water. Someone else needs to pull you out. Don't blame yourself for rescuing me.'

'Now you make me sound like the RNLI.'

'Well,' I smiled 'They have been known to save the odd drowning man from time to time, haven't they?'

Anyway, it all seemed very academic now. To be perfectly honest, Anna seemed more interested and far more emotionally engaged in the whole concept of divorce than me. (Looking back on it now I guess she was just worried about feeling obligated to me, if she'd been the cause of the break up, but of course at the time I didn't have the wit to figure that out.) I was still a little too tired to really focus on anything properly. Vaguely, I tried to imagine myself telling my mother that Marion and I were splitting up, to which, she would initially smile fondly and without any comprehension at all say, 'How lovely.' Although the next time I ran the scene she peered at me with her pale watery eyes, whispering, 'How very disappointing. But it's what we've come to expect from you, Alistair, isn't it?' The trouble was Mother now hovered between two worlds and two personalities. To be honest, I preferred the new Mother, who couldn't remember who she was. Perhaps I just wouldn't tell her. Not before Christmas anyway.

What really perturbed me was the way in which Chris had found out about Fay. You think you've left your past behind, closed a door on a situation or event, and then quite unexpectedly the door flies open again, and some idiot waltzes back in with your past life stuck to their shoe like dog's mess.

I had no excuse, I confessed to Anna, except for the fact that I had been a very selfish, self-centred person, and I hadn't loved Fay at all. That sounds awful, but I really was a very lost and lonely man at that point. And Fay had her own problems, which people seem prone to forgetting.

'Being with you,' I assured her, 'even just these past few months, has changed me beyond recognition.' I interlocked my fingers with hers across the kitchen table. 'You make me whole. Who I was before was a half-life. I don't think I properly knew how to feel for anyone else.'

At this very moment, to my utter chagrin, Thaddeus burst through the cat flap, his tail like a bottle brush and his eyes round and crazy. The dark intimate atmosphere annihilated as he skittered like a crab on roller skates.

'Something's frightened him,' I stated, a slight irritability in my voice.

'Never? So that isn't his usual entrance?' She laughed delightedly. 'This must be the legendary Thaddeus.' And that was it. She was hopping about the room chasing Thaddeus round, until he conceded to letting her pick him up. With no sense of loyalty to Marion at all, Thaddeus, spent the next hour sat on Anna's lap, nudging his demanding orange face against her hand. I washed up the cups while Anna asked me endless questions about the cat, followed by tales of every creature she'd owned, which, to my surprise, ranged from stick insects through to a chinchilla called Jeffrey.

'Chinchillas have the densest fur of any mammal; I think it's 20,000 hairs per square centimetre. Isn't that amazing? It's supposed to be finer than a spider's web. Did you know that?'

I had to confess that I was not aware of such a nugget of information, but that I would store it up for use at future dinner parties and so forth.

Why Jeffrey?' I enquired.

'No reason.' Anna said lightly, 'just seemed like a silly name for a chinchilla. And Thaddeus?'

'Well,' I began slowly, 'that was Marion's choice. It means 'gift of God' or 'praise to God', something like that.' Then adding by way of explanation, 'She

was rather low when we got him, was going through a bit of a religious phase...
I wanted to call him Bastet.'

'What? Bastard!' Anna cried.

'No. Bast -*et*. You know - the Egyptian cat god, religious too in a way, actually. But Marion thought: one, it was typically pretentious of me, and two, like you, she said it sounded too much like bastard, and didn't want the neighbours to think I was late back, when she called him in at night!'

Fondly, I smiled at the memory of those days, when this tiny ginger kitten seemed to bring some hope into our lives. There he slumped now, all twenty stone of him, - a few teeth missing, one raggedy ear, pungent fish breath - our 'gift from God'. But I had to hand it to him - he still had a way with the ladies.

It was getting close to his feed time, and as I opened the fridge door, he leapt off Anna's lap. You always fall for it, I chuckled triumphantly to myself. Noisily, cocking his head on one side to enable him to eat with his remaining good teeth, Thaddeus devoured his stinky mush.

By four o'clock, it seemed so gloomy it was as if night had already gathered outside. When we were not speaking, the silence felt warm and safe around us. Only the fridge hummed, and the cat's mouth made regular wet ticking sounds. Anna stretched in her chair, and stared outside.

'Hey! Just look at that!' she cried, in the breathless tones of a child, 'It's snowing again!'

I turned my face to the window, and gazed as plumes of snow, soft as white ash, descended to the earth. We stood together at the window, fixated by the slowness of the gentle falling motion. Many moments later, still staring into the mesmerising swirl of whiteness, I whispered, 'How about I light a fire?'

'You have a real fire?'

'Yes. Real logs, real flames, really real - not pretend.'

Holding her hand, I led her to the sitting room, which was my favourite room in the entire house. I drew the heavy green curtains, turned on a lamp, which gave out a pleasing soft hue and set about lighting the fire, while Anna drifted about the room seemingly absorbed by our things. Watching her studying our shared paraphernalia caused a funny tingle down my spine. She scrutinised every painting and print, picked up and examined one of the pair of Staffordshire figures, War and Peace, (*circa 1855 I believe*) which my grandfather had left me, read the titles on the book spines, traced her fingers along the back of the sofa, and stared and stared at the photograph of Marion, which stood self-importantly, in a silver frame on an occasional table.

'Is this her?'

'Mmm, yeah,' I said trying my best to sound unperturbed, indifferent even.

'When was it taken?'

'Oh, that? Several years ago. She's about forty-two there, I think. She'd just won some sort of award or something.'

'She doesn't look *that* bad. She's not *that* fat either.'

'Well, as I said, it was a few years ago.' Thankfully, the fire came to my rescue.

As the flames sprung up lustily in a feeding frenzy, I said proudly, 'What about this, then?'

Right on cue, Thaddeus entered the room, the volume of his purr increasing as he approached the fire. He sat in front of it, right in the centre of the rug, narrowing his eyes with contentment. Immediately, Anna was down on all fours and curled her body around his, stroking him rhythmically - a tremor of pleasure rippled through Thaddeus' body.

'He's so gorgeous,' she murmured, (What is it with women and Thaddeus?) and then glancing up at me, said hopefully, 'Are we going to have a drink?'

Oh, God, Oh, God. Suddenly, I had a vision of where all this was going to end up. On the rug, in front of the fire job, with Marion coming back unexpectedly… …I mean Anna had no idea just how vicious she'd be if she found her here. Even I didn't want to be caught in a 'funeral bak'd meats coldly furnishing the marriage tables' situation. As the reality of Anna being in our house hit home, I began to feel increasingly nervous. What had I been thinking of? However, I couldn't just tell her to go; perhaps I'd give her one drink and suggest we decamp to her place. Marion should be away for days I tried to reassure myself.

When I came back with the wine, Anna had really made herself at home, putting on a record, (a compilation of adagios) and turning the lights off completely. She'd returned to lying on the rug, only this time had lifted Thaddeus onto her chest, where he was rising and falling with her breathing, while they beheld one another's image. The fur along Thaddeus's spine, spread out in fiery points, glowed like a raging sunset.

'Mind he doesn't start drooling on you,' I said uncomfortably.

'You wouldn't do that Thaddeus, would you?' and she stroked his head so firmly that for a moment it looked like he'd had one too many facelifts. As his face sprang surprisingly back into shape, he sneezed violently, and sprang off her body.

'See,' I said.

'That was sneezing, not drooling.'

'Same result.'

Sitting up, and reaching for the glass in my hand, Anna said, 'You don't seem that fond of him.'

'He's Marion's cat really.'

'That doesn't mean you can't love him though, does it?' She was lying on her side now, propped up on one elbow, the glass dancing with the light from the fire. 'She'll have him then, I guess?'

'Without a doubt; he's like a child to Marion really, just like a baby…' My voice trailed off. I loved him too…but, in a more appropriate way, for a pet. Anna had asked me a few weeks ago why Marion and I didn't have children. We had careers. Well, Marion had a career to pursue, and so the moment never seemed right. Then things became so shaky, it would have been ridiculous to add children to the equation. Anna had accepted this untruth.

And now she lay, in the blazing glow of fire, in my barren marital home, stretched out like honey dropping languidly from a spoon. She was so beautiful: the warm tones of her skin; her luxuriant posture emphasizing the sublime curve of her body, as it swept down into her waist then rose again to the highest curve of her hip, then the downward rush along her thighs towards her feet. My eyes rode her body like a rollercoaster car. A familiar sense of intense desire, awakened in my marrow, permeating through my bones seeping into my flesh. I was getting dangerously close to having to make love to her, and it was only late afternoon, plenty of time for Marion to return due to some travelling mishap or something. But she wouldn't, would she?

Bach's adagio (BWV 974) paced elegantly about the room, the pianist fingers pressed lightly on my soul, gently, gently seducing me. Just a few moments - to touch her flesh, warm from the flames of the fire, to be in the rich glow of light with her, to seal the bond between us once more after the severance of last night.

I lay down next to her on the rug, and she ran her hand down my body in a not too dissimilar way to the way in which she'd just petted Thaddeus. No wonder he'd shuddered. Then Anna kissed my face, my hands.

'Lie perfectly still. On your back; with your eyes shut,' she said softly. So, I did. Slowly, while I lay motionless on my back, she began to undo my shirt buttons; an intensely deep sense of peace and relaxation begun, little by little, to seep into every fibre of my being. My conscious mind began to drift. Her hands, the palms, fingers, knuckles, nails, her mouth, lips, teeth, tongue, and even the almost imperceptible sweep of her hair, caressed my body. I did nothing, but experience… My body yielded up to me treasure from deep within. All these years trapped in this flesh, bones and sinew, and now it astonishes me, with this as yet unrevealed nervous system. Sensation after blissful sensation. Anna had a way of taking me so close to the edge that I could have passed out with vertigo, only to then pull me back from the brink, just in time.

'Now,' she whispered, so near to my ear I could feel her lips moving, 'it's your turn to give me a massage.' My eyes blinked open; the ceiling appeared to be a long way away. 'Well?' she said expectantly. Casually, I rolled over to be greeted by the surprising, but totally engaging sight of Anna lying completely naked on the rug next to me.

'How did you manage that!?'

'One-handed undressing. Obviously.'

I gazed at her body in wonder. I wish I could find the words to convey how utterly perfect she was. Firelight was probably even a flattering light for me, and God knows I needed some help, but because she was already so exquisitely lovely, the firelight transformed her into something divine. In a past life I must have done something very good, for nothing I had done in this one deserved that I should behold such a vision. I stretched out my hand until my fingertips hovered just above her belly. Gradually, my fingers descended to meet her gilded skin, where with the lightest of touches I swirled in a circular motion around her navel, then swept down her body with the sweeping motion of slalom skier. The back of my nails retraced my path upwards, deftly gliding over every smooth rise and fall of her lovely form. I continued to caress every part of her body, sometimes fleetingly, sometimes lingering. She, according to the rules kept her eyes shut, while mine drew her image into me, as if she were the last thing I should see before being cursed to blindness. Anna's back was arched with pleasure and she was moaning and pulling me towards her in that way that told me the massage was over. We were just at the moment of both fumbling around trying to get connected, when I happened to catch something in the corner of my eye - the outline of a shape in the doorway.

My heart stopped. Literally.

It was within a fraction of a second that I realised what it was. From the angle I was on the floor, Thaddeus who was sat on the back of the sofa, starring down at us, had appeared to be a head and shoulders in the doorway. I collapsed on top of Anna gasping and laughing with relief.

'God! I thought the cat was Marion.' …Unfortunately to my utmost embarrassment, I was not the only thing to collapse through shock. And to my living shame no amount of coaxing would revive it.

'I'm so sorry,' I mumbled, while we were getting dressed. 'It's never happened to me before. It was that bloody cat.'

Anna just thought it was the funniest thing ever, and the fact I was trying to blame my impotence on the cat even more laughable.

'It wasn't the cat that frightened you into resembling a jelly. It was the fact you thought it was your wife. You're petrified of her, aren't you?'

This last comment made me feel rather defensive. Surely, even if my marriage was over, Anna could appreciate the awkwardness of one's soon to be ex-wife walking in on such a situation?

'Oh, come on my little stress ball, you've had a very trying twenty-four hours. Let's go back to my place, grab a pizza and watch the TV, eh?'

Which is what we did, though not before I'd put down a hefty supply of cat biscuits. Before we left the house, I made Anna put her scarf around her face, and her hood up, so as no one would see us together. I parked round the corner as usual, and she walked to the house first, with me following a few minutes later, after a brief visit to the takeaway pizza place. I couldn't live like this for much longer. Tomorrow I'd start to have a look at other universities with similar courses to the one Anna was studying and see if I could arrange a transfer of some sort. Then I could resign. They'd probably be glad to be shot of me. I could find other work, teaching, whatever. I didn't really care what I did, as long as I could be with Anna.

Chapter Twenty-two: It's them pills I took

All night long my mind had been racing with exciting plans for my future, though strangely mingled with a gnawing sense of regret and nostalgia for the past. I stood as Janus in a doorway, which was both the exit from a past life and the entrance to a new one. Was Hartley right to say, *'the past is a foreign country: they do things differently there'*? In the context he wrote perhaps, but I felt it was my future, where I would experience the thrill of unfamiliar territory. Tomorrow and tomorrow, where I would know life, and live life, as a different man in a new land. I couldn't wait to leave the shores of my past life soon enough. Restless, I got up unusually early, and was washed and dressed before 7.00 am. Nobody was ever around at that time. Softly kissing Anna, who still lay sleeping, I left a note on the pillow, and slipped quietly away.

The snow had settled, transforming the dirty, grey, dingy city into something quite beautiful. *'The dung heap cover'd o'er with snow.'* I revelled in the gentle creaking sound my shoes made as they compacted millions of crystals. There I stood, a Titan on a mountain of stars, crushing them under my mighty weight. Creak, creak, creak. Molecules colliding together, merging. Childishly, I walked round in a tight circle retracing my steps and then strode through the street, breathing in the air which seemed lighter, purer, as if the feathery, snowflakes had given it a light dusting on their descent to earth. Just as I turned the corner, I noticed a patch of yellow snow, still steaming. Like acid, burning its way through the veneer of snow, it worked – dissolving – revealing the dark road beneath. Abandoning the car, I walked all the way into town, never once tiring of the deeply satisfying creak of the snow compressing beneath my feet.

Several streets away from the department, I knew of a rather good 'greasy spoon', where I treated myself to a full English breakfast. The café floor was wet from people's shoes, in spite of everyone entering accompanied by the thud, thud, thud, of exaggerated stamping on the doormat. There was a jovial, holiday atmosphere, and the oval plate of all things cholesterol had never looked so good. I was happy to be alive!

At 8.30am I arrived at the department and, after dealing with some correspondence, I had a look through various prospectuses from other universities, one or two of which looked very suitable for Anna's needs. When I thought about it, with my extra input there was no reason why she couldn't pick up a very good degree, even a first perhaps. Gleefully by-passing the pages on accommodation, I tried to imagine what kind of house Anna and I would create for ourselves. It would be slightly more bohemian, a little more artistic and eclectic that the one which Marion and I had spawned. Anna's creative side would be reflected in every room. Possibly there would be an ethnic influence, but nothing too posturing; Anna wasn't like that. She hated people who assumed postures and took fake identities for themselves in order to appear more interesting than they really were. Like those girls who put henna in their hair, wore dangly earrings, and yet in reality were about as far out as a high tide.

There was a department meeting at 9.30 am, so I grabbed a coffee from the machine and strolled in only five minutes late.

'Morning, everyone,' I said brightly, surveying the crème de la crème of academia posed for action, seated around a large rectangular table, like the doppelgangers of the disciples at The Last Supper. David, head of department sat Christ-like at the centre, while Ruth, a worthy Judas was bending towards his ear, no doubt dropping poison therein. As I took my place around the table, she looked up and glanced up to the clock. There was something subtly different about her. But what?

'Good morning, everybody,' intoned David, radiating his 'let's all try our best, shall we?' smile. The similarities between the department Jesus and the twelve ended with that single visual image. David's real persona was not Christ-like at all, but that of a good natured, firm but fair headmaster. 'And well done for making it in through the snow and ice! I'll try to keep this brief, last meeting before the Christmas break and so forth. You should all have a copy of the agenda.'

He scanned us all for confirmation of this over the top of his half-moon glasses; we all dutifully indicated that we had. (God, how I hated these meetings.) Steve Woods, the youngest and newest member of the department particularly suffered the attentions of 'Sir'. David had a way of beginning sentences to Steve with 'Now Stephen, sorry, *Steeeve*' (and he always said *Steve* in a long drawn out way as if he thought shortening names a rather odd concept to wrestle with.)

'Not Stephen?' He must have asked him that a dozen times or so when he first started. Anyway, it would always be, 'Now Stephen, sorry *Steeeve*, this may all seem somewhat new and daunting at first, but you'll soon get the gist of it. Do ask any of your learned colleagues for advice...etc.' And we learned few had to smile encouragingly at Steve, while David looked on fondly over his half-moons. I realised I couldn't wait to hand in my resignation.

The meeting was as tedious as ever. Eventually, I became aware of David adopting his 'AOB' voice, followed mercifully by negative murmurings. His Headship reminded us to all be at the Christmas gathering at his home next week, 'And *Steve*,' he said emphatically and proudly for having got Steve's name right for once, 'Do bring along a friend, girlfriend, partner whatever they're called these days. You'll find you'd both be warmly welcome, to what is after all a most enjoyable evening; relaxing end to your first term with us.'

Several of us shifted uncomfortably, with Tom and me in particular avoiding making eye contact. The evenings at David and Mrs David's (as his wife was known because as far as anyone could ascertain her character seemed totally subsumed in his) were a long-running joke amongst certain members of staff. There was something so agonizingly embarrassing about seeing David 'at home' – 'relaxing', like the shamefaced feelings aroused by a scruffy page of 'reader's wives' discovered in a ditch as a boy.

The meeting began to break up. People gathered papers and fell into small groups talking.

'Alistair, how are you?' Ruth enquired with a tone of concern, which didn't ring true.

'Fine, thank you.' I replied defensively.

'Oh,' she said, the volume of her voice increasing slightly, 'I understood you were really quite sick yesterday. Am I mistaken?' *(*You Duessa, I thought. Don't think I don't know what you're doing.)

'Yes, I was. I had a migraine.'

'A migraine as well? Oh, poor you. As far as I understood Marion rang through to say you'd got a stomach bug.'

By now, I was aware that several other people had finished their conversations and were tuned into ours. 'No, just a migraine. They can cause vomiting you know. In fact, every time I stood up, I was sick.'

'Terrible,' Ruth said, 'but you're all better now.'

'I didn't know you were a *'megraine'* sufferer, Alistair, dear?' interrupted Auntie Joan sympathetically. 'Mine are atrocious!' She said the last word as if it was a violent sneeze. 'I should never, never, but never be tempted by chocolate. But you know how it is – "I can resist anything except temptation".' And she chuckled briefly, before saying soberly, 'Chocolate - gets me every time; red wine too if I go over a glass and a half.'

Ruth was smiling unpleasantly, and touched my arm with insincere comfort.

'And what's your trigger Alistair? What is it that you can't resist that sets your head a-throbbing?'

'Cheese?' interjected Tom distractedly, 'Cheese, red wine, chocolate. All triggers.'

'It's something in the grape skins, with wine' said Auntie Joan knowledgably, she'd obviously made quite a study of this, 'Tyramine erhm…pheny, pheny, No. Senility strikes. Wait a mo. Phenyle…ooh.' I groaned inwardly, would someone please put Auntie Joan out to pasture?

Now young Steve made a valiant attempt to join in with the department at its woolliest.

'I sometimes get headaches if I don't eat. Low blood sugar, I guess. But I've never had a true migraine. I expect it's awful.'

'It's torture.' Joan closed her eyes and shook her head at the very memory of migraine 'machete-ing' through her brain, 'But Steve, with regard to your problem, you might like to take a tip from one who's been around the block a few times: low blood sugar, all you need is glucose. I carry glucose tablets everywhere I go for that very reason.' Joan smiled, producing a pack from her handbag as evidence.

With ever growing confidence Steve continued, 'Do you get those bright lights? You know the aura.' And he waved his hands about in front of his face and went cross-eyed.

'Now, I can't say I do, really,' answered Joan, almost sounding disappointed.

'Do you Alistair?' pressed Ruth. 'Do you experience an array of dazzling lights before your migraines? It's just like a migraine advance party isn't it? Building up to the main thrust.'

'Steady Ruth, you make it sound like foreplay,' muttered Tom dryly.

Oh heavens! I really did not want to be having this conversation. And I would have words with Tom later for his unhelpful contribution. Steve, unaware of Ruth's agenda, seemed more than pleased his line of enquiry had generated some banter, and gave out a guffaw. Joan looked slightly embarrassed.

I refused to be unnerved by Ruth.

'Actually,' I began calmly, 'I have experienced aura once or twice - zigzag lines, a strange unidentifiable smell and very occasionally visual distortion, which was really strange.'

'Sounds like quite a trip!' laughed Steve. 'Did you know they reckon Lewis Carroll conceived some of *Alice in Wonderland* through aura experiences? It's not unheard for some people with migraine to experience a feeling of distortion about the shape and size of their body parts!'

'Really?' said Ruth her eyes widening.

'They call it 'Alice in Wonderland' syndrome' Steve added.

'Well that explains everything!' Tom grinned. 'All these years, Alistair, you've been suffering from 'Alice in Wonderland' syndrome, and we never knew it. Deluded about the size of your body parts! So that's where you get your confidence from.'

'Thank you, Tom,' I warned playfully.

Everyone laughed, even Ruth. Steve grinned like the Cheshire cat from the aforementioned book. He was really facilitating the convivial banter now.

'But seriously Alistair, what do you take?' Joan asked, obviously keen to steer the conversation away from proportions of body parts.

Erm, what d'you call them?' I drummed the desk noisily, 'You know they advertise them with a couple of rutting stags.'

'Rutting?' repeated Ruth.

'Yes, banging their heads together. They're called Head... Head something.'

'Headache pills?' suggested Tom, who I could tell was beginning to grow as weary of this conversation as me. Anyway, Joan didn't hear this aside on account of rummaging through her handbag again, with her pudgy soft hands.

'This,' she announced proudly holding aloft a thin box of pills, 'is the very latest thing on the market 'Migrate'' and then she began to read aloud from the packet: 'A major breakthrough in pain relief for *megraine* suffers, also effective for sinus pain and neuralgia, oh, neuralgia,' she nodded sagely towards me. 'Lovely ad too, no stags, but a murmuration of starlings in this woman's skull that finally burst through and dissolve into dust, all to the tune of *Ride of the Valkyries*, although I think the flock of starlings should be something with talons, like eagles or vultures.'

Steve offered the little-known ornithological snippet that birds of prey didn't murmurate - which was generally ignored. Tom, who'd been perched on the edge of the table looking increasingly bored sat forward and clasped his hands together. 'Could the migraine sufferers' support club conclude their meeting now, so we can joyfully sort out who's going to buy David and Mrs David's 'Thank you's' for hosting next week's Christmas wake, party, I mean?'

'There's no need to take that tone,' reprimanded Ruth, 'anyone would think you had a migraine coming on.' Steve snorted.

As usual, it fell to Joan to venture into town and purchase a suitable gift 'from us all' to Mrs David, and Roger (boring, beardy medieval English buff) eagerly agreed to hunt down the annual gift of an unusual rare bottle of single malt whiskey for David, to add to his annually growing collection of unusual rare bottles of single malt whiskey. My mistake was not to make a very hurried exit. For I found Ruth and myself awkwardly last to vacate the room.

'Well, that was all very informative, wasn't it?' She sighed, peering at me intently.

'Well, you know Auntie Joan.'

'Come on Alistair, you know I'm referring to you.'

'What do you mean?' I asked feebly trying to buy time.

'What we talked about. It's been going on for weeks, hasn't it? Can't you see the potential damage you could cause to everyone involved? Missing work through fake illness could be the least of your problems.'

'Are you suggesting I lied about being ill yesterday?'

'I'm suggesting I saw you leaving a student's residence this morning at 7.15, and I've drawn my own conclusions. Not difficult to do. You are rather transparent, Alistair.'

'Ah,' was all I could say.

'I happened to be in the area, quite by chance. A friend of mine has flu. I was walking her dog, first thing.'

It seemed to me that since the night of the snow everything that could conspire against me had conspired against me: Greg, Marion, Ruth exercising some bloody dog! There were no lies I could think of by which I could escape. Then I remembered the truth. Well, a half-truth, which is sometimes all you need to help you out of a hole.

'Actually, yesterday, through the day, I was unwell. You may as well know now, everyone will soon, Marion's announced she's leaving me. You may not think I've much justification to stay at home feeling shell-shocked, seeing as you seem to have made such a study of my marital and extra-marital activity over the past few years, but I didn't feel on top of things yesterday, OK?' She stared even more intently at me; her eyes looked glazed.

'I'm so sorry. I should apologise for accusing you of faking illness. I guess you had every right to absent yourself with a white lie, but...'

I suddenly had a vision of Ruth speaking to David at the start of our meeting,

'You weren't telling David this morning, when I came in, were you?' I blurted out.

'Of course not,' she answered firmly. Then weirdly, an inner smile bubbled up from beneath her face.

'What?' I asked mystified.' Why are you smiling?'

'It's nothing.' She shook her head as if trying to throw off an image. 'No, really, it was just you thinking I would speak to David about such things at the start of a staff meeting…just struck me as amusing - the inappropriateness of it. Sorry.' I wasn't convinced. Something strange was at work here.

'But, let's get back to the point. For all concerned, I still can't implore you enough to give up your relationship with…' she lowered her voice 'Anna. I mean, good God, it's already wrecked your marriage.'

'That's presumptuous,' I retorted.

'Well, hasn't it? I guess Marion's only just found out?'

'Marion has her own fish to fry if you must know.'

For a few seconds she looked slightly stunned, then shrugged saying, 'I can't say I blame her.'

'Will anyone?' I said bitterly.

Ruth continued to scrutinize me in a way, which I found most uncomfortable. She took on an imploring almost pleading tone.

'But Alistair, you will get hurt and so will she. I can see it coming. One should really, with maturity, learn to resist such impulses.'

'Such impulses?' I almost laughed; in fact, I did. But Ruth's face was deadly serious. 'Do you imagine for one moment, Alistair, that you are alone in falling in love with someone who is out of bounds? That there aren't times when each of us has to struggle to resist inappropriate feelings?'

'Inappropriate feelings? Since when was falling in love an inappropriate feeling?'

'You know exactly what I mean Alistair - but I'll spell it out for you if I must - when it's with the wrong person.'

'And who is your 'wrong' person?'

'I was speaking about a principle, not a personal experience.'

'Ah, well that explains everything - because if it was from personal experience you would know what bollocks you're talking.'

'Resisting the impulse to swear would also be appropriate right now.'

There was something about this woman that just made me want to throw a tantrum. I was almost spitting venom now, let alone swearing.

'You've no idea. No idea at all. Please don't interfere in my life any more. I've told you before, I am at a loss as to what makes you think you have a right to speak to me like this, or what your motivation is. Anna is fine. I am fine. And if it all goes belly up at least I'll have died trying, which' I added scathingly, 'is more than some people can say.' I tried hard not to register the pained look that passed across her face. Then quite surprisingly, she said calmly, 'I know I'm probably the last person you want to talk to, but I can be a good listener. I can be there for you if you need me. But time is short. Tongues are already wagging; do you really want to put yourself and Anna through all that?' She placed her hand on my shoulder and let it linger there. 'David has worked so hard to build up the department's reputation. We all have. Nobody wants this to look like some hotbed of sexual impropriety.'

'Oh, really, Ruth!' I snorted, walking towards the door, 'This is the twentieth century. Anyway,' I continued boldly, 'I'm going to make it easy for you very soon. In the words of Richard Nixon, soon, "You won't have me to kick around anymore."'

'You're leaving us?'

I looked back at her with 'devil-may-care' glance. 'Yes.'

She stood silently, absorbing what I'd just announced. To be honest, so did I. It was then I noticed what was different about her. She'd changed her glasses for a smaller oval pair. 'You've changed your glasses, haven't you?' (Which come to think of it was actually really inappropriate and somewhat ridiculous in the circumstances). Her fingers touched the frames self-consciously. She looked slightly abashed.

'Are you sure, Alistair?'

'Yes, they used to be big, circular ones, these are smaller.'

Her face broke into a genuine smile. 'I meant about leaving.'

'I think so.' I said with a little laugh, and tapped the side of my nose to indicate discretion.

What a strange encounter that had been. We'd hardly exchanged two words since September except for absolute work-related issues. And now this. There are some people you just cannot fathom out, and I began to realise Ruth was one of them. Who or what was she really concerned about: Anna, me, Marion, herself, the department's reputation, or that loneliest of places, the moral high ground? And what was all this about 'resisting impulses'? Was she jealous of me having Anna, or of Anna having me? As I've said before, her sexual orientation was a mystery to me. Most people you can tell, can't you? But Ruth…there must be someone she's wanted, who she couldn't have, but who? She had seemed softer on this occasion, less condemnatory. Perhaps she had slightly shifted her opinion. After all no one could deny that Anna and I had made one another deliriously happy. Maybe she could see that this time it was different and that relationships such as mine were not always so terrible. Nonetheless, she still wanted me to end it.

I heaved an enormous sigh as I entered my room. It would all be in the past soon. Tongues could wag like ecstatic Labradors' tails for all I cared. Soon it wouldn't matter.

Chapter Twenty-three: We who were living are now dying

'How dare you!' exploded Anna, narrowly missing me with the prospectus she'd just propelled in my direction. 'You can't organise my life for me! I have no desire to move from this city and the university at all. I worked bloody hard to get here. I like it here!'

I'd not seen her so angry since the time she quizzed me about my marriage and how serious I was about her. I picked up the prospectus, no doubt looking as violated and wounded as a kicked whippet, and folded back the bent corner of the cover.

'It was just a thought.' I said quietly, lifting my eyes towards her. 'It seemed a way of making our lives together easier.'

'But our lives are not 'together' like that, are they?'

'They could be.'

'No, Alistair. I don't want to be together like that. I'm nineteen.' There are sometimes when a truth hits you so suddenly and with such force it's like being stunned with an electric cattle prod. This was one such time. Clutching the prospectus close to my chest, I sank backwards onto the sofa, hot tears seeping through my tightly screwed up eyes.

'Oh, please don't get upset. I didn't mean to get angry. I just can't bear someone trying to control me.' She sat down beside me, and slipped her arm around my shoulders. 'Look I didn't say we'd never live together, but now is too soon.'

Then prising the prospectus from my hands with her other hand, whispered, 'Really everything is fine, just the way it is. If you and Marion get divorced, it *will* be easier. We must be more discreet that's all.'

'I *have* to be with you.'

'You are with me. But here, I want to stay here. With things just as they are.'

She kissed me gently, nuzzling her mouth against my neck. I knew I'd lost to her, was lost to her. In my mind, Janus took a step back, and a door slammed firmly in his face.

Over the next few weeks, it didn't matter which way I turned, doors marked 'Exit' were repeatedly barred. Marion returned from London, precisely when she said she would, laden with carrier bags from possibly every shop in Oxford Street and Regent's Street, and one or two dark green bags with distinctive gold lettering.

'You've gadded about,' I remarked nodding at the growing pile of bags in the hallway.

'Mmm,' said Marion tight lipped. 'Would you mind fetching my case? It's rather heavy.'

Struggling to carry the case, so as not to drag it through the slush on the path I grunted, 'What on earth have you got in here?'

'Just clothes. Oh, and several pairs of new shoes. It's probably the books making it heavy.' Thaddeus emerged from the kitchen blinking and sniffing at the rush of cold air pouring in through the front door. He strode towards Marion and rubbed warmly up against her calf.

'Hello Thaddeus,' she said flatly, and disappeared into the kitchen.

'Tea?' she called.

'Erh, yes please.' I patted Thaddeus on the head; he was looking like a child whose ice cream had just dropped out of its cone.

I entered the kitchen, 'Well?'

'Can't you guess?'

'No.'

Marion gave a dismissive snort and continued to make the tea, with a level of concentration more suited to setting up a science experiment. She turned both the handles on the teacups to face the same direction, studied the teaspoon for cleanliness, and measured out three heaped teaspoons of blackened tobacco-like Earl Grey into a functional stainless-steel teapot.

'I should have known, shouldn't I?' she said achingly, pouring steaming water into the teapot. 'Christmas!' She went to the fridge and stood in its doorway in the thin strip of light holding the milk. 'Christmas!' she repeated sourly, and shook her head as if in disbelief. I moved towards her and took the milk from her.

'Let me finish the tea.' I shut the fridge door and indicated for Marion to sit down, which she did. 'Always the same: too close to a birthday, anniversary, holiday, his brother's wedding, and now, Ch-r-r-istmas!'

I was beginning to fathom out what had happened; my heart began to plummet.

'How could he possibly spoil their Christmas? Especially as it would be their last one together as a family?' She gave a hollow laugh. 'And of course, January will be Lizzie's birthday. Her twenty-fifth... he's been promising her trip to

Paris for ages.' I handed Marion a cup of tea; she inhaled deeply as if the delicate fragrance of bergamot might sooth her anguish.

'So, you're stuck with me. For the time being, perhaps forever the way things are going.' She looked up at me, her head fell to one side, 'I *am* joking, Alec,' she said.

'Oh, I know.' I replied dully.

What followed was rather memorable. For the first time in ages, Marion and I had a proper conversation. It seemed that *'our'* battle was over, and now we'd found a common ground with one another, in defeating new enemies. Our causes were not so different. Strangely, we were both fighting to possess people, who really belonged somewhere else. We did not acknowledge this truth, but it hovered between us like a swarm of blue bottles over a steaming farmyard mound.

We were even supportive of one another. I repeatedly assured her that things would eventually work out with Edward, and that I believed he and Marion were right for one another. We were almost civilized. Marion even managed to say that while in no way approving of, or encouraging my pursuit of a young girl, such as Anna, she could see how besotted I was and had decided to be utterly *laissez-faire* about the whole situation. She completely surprised me by saying she'd already rang Joy and told her that Anna in fact wasn't one of my students after all, but a dental nurse. I don't want to be implicated as instrumental in any impending situation whatsoever, she explained.

'Marion!' I exclaimed, 'I thought I was supposed to be the one always fabricating things?'

She assured me that it was only a white lie.

'When I was in London, I suddenly felt very weary of the whole situation. I feel tired, Alec...really tired.'

I thought, well not too tired to have brought up half of the entire Christmas stock in the capital, but I kept quiet, and patting her hand murmured softly, 'Marion, I know you do.'

We were both tired. I thought again of my conversation with Anna, where I'd compared leaving my marriage to escaping from a whirlpool. Sometimes I thought both Marion and I should just abandon our escape plans, and after one last whirling dervish glimpse of life, would agree to spin, still intertwined, in an ever-downward spiral; sucked beneath the surface, a look of bored inevitability on our faces.

Anna's uncompromising reaction to the prospectus and the proposal of a new life together elsewhere had certainly drained me of energy. Crestfallen I was. To continue, for the next three years in this shadowy way depressed me hugely. I suppose Marion had been at it for years; never ringing Edward in certain places, avoiding being seen with him in public. Not being the one in the driving seat. It all struck me for the first time, and I felt sorry for her. I really did. And just when she'd hope it would all change…. I thought of how she must've been dreaming of waking up with Edward in that special glow of Christmas morning, and of how she'd have spent the journey down to London anticipating the relief of their 'coming out'. I presumed that like me, she'd have already mentally furnished their new flat. And no doubt, nervously played out the scene, where she'd meet Hattie, who she'd watch growing up from the safe distance of photographs and Edward's devoted bulletins, for many long years.

As if life wasn't bizarre enough for us at the moment, we spent that evening writing Christmas cards; both holding the unspoken hope in our hearts that this would be the last time we ever signed ourselves as 'Marion and Alistair'. Although I'd tried to argue the sending of cards seemed a little futile this year, Marion thought it a matter of politeness. And that was that. We listened to Handel's Messiah which had been a tradition for this task, since we were first wed and we saw no reason to break with tradition at this juncture. It wasn't really a problem to stay in on Wednesdays anyway, as Anna had joined the Film Society, which met that night, so the distraction suited me.

'Goodness, it's cold in here,' complained Marion as we worked our way industriously through the endless mountain of mangers, magi and Madonnas.

'Didn't we send this Fra Angelico 'Angels' one last year?' I queried, as that unsettling, but enjoyably weird sense of déja vue crept over me.

'Heavens, I don't keep a record of it, Alec. Nobody's going to remember even if we did. People just glance at the name, stick it up for a few days and throw it away.'

'We did. I'm sure we did.' Marion gave me a world-weary look over the top of her glasses and I resumed signing.

'Really, it is cold in here.' She shuddered. 'Can't we light a fire?'

I glanced nervously at the pile of ashes already in the grate; Marion followed the direction of my eyes.

'Did you have a fire while I was away?'

'Uhm. Yeah. It's been dreadfully cold the last few days.'

'Not like you to bother.' I could hear the cogs working in her mind. She drew her lips together with such a mean tightness they resembled Thaddeus's rear end. 'Didn't you stay with whatshername?'

'Anna? Well, uhm…yes…'

'You wouldn't have had her here, would you?'

'Of course not,' I retorted rather too forcefully, adding more calmly, 'Look. I thought we'd decided to finish with all of that. No more Spanish inquisition. We're not entitled anymore.' Marion slowly removed her glasses, revealing a red ridge 'burnt' across her nose, which she massaged with her thumb and forefinger.

'It is still my home, Alec… still my home, until I, and all my things have gone.'

'I know it is.' She didn't pursue the topic any further and I, with my insides completely jittering, set about making a fire, but it didn't catch as easily as before and Marion crouched down beside me blowing into the grate, her cheeks ballooning like the throat of a bull frog. 'Get some fire-lighters,' she ordered.

'I can do it without.'

'You're not in the bloody boy scouts, Alec. Get some fire-lighters.'

Reluctantly, I did as I was told and went in search of fire-lighters.

'Look in the cupboard under the sink,' she called from afar. The firelighters weren't there, nor were they in the box in the pantry, nor the cupboard under the stairs.

'Have we actually got some?' I said returning to the sitting room.

'No need,' Marion said smugly, rubbing her hands together in a Dickensian fashion. Looking at her by the fireplace, on the very same rug, so triumphant in her fire-lighting victory, I felt a sudden rush of pity for her. Squatting, as she was, her knees looked large and unattractive, bulging beneath a slightly thicker denier than she used to wear. I watched her struggle to her feet, holding onto the mantelpiece for support. Heard her joints click. From the stereo speakers an exultant soprano built to an exuberant crescendo to remind us all: *'But who may abide the day of His coming, and who shall stand when He appeareth? For He is like a refiner's fire.'*

Bright, fierce yellow flames roared with fervour, the refiner's fire, danced in my eyeballs.

'Well,' Marion said, with jubilant tone, 'I think I deserve a drink, don't you?'

What to do about the staff party? I broached, between licking envelopes, and sipping whiskey. Thankfully, Marion said she couldn't face it and it was decided that I should go alone. So last year was your last ever staff party I had said to her. Do you imagine that is of any significance to me at all? She'd replied. Well, I always like to know when something is the last thing, the last time. That's because you're a stupid sentimentalist. Probably...

Later, in the evening, Marion decided to unpack her shopping bags and show me her booty.

'Oh honestly!' she said returning from the hallway. 'That bloody St Barnabas! Look at this!' and she plonked down Anna's wad of carol flyers. 'They must've got some kids to deliver them. I've a good mind to ring up and let them know. They've got some new young vicar, haven't they? 'Father Stuart' I think he's called. 'Father! He looks all of about twelve!'

Stretching out to relieve her of the flyers, I suggested that I'd take them back to the church the next day. She said that it wasn't worth the effort. And before I could stop her, she placed them carefully on the fire. Then strangely, she stood watching them burn, as if fascinated by their combustion. She took the poker and slid the layers apart; bits of paper began to swirl around in the updraft. It was as if she were dissecting a Danish pastry, prising the flakes apart. The middle layers, no longer protected, caught light. She held them down in the flames, pressing with the poker. Uncomfortably, I shifted in my seat; this seemed terribly wrong to me, and guilt slithered up and down my spine. Eventually, there was nothing left to destroy, and she replaced the fireguard, exuding the glow of satisfaction of someone content that a job had been well done. Anyone would have thought she'd just sent up a smoke signal to announce a new pontiff had been chosen for the world. Smiling quietly, she went back out into the hallway to collect her carrier bags. Marion began to empty them one by one, holding up each gift as if she were an auctioneer's assistant. She finally found, what I realized, was her prized quarry.

'Aha! Here it is. Do you think your mother will like this?' she asked proudly, cradling a small hamper, which proclaimed itself to be "The Ultimate Ginger Lovers' Selection". I took the hamper gingerly, (sorry, couldn't resist) and studied the various ginger delights, which included: crystallised ginger, ginger marmalade, chutney, sweets, biscuits, a small jar of gourmet powdered ginger, all nesting in shredded golden tissue.

'Ginger has great health benefits,' Marion said with authority. 'I read it on the tag.'

I turned the tag over, and perused the seemingly endless list of health-giving properties of the yellow root.

'Truly a wonder drug… Mmm?' I mused ponderously.

'What?'

'I'm not sure mother's quite up to having her 'internal organs warmed.'

'Please, Alec. Let's not go there.'

And we both laughed.

****

Somehow the sands had shifted. Something had changed, I'm not sure what, but I felt we were all becoming quite different people.

Chapter Twenty-four: HURRY UP PLEASE IT'S TIME

Over the next few days, I saw very little of Anna. She was busy Christmas shopping with friends and there was a plethora of other Christmas jollies in which she seemed to be involved. It hurt that I couldn't accompany her to these things, for obvious reasons. However, there was a deeper grief which crept over me, as it dawned on me that, whatever the circumstances, I would not be able to accompany her. I was forty-eight. The gulf between us widened immeasurably when we moved beyond our own charmed circle of two. These thoughts I buried.

Anyway, I was busy as well. It took me nearly three hours to buy Anna's presents. Inevitably, the town centre was crowded and sweating fatly with the shiny grease of excess. Everything bulged at the seams, from the car parks, to the lifts and escalators, to the displays of goods in the shops and of course the customers, hot and bothered in coats and hats, which were fine for the freezing dampness outside, but bearskin like once in the central heating air-free zone of the department stores.

I felt like an inconsequential Mr Potato Head, who had fallen to the bottom of an overstuffed Christmas sack. An action man's boot on my head and a large slightly scary, bossy, brassy doll elbowing me in the ribs. In fact, there are a lot of women shopping here today just like that: big shiny cheeks, blatant shade of lipstick, brash dyed hair, glazed eyes swivelling in their heads as they hunt for bargains. Hamble from *Playschool*, popped into my head. Remember her? Years ago, I happened to see *Playschool* when I was off work sick with flu, and didn't have the strength to get up and change the channels; gave me bad dreams actually. There was something sinister about that doll. Again, we're back to evil masquerading as good: *The dung heap covered o'er with snow.*

I looked about me. Here it was again. The whole festering pile of waste and excess steamed quietly beneath the twinkling, glittering surface. Fake polystyrene snow lay in warm drifts in café windows moist with condensation. Mechanical elves in shabby felt costumes hammered mindlessly at dusty wooden trains, which no self-respecting child would thank you for. All manner of Christmas-shaped food beckoned from within its cellophane, or paraded itself as an evocation of some nostalgic Christmas past, somewhere between the *Adoration of the Magi* and Dickens' plum pudding, and all stops in between, but not here; please, not here. Tinsel radiated like a scintillating web from every ceiling, and coloured fairy lights made everywhere an out-of-season amusement arcade. And in every shop, money-spinning Christmas ditties jingled out from hidden speakers, invisible yet all pervading, like the very air we breathe.

Nobody therefore heard the dire grating noise, or saw, through the dazzle of lights and tinsel, a slow-moving shadow. No one but me wanted to cry out:
'What rough beast, its hour come round at last,
Slouches towards Bethlehem to be born?'
Bah! Humbug! There were times I took life too seriously. Shopping as you may have gathered was not my first love, neither was it my last. In truth, it didn't make it on the list at all.

Valiantly, I survived the department store, and found myself expelled onto the street an hour later complete with several gifts. For Anna I had bought: a soft-toy ginger cat, a necklace, purportedly made by the indigenous peoples of South America, a couple of ethnic-style scarves and a Joan Armatrading album. Marion, I thought would be pleased with a three-pronged device for extracting weeds and some posh leather gardening gloves. I got Mother an ornamental teapot, to go with the ginger bits and pieces, and a neat little gadget called 'croc teeth', which helped you pick things up off the floor.

I was almost done, only the bookshop to go, which naturally did very well out me. In the course of two hours' perusal, for Anna I selected: *The Complete Poems and Plays of TS Eliot*; a recipe book which declared in bold lettering *'Anyone Can Cook.'* I searched the inside covers for a disclaimer, and, finding none, presumed I'd found the answer to endless nights of what Anna called 'Toucan' cookery (open contents of two tins - mix, heat and serve over either pasta or rice. However, this was a step up from the slightly exotic sounding, but even less inspiring 'Woncan' cookery); and a beautiful illustrated second-hand copy of *The Water Babies* (just because the pictures were so exquisite.)

I also found Marion a small book of amusing sayings about cats accompanied by apt photographs or drawings. This would be from Thaddeus. All done!

As I made my way back to the car, with all my gifts, and knowing the shopping ordeal was over, I allowed myself to reflect more kindly on the dung heap. The world around me, for one brief moment, sparkled and glistened. I let myself be taken in, charmed and dazzled, by all things shiny and luminescent. I was a happy magpie.

That evening was spent carefully wrapping and labelling gifts. The last thing I wanted to do was to get anything muddled up. Meanwhile, Anna was at the film society Christmas bash, *A Wonderful Life*, which was to be followed by a trip to the tandoori. If only life and death itself were so straightforward. Marion had gone out for a Christmas drink with Joy and Caroline, on the strict understanding she did not talk about my private life.

'Oh, they'll spend all night probing me about Edward. Your infidelities are old news really. As far as they know this is virgin territory for me.'

I suppose that was supposed to make me feel better.

The following day I didn't manage to see Anna either. My study looked a mess again and I wasn't keeping paper work filed properly. I spent the entire day tediously filing, sorting and throwing things away. It was my second pet hate to shopping.

That night was the 'staff do' at David's and he came round to each of us through the day to remind us: lest we forget.

'I must apologise, David,' I said, trying to sound as pained as I could, while pushing more papers into an already overflowing bin. 'I'm not sure if Marion can make it after all.'

'Oh?'

'She got the dates mixed up, and now finds herself double booked.'

'Oh,' he said again, only this time on the downward cadence.

'She's so sorry. She tried to change the dates with her friends, but you know how it gets this time of year. Everyone's so busy.'

'Busy! Naturally: it's Christmas! Not to worry, not to worry one bit. These things happen.' He glanced nervously about the room, 'You'll still…' and he raised his hand as if he were toasting me.

'Of course, looking forward to it.' And I echoed his gesture.

'Tonight, then!' His eyes shone with happiness. He was such a boy, beneath his half-moons.

Poor David. I knew Tom's wife Eve had refused point blank to come. She made no secret of the fact that she thought most of the department to be dull, poker up their arses types, who wouldn't know a decent party if it sat on their face.

To some extent this was a fair criticism, but I wouldn't have expressed it quite like that myself.

Tom and I caught a bus out to David's leafy suburb. We planned to get a taxi home, as one couldn't survive the evening without copious amounts of alcohol. Even before we arrived, we stopped off at 'The Dog and Duck' in the main street in order to steel ourselves for the evening's entertainment. It was the kind of pub which was more restaurant than pub; although they didn't overstate the case, only claiming on the board outside, 'We serve food' so no contravening of the trade description laws there then. Although I had a sneaking suspicion tonight's *food* would have a poultry theme.

This evening, it was already packed with an assortment of humanity on their annual works Christmas do. It seemed the one occasion on which women, who normally kept within the boundaries of questionable taste, let their judgement take a complete holiday and actually believed they looked fetching in all manner of ill-fitting outfits, so long as they sparkled. Something... a little glamorous had seemed *de rigueur*, but oh, how wide of the mark... On the table next to us: a pair of bosoms, like a brace of basted turkeys, glistened from beneath a tight wrapping of tin-foil-like-satin; another whose little black dress would prove a tad small for your average six-year-old seemed to be struggling to respire; while another stood by the table, back to us, with a bottom the size of two fully inflated space hoppers bouncing beneath clingy red lurex.

All the women had made an effort - all forlornly trying to prove to one another that outside the workplace they were actually quite different. They had a fun, wild side. Those with glasses had ditched them for the evening. If you normally wore your hair up, you wore it down, and vice versa. It was the one season when the glittery eye-make up showed you were entering into the spirit of things and not still 'making your face up' with your first teen eye-shadow set. It fascinated me.

Men on the other hand were their usual 'no-sense-of-occasion' selves. Older colleges, who I guess usually wore ties, now unwisely went casual in open-necked shirts, which revealed an alarming amount of grey chest hair, creeping upward like a decrepit werewolf hand threatening to strangle them. Younger colleagues, already 'lagered up', were loud, leery and lecherous. In fact, everything they were could be found in the L section of the dictionary.

Above the raucous laughter, and the endless banter of innuendo, 'Wizard,' endorsed that they: 'wished it could be Christmas every day.' And even this early in the evening it seemed that most people in the pub agreed with them.

'Bloody Nora!' Tom laughed, his eyes rolling. 'Shall we just stay here for the evening?' Before I could reply, the space hopper bottom rebounded against my elbow just as I was about to take a sip of my pint, causing the glass to damn near break my front teeth.

'Oh, sorry love,' apologised its owner rounding on me. Christmas pudding earrings swung from her fleshy earlobes, while her shimmering lips stretched into a wide smile over teeth all of which seemed to be trying to mount their adjacent neighbour. Her mouth dropped slightly.

'Ave I made yer spill yer beer?'

'Only a bit,' I replied nonchalantly, unperturbed, smiling through my own recent dental trauma, and a growing sensation of dampness in my lap.

'What am I like? My bloody arse!' She laughed patting the offending inflatable. And I laughed too, to show that no offence had been taken, but I think she mistook my good humour for delighted admiration of her glittering derrière.

'Ere, 'ave this serviette,' she indicated boldly, pointing toward my groin, and I dabbed at my trousers cautiously, with more than a little self-consciousness.

Her front bottom (as my mother had impressed upon me was correct terminology for that area of a girl's lap) was now directly in-line with my eyelevel, and I couldn't help but notice how the material of her lurex garment was so tight that there appeared to be a couple of ferrets jostling for position therein. Heavens! With a face like a shiny red Christmas bauble I smiled up at her, swallowed hard, and folded the serviette up purposely to try to indicate the situation was now concluded.

'You don't work at Terry's, do you?' She had the air of one who'd just discovered escaped convicts in their midst.

'Sadly, no,' I shouted above the growing din, 'on our way to another do actually.'

'Pity,' she yelled back and winked at me, with another word beginning with L – 'Lasciviously'. No L. No.L. Not in this pub ironically, I thought, playing a little word game with myself.

'Well, 'appy Christmas anyway, love!' And she leant over the table, whipped a piece of plastic mistletoe from behind her back, and planted a moist lipsticky-kiss on my cheek. 'Oo, I'm Bev by the way,' she added. 'Guess I should've introduced meself before kissing yer.' She laughed, the ferrets tussled briefly, and I let out a nervous, fluttering sound, similar to laughter. 'Here's a thought,' she posed with her finger to the side of her mouth; 'Why don't you boys pop in after *your* do, and join us for the disco? It's upstairs in The Lemon Tree Room - by that time no one'll care that you haven't got a ticket.'

'Thanks. If there's time, we might just do that.' The terror in my voice was barely concealed beneath the surface. Bev's tongue hovered momentarily against her glossy upper lip, then shot back into her mouth which she let hang open, slightly, her lips moist and parted. It looked so rehearsed; I wondered if it had been a seduction tip in some ghastly woman's magazine about 'How to get your man.'

'Later, then…' she breathed. She moistened her lips once more and turned back triumphantly to the excited brouhaha of her work mates.

'Come back here?' I whispered out the side of my mouth, into Tom's ear, 'you have *got* to be joking. She'd eat me for breakfast.'

'You wouldn't survive till breakfast!' He laughed warmly and let his soul soak up all the jovial effusiveness of life that bubbled around us.

At that moment, *Day Trip to Bangor* jauntily skipped in, and half the pub began swaying from side-to-side where they sat, singing along in slightly slurry unison. It was a very catchy tune and most people in the pub seemed to know all the words. My favourite bit was where the day-trippers ate jellied eels while riding on a ferris wheel, which made one of them… I think her name was Elsie, feel nauseous. This had been preceded by scoffing lashings of ice-cold chocolate ice cream. No wonder she felt queasy turning round and round on a giant wheel with a stomach full of eels and ice cream.

Yes, I thought cynically, that's what makes us all feel a little queasy, 'the wheel going round.' The cosmic universe gave a hollow laugh, and I took a sip of my warm beer. Meanwhile, some of the office gathering had risen to their feet and joined in an impromptu folk dance. Bev grabbed a length of tinsel and, wrapping it round her neck like a feather boa, twirled round in circles with a joyful bouncing rhythm. Smiling inanely, the assembled company clapped and wailed along without a care in the world. It was what made life worth living...

About ten minutes later, just as we were about to leave, John Lennon's *Starting Over* struck-up. Eager for a second performance, Bev and the office wag grabbed a beer bottle each, held it like a microphone and crooned along like a couple of Elvis impersonators. She spotted us escaping through the happy throng and with a wink, sung her song directly to me. In spite of myself, I blushed. 'Later,' she mouthed and gave a little wave. How little we knew...the irony of the lyrics was not lost on me now: a man singing so optimistically of the future... only weeks from death.

Chapter Twenty-five: While I was fishing in the dull canal

Half an hour later, we walked up a quiet suburban street, where the only evidence of the time of year was the soft glow of tree lights in the bay windows of the Victorian houses. David and Mrs David's front door also sported a dark, funereal wreath of twisted holly and ivy.

'Just don't look at me when he receives the 'Thank You' bottle of single malt,' Tom warned with his finger poised above the bell.

'What? Not even when he says, "Ah! Splendid! Splendid choice!"?'

'Especially, when he says, "Ah! Splendid! Splendid choice!"'

We nodded solemnly and he pressed the bell... we waited for a few seconds. In the silence, we began to pick up the strains of King's College choir singing Christmas carols. The door was flung open widely, framing David in the subdued lighting. He was wearing a red bow tie. 'Good evening gentleman! Welcome! Come in, come in. Tom...' he paused warmly pumping his hand up and down, 'and Alistair.' He grasped my hand tightly. 'Lovely to see you both, do come through.'

As we followed David down the hallway, the rich, spicy sickliness of mulled wine filled my nostrils, and King's Choir mingled with the scent like a musical Christmas vapour.

'Angela, Angela!' he called out as we processed. Mrs David dutifully appeared from the kitchen, oven gloves still on, like a pair of domestic handcuffs.

'Tom and Alistair are here.' Angela threw off her fabric manacle, tossed it over her shoulder and stretching out her hand towards us enthused, 'Tom! How lovely to see you again. You do look so well.'

'In spite of all the children!'

'Ah now, I didn't say that!' she laughed. Still smiling broadly, she turned to me, but the light went out of her eyes as she took my hand. There was something behind her eyes, like the unspoken sorrow of meeting a bereaved acquaintance and not being quite sure whether or not one should offer condolences.

'And Alistair,' she said, a social smile struggling to stay on her face, 'how are you?'

'Never better, thank you.'

'Oh, good.' She sounded almost disappointed. There was a tiny awkward pause. 'Mulled wine for you two?' David asked. 'Or there's the whole gamut of alcoholic beverage lined up on the kitchen table, if you'd prefer.' (By which he meant red or white wine and some bottled ales.)

In spite of the party's long-standing unpopularity, the house was quite full. Tom and I edged our way into the lounge, beers in hand, scanning the room. Which group to infiltrate? Damn! The first eye I caught was Auntie Joan's, who immediately raised an incongruously, bangle-clad arm to beckon me over. She was sat on the sofa – alone - with a large space beside her. Oh, heavens!

'How's the head?' she said casting a rueful look to my beer.

'Oh,' I said peering into the froth-less pint, 'this is a bottled beer, Joan; it doesn't have a head.'

'I meant *your* head. You silly! Alcohol and migraines…ring any bells?'
Oh, please no, I thought, not this old chestnut again. There was no way out. I'd give her two minutes, then escape.

'I don't think drink's ever been a problem for me.'

'Oh? Well, that's where you're so fortunate. I could have said the same until the dreaded menopause – unbalanced my body chemistry dreadfully. ... Does my mentioning menopause discomfit you, Alistair?'

'Of course not, Joan,' I smiled reassuringly with cheeks flushing as if in empathy.

'Sadly, this will have to be my last glass of wine for the evening. Can only ever drink two, then it's the orange juice for me, I'm afraid.'
I shook my head, muttering something like, 'and at Christmas too', and noticed Tom engaged in lively conversation with Steve, and a beautiful Indian girl, I took to be Steve's girlfriend. Joan was looking miserable as the tragedy of her only being allowed 'two glasses' hit home.

'I feel it most at Christmas,' she whispered forlornly and put the glass to her lips for another fatal sip.

'I would've thought most of the alcohol evaporates in mulled wine though,' I said offering some comfort.

'Do you think so?' She brightened momentarily, and then added, 'Ah, but what about the Tyramine?'

'I'm sorry, Joan - I really couldn't tell you.'

She swirled the remaining mulled wine in the bottom of her glass and poked thoughtfully at the sliver of orange rind with her finger. I sat forward as if to make my move, but her reactions were rapier-like. The bangles rattled as she put her hand on my knee.

'Now Alistair, you and I have known one another for a good few years now, haven't we?' I slumped back, defeated.

'And in those years, I've come to learn you're a good listener, a good listener and a good friend. And as our dear Mr Addison said, and I quote: "Friendship improves happiness, and abates misery, by doubling our joys, and dividing our grief."' She gave my knee a gentle squeeze, 'So true, don't you think?'
I sank further into the sofa, trapped once more in her sticky gossamer threads, fervently hoping that her shared misery was not going to be menopausal in its theme.

A reprieve of sorts: in the ensuing half an hour, Joan successfully 'divided her grief' by sharing the sorry tale of the demise of her elderly dachshund, Henry, who had recently gone the way of all sausage dogs, (incontinence featured heavily.) This was followed by Joan 'doubling our joy' as she accompanied the choristers during a resounding rendition of 'Torches.'

Thankfully, before she could perform any more socio-mathematical operations, Angela came to my rescue. 'Food's ready everyone!' she announced loudly from the doorway. David was jostling in behind her.
'Yes, come on folks,' he encouraged, with his head bobbing over Angela's shoulder. 'Don't stand on ceremony. It's every man for himself here!'
'Everyman *for* himself. Now there's a conundrum' declared Robert, the boring beardy medievalist. 'If Everyman's *for himself* then he can have no good deed to accompany him. So, who will come to the table admitting that, David?' and he gestured opening the question to the assembled company, while chortling into his facial hair. We all laughed politely, if somewhat uncertainly, but no one moved. Any minute now I thought...chance to take up a new position, whilst lost in the stampede for the buffet. I was poised. Still nobody moved. Conversations began to resume. Joan shifted forward purposefully.

'Come on, Alistair, let's lead the way. Someone's got to be first.' (Joan had obviously sussed plan B) Dutifully, I helped her from the sofa, her bangles slid noisily down to her elbow, 'And *we* need to keep our blood sugars up too,' she added confidentially, while keeping a firm grip on my arm.

The crowds parted like the red sea, while Joan acknowledged the other party goers with the beatific air of the Queen Mother. I caught Tom's eye, and thought it seemed a real possibility that a man could literally 'burst' out laughing. Meanwhile, Robert held his hands up with a 'well, who else?' look on his face, but I think he was only sharing his peculiar brand of humour with himself.

David bowed us into the dining room, where Mrs David, – sorry – Angela, stood grimacing at the head of the table, brandishing a silver fish slice.

'It's all help yourself,' she explained briskly, 'although I thought it would be easier if I served the trout.'

(I was about to say, oh, don't bother I'm sure the old trout can manage by herself, but I thought better of it.)

David handed Joan a plate.

'Caught this beauty on my last trip to Loch Hope, Alistair. Five pounds. Good size for a sea trout.'

'Very impressive.'

'Put up quite a fight. Caught it at night, with a flick of a white moth fly.' And he began to wave his forearm backwards and forwards to demonstrate his technique.

We stood admiringly, while David now progressed to wrestling with the creature from the deep.

'Mind the lamp!' cried Angela raising her hands in alarm.

'I can see it!' he replied, irritated at being interrupted. 'Then grab the priest, quick whack on the forehead, and back for his mate!'

Joan winced.

'The priest?' Joan mumbled in confusion, 'I never knew you were a Catholic. Whatever made you hit him?'

'No, Joan dear,' said David, his fishing tackle packed away now, 'a priest is the name of a metal thing you kill fish with.'

'Oh,' whispered Joan, 'and his mate?'

'His mate's outside;' explained Angela, 'not enough room for him on the table. Now Joan, can I help you to some? There's homemade hollandaise in that gravy boat thing.'

'Erh, thank you, Angela… just a little.'

The sea trout's eye, now white like a full moon cataract, stared blindly at me.

'Alistair?' Angela said. Did I detect something of a challenge in her voice? 'David's hard-won sea trout for you?'

She was holding aloft a piece of the trout's pinkish belly on the fish slice. For one horrid moment I thought I saw the blind eye glance downward trying to fathom out what was happening to him.

'It looks fantastic, but unfortunately fish doesn't agree with me,' I lied.

'Oh, what a pity. Never mind. Ah, here's Tom; I'm sure he'll be partial.' Naturally, Tom ate heartily. He established himself by the mantelpiece, where his large frame enabled him to rest an elbow on the shelf. Being at the far end of the buffet table also enabled him to dip in and out of the food at leisure.

'Great vol au vents, Angela!' he said, spraying little flakes of pastry into the air.

'Prawns,' she mouthed across the room, wiggling her finger like that weird Fingerbobs puppeteer. I began to wonder if David and Mrs David communicated in mime often. They seemed very fond of it. Perhaps they played charades together in the evening when nobody was looking.

Joan had steered me back to the sofa, and we sat awkwardly together, balancing our plate of cold meats, quiche, salads and pickles on our laps.

'I could do with a tray,' mused Joan, looking around the lounge as if she might be lucky enough to spot one floating by.

'I'll see if I can find you one.'

'Would you be a dear?'

Just as I was returning with the tray, the doorbell rang. Immediately, David leapt out from the dining room. 'I'll get it!' As he reached the door, he shouted back, 'I've got it!' Slightly transfixed by his urgency, I hovered in the hallway with the tray. He smoothed his floppy fringe back from his brow, and opened the door swiftly. Lit by the porch light, I saw at once it was Ruth.

'David...' she said.

'Ruth...' he said.

Good God! I thought - surely not? But it was unmistakable: the unspoken volumes in that brief exchange. The depth of warmth in their voices, the way her eyes held his, a moment too long, an almost visible spark of energy arching between them revealed an intimacy that went beyond that of colleagues. David glanced upward, tilting his head to the bunch of mistletoe hanging above them. Ruth's eyebrows rose in question and she gave a small smile. Just as David was inclining his head towards her, she saw me in the hallway; she nodded over his shoulder in my direction. I knew that look. Knew, she knew, I'd seen.

'Alistair,' she said simply.

David turned and recovered himself instantly.

'Ruth's here, Alistair. Doesn't she look frozen. Brrr! Come on in, come on in. Out of the cold.' She stepped into the hallway, tiny beads of snow on her coat melting instantly to droplets. In a single moment I saw how and why she'd changed in the past few weeks; when I'd been too wrapped up in myself and Anna to notice. God, the irony of it. The hypocrisy! Could it really be?

'I was just getting a tray for Joan.'

'Ah, good man.' He gave me an appreciative pat on the back. 'Yes, Alistair's been doing sterling work looking after our dear Joan all evening, haven't you?'

I made a long-suffering smile and taking a step backwards, held my tray up like a shield, 'Once more unto the breach and all that.'

But like a complete idiot I backed into Angela, who was striding purposefully from the dining room, the translucent skeleton of the sea trout on a platter in her hand. 'Ooh!' she cried just managing to prevent the sea trout's remains from slithering to the floor.

'I'm so sorry, Angela.' - Damn! - There was a blob of mayonnaise on Angela's mulberry-coloured blouse, where the tray had slammed up against her bosom. As yet she hadn't noticed. The trout's blind eye scrutinized me. An accident - it was an accident. Not guilty my friend. Not this time. *'Confess.'* I'll only embarrass her. *'Coward!'* sneered the trout.

'Look! Ruth's here, Angela,' announced David, doing his best to ignore my blundering about.

I watched Angela's face so closely, saw the tiniest of muscles flickering beneath her skin. (She knows, I thought. Poor Mrs David knows or at least she's got a very good idea. What was David playing at? He and Mrs David were an institution.)

'Ah, good evening, Ruth. How kind of you to come, 'she said with all the warmth of hoar-frost. 'There's more of David's sea trout in the kitchen. Don't fret that you've missed it all arriving late.'

'Thank you, Angela. It's very sweet of you, but I must confess I've already eaten. I do hope David told you I had a former supper engagement?'

'Whoops!' said David slapping his forehead and rolling his eyes. 'Forgot.'

'Then perhaps David can get you something to drink?' (Hemlock, for instance?)

'That would be perfect,' Ruth said with a serene smile.

We all hovered uncertainly.

'The drinks, David,' Angela prompted rather firmly... 'in the kitchen.'

'Oh, yes. Do come through.' David gave a theatrical obsequious bow. But, just as the assembled company were gathering for the push towards the kitchen, David spotted the smear... 'Angela dear, you seem to have something on your blouse,' whispered David, gesturing towards her breasts. All eyes lighted upon Angela's soiled bosom. She glanced first downward at the creamy streak - then immediately at me.

'Must've come off the tray when I ... uhm...'

'I'm sure it'll sponge off,' David assured, suddenly aware of his 'faux pas.'

'This is silk, David,' Angela said flatly.

'Oh, what a pity,' Ruth said, her gaze unwavering. 'Anything greasy is such a devil on silk.'

'Angela'll have some stain removing trick up her sleeve, won't you, dear?' However, David's reference to Angela's laundry skills did nothing to diffuse the situation. I don't think it was quite the accolade she wanted in front of this woman, who seemed to be exerting such effortless superiority over her. She composed her face into a resigned 'whatever next?' look. Rather unhelpfully I ventured, 'Salt. Would that work?'

'Or white wine?' added David.

'Perhaps I should rub it with this dead trout's head? Really, I haven't clue. I'll take it to the cleaners in the morning. Anyway, Alistair, I think Joan's rather anxious for that tray.' Angela nodded towards the living room. I knew I was being dismissed. Angela stiffened as she followed David and Ruth into the kitchen. This was a revelation. Well I never!

The other old trout with the bangles was forking shreds of coleslaw into her mouth, and was a good three quarters of the way through her plateful. I think she could've managed without the tray well enough. Anyway, she grumbled playfully about my tardiness, took the tray and resumed eating, while my mind gnawed away at a very juicy titbit.

Fortunately for me, Joan had taken my hypothesis on the lowered alcoholic content of the mulled wine as a good enough proof for her and now moved on to her fourth glass. She accompanied this with a large helping of sherry trifle, soon after which she mumbled something about needing to sit somewhere quieter and stumbled off in the direction of David's study.

The rest of the evening passed away, just as uneventfully as one who slips from this world to the next in a coma. Having lost Joan, I was then cornered by Robert, who had a bit of dried bogey protruding from his left nostril, which quivered on his stiff nose hair every time he breathed in or out. Although, too embarrassed to say anything, sustaining a tedious conversation about the problem of installing a new damp course under the original flagstones of his old property, while transfixed by the dancing nasal offspring, was a strain indeed.

Eventually, Ruth sidled up to me and suggested we rouse Joan, as one or two people seemed to be making a move and we ought to present the gifts *tout de suite*. Considering what she knew I'd worked out tonight, she seemed remarkably collected. However, I suppose she thought there was a mutual trust between us now; each of us having a firm grip on the other's short and curlies.

We discovered Joan, still recumbent on the chaise longue in David's study. She'd pulled the beige sofa throw around herself, so she looked like a giant, shabby, fat chrysalis; her sonorous snoring, the only sign of life.

'Perhaps you'd better…' I whispered hesitating in the doorway. Ruth nodded in agreement.

I retreated to the hallway; King's College brightly sang out that they, *saw three ships on Christmas morn*, but my mind saw Anna - not for the first time that evening, I have to say. Anna: blissfully naked, smooth, warm, all embracing. Her eyes so bright they dazzled me as sunlight fragments upon a lake. By some miracle, by some bewitching spell, she loves me. She sustains me wherever I am. I'm kissing her now. My insides plummet. The exquisite cliff-falling sensation whenever she is near; just the image of her face and my entire body surges with life; my soul banging up against the limits of my physical being - it was incredible.

Steve emerged from the living room on his way to recharge the two empty glasses clinking in his hand. He grinned in that young easy manner, 'All right?'

'Fine, thank you,' I smiled back. 'Just waiting for Ruth to rouse Joan,' and threw a glance into the dimly lit study.

'Ah, too much Christmas spirit.'

'Probably.'

He smiled again and raising the glasses disappeared into the kitchen saying, 'Not enough training. We should get Joan down the pub more often.'

Funny that, isn't it? You can be a thousand miles away in your mind. Doing anything, with anyone, and yet in the midst of a crowd nobody knows where you are, who you're with, what you're doing. It always strikes me as quite unbelievable. You can even hear a symphony in your head in the most silent of places…and no one else will hear a single note. Steve probably thought I was waiting there, thinking of nothing in particular - just my usual vacuous expression, which tells the world nothing of my internal life. Inside, I'm so on fire I could self-combust. Doesn't a light burst forth from my soul and radiate all about me till I'm like the exuberant dancing figure of Albion in Blake's *Glad Day*? So taken am I by this image, I actually move in front of the hall mirror and check myself for escaping rays of light, of life.

A few minutes later, Joan emerged from her cocoon, not so much a butterfly, but a dusty, tired old moth.

'The present, Alistair,' she muttered, flapping her arms distractedly, 'it's in a carrier by my handbag.'

'She thinks it's under the table in the dining room,' said Ruth, as she guided Joan down the corridor towards the downstairs loo. 'Would you mind, Alistair?'

Eventually, all was well and we dutifully gathered in the front room. Joan had retrieved the mystery present, and Robert was poised, wrapped bottle waiting patiently at his feet. He tapped the edge of his glass musically, cleared his throat and drew himself up to his full height of five-foot four.

'Well, it seems to have fallen upon me to perform the most pleasant task of proposing a toast of thanks, from us all…' (He smiled fondly around the room as if he felt he really belonged to something good, and I felt like such a heel for thinking he belonged to the noble order of ennui in extremus.) He held his near empty glass aloft: 'To David and Angela, for their truly splendid hospitality here tonight.' A few muttered, 'Hear! Hears!' a little ripple of applause, muted only by the fact many people were still holding onto wine glasses. Several began to rise to their feet only to sink down again as they realised Robert hadn't finished – not by a long way. 'I can't recall,' he continued, 'how many years it is that they have been kind enough to invite us all here, to their charming home at Christmas, and make us all so welcome, but I do know, and I'm sure you'll all agree with me on this point, that *quod erat demonstrandum*, 'the proof is in the puddings' of which I had no less than two delicious helpings this year.' His eyes scanned the room theatrically waiting for the convulsed laugher, a few obliged with 'hm, hm' noises. Undeterred, he continued... 'In that same vein,' (presumably the one now flowing with cholesterol) 'Angela – I'm sure Bethany, who sadly can't be here tonight due to gastric flu, would love the recipe for your exquisite Boodles Fool – we so look forward to it every year.'

Tom began to smirk; I had to intently study the raised pattern on the carpet. Robert still continued, 'Each year never fails to thoroughly, and unequivocally, exceed the expectation of the last and will no doubt continue to exceed the expectation of the last -' I was still trying to fathom out if that last bit made any sense at all or indeed if he was talking about the party in general or still drooling over the fool, when Joan, who'd been swaying like an aspen in a gentle breeze, suddenly and quite frighteningly broke into frantic applause. Robert gave her a nervous glance. The rest of the assembled company realised this was possibly their only chance to cut Robert's speech off at the knees and the clapping quickly gathered momentum into a full-scale round of applause.

The clapping petered out and one or two people felt compelled to add their individual gratitude as some do on such occasions (on this occasion as a means of underlining all speech making.) 'Lovely spread, Angela!', 'Great trout, David!'... even 'Vol-au-vents to die for!' got an airing.

Robert raised his hands like a conductor hushing an orchestra, but a voice, rich and boozy, disobediently rose above all others.

'Angela, my dear. Juss to say how loverly everything has been tonight. You, and David, are our most graciousss hosts as ever.'

Joan lifted a square-shaped package from the side-board, took one or two hesitant steps in Angela's direction, where much to my relief, she delivered it without falling over.

'To say thank you for tonight...' A pause for a hiccough which never came... 'And I suppozze, a very, very, very... (second hiatus for relevant seasonal greeting to be pulled from Joan's back catalogue) 'Merry Christmas. For Christmas is upon us all once more.'

Before she could say anything else, she was helped into an armchair, where she concentrated very hard on staying upright and awake.

Angela thanked Joan and everyone for coming, wished us all a happy holiday with our friends and families, and then sat on the arm of the sofa quietly sliding her nail beneath the paper of the present. Now poised with bottle in hand, Robert, not to be outdone, seized his moment as his second favourite duty of the evening befell him and loudly announced, 'No prizes for guessing what's in here, David.'

'I can't imagine!' responded David examining the parcel, with just the correct level of incredulity. We all laughed in that warm social way so beloved of these occasions. Tom was by my side now. 'Wait for it... Wait for it' he whispered. The golden paper was unfurled... 'Any second...'
We were not disappointed.

'Ah! Splendid! Splendid choice!' enthused David, holding the bottle aloft for all to see. Robert beamed; his mission successfully completed. A second round of applause was led by Tom, who obviously needed some sort of release. And then Tom and I exchanged a look of such triumphant joy, it was all I could do not to kiss him.

'Angela, what's that you've got there?' asked someone's wife loudly as the clapping died down into an awkward lull. Angela stood up with the bewildered look of perplexed gratitude of one who has just received a gift about which they have absolutely no clue as to what it is at all.

'It's a sort of wheel.'

'Oh super. You'll soon have a stomach like a wash board.'
Angela continued to look mystified as did everyone else, apart from Joan who'd gone into an oblivious happy trance.
'What do I do with it? Roll myself flat?' Angela begun running the wheel back and forth across the bulge beneath her plaid skirt.

'Oh goodness no,' laughed the same woman, 'you roll it on the floor,' she explained by demonstrating in mid-air, 'but while crouching on all fours.'
Angela's eyes widened.

What was Joan thinking of? I knew she was losing it, but a stomach toning wheely thing for Angela, on such a public occasion?

She stood quite alone, on the edge of the room; her best blouse indelibly scarred by a greasy smudge - the rival for her husband's affections a witness to her humiliation (and in her own home too) after all her labours to make the evening a success for him. It doesn't take much to crush a person, a daub of mayonnaise in the wrong place, an ill-thought-out gift, one's life-long partner slipping from your grasp.

Joan, sensing a change in the atmosphere, looked up anxiously. She too focussed on Angela, whose fixed smile was frozen solid by now.

'Thank you, Joan. Soon have me in shape, eh?' she said. Even David looked as if his heart had gone out to his wife.

'What? No dear, I gave you the squirrel proof bird feeder. Where's the bird feeder?' She looked around the room accusingly.

Well, to cut a long story short, Joan had muddled the wrapped exercise wheel, as requested by her nephew, with the wrapped bird feeder suitable for the boss's wife, who loved garden birds. It caused a round of mirth to break out amongst us revellers, and prompted one or two anecdotes about muddled or unwanted/ unsuitable/ embarrassing gifts and otherwise. From all outward appearances you'd have thought Angela had enjoyed the jape as much as anyone. But I knew differently.

However, even I must admit I hadn't noticed what a big bratwurst sat under Angela's waistband until that moment. I guess I wasn't the only one. Poor Angela. Oh, and of course, I don't suppose I need to tell you, we gave 'The Lemon Tree Room' a wide berth on the way home - a very wide berth.

Chapter Twenty-six: April is the cruellest month

It's funny, isn't it? I remember that evening so well. You never really know which bits of your life will become memory and which will disappear beneath the rising tide, do you? Maybe it's because I knew that department party was likely to be my last. And somewhere deep down, where even I couldn't see it, I felt something of that love which Robert obviously felt for them all. I just don't know really. But it matters to me now. Thinking back about them all, maybe without knowing it, I had belonged to something good. And it's only now I see how just 'ordinary life' could be so memorable, so magical, if only I let it.

I suppose I should explain that the Christmas party was the last episode I wrote about in that first autumn after I'd lost Anna. As I take up writing about this extraordinary time in my life again, it's many months later; I'm certainly no longer in my Victorian house opposite the park, so don't picture me there.

But when I'd started writing in the autumn after I'd lost Anna, I felt it was the only thing that was holding me together, wandering through the past. It seemed safe, while everything else crumbled around me. I'd carried on at the university. One can't say teaching; that would be over-stating the case. To be honest my teaching life was in rapid decline. I was frequently absent; ringing in with a variety of maladies from migraines to stomach upsets, to chest infections. Some were real, some I must confess imagined. When I did make it into work, I was less than useless. My lectures fell apart as I struggled to make sense of what seemed to me to be increasingly incomprehensible notes. I was mumbling, incoherent, easily distracted. In tutorials I often found myself staring out of windows … miles away. Once or twice I fell asleep. But I hardly slept at night anymore, so that was understandable. Students' essays lay unmarked in jumbled piles under dirty coffee cups; one or two essays I mislaid altogether. It happens. It wasn't long before complaints began piling up too - some even accusing me of drunkenness. Although, in my defence, while I'd admit to drinking frequently, I was never drunk. But these kids… they smell a faint waft of last night's booze, you doze off for a few seconds, stumble over a chair leg or whatever - and they all assume you're intoxicated. What do they know?

However, things have a way of falling apart, sometimes you can fix them and sometimes you can't, and you have to throw them away. I fell into the latter category.
At first, there had been some muted sympathy from the few who knew the details.

Well, I had to tell David in the end, didn't I? He sucked in his teeth and sagely explained to me that this is precisely why relationships of this sort should be discouraged. However genuine one's feelings seem, he told me with a weary sigh, there is sadly only one outcome: misery for some or all involved. In view of all I had already lost, he would take no further action. Considering I had no doubt learnt a very hard lesson, he said that he presumed there was no need to ask me for my complete and utter assurance that such 'involvements' would never occur again. Ruth fluctuated between an unspoken: 'Oh God, if only you'd listened to me when you had the chance,' mode, and a new desperate expression etched in anxiety upon her face - the haunted shadow of a shared secret, now darkly buried, deep within us both. Tom was a mixture of anger and pain. He wanted to hit and hug me by turns. Such tolerance, however, increasingly turned into warnings of needing to pull myself together.

'You're so close to being asked to leave, another few months, that's all the grace they'll give you – get a grip on the situation, Alistair. If you lose your job, what will you have left?'
These words of Tom's were, I supposed, to help me. Maybe in hindsight I should have taken heed of the warning, but I was incapable of helping myself. Maybe losing my job would benefit me in the long term...for everything about being at the university tortured me.
I saw her - and yet, I didn't see her - everywhere.
She was like the light from a dead star, seemingly so tangible, and yet only really real in the past.
God, I missed her. I missed her so much. I miss her still. I will always miss her...

By spring Tom's prophecy came to fruition. He had indeed been a voice crying in the wilderness, for his words had blown away in the wind, and I did not care. In a meeting, which I thought was very sensitively handled by David, it was suggested I might find other work more suitable for my needs. I made it easy for them in the end. Well, I had to. I loved them now, didn't I?

'Don't worry, David. I was going to hand in my resignation at the end of term,' I lied.

'We'll all miss you Alistair - you and your inimitable teaching style,' he lied back. We shook hands. Behind his glasses I thought I detected tears in his eyes - maybe not. So, I left of my own accord.

It was Easter: a time of new life; a time of new beginnings. It was April, 'the cruellest month' a time for 'mixing memory with desire' a time for 'dull roots to be stirred'. On the morning when I took the last of my possessions from my study, it was pouring with rain. As it trickled down the back of my neck, I held my carrier bag of papers close to my chest, and told myself that this was a good sign.

Chapter Twenty-seven: The nymphs are departed

The previous Easter, Marion finally got her heart's desire, her new beginning, and left me. It happened quite out of the blue at the end of the Easter break - took us both by surprise. As you know, just before Christmas, Marion had been let down again by Edward, and it had seemed as if we'd never unravel the messy knot which God had joined together. What happened that day? Let me think, cast my mind back, many months. Yes, that was it.... the phone call.

'Good afternoon. May I speak to Marion, please?'

'I'm sorry. She's out at the moment. Can I take a message?'

'Am I speaking to Alec?'

Now, this was strange. The only person who ever called me 'Alec' was Marion.

'Yes,' I answered slowly, 'speaking.'

'I need to speak to Marion urgently. Can you tell me where I might contact her?' And then as if by way of explanation added, 'It's Edward.'

Well, the strange thing is - you may not believe it - but this was the first time I'd ever heard him speak. Immediately, I felt intimidated. His was the voice of a smooth, self-assured, self-possessed man, and although I detected some crisis was afoot, Edward's voice remained calm and superior.

'I'm terribly sorry, I believe she's at the hairdressers at the moment,' - my own voice struggling with my version of casual superiority - 'but I'll tell her to call you as soon as she comes in, shall I?'

'If you would be so kind; I'm at home. She has the number. Thank you so much.' And he put the phone down. I was dismissed.

'He said *what?*' Marion asked with incredulity, while carefully removing her jacket so as not to disturb her freshly pronged hairdo. She'd recently taken to having it coloured. God knows why. Is chrome yellow really a becoming colour for a woman of Marion's age? She obviously thought it was, this being the second time she'd sent her crowning glory off the chromatic scale.

I repeated myself with slow deliberation. 'To ring him at home, as soon as you were back.'

'At home? Not at the office?' She marched passed the mirror, unable to resist pausing to admire herself. 'Did he leave the number?' she asked, pretending to wipe a trace of lipstick from the side of her mouth, while secretly dazzled by this 'blonder' more youthful-looking self.

'No. He said you had it.'

'Well, yes I do. I've hardly ever used it though. What on earth could've happened?' She turned round keeping her head unnatural still. 'Did he sound upset?'

'I couldn't tell you. Just bloody call him and you can find out for yourself.' I held the receiver up to her. It sang its dull monotone. When she took it, I retreated purposefully upstairs. The house was very quiet. I perched on my bed, picked up a paperback I was reading and opened it where the comb I was using as a bookmark pushed the pages apart. But of course, I wasn't really reading anything. I was listening. I still have remarkably good hearing; can still hear a mosquito, anywhere in the room at night. The noise they produce is coincident with a high G apparently. Fascinating. So, hearing Marion loudly exclaim, 'Oh, My God! Well I never!' wasn't difficult at all...

Marion almost ran up the stairs, which in itself heralded the enormity of the speech she was about to deliver. Breathless, over-excited, red and chrome-yellow, she barged into my room.

'It's Edward,' she gasped. 'I have to go to him.'

'Is he ill?'

She shook her head.

'Well, what then?'

'Lizzie's gone. Taken Hattie with her.'

I calmly replaced the comb bookmark and regarded my wife. Her eyes were wide and glassy.

'Lizzie's left Edward. Run off with a policeman! Must've met him when she had her handbag stolen in January.' She began wringing her hands in a rather melodramatic fashion. 'Edward's beside himself. They've gone off to Margate of *all* places.'

In all the years I've known her I don't think there's ever been a moment where I was at such a loss to interpret how she felt: excitement, panic, amazement, indignation, outrage, shock, fear, hope, all rose to the surface and disappeared again like bits of mixed veg in a pot of boiling minestrone soup.

'When I think how *loyal* Edward has been,' she announced with a voice full of indignant self-righteousness, not a trace of irony. 'How patient *I* have been. And Lizzie and bloody Dixon of Dock Green... three months! Less probably.'

That bit of vegetable sunk and a new one took its place. I didn't recognize this one at all. It was something like 'serene benevolence,' an alien ingredient in Marion's emotional recipe.

'And now Edward needs me. Really *needs* me. I must go to him at once.'

For a moment she gazed out of the window, with such a distant sense of purpose I was put in mind of Julie Andrews in *The Sound of Music*. This was not the time to harbour such a thought. The deep alto of Reverend Mother warbling *Climb Every Mountain* momentarily soared into my head.

Then, thankfully, came the anger again, although this time accompanied by fear and anxiety. 'He'll fight her for Hattie though. He's been a devoted father - adores that child.' (I think that would be one battle Marion secretly hoped that Edward would lose.)

And so, she left, within the hour. A suitcase carelessly packed. A lifetime swept under the carpet. She didn't even think to say goodbye to the cat. (Not till later that is, when she rang from Edward's at about ten-thirty that evening to check if I'd fed Thaddeus.) I asked after Edward, which I thought was very grown-up of me. He's sleeping now she had replied in her newly discovered, bed-side manner voice, 'utterly emotionally exhausted.'

I pictured Marion in Edward's flat. Obviously, I'd never seen it, but I knew his type. Edward lay snoozing on his pristine divan, white Egyptian cotton sheets, matching bedside tables from some exclusive furniture shop in Hampstead. I imagined Marion running her finger across the dustless surfaces of the glass dining table, so excited, yet petrified to be in the other woman's house. Quietly, she began to sing 'My Favourite Things' (she was alright with the first verse, but could only remember the second verse was something to do with schnitzels and strudels, so she had to content herself with repeating the first verse until she felt her equilibrium restored). Was this to be my lasting and enduring image of my wife? A wimple clad governess with a fondness for Austrian cuisine?

'It was all rather rushed, wasn't it?' she admitted. 'I'll have to come back for my things at some time.'

'Whenever.'

'Are you humming, Alec?'

'Not that I was aware of.'

'Mmm. Well, goodnight.'

'Goodnight, Marion.'

Anna had gone home to visit her parents and I knew they were going out for a meal tonight to celebrate her father's birthday. He was forty-nine. They didn't know about me. We'd discussed the possibility of introductions several times, but it had always been shelved as a bad idea. So, I was totally alone.

I wandered through the silent stillness of the house, and found myself strangely drawn to Marion's room. Nervously, I pushed the door open, almost expecting to find her there like some spectral vision waiting for me, but the room was empty. She'd left in such a haste she'd uncharacteristically left several drawers open with clothes trailing out of them. Now, with all the care of a bereaved husband, I took each item and folding it lovingly, neatly, replaced it in the drawer. Just the way she liked it.

The silence burnt my ears.

Marion had gone. Soon, gone for good. I was free. Free at last. I sat in my prison cell, looking at the open door…and wept.

Chapter Twenty-eight: My nerves are bad tonight

I guess what I'm supposed to do now is pick up the story where I abandoned it and slide effortlessly back into it. Tell you all about that first Christmas that Anna and I didn't share, because she had to be at her parents' place; or how Marion and I spent our last Christmas together resenting each other's presence over a flaccid turkey dinner. Or I could recount our visit to mother on Boxing Day, because that really was memorable, (not least Mother's reaction to the 'all things ginger' present).

'*Do* I like ginger, Alistair?'

'Yes, mother you do. You like it a lot. You always say, nothing beats a ginger biscuit.'

Marion's face was becoming slightly twisted with anxiety.

With her yellowing finger nail, Mother prodded at the cellophane, and then wiped a small trace of spittle from the corner of her mouth with a little lacy handkerchief she always kept scrunched up in her hand just for this purpose. Years ago, if she received a present she didn't like or want, she'd thank the giver politely and wrap the paper back around it, while making a mental note to pass it on to one of her friends, or donate it, with a flourish of generosity, to the church tombola. But this artful concealment of how to deal politely with the unwanted gift was now lost on Mother. She just shook her head, 'No, I can't eat these ginger bits and pieces, Alistair. I'd be belching all afternoon.' With some difficulty she lifted the basket upwards like an offering. 'You have it Marion. I can't be doing with ginger. Lemon, maybe, ginger, no.'

On the way home, 'The Ginger Lover's Basket' sat on the back seat of car, in silence, like an admonished child, who had disgraced itself during a trip to granny's.

'Don't say a word, Alec.' Marion gripped the steering wheel tightly.

'I wasn't going to,' I replied truthfully.

****

Oh, where was I? Oh, yes…Then I might throw in a bit about my trip to Wales with Anna and then we'd be neatly back to where Marion left me, and I could continue to tell you all about the events of the summer, which led to losing Anna, and so on, until the breaking of my heart was complete. But at the moment I can't be bothered to write about any of that at all. Maybe I'll just stop writing now all together. I don't think it's doing me any good at all. It's making me ill; filling my head with too many memories. All these emotions sludge around in your veins, clogging up your heart like cholesterol. *The past is a foreign country*; and I am travel weary.

Now, not only have I lost Anna, Marion, and my job, I have just heard from Marion that she needs her half of the value of the property. She said that I'd had a good year to sort myself out. 'But Marion, you know I've just lost my job. I obviously can't pay you off.'

'Oh, I realise that,' she'd replied. But they'd finally got a buyer for Edward's flat, and property, especially the little mews house they'd set their heart on - London location- well, it came at a price. 'Prices in London are sky-high, Alec. You've no idea.' She asked could I speak to an estate agent as soon as possible? It was only fair. There would be plenty, she had said, in my half to buy a small flat, a little terrace whatever.

So, I guess it's goodbye to my home too.

I think you could say I'm about as low as I can go - I have to reach up to touch the bottom. Is that a cliché? A plagiarised phrase? I don't know, and I don't care. It's in my head and I have no idea if the voice in my head is me talking to myself or what anymore. Where do anybody's thoughts come from? I'm so lonely I have to have conversations with myself or invented people, or listen to Thaddeus. Ironically, there are some days when Thaddeus won't shut up at all. Goes on for hours - singing songs from the shows, quoting random lines of poetry, speeches from Shakespeare – amazingly knows them 'word for word' - and yet on other days he makes me quite irritated by pretending he can't speak a jot of English and just meows. Ginger cats are notoriously untrustworthy.

I'm not becoming schizophrenic or anything; let's get that straight; everybody in my world is real. But my mind has somewhat departed lately. My thoughts arrive externally, orchestrated somewhere else by others' mouths. Or am I just remembering snippets lost in my memory, the odd line of poetry, a long-forgotten speech? This memory bank of words and images; who possesses them once they're in my head? Where does the imagination end and insanity begin?

I'm just not sure if I have still have a voice or not some days. Just to test if it's still there I sometimes join Thaddeus in his musical repertoire. He was absolutely bewitched by my rendition of *Some Enchanted Evening*, (in fact, I think he was possibly a little intimidated by my performance, as he refuses to sing it himself these days.) Sometimes I just talk to people I wish were here.

Oh, hang about - Thaddeus has just come through the cat flap, and he, as you know, loves my voice. Right, now I'm going to sing his favourite, *Some Enchanted Evening*, very loudly, and very passionately, but if that is not your thing, please leave the room immediately.

Yes, the only real significant other I still have is Thaddeus. Would you believe it? At first, Marion couldn't take him because there was a 'no pets' rule at Edward's smart block of flats. It then transpired that it would be impossible for Marion to have Thaddeus anyway, because even when they moved from the flat, which was on their agenda, Hattie had allergies, and reacted to cat hair even if the animal wasn't actual present. Sorry - but Hattie would be a frequent visitor, if not a permanent fixture if Edward got his way, and her needs came first. 'Oh, of course,' Marion said reasonably, swallowing a rather stubborn lump in her throat.

'I imagine you're quite happy to keep him, Alec? You've always held a secret soft spot for him. I'll share in the cost of his vet bills and so forth.'

How magnanimous I thought - the responsible absent parent.

'But what about his school fees, Marion?'

'Very funny.' She laughed.

To off stage right I heard her say wryly, 'Alec asks if we'll consider sharing Thaddeus's school fees, Edward. Edward?' Edward didn't so much as chuckle.

Within a week or so, the house was on the market. It was, I have to say, at a very reasonable price. Marion wanted a quick sale. To those of you who have never experienced the excruciating agony of having complete strangers come and critically view your home I have only one word of advice: don't. I know our house wasn't an estate agent's dream. Phrases like 'possibilities for some exciting renovation to this otherwise fine traditional property' come to mind, which meant he thought the kitchen and bathroom were achingly awful and no self-respecting buyer could possibly bring themselves to cook, eat, bathe or relieve themselves in the presence of such antiquated facilities.

The first couple, Mr and Mrs Alcock obviously agreed. Mrs Alcock was one of those Hamble type women I encountered last Christmas. She had glossy, unnaturally black hair set in large stiff curls, and was wearing a shiny, satin-effect harlequin blouse which stretched tautly across her chest – goldish filigree-styled buttons, did their utmost. And I'd never seen a woman wearing orange lipstick before. Meanwhile, Mr Alcock sported a bright blue shirt with a white collar, which set off his fat, bristly, red neck very nicely. I did not want these people living in my house. The first thing they did when they went into the living room was sit on the sofa, without being asked.

'We'd have to find another position for the telly,' Harlequin Hamble proclaimed, rocking from side to side. 'The light's shining directly on the screen.' She looked irksomely at the large bay window behind her. 'Don't you find it impossible to *view* with the sun on the screen, Mr Johnstone?' To be honest I don't think I'd ever watched the television in the daytime before, apart from the odd occasion when I'd been ill, and then that was usually in the winter.

'No, not really.'

'A new aerial point is a very simple procedure should it be required,' assured Barry, our trusty estate agent.

'What about this magnificent fireplace, Mr Alcock?' Barry announced, and he and Mr Alcock took a few steps towards it. I knew Barry was thinking he should have advised me to have a cheery fire going, you know, to show off one of the best features of the house. The two men stared into the empty grate, which gawped back, open-mouthed, clinkers littering the floor like a mawful of broken fillings.

'Bit old fashioned for my taste,' said Mr Alcock with a phlegmy cough, and then pressed his fingers onto the mantelpiece as if testing its weight-bearing potential. 'Probably come out easy enough though. Nice gas fire. That's what I'd put in. Instant heat. No mess.'

By the time we got to the kitchen, Harlequin Hamble was giving Mr Alcock the 'over my dead body' look. My heart sunk further as we ascended the stairs. Why couldn't we just abandon the whole charade?

'Mr Johnson was telling me that he and his wife had been planning for a new bathroom suite until quite recently. It's probably a good thing they didn't get round to it because now whoever becomes this fine property's owner will be able to choose their own.' How very astute of Barry to have realised that our choices of bathroom suite would not coincide. However, I had no recollection of discussing any long-held cherished dreams for my bathroom suite with him at all.

Later that afternoon, Barry rang and repeated his advice that while a 'lived in' home appealed to its owners, it was rarely a good selling point, and would I mind awfully, perhaps packing some things away, tidying up a bit. To people in 'my position', they often recommended 'Kerry's Kleaners', who apparently could work wonders - and were very reasonable. 'It may seem terribly presumptuous, Mr Johnson, but there are ways of improving the marketable potential of one's home.'

After one or two further lukewarm to icy buyers had sneered at my home, I surprisingly took his advice. Much of the debris of my life I concealed in boxes. It looked far less chaotic contained in cardboard cuboids. The lovely 'Kelly's Kleaners,' who seemed particularly satisfied with the level of squalor they found, paid a call. I suppose it heightened their level of post cleaning satisfaction; must have some mathematical relationship to the amount of filth present prior to cleaning

X= amount of dirt and grime multiplied by PCS (post cleaning satisfaction) So the higher the value of X, the greater the value of X(PCS) or something like that.

Anyway, the upshot of all this domestic activity is the next couple who come to view it fell immediately in love with the place, and I have what is professionally known as 'a buyer' in the form of a young trendy couple, Jed and the lovely pregnant Zoë. He was something in the health food business, which surprised me, because he looked more like a hippie than a business man, while Zoë with her round belly, encased in a rainbow jumper and pale blue dungarees gave the impression of being an adult-sized toddler. She was all enthusiasm and energy. Not only was she a primary school teacher, but a yoga teacher too. While we perused the garden on that fine bright morning, she asked me if I, or my wife, had ever tried yoga. Hiding a smile, as a picture of Marion squatting floated by, I had to confess we had not. 'It's so relaxing,' she breathed, her cheeks flushed in the wind. 'Gosh Jed, it's been a while since I've managed the camel pose, hasn't it? I could just see myself out here on a blanket in the summer, doing my post-natal stretches while the baby takes a nap.'

Barry gave me a sly smile, as he picked his way through the celandines, but I was more captivated by the look exchanged between Jed and Zoë. My heart clenched with envy.

They loved the house. All its old foibles seemed to make it all the more enchanting to them. And the open fire... well, Zoë nearly had a 'mmm coalblazinlogburninwoodsmokinhotheatinlovemakinlipsmakinrealfire' orgasm on the spot. The garden they thought was 'just heavenly', and Jed was already voicing his plans to renovate the neglected vegetable patch even as we were sauntering back toward the house. As we went up the steps to the house, they were a little ahead of us. Behind their backs Barry winked at me and mouthed, 'in-the-bag' giving me the thumbs up.

He was right, of course. Funny, though. It came as such a shock to realise that I would actually have to move out now. This was it. I was going to have to go.

The fine Victorian house opposite the park was reduced to a two- up-two-down terrace backing onto another row of two-up-two-down terraced houses, and facing another two-up-two down terrace opposite. I would've quite liked a flat really. They seem more anonymous, less pedestrian. But Thaddeus needed a garden, although the new backyard would be over-reaching itself to describe itself as such. Nevertheless, cats, as you know, have no boundaries, so I reckoned Thaddeus would have the run of everyone else's pocket backyard too.

'You're going to meet a somewhat more plebeian variety of feline than you've been used to,' I warned him as we sat disgruntled, several nights before the move, amongst the cardboard boxes stacked around us like oversized building blocks.

'No more Xanadu from number 20, or that Pudenda, whatever she's called. You know the one I mean, silly Persian, you like to hang out with - only allowed out in temperate weather.' Thaddeus pushed his high cheekbones firmly against the hard edge of a box, and, enjoying the sensation, began to rumble deep in his throat.

'Still, I'm sure you can hold your own,' I encouraged, scooping my hands under his belly to lift him onto my lap. He went into his limp plump horseshoe shape. Burying my face into his warm, dense, golden fur, I felt such a rush of love for him that I was quite taken aback.

I didn't like the new house much. In fact, I didn't like it at all: it smelt strange. Having declined to buy the previous owners' curtains and carpets, I found by some error of communication they had left them anyway. Now all my furniture and boxes were stacked on top of them, I wondered if I'd ever get rid of the random brown swirls, which reminded me of spiral galaxies, but only in shape, not beauty.

When the final box was laid down, I gave the removal men what I thought was a fairly generous tip, and I was left alone. Thaddeus, who'd refused to settle in his travelling cage, had been released and slunk upstairs for a sulk. I sat down on the arm of the sofa. Even without Marion's things, and all the stuff we'd discarded, the boxes seemed to completely fill the space of this house. If I had the courage, I'd take them all to the tip now. Not open a single one. Be free of it all. But I couldn't do that - sentimentalist that I was. So, I stared at the boxes for a bit longer.

Could I really make this my home, just by turning these boxes inside out? Tipping the innards of my life out of these containers, only to hang them on the walls; stack them neatly on bookcases, arrange the viscera of my life on shelves? The walls of this dismal little house stared down, disappointedly realising that it would never be loved. Not by me. I returned the disappointed gaze. I sensed its embarrassment in its shabby plum-coloured floral print dress and fallen pride that I did not appreciate walking with the universe beneath my feet, a feature so admired by the previous owners. I felt sorry for the house…just for a brief moment.

'It's hard for you too, I guess?' I said into the silence. I sat in the womb of this house, more like a malignant tumour than a cosseted safe little foetus.

'I won't stay here long, I promise,' I announced to myself and to the house. Still staring intently at the walls, to gauge their reaction, I began to listen to the sound of my breathing. It happens all by itself until you start to think about it. The more I listened to the soft sucking in and out of air, the harder it became. Soon there were long pauses followed by long heaving pulls of drawing oxygen into myself, and then a rapid expulsion of breath. Can you make yourself hyperventilate? Slowly a slight sensation of dizziness developed. I breathed in. Held my breath...held my breath...held my breath. Could I black out? Then I heard Marion say abruptly, 'Oh for goodness sake, Alec. Pull yourself together and go and make a cup of tea. Open a bottle. Stop being so pathetic.'

We'd found the kettle earlier. Well, the removal company had sent this pamphlet written in breathless tones of excitement about *Your Moving Day!* (which was in italics, with a couple of speed lines, to make it look like it was actually going somewhere itself.)

'The big day is here!' it announced at the top of its voice. Advice had included packing the kettle, tea bags, coffee, sugar and biscuits in a recognisable box, so you could easily locate it the other end. 'After all, you, your family and all the removal men will appreciate a well-deserved cuppa in your new home! And don't forget to pack a tin opener and a corkscrew! After all, you've done it! Your moving day is over! You might want to have a celebratory drink while starting your unpacking!'

I'd never seen a pamphlet so overloaded with exclamation marks. In fact, it had more explanation marks per sentence than anything else I'd ever read!!!

The water gushed harshly from the tap. Was it my imagination or was it tinged brown? I let it run for a while, filled the kettle and waited for it to boil. Slowly, steadily, noisily, it rumbled and whined to a crescendo. Outside a beautiful late June afternoon only served to remind me that somewhere, in a fine Victorian house overlooking the park, a young couple would also be boiling the kettle, looking out of their new kitchen window at this beautiful late June afternoon. I know they'll be admiring the buddleia bobbing in the breeze, each tiny perfect flower, forming part of the larger bloom of vibrant purple beauty... butterflies uncurling their tongues like tiny springs into the fragrant nectar, hoverflies dancing with dizzying uncertainty and bees droning through the warm sun-filled air. They'll take their tea outside and sit on the far bench in the shade of the poplar tree and hear its whispering leaves rustle with joy. Squirrels will race along the top of the fences, then scamper in jagged leaps up the rough bark of the oak tree, whose leaves are so fresh and green they dazzle you. In amongst the trees at the bottom of the garden, which provide total seclusion from the neighbours, cornflowers and saffron-coloured marigolds awaken lost memories of childhood. And in the flowerbeds, a myriad of late forget-me-nots dance and bubble like an iridescent river. By dusk, their mysterious luminosity will hold your heart. Catch your breath. But that's still to be discovered. For now, these two will just sit and glow in that warm corner of a piece of heaven that was mine until this morning. Looking upwards, they'll be delighted to see the clean-cut silhouette of house martins swirling and darting around the eaves of the house. And just as one would have hoped, the sun is beaming down into the southwest-facing garden, enriching the warm red brick of the house and the pale honey-coloured chimney pots, beneath the blue, blue sky.

Here the blue, blue sky sits behind the row of houses, which back onto my row of houses. I have less impression that it is sky, and more the feeling that it's a painted backdrop. You know the kind of thing - a clumsily painted flat, wobbling at the back of the stage in a local am-dram production of *Oliver!* (another abuse of the exclamation mark if you ask me!)

It's the *Who Will Buy?* scene and the answer to the pressing question of 'What am I to do to keep the sky so blue?' seems fairly obvious - pop down to your local DIY store and stock up on some more ghastly pots of 'sky blue'. I have a sneaking suspicion that shortly this unnaturally cheerful sky will be removed by two burly stage hands, and a darker more malevolent flat will wobble on - featuring the company's best attempt at 'a menacing night sky', beneath which the unfortunate Nancy can be brutally murdered. Annoyingly, this Bill Sykes thought prompts the memory of Oliver Read swaggering menacingly about, and a wide-eyed, straggly bearded Fagin, his coat tails flapping like wet seaweed, dancing around entreating, "No violence".

I try desperately to shake off this train of thought. I have a 'love-hate relationship' with musicals. Their utter ridiculousness appeals hugely to me, and I have whiled away many a dull moment, imagining bank managers, dinner ladies, and even Marion's gynaecologist once, bursting into song and putting serving trolleys or stirrups or whatever into good use during a vigorous song and dance routine.

The tunes are so irritatingly catchy. Even as I stare out of the window trying to empty my mind, Jack Wilde comes striding jauntily into view, kicking his heels, and chirpily suggesting that I *Consider myself...at home...*

'No thank you,' I reply, and push him into a barrow piled high with apples. One thing I know for sure, there'll be no singing and dancing here for a long while, possibly forever. Sorry, Thaddeus.

The houses must be all of twenty feet away. In one upstairs window opposite I can actually see the outline of a huge man through the frosted glass. From the length of time he stands there, approximately a minute, I guess he's peeing, and make a mental note to keep the blind in my bathroom permanently down.

Taking a sip of tea, I began to look for the box marked, 'Fragile - bottles!' Anyway, after a good ten minutes, I found it in the hallway. Some idiot had put it under another box marked 'Kitchen', which was itself covered up by a plastic bag full of damp bath towels.

When I returned to the kitchen to find the corkscrew, I realised there was now someone in the garden opposite. In the fading afternoon sun, a young mother, fag drooping from her lips, was pulling laundry from the washing line. Oh dear. At the top of her large arm was a red and black shape, which I could only assume was a tattoo. A fuchsia pink vest sporting some slogan in large black letters stretched across her low-slung bosom; the witty *mot juste* lost between the folds of her ample bosom and belly. At her feet, a toddler of indistinct sex, wearing nothing but a nappy, t-shirt and a pair of wellies, tugged at her denim skirt, while absent-mindedly sucking at a dribbly orange ice lolly. And to complete the picture - a Staffie snapped wildly at an empty plastic coke bottle, which it was chasing in frantic circles around the patchy lawn.

Suddenly, Thaddeus didn't seem quite so butch. In spite of the raggedy ear and the broken teeth, he was still a fat, fluffy, ginger mummy's boy at heart. The prospect of a permanent litter tray loomed fug-like in my mind. I was still locked into the memory of cat litter - thick, dark greyish moist clumps of it stuck to the bottom of the tray; scatterings of it flung around the kitchen floor as if a road gritting lorry had passed through the kitchen in the night; and the horrid sight and smell of cat poos, half emerging from the greying dust and granules, like a charred jointed finger pointing accusingly at the sky - when from the house adjoining mine, came the sudden blast of the theme tune to a TV quiz show.

'Yoooou jeeeeerst myyyte beeee luck, luck, lucky!' the host drawled, followed by a well-rehearsed retort from the audience: 'I'm gonna be luck, luck, lucky tonight!' I winced. So, this was to be my life…

The sun went down, the telly blared on, the neighbours that backed on to me had a row in the garden, and the dog, who'd ended up being shut out there when the row had gone screaming and banging indoors, set to barking – continuously. Then I heard someone else shouting, 'Will you get your fucking dog to shut the fuck up!'

While all this went on, I just sat and drank. Hours must've slipped by. I had yet to unpack the stereo, and as the TV had recently broken, I couldn't even block out the neighbours' noise with a blast of my own. However, at eightish, slumped in the dusky plum interior of number 25, I was startled by another noise - the doorbell. Well, I've already told you how I feel about doors, front doors, anyway. I was actually really scared. Perhaps, it was the man from the house backing on to mine, having finished arguing with his wife, thought he'd have a go at me. No doubt thinking it was me who'd told his dog to quieten down in no uncertain terms. God, the people I'd bought the house from had seemed so nice and normal, (even if they did have questionable taste in soft furnishings). Elderly couple, moving to a sheltered retirement bungalow on the coast, so as they could be nearer their daughter. They'd said nothing about the noise, the aggressive neighbours, nothing. The bell rang again more persistently. We've been here before, haven't we?

Without warning a sudden thrill began to rise rapidly within me; a mad, swirling, ridiculous hope, a bursting ball of light. I refused to give it life. I drowned it in a grain silo full of darkness. It choked. The extreme despair which followed felt more familiar. It was almost comforting. I knew where I was with despair. My journey into the gloom could continue undisturbed. The blackness of the tunnel resumed. The searing pain of the brightly lit station subsided. Don't respond. She isn't on the doorstep. She doesn't exist for you anymore. Just hold on. Eventually this ride will end when we run out of track and hit the wall. Just relax. We will pass one or two red lights shortly, but don't worry; this train cannot be stopped.

Just had to hold my nerve... the second bottle of cheap red was actually beginning to taste quite good by now, so I took a long deep gulp. Shit! The fucking doorbell rang again. Only this time it was followed by someone fiddling with the letter box. Now, I thought, he's posting something offensive through my letter box. What? ... A dog turd, of course. That's what he'd do. That type of person, in an area like this. I peeped around the corner of the living room door frame and in the faint light focused on the letter box. An eye flashed in the gloom.

'Alistair, you silly bugger, come and open the door. It's me, Tom.'

'Oh... sorry, Tom,' I yawned, stretching and shaking my head, 'must've dropped off, such a day.'

Then the smell hit me. Even before I'd opened the door

'Guess what?' he said. 'I've bought you your supper – fish 'n' chips!'

Chapter Twenty-nine: a pocket full of currants

Tom left just before midnight. I am indebted to Tom for many things in life, but on that occasion, he saved my life with a large portion of fish'n'chips. He'll never know it of course, but I think it's true.

During the evening, he helped me make up the bed and began to unpack some of the kitchen bits and pieces. He put the War and Peace figures on the glass fronted drinks cabinet, sorted out the stereo, and put one or two photographs around the place.

'You can always move stuff around later,' he said, filling a bookshelf with old volumes of Dornford Yates for which I had a nostalgic weakness.

Opening another box of containing poetry, he looked up at me and asked, 'You don't arrange these alphabetically, do you?'

'No.' I laughed as if this was an absurd notion, knowing later I'd have to arrange them chronologically.

'I'll be round tomorrow afternoon,' he assured me as we stood in the hallway. 'Now, you get off to bed. And Alistair...' he paused, his hand on the door handle. 'I know today's been particularly tough, but slow down on the booze mate; otherwise a year from now your social life will consist of nothing but AA meetings – and God how ghastly would that be? A whole bunch of new friends, and every single one of them on the wagon. What a bummer for New Year!'

I laughed half-heartedly. 'No chance.' Then placing my hand on his forearm said 'Thanks; for all your help. Really, Tom, you've no idea...well, thanks...' My voice faltered.

For a brief moment our eyes met; we could read each other's thoughts so easily. We hadn't mentioned Anna all evening... until that moment. There was an uncomfortable pause. And then...

'Better get back,' he said glancing uneasily at his watch. 'Eve'll be wondering -'

'Oh, yeah, of course,' I interrupted. 'You'd best get off.'

His large form lumbered down the road towards his car. 'Take heed of what I said Alistair,' he called back. 'And keep your pecker up!'

In the bedroom, I drew Mr and Mrs Burbridge's curtains. There was no lampshade as yet and the overhead light seemed blinding, so I turned it off and got undressed in the faint light from the landing. Only last night Mr and Mrs

Burbridge were lying here in this very room. Only last night, I had slept restlessly in the bedroom of my fine Victorian semi-detached, never to return... ever. And only last night, Jed and Zoë would have made love (in whatever way couples do when they're expecting) in their flat above the bakers, for the very last time. And all the others in our chain, the last time in a place we knew. A place we belonged to, that would forever hold a memory of us and all that we had been there.

Everyone, except me, would be full of nostalgia and anticipation. But my nostalgia was tainted with such failure, loss, and regret. It ached within me like arthritic bones on a damp November day. My anticipation rating was zero.

When I finally surrendered to sleep, somewhere between two and three in the morning, I must admit that I unexpectedly dreamt the kind of dream I enjoyed. A surreal, complex piece with a cast of thousands; all people I knew if only I could see through their disguise. I was sure the plot had been fantastical, if only I could remember it. I was being pursued. I remember that. And I flapped my arms while running away and soared into the air. I wasn't surprised. I always knew I could fly if I'd wanted to.

On waking, I discovered Thaddeus lying across my left leg, which was slightly dead with pins and needles. As I lifted him across the bed he began to purr heavily and then, blinking open his eyes, gave a great gaping yawn and stretched out, extending his claws from the tips of his toes. Content. Perhaps a night's sleep had done us both good.

Later that morning, I realised I would have to venture into the garden to put some rubbish in the bin. Last night's fish and chips didn't smell quite so appetizing and the litter tray was already nauseatingly crumbly and stank in that nasty 'meaty' way. Not pleasant.

However, I was waiting for an opportunity when the neighbours at the back of me were safely in their house (I couldn't face a confrontation) but they seemed to drift in and out their back door like flotsam in a scummy surf. They always had a cigarette hanging loosely from their mouths and he seemed able to continue to talk with it almost glued to his lip. I know I still smoked, but I had given up for a while when I was with Anna. She'd never really been a serious smoker and in the spring after Marion had left me, she suggested I give up. She couldn't stand the smell on my breath. Well, I had to give up, didn't I? But I can't say it was easy. However, that's another story. Stupidly, I was rather disgusted by others smoking; unfairly condemnatory, considering I was smoking again quite heavily myself. But then there was much that disgusted me about myself too.

Eventually, I thought I could see a window of opportunity and I opened the backdoor quickly to avoid letting Thaddeus out.

But just as much as I had been watching out for them, I think they were watching out for me. I had hardly lifted the lid from the bin when a voice launched its gravelly way in my direction. 'Mr Johnson? It is Mr Johnson, in't it?' The voice was so loud and penetrating I couldn't simply pretend not to have heard it, without having to feign stone deafness from that point onwards. I turned in the direction of the speaker, and sure enough my neighbour, still in fuchsia pink vest, was bowling up the garden towards the low fence, bosoms swinging freely. I waved my hand in an appeasing gesture, nervously perplexed that she knew my name.

'I'm right, aren't I? Yer Mr Johnson, eh? You were teacher down Uni?'

I nodded slowly, growing increasingly mystified. Lovely young lady that she was I had a sneaking suspicion she was not an ex-graduate of mine. How else could she know who I was?

'Yes... I am Mr Johnson ...' I confirmed, and offered my hand across the fence as my natural sense of good manners took over. 'But please, call me Alistair.'

'Pleased to meet you... Alistair.' she said somewhat bashfully, then clutching herself like a little girl added gleefully, 'I bet you're wondering how I know yer name.'

'Well, I eh...yes, I was.' I smiled at her, relaxing a little. She looked much younger up close, and in her present mode not threatening.

'Me mum came over late last night... She asked who'd moved in over the back.' She paused slightly, and looked from side to side as if checking the coast was clear. 'Well, to be honest, Mr Johnson, I'd seen you and another man at the bedroom window a little earlier, so I says, "A couple of old queens and a big ginger pussy,"- no offence - but she did laugh. Then I saw you again, down in the kitchen, and I said, "No, seriously, come an' look, there's one of 'em." She laughed even more when she saw *you*. She said "I don't think that man bats for the other side love! *That's* Mr Johnson."

Well, I was rather thrown at having my supposed sexuality decided on such flimsy evidence, but waved it off with devil-may-care air. (Did I really look like an old queen? I'm not sure what epithet bothered me most; the 'old' or the 'queen?) I don't think Tom would quite see the funny side so easily. Anyway, I could tell she was obviously bursting to divulge her information source. This was a tricky one. What a great fresh start. Who the heck could it be?

'I bet yer dying to know who me mum is?' she teased, twirling on one foot. Giving her, her moment, I laughed nervously.

'Oh, go on then. Who's rumbled me?'

'Mary!' she said triumphantly.

'Mary?' I repeated none the wiser.

'You know. Mary, me mum. She was one of yer cleaners, at Rectory Road... 'member?'

'Oh! Mary. Oh, yes. I remember Mary.' (Irish Mary, with the red face.)

'Well, she's me mum!'

Smiling, I shook my head in exaggerated disbelief, 'Small world!'

'She says she's gonna come round and say hello later. Says she'll give yer a hand to get sorted if you like. Says that me and Gary should introduce ourselves. She says you're a very nice man, Mr Johnson, er, 'Alistair' I mean.'

Some things in life are truly humbling. And meeting Mary's family was one of them. I knew I could be stuck up and snobbish. I wrote people off too easily. Made judgements based on the most superficial of evidence. I was wrong. Later that morning, my new neighbour whose name turned out to be Monica, invited me to climb over the low back fence and come and join her and Gary for a cup of tea. (She was apparently, Monica told me, named after Saint Monica, the patron Saint of alcoholics and disappointing children, making me laugh when she said, 'I mean what kind of mother names you after the saint of disappointing children? No wonder I didn't pass a single bleeding exam.')

They were both in their early twenties, both lacked qualifications and had messed around at school. I know this because it was one of the first things they said to me after asking how I liked my new house, which I lied very convincingly about. It was almost as if they had to apologise to me, as if they felt compelled to pre-empt any attack on them by spending life very obviously in the 'Nothing to Declare' lane. Neither of them had ever had a job, although Gary still went down the job centre most days.

'It ain't like we haven't tried, is it?' Monica said dispirited. She lifted a packet towards me, 'Another Jammie Dodger?'

I couldn't imagine what life would feel like to be twenty with no vision; no hope; no ambition. God, when I was twenty I thought I could be anything I wanted to be: the next F.R. Leavis or add my name to the list of great twentieth-century poets; or in my less deluded moments the least I saw myself as was a well loved and respected teacher of English literature, a sort of Mr Chips…without the sad bits.

All Gary wanted was a job, any job, but preferably one in a DIY store. He was good at DIY. He proudly showed me the kennel he'd constructed for Jemmy, the Staffie, and I have to admit it was well made.

'Is Jemmy short for Jemima,' I asked, thinking it seemed a slightly delicate name for the beast snorting grumpily in its sleep.

'No,' he grinned. 'It's just Jemmy. Like the crow bar.' He yawned noisily, and stretching skywards revealed his armpit hair, all pale and straggly. 'She's a lot better now. But when we first had her, she were a nightmare. Ripping into all t'furniture. Even took off a skirting board, and turned it int' pile o' wood chips!' Snarling, Gary made a frantic tearing gesture with his hands, and then grimaced into the kennel mouth. 'Yer barking mad, aren't yer?' He laughed.

'Ha!' I exclaimed and joined him in gazing indulgently at the boisterous hound of the Baskervilles stirring in its lair.

It seemed like a good opportunity to broach the subject of Thaddeus.

'No problem,' said Gary, waking Jemmy up by gently bonking her over the nose with a bit of twisted rope. 'Jemmy loves cats, don't you, girl? We had two cats when we got her, but one's gone walkabout, haven't seen it for weeks anyway, and t'other one, just sleeps under the bed all day.' Jemmy was too busy wrestling with the piece of rope clenched in her powerful jaws to make comment, but I was slightly reassured - slightly.

Over the coming weeks, Mary, Gary and Monica helped me survive. Mary, true to her word, dropped round that afternoon, to say 'hello'. She was on her way to the university. We shared several large gins together; well, Mary just had tonic on account of her rosacea and smoked three cigarettes in forty-five minutes. 'I don't know that you've ever noticed Mr Johnson, but I have a more than rosy glow about me sometimes. Now, I tell yer it ain't the drink! No. That sets it off terrible. One sip and it looks like I've attacked myself with a cheese grater!' I laughed and secretly thanked God that I didn't have such an allergic reaction to alcohol.

'There was a lot of nasty gossip down at the University, but I'm not a woman for gossip – and I don't judge people - that's for the Big Man. To tell the truth, I quite miss our little chats and I think you need a bit of looking after right now. Am I right or am I right?'

My mouth fragrant with lemon and juniper opened to speak, but Mary had drawn all the breath she needed in a microsecond.

'Now, the first thing is the wallpaper, I think. Mrs Burbridge was a lovely lady, but she did have a soft spot for floral prints Mr Johnson, didn't she? Not what a *man* wants, is it now?' she added with a wink.

Over the next few days, she dropped in and out of my life helping to transform the plummy interior into something more suitable. One evening we stripped the wallpaper until it hung in clumps from the naked plaster, like 'weed in' raggedy bloomers. Another morning, Mary and Gary hung the new wallpaper (Mary being the most frightening vision on a ladder I have ever seen). I'd chosen a calming sage-green interspersed with a tiny racing green fleur-de-lis motif. Deemed too useless at everything else, I was given the job of pasting. Meanwhile, Mary declared proudly that decorating was her hobby.

'Every room in my house is decorated once every three years on a rota. And I keep my place spotless, Mr Johnson. Empty the ashtrays three times a day. And that's the truth, isn't it, Gary?' I have to say she and Gary were as skilled as any professional in this wallpapering malarkey.

When we'd also hung a few prints from my former life, Mary announced it looked like a 'bleeding gentleman's club.' 'We'll all need a smoking jacket to come here now!' She laughed. 'Well, it'd be nice to sit and relax with a fag. You can't smoke in-doors at Monica's. The babby's asthma's too bad these days.'

I offered to pay them, but Mary was quite affronted. 'You'll do no such thing, Mr Johnson. It's been our pleasure - hasn't it, Gary?'

'Yeah.' He shuffled awkwardly from foot to foot. I think he could've done with the cash. Later in the week, I bought him a power drill as a 'thank you' present. 'Brilliant! It's brilliant...but, it was a favour, to a neighbour like.'

'Well, put it to good use,' I said. Giving and receiving of presents always embarrassed me.

At night, Thaddeus slept on my feet, tired from his excursions around his new territory... so far, so good. But I still breathed a sigh of relief when I heard the cat flap bang as he shot back into the kitchen. Jemmy's love of cats was not apparent to me, unless I was misunderstanding her persistent snarling and barking at Thaddeus, as he sat on the roof of Gary's tiny shed. To me it looked as though Jemmy thought Thaddeus had a passing resemblance to a skirting board, but I may be wrong. Anyway, Thaddeus wasn't as daft as he looked. He was a bit of a tease really. I once heard him hiss out the corner of his mouth, *'O keep the Dog far hence.'* I had to laugh; the move had obviously brought out his mischievous side. He had quite a sense of humour really.

His presence took the edge off my loneliness and sorrow, which at night lay like a raw open wound. Some hours of the night are interminable. I prayed that death would not involve anything like eternal life... I have seen enough of eternity between the hours of two and five in the morning to last me a lifetime - and beyond. I could not bear that bit in the requiem mass, 'Rest eternal grant them, O Lord; and let light perpetual shine upon them.' Whoever wrote that had never suffered from insomnia. Who could possibly rest for eternity with a bloody light shining on them? No. Eternal life was obviously the long night of never-ending insomnia. I longed for dreamless sleep. Total darkness. Oblivion.

2.13 am: Time would not pass. Sometimes it stood motionless; the hands on the clock frozen. I watched each minute struggle to the next, only to arrive exhausted... rest for hours... before setting off reluctantly to the next minute. In the dim, dark-grey blackness of the night, I studied the swirls of Artex on the ceiling. Just like the living room carpet, this ceiling held a grim wonder for me. Our galaxy was, I'd decided, just to the left of the central light which I designated as God, the creator. I felt we should be near to him. Somewhere in this galaxy, this solar system, this planet, this country, somewhere... Anna lay sleeping. I curled my body protectively around hers. Sorry. Oh, Anna. I am so sorry.

But at the end of these nights, during the hours of the day, my neighbours made it bearable for me. In many ways I felt cared for. Even the noisy next-door neighbour turned out to be a deaf old man name Bill, who at eighty-six still kept an allotment. Once, he gave me a little bunch of asparagus. It was the finest I had ever tasted.

After the first few weeks of unpacking and decorating, I saw less of Mary, but she'd climb awkwardly over the back fence from time to time, banging on the backdoor with her thick knuckles; her heavy red cheeks wobbling. It must've been sometime in July when she'd clambered over the fence clutching a rhubarb crumble and a small jug of cream, reminding me of a contestant from 'It's a Knock-out', that it happened…

There was one box I had been avoiding opening: a Pandora's Box whose contents I knew only too well. It was quite heavy. I knew the weight wasn't the reams of paper, but the old typewriter that lay upon the wallet of papers. On my moving day, that box, along with Thaddeus' travelling cage and a few photo albums, were the only items that travelled with me in the car. I'd put the box in the corner of my wardrobe, where it had stayed lodged against that back panel for weeks. There, in that most magical of places, it waited, leaning heavily against the one surface in every child's imagination, which held such hope, followed by such bitter disappointment - the back panel of the wardrobe. Come on, admit it. I can't be the only person, man and boy who's flung suits and jackets apart in the mad desperate longing that this time it would be true. Just once to feel the rush of cold air against my face and glimpse the faint glow of a street lamp through a swirl of snow.

So there, my Pandora's Box sat, poised between two worlds: one possible, one impossible. Its whispering contents, only half-formed. Most of the time, I could ignore it. But today, for some reason, I'd pulled it from the darkness and carried it carefully downstairs into the light of the sitting room.

I studied the box from every angle - **This way up**. Through the open window, I could hear a few birds chirruping as they sat on the rotary washing line. A shaft of sunlight seemed to hit the box directly, and swirling in the light, a million pieces of matter danced in frantic eddies. From dust you are and to dust you will return. A good part of me had already returned to the dust. It isn't a process which only happens at the end of your life. It happens every day; from the day you were born. I blew into my dust. It spun frantically, falling in every direction. In space you can fall forever. But not here - on Earth - because we have a sign: it says '**This way up**.' And there is only one way to fall: down. I know this.

I am still falling now.
Maybe it is possible to fall forever?

Maybe not.

Using a kitchen knife to cut through the packing tape, I then folded back the cardboard flaps. The typewriter felt strangely cold in the warm air, but I loved its weight. It was a very comforting weight. It felt like it looked. I didn't like things, which were unexpected in their weight. You know, like when you brace yourself to pick up what you think is a heavy case and nearly give yourself a hernia, because it's actually empty. That's why I loved Thaddeus so much. He looked like a big fat cat, and he was just that. No illusion.

The typewriter's feet pressed into the Andromeda galaxy. I always sat in the centre of the Milky Way. Again, it was just to the left of the central light, and could further be identified by the distinctive brown coffee stain on its uppermost spiralling arm.

As these were the only two galaxies I knew, the box sat on an unknown galaxy.

After some time, I knelt forward again, reached into the box and fished out the wallet from the bottom. It wasn't that thick really. A hundred or so pages of life don't amount to very much. The next thing I did, I suppose is a little obvious - I began to read. Although almost every sentence about Anna shot through me as if delivered from a cross-bow, I began to connect to feelings of such intense happiness that I was quite overwhelmed. It was while reliving my hotel bath time with Anna, that I was interrupted by the familiar cement mixer tones of my good neighbour, Mary.

'Are you there, Alistair?' she hollered, 'cos I'm coming over if that's alright?' Slightly flustered, I stood up, sheaf of papers still in hand, just in time to see the equally overwhelming sight of the Mary cocking one of her swollen legs over the fence. Hastily, I made my way through the kitchen, to the open the back door for her. Mary's face was the same colour as the aforementioned rhubarb.

'Oh! It's a warm one today for sure,' she panted. 'This lovely bit o' rhubarb's from Bill's allotment. He gave it to Monica, but she doesn't know nothing about fruit that don't come out of a tin marked pie filling! So, I've made three crumbles: one for them, one for Bill, and one for you. Oh, and here's a spot of cream left over from what Monica had.'

'Really Mary, you're too kind. Come on in, I'll make us some tea. I was just about to have some.'

'You! Drink tea? That'll be a first!'

'Now, I'm not as bad as you like to make out,' I reprimanded her while filling the kettle.

'I hope not, Alistair, I sincerely do.' She glanced about the room hopefully. 'You wouldn't have a spare fag, would you? Not enough hands, what with bringing the crumble an' all.'

While I made the tea, she stood in the doorway of the kitchen grilling her flesh in the sun. Little scarlet spidery veins crept this way and that under the glossy crimson sheen of her cheeks. I imagined her lungs like two fiery furnaces radiating redness and heat through every capillary, through every pore. Mary blew smoke into the air with such a sense of purpose and satisfaction it was as if she thought she was adding something to the loveliness of the summer's afternoon. Her exhalations were white petals flying from her mouth in a tumultuous tumble. They span like enormous soft snowflakes. One could hardly see through them...blindingly beautiful; soft against your skin. Drifts of them banked up on the kitchen window ledge. Disintegrating now, crumbling into a fine powder, that slipped over the edge and poured like an elegant, soundless, waterfall.

She watched me making the tea, while deliberating on whether to paint her own kitchen sunburst yellow or peachy peach. Then she stubbed out her cigarette and with her usual rolling gait waddled across the kitchen towards me. She sipped the boiling tea without hesitation, and nodding casually towards the papers I had laid down on the kitchen table, she asked with typical directness, 'So what's this then? You not got marking any more, have you?'

'No, no... this isn't marking.'

'Well, what is it then?' she said squinting in the sun. 'You're not writing a book or something, are yer?'

I smiled and shrugged, 'Shall we take our tea outside or inside?'

'I need some shade for a bit.' Mary wiped her sausagey fingers across her brow. 'Phew. That's a very hot sun.'

We sat in my 'gentleman's club' as Mary liked to call it and she lit another of my cigarettes. I had one too.

'Are you not going to tell me, then?'

'Tell you what?'

'What you're writing.' She waved her fag in the direction of the typewriter which sat squat and solid on the floor like a mechanical toad. 'I don't have to be Sherlock Holmes to work out you're doing a bit o' writing now, do I? I can't help being a bit nosey that's all – 'tis in the blood. Now, is it your memoirs? A novel? I like a good read meself. So come on, what is it?'
For the first time I had to ask myself the same question. What was I writing?
'It's just some ideas…a few thoughts.'
'Tuh! That looks like you got more than a few thoughts there.'
'Well, a few thoughts strung together with a lot of words.'
'You're writing a novel, aren't you?' Mary said knowingly. 'Don't be shy now, you can tell me.'
'It's not really a novel, no… And, I've given up on it now, anyway.'
'Given up! Whatever for?'
'It's hard to explain, and what with moving and everything…' My voice petered out, but Mary's didn't.
'Oh, dear God, no. You can't be doing that. No. I like things to be done properly. And to be done properly they have to be finished.' She pulled herself forwards in her chair and leant across towards me. 'I think this is very important, Alistair, to finish things. Take decorating for instance. If I get half way through stripping a room and think oh, bugger it, I have had enough of this and go off to do something else, all I've done is make things look worse, not better. Only when it's properly finished do you get to feel satisfied with anything.'
To start arguing that some things were not so black and white would have been futile. So, I found myself agreeing with Mary. All unfinished articles in life were useless, if not totally worthless. She thought of countless examples of course, from half-cooked roast pork dinners to jumbo jets. Even people were an unfinished work in progress, she insisted, for whom 'The good Lord, himself, would provide the final topcoat.' After life has given us a good rub down with a bit of coarse sandpaper, no doubt.
I guess she had a point really.
'So,' she said emphatically, 'if I've learnt anything in life, it's to finish what you've started. And if you don't want to live in a room half-stripped for the rest of your life, Alistair, I suggest you get back to bashing them keys.'

She struggled from her seat and stood gazing down at the scattered papers resting by my typewriter. With her white twisted toes, with their red painted toenails splayed out over her rubber flip-flops, a painful bunion protruding so close to my words, a slither of disgust trembled through me. I thought my typewriter can see right up Mary's skirt at the moment. I pictured her enormous, lumpy, dimpled thighs…and a lot more besides. In fact, for some reason, unknown to me, I visualized her completely naked - it was terrible. There was no hope for me. Even with the most well-intentioned, kindest of people I was a lost cause. My mind took me places I never wanted to go. 'Stop it!' I suddenly shouted out.
 Mary threw a look at me, her face looking as alarmed as I felt.
 'Oh, I wasn't reading it or anything. I can't see without me glasses anyway.' She sounded embarrassed and apologetic.
 'No, it's nothing you've done, Mary. I don't know why I said that,' I lied.
 'It just came out…Probably spending too much time on my own…'
 She gave me a curious stare, and then said softly, but firmly, 'Write your book love. Get it out your system. Whatever it is - finish it. You'll feel a whole lot better.'

Chapter Thirty: What you get married for if you don't want children?

So here goes. On the advice of my ex-cleaning lady I attempt to finish what I started. To be rubbed down repeatedly with sand paper until I am through, ready for my eternal gloss paint, which at this point in my life I can honestly say I am quite happy to live and die without. To spend forever unfinished and imperfect didn't seem such a bad option. At least one wouldn't spend eternity in a state of perpetual smugness. But for those of you, like Mary, who love decorating know, preparation is everything; and I have hardly been washed down with sugar soap yet - let alone got down to the real nitty-gritty.

How beautiful it is to return to the past: to enter a room in your mind so glorious... to be in a 'before' time, when anything seemed possible. There are so many rooms in my mind where I open a door to find Anna standing there. It is almost as if she has come to inhabit every memory I ever had. In recent months I've tried so hard to keep all doors firmly shut. But now I have given myself permission. I wander down the corridors of my mind, like a child blindly running my hands over the mysterious contents of a pre-dawn Christmas stocking. I'm looking for a moment, when potential was everything. When I did not know what outcome awaited me. Softly padding along… You see, there's one very special feeling I want to reconnect to. (Look at me - A heart so gripped by joy- This is the 'before' time.)

Ah! Listen… did you hear that? There, again!

'Find me…' I hear her whispering playfully. 'Find me, Alistair.'

I found her… A smile spread through every corner of my being…Here, the two of us, hiding beneath the Indian print quilt. It was a funny little habit we had - chatting under the covers.

'Italy?'

'Yes. Do you fancy it?'

'Where in Italy?'

'Tuscany; a little village, high in the mountains. You'll love it - I know you will.'

'Just you and me?'

'Just you and me...'

Making a rude and unwelcomed entrance, another memory barged in through the thin walls of my mind.

'Marion! What are you doing here?'

'Just come to collect a few things, Alec. You knew I was coming. We discussed it on the phone two days ago.' She was standing on the doorstep, wearing a safari suit - she knew me so well - 'Don't even think about it, Alistair,' she warned striding down the hallway. 'It was a present from Edward. He thinks I look very handsome in it.' (Since when did Marion like looking 'handsome'?) I followed her around the house, while images of Marion astride a swaying elephant popped in and out of my head. She hunted around the house for the items from our home, which she felt, were hers. There were very few things she wanted really, apart from her record collection, which I wasn't sorry to see the back of anyway, one or two prints, masses of books, her mother's grandfather clock, which she'd get an antique firm to move later, a few *objets d'art*. We argued briefly over a framed photograph of Thaddeus as a kitten.

(He was about ten weeks old, and was peering out from the washing machine. This had been preceded by Marion and me frantically thinking we'd lost him. The hour or so before we found him, the accusations had flung between us like a tirade of bullets. 'Did you leave the backdoor open when you put those scraps out for the birds, Alec?'

'Could he have climbed out of the downstairs' toilet window, Marion? - You left it open after that nasty bout of diarrhoea you complained about this morning.' How could our parenting skills have become undone so quickly? It was while standing silently in the kitchen, with her eyes full of anxious tears, Marion heard a familiar rumble. 'Alec! Come here! I can hear him. Thaddeus is somewhere in here...' It didn't take us long to locate him, curled up happily on a jumble of clothes, Marion had loaded in the machine earlier. Thank goodness we didn't put the washing on, she'd sighed. Thaddeus woke up, blinked, stretched and yawned, his tiny needle teeth white and pure. She was just about to grab him, when I suggested taking a photo. He looked so adorable; he really did. So, this was the photograph, his fluffy inquisitive face peering at us from the porthole of the washing machine. In that instant, we both knew that he meant more to us than we could ever fully express to one another.)

'But Alec you have the real thing,' she said forcefully, wrapping Thaddeus's image in some tea towels she was obviously also attached to.

'But it was my idea to take the photograph.' In spite of my best efforts to sound reasonable, this had come out like a child's whine. She gave me 'the look'.

Defiantly, I added, 'It is the best one we've got of him that small.'

She rolled her eyes. 'OK Alec. OK…I'll get you a copy done, all right?' She continued bustling around the room gathering up her life with me.

'Where is Thaddeus by the way? I hope you've been looking after him properly.'

'I guess he's in the garden. You know how he loves to lounge about outdoors once the weather warms up.'

'I must see him before I go. I'm presuming you *did* take him to the vet last week for his cat flu jab, didn't you?'

She was gazing out the window now hoping to catch a glimpse of him, her new safari suit, starched, stiff, and ridiculous. Marion…in spite of everything she still drew something from my heart. In a jokey, affectionate way I ventured,

'How on earth does Edward cope with having you permanently in his life, Marion?'

Reflected in the glass, a fleeting smile danced across her face. For a brief moment I glimpsed the memory of something vaguely attractive about her. Suddenly, the laughter lines around her eyes touched my heart; I noticed her chrome yellow hair had been toned down to a more becoming ash blond; and her mouth looked softer, less judgemental. Still staring out of the window, she said slowly, 'I'm an altogether different person when I'm with Edward.'

'I know,' I said, because I did know. Something in me suddenly understood something quite profound, and I surprised myself by saying, 'Perhaps that's why you love him so much,' which Marion could've easily taken the wrong way. But for once she was perfectly attuned to my thoughts.

Gently, I placed my hand on her shoulder - she reached up and held my hand in hers. Then quite without precedent, lay her head upon our two joined hands and brushed a kiss across my fingers.

'Yes,' she mused, 'it's true. It's not just the other person we love for their own sake, is it? It's the person they make us become that we really fall in love with, isn't?'

She broke free of my hand and turned to face me.

'I'm sure you've found that you are a much better person with Anna than you ever were with me. The person you always thought you should be - wanted to be. Am I right?'

I smiled in acknowledgement.

'You and I never could bring out the best in one another, could we?'

'No. Not very often; but we tried for long enough, didn't we?' She sort of laughed as if our past lives were a fondly remembered comedy show. We broke apart again, and she continued to gather her strange assortment of things, which were packed unceremoniously into grocery boxes.

That was the last moment of physical affection that passed between Marion and me.

There isn't much to say about the rest of May and June, except that they were very busy months. Anna was studying for exams and I was constantly harassed by students from all year groups, who were panicked about one thing and another. Most had just realised too late that they just simply hadn't had put in enough work. So many chickens came home to roost in those few summer months it was like a mass domestic fowl migration. In addition to all this activity, it was particularly fine weather, and nothing seemed crueller than exams and extended essay deadlines spoiling what should have been the most halcyon and carefree days. These were not my favourite months at work.

However, it was so completely bearable this year. I had evenings to spend with Anna, although often helping her revise, coupled with the exhilarating prospect of a long, hot, summer in Italy -together. The regrets of a few over-indulgent third years couldn't touch me this year. My star was in the ascendant. I was soaring.

Chapter Thirty-one: The time is now propitious

It fell to me to organise all the practicalities for our trip: tickets, passports in order; the Morris had to have a full service and be declared fit for travel; and Thaddeus was introduced to a new sitter in the shape of Xanadu's owner, with whom I had recently become friendly. All set then.

I have never felt as excited as we set out together at 4.00am that morning to head down for the ferry port. The dawn, such a rare sight to both of us, was stunning. A pale ivory-gold sun, at first shimmering, fragile and uncertain, hovered at the edge of the world. Then with increasing power, it rose over the brim of the earth; its wavering form becoming more defined. It was so clean and reborn... and yet... it had never died. Against the dark horizon of the countryside, the sky bled into layers of golden ochre, flecked with pale apricot. And the sky rose above us, a hesitant greyish cornflower blue, streaked with clouds that had been brushed by the wind into soft peach-coloured wisps.

'Have you ever seen such a dawn?' I breathed.

'I can't remember,' Anna said.

'Then you can't have done. Otherwise you would remember.'

'I guess so.'

Our journey down through France was delightful, but fairly uneventful: the car behaved impeccably; the hotels perfectly adequate for one night - although the one just outside of Dijon had been such a study of idiosyncrasy, both in its décor and staff, one might well have expected to have encountered one or two characters from a certain famous French fairy tale wandering down its corridors.

Each morning however, we ventured further south, fully replete with croissants and coffee. We had the car windows down, wore flattering sunglasses and flew along to a selection of tapes Anna had made especially for the journey. Some were a classical mix, others a collection of rock and pop tunes, but I didn't mind that; I wasn't a total stuffed shirt. In fact, we went through the Mont Blanc tunnel to a Bowie track I loved, and there was plenty on Anna's uplifting 'Guilty Pleasures' cassette to sing along to when exuberant spirits got the better of us. ABBA featured quite often, although I have to say there was something strangely heart-rending about some of the tracks Anna had selected. Nevertheless, the overall effect was joyous. Marion and I never sang together, the only exception being various church services, lustily belting out *Jerusalem* or mournfully droning in unison on the subject of walking in 'death's dark vale' during funerals. What a difference with Anna. Without a moment's self-consciousness we sang out together. Her voice pure and lilting, mine growing in confidence following her lead.

Happiness ran in my veins.
It was in every breath I took.
I could taste it on the warm breeze.

Then at last…Italy. How I loved her. A country shaped like a high-heeled kinky boot and every bit as sexy. Places like England and Germany were such masculine countries if one could categorise places by gender, but Italy, she was a fantastic woman of a country. I adored her. She was a woman whose skin was warm and golden bronze from the Mediterranean sun, who loved to sit outside in the balmy evening heat, with red wine, olives, olive oil, pizza with meltingly soft mozzarella, a sudden tangy saltiness of anchovies. She rides a Vespa, and bathes in the sea at Amalfi, and when she speaks, she sounds like a siren…she will seduce you to your death with her beauty.

Eventually, we wound our way up through the hillsides, and trundled slowly down the narrow roads leading to Tom's parents' villa. It was already past one o'clock in the morning and the village was silent and almost entirely in darkness. After some difficulty with the key, we entered the unlit vestibule - there, at last. The villa interior was relatively cool, with its thick stone walls and shutters blocking out much of the day's heat. With as little sound as possible, we unpacked the car and, after Anna had enjoyed an exciting exploration of the villa with which she immediately fell in love, we traipsed upstairs exhausted. It had been a very long and tiring, hot day's driving.

Tom had suggested we slept in the main bedroom, because not only did it have its own bathroom, but also the finest view. An ancient traditional iron bedstead, with an oval painting depicting *The Assumption of the Blessed Virgin Mary,* mounted centrally between its bars, sat squarely facing the shuttered window.

'Good grief! That's going to be a bit off-putting, isn't?' laughed Anna when she noticed the serene-faced virgin looking heavenwards above the pillows.

'At least she's averting her eyes.'

'Still…not every cherub is,' said Anna uneasily.

There was nothing to embarrass 'Our Lady' that night anyway, or cause any cherub to hide his eyes beneath his wing: I was shattered. Three days of travelling, albeit at a fairly leisurely pace, had taken its toll. Thankfully, Tom had organised for a local woman to act as a housekeeper when required and the bed was all ready, expertly made with exquisitely fresh, clean, white cotton linen. After a brief shower, I slipped between the cool, soft sheets and felt my body dissolve into a state of complete blissful relaxation. There was hardly time to register the crickets' night-music or the slightly annoying sound of a dripping tap in the bathroom, before I was lost in a peaceful slumber.

When I awoke, I instinctively reached out for Anna, but she wasn't next to me. The air was already warm and the room flooded with light. Sitting up, squinting into the morning sun, I realised Anna was sat in the deep window recess gazing out at the view. The shutters were folded right back and one could already hear a few indistinct Italian voices rising with the heat. Quietly, I turned back the light counterpane and stood on the cool tiled floor. Softly, I paced across the room. Gently, I placed my hands on her shoulders and leaning my body against her back, joined her in beholding the sight that lay before us. Anna still stared outward.

It was indeed magical to have arrived late at night, when one could see nothing beyond the walls of the villa, and to witness this moment of transformation. Now, drowning in early morning sunlight lay one of the most beautiful sights I have ever seen. I committed it to my memory then and can still see it all now.

As one looked out beyond the rough texture of the stone walls *where sat we two, one another's best,* layer upon layer of breath-taking beauty rolled out before us: a litany of beauty processing before our eyes. In the immediate foreground, the garden spread out below us, dotted with huge terracotta pots overflowing with an abundance of flame-red flowers. On the edge of the garden, a group of ancient gnarled and twisted olive trees stretched their aching, old limbs towards the sun. They teetered on the edge of steep vine-covered terraces, which dropped in waves down the hillside. Clawing desperately at the sky, the trees seemed to be trying to hold on - keeping the inevitable slide downward at bay. In the valley below, the dark green tips of cypress trees pushed themselves through the mist, erect and stately, like rows of giant asparagus. And the mist itself, fine, cobwebby, hiding some yet to be revealed treasures beneath its soft veil of organza. Beyond the mist, far, far away, rose the distant mountains. The air already hummed and droned with insects, and in the midst of the valley I could make out the distinctive shape of a bird of prey, effortlessly circling on the thermals; its haunting cry, like an icicle, dropping through the incandescent sky.

'I knew you'd love it,' I whispered, stroking Anna's hair. More than ever she resembled a medieval princess, sitting rapt in wonder, a halo of light surrounding her. She said nothing, but turned and kissed me. She rose and took several steps towards the bathroom, then turned her head to me. 'It's just perfect, isn't it?' she said, echoing my thoughts.

Now I don't want this to end up sounding like a travelogue so I'm going to be economical with the tales of our time in Italy. It will suffice to say for the moment that the first week or so was the happiest of my entire life. If Marion and I could've made a holiday here a trip to the Underworld, it goes without saying that with Anna it was an excursion to Elysium.

Every day the sun blazed, while we lay drowsily in its heat. Occasionally, the peace was disturbed by the loud thrum of an enormous petrol-coloured beetle, the Chinook of the bug world, clumsily circumnavigating the garden, or the incessant frenzy of cicadas frantically playing their high-speed maracas. Apart from these intruders, and other less demanding creatures, the entire garden was our dominion.

Once or twice, we ventured down to the market in town and returned with bagfuls of luscious ripe fruit and vegetables bursting with readiness. At lunchtime, these accompanied a glass or two of wine, an array of interesting cheeses, air-dried hams and sausages, and bowls brimming with glistening green and black olives. After an extended lunch, we settled by the pool reclining like two over-fed lizards – not like lizards in appearance (hopefully) just our languor – our need to soak up the sun to live.

To be honest, the sun got a bit much for me in the afternoon, so I had to lie in the shade of a massive vine, which had been trained along a rustic wooden pergola. I used to look up through the feathery greenness of the vine leaves at the blue, blue sky above me. My eyes would trace the twisting chartreuse green tendrils that frayed around, little wild spiralling helix searching for purchase. I was like a resplendent Bacchus, who had nothing better to do than gaze in wonder at these ripening juvenile globes, while drinking in their ancestors. Big clusters of grapes dangled above my head; they were so firm and tight at that moment, but in a few months....

In between times I read novels, or from behind the darkness of my sunglasses watched Anna swimming, snake-like through the water. It was very private round the back there and her bare skin had the lustre of pure gold beneath the surface of the pool. If I could choose, just one week of my life to relive over and over again until the end of time, that would be it.

Anna, can you believe it, had only ever been abroad once before; a school trip to Normandy in her fourth year. Her family had always taken holidays in Britain, as finances didn't allow for foreign travel; furthermore, her mother had an acute fear of flying. It had been a tense few days waiting for Anna's parents to allow her to travel to Italy; but Anna had spun a fairly convincing white lie about coming to stay here with an Italian girl she'd met at university, who was also studying English. 'I feel we should speak to her parents about it first,' her father had protested. 'just to check it's convenient to them and so on.'

'Dad, I'm twenty soon. I don't need you to communicate on my behalf. Anyway, you don't speak Italian and they don't speak English. Please. Luisa is lovely. She'll look after me and I'll help her and her family with their English.' It sounded a wonderful arrangement, didn't it? However, as the date of our departure grew nearer, I felt increasingly uneasy about this deception. 'Why can't you just tell him the truth? Are you embarrassed by me?' She laughed aloud at this suggestion.

'Of course, not.... but ... it would worry them unnecessarily. What they don't know can't hurt them.' I pointed out that this implied they would have a negative reaction to me as their daughter's suitor.
'I love you,' I said emphatically. 'I'll always look after you. I'll *always* love you.' I didn't add, 'What more could they want?' but I guess it was implied in my tone. Studying my face closely, she sighed.

'Try to see things from other people's point of view occasionally.'
'I thought I was.'
'Never mind, Alistair. You do your best.' Anna picked up another pile of postcard revision notes she'd made herself and begun to shuffle them like a deck of cards, 'They're quite happy with the Luisa story. I don't want them to know I've lied.' She thrust the cards towards me. 'Go on. Pick a card. Test me.'

'It's blank.' I held it up, turning it this way and that.

'Trust you to pick one I haven't written yet.'

Yes, so as I was saying, this was Anna's first time abroad, (unless you count the Fourth years' wet October Normandy experience - the Bayeux tapestry, followed by endless 'ambougeur and frites, and spotty youths practising their *bonjours* on school-trip weary local shopkeepers.)

Visiting a country like Italy for the first time, I told Anna, is like falling in love. And every time you return to her, your love will be rekindled with all the passion of the first flush of love. 'Isn't it true?' I had asked her one evening, while eating out at a bijou restaurant on the edge of town overlooking the hillside. 'Don't you feel you're falling in love with her?' I paused briefly from my devoted attention to a particularly succulent dish of pasta with a wild boar sauce pungent with juniper berries, 'Aren't you seduced by every sight and sound around you?'

'Not forgetting smell...and taste of course.' Anna pointedly lifted her glass of wine to her lips.

'Well, naturally,' I agreed, my eyebrows flicked up and down knowingly.

She smiled warmly at me. 'This country, Italy, brings out the *bon viveur* in you like no other, doesn't it?'

'It doesn't take much I'm afraid to reveal the true me. Such an easy lay for all things sensual.'

'I could almost believe you're more in love with this country than you are with me?'

'No, no, never,' I replied shaking my head vehemently. 'She enhances your beauty for me, makes me love you even more.'

'Perhaps, we should all have a threesome sometime?'

'We already are,' I said with a lascivious smile spreading across my face.

'Really, Mister Johnson! For the first time since I've known you, I do believe you're drunk!' She was staring at me absolutely wide-eyed, with disbelief. 'You're pissed, aren't you?' I furrowed my eyebrows and held up my right hand with my thumb and forefinger hovering a centimetre or so from one another, 'Just a little.' I assured her, squinting at the tiny gap. 'This little much.'

She didn't care of course. She wasn't like Marion, who always clambered onto her high horse, for a good old gallop about, if she even got a whiff of public intoxication. Anna was free of all the boring middle-class restraint - its false niceties. 'But you're always over-doing it, Marion,' I shouted back at her once, after a particularly intense chastisement. (Yes - the dinner party at one of her publishing friends, when drink had emboldened me to play the devil's advocate and I upset the host's young and under-confident wife. She had just sung the praises of Dickens, and I, just for fun, proclaimed Dickens to be an overrated windbag, whose prose held great troughs of tedious page filling guff - well, I was very drunk at the time. It all ended in tears – yes, really! Mmm, that particular occasion had sent Marion on an all-day hack.)

'But not in public, Alec,' she berated, cantering in from the kitchen. 'That's the difference! Growing up, you see, is knowing when and where you can be off your guard; when you're allowed to be the broken dysfunctional mess we all are, and when it's right and proper to keep that mess hidden away.'

'That just makes everything we are, everything everyone is, a bloody lie!'

'Yes! You've got it Alec. And *that's* how it is, my dear. *That's* what makes it all work.'

Thank goodness Anna could drive. She hadn't been drinking quite so much since we'd come away, said she felt dehydrated if she had too much red wine. Never been like that before, I guess it must've been the heat, as she wasn't used to it. Anyway, we meandered up the hillside back to the village safely enough, and in spite of being as Anna had rightly observed, 'unusually drunk,' I managed to give the performance of a lifetime, even though I say it myself. What about 'Our Lady' and her chubby cherubs? Well, Anna had draped a bra over the portrait, to spare their blushes. We just had to remember to take it off on Wednesdays when the housekeeper called to clean, and change the linen.

The next morning, I awoke to the now familiar sight of Anna sitting in the window meditating on the wonderful vista stretched out before her. I'd been dying to make some witty *bon mot* invoking *A Room with a View*, but as yet everything I thought of just seemed corny and stupidly obvious, so I'd shelved that idea. But every morning the same thought popped into my head like an annoying riddle that wouldn't go away. Reluctantly, I pushed Forster and his entire pension of guests back into their box, until tomorrow morning or at least until the evening, when Anna also liked to stare, and stare. 'You'll never tire of it,' I yawned, propping myself up on pillows, like a sick child on a day bed.

'No, I don't think I could.' She answered without looking round.' So, Alistair, how are you this morning?'

'Surprisingly well - fine, actually.' Pouring a glass of water for myself, from a jug on the bedside table, I took a sip. 'Ah, that's better. Now, I think the problem is I keep ordering all this wine, thinking it's for two of us, and you're not keeping up to speed, so I end up drinking more than I realise.'

She spun round with a face of mock anger. 'Oh, so the fact you can't control your drinking and are perpetually hung-over is my fault, is it?'

'No. But you used to drink more, in England… and I guess I keep drinking your share.'

Anna walked across the room to the bed. She was only wearing a thin white t-shirt, and as the sun lit her from behind, I could see the outline of her body beneath. Every now and again, it still shook me to the core that she was with me.

'We've only been here a week or so. I'm still getting used to this heat.'

Then she said slowly, 'This hot, hot, climate.' (I knew that glint in her eye well enough now.) 'You have to learn to say no, and mean it, my boy…'

She slid into the bed next to me, and whispered things about last night, which I feel should remain private - but included the phrase, 'the most amazing lover' – as I said earlier, this was the one week of my life I could happily repeat forever.

Chapter Thirty-two: a burnished throne

But life, as they say, must be lived forward. However wonderful, you can never go back. It's always lost to memory. If only I could have stopped time - I could have died a happy man. Happiness? Happiness, what is that? A feeling? A sensation? A sense that God is in his heaven and all's right with the world? To glimpse the creation, before the Fall, when love worked? How can you possibly know light if you've never known darkness? How could *I* possibly know this was the happiest week of my life, if I had not experienced misery before, and annihilation after? Trust me, I would have known. I knew it instinctively in every living cell. I didn't need to lose it to appreciate it. What more have I learnt? Just a gulf of sadness.

Pain is always the most bitter when tasted after intense happiness.

Nessun maggior dolore
Che ricordarsi del tempo felice
Nella miseria.

There is no greater sorrow
Than to be mindful of the happy time
In misery.

Somehow... into my Paradise... a serpent slipped... unnoticed. This serpent was six-foot-two, with eyes as deep and dark as polished granite; His tawny skin glistening, satin-smooth – almost feminine – but for the taut muscular structure straining beneath.

Amongst the other builders, he didn't particularly stand out. Thinking back now, if I had to make an objective assessment, I would have said the carpenter was the most attractive, but no, it was the plasterer. Stripped to the waist, smoothing wet, silky plaster onto the cracked walls, with a sweeping motion so fluid, he put me in mind of the powerful elegance of a male ballet dancer.

Looking back, I can see it all so clearly; but at the time, I was blind. I didn't see anything. Psychologists call it inattention blindness. Magicians use it all the time. Just divert your attention, get you to momentarily focus elsewhere, and in the blink of an eye, something precious - vanishes. It was just like that - I didn't see a thing.

They were going to work on Tom's place for a week, then go off to do other jobs and return to us to decorate, complete the repair jobs, which they couldn't manage now, because the suppliers had let them down – typical.

A week was all it took to destroy my life.

They arrived surprisingly early on Monday morning. Four of them on the first day: Sergio, the governor, probably my age, but looked infinitely older; amused me by always wearing a moth-eaten sleeveless pullover, no matter how hot the weather.

The carpenter, Marco, was ironically not unlike Jesus actually, with longish tousled black hair and a thick beard. At lunch times, he sat alone in the garden, smoking thin rollups, while strumming a battered guitar and singing softly to himself. He had a dangerous gypsy air about him. I'd have put money on it being him - if I'd been asked.

Dino, the sixteen-year-old dogsbody - very smiley, very useless, from what I could see.

And last, but not least- Fabrizio. He smiled and shook my hand that morning...nothing extraordinary in that. He had a pleasant enough face, but not so beautiful as to raise alarm bells, although his eyes were unusually dark, almost black. Eyes you couldn't easily read.

Only Sergio spoke a little broken English, and my Italian only stretches as far as restaurants, but communication wasn't really an issue. Tom had organised it all from England, all I had to do was keep an eye on things. The builders had a full spec. of what to do. Any problems, speak to the architect directly. It all seemed straightforward enough. I led them to the various points in the house cited for repair work and left them to it.

I'd been looking forward to that day for some time, not because the builders were arriving of course, but because Maggie was due to arrive back home. In fact, she arrived back from a jaunt to Genoa last night, but had telephoned a few days previously, inviting both Anna and me around, so that we might, 'drink some gin in the garden and play boules (her latest interest) before enjoying a sumptuous supper with the Blythes – you remember them, Alistair? Delightful couple, such fun... Sally's such a scream - still as mad as a box of frogs!' Oh, and you should see Duncan, must've lost at least two stone since you saw him last, if not three...' How Maggie had found out about Anna, goodness knows, but she was 'simply dying to meet this delicious girl.'

Anna and I spent the morning in town as I wanted to buy a present of some kind to take to Maggie, and I knew of a tiny pottery shop, where I might find just the thing. We'd parked in the centre of town and strolled together through the back streets, which gently climbed up the hillside. Anna was strangely quiet. 'Are you all right?' I enquired. She did look awfully pale. 'No. I'm not actually. I feel really tired...sort of weak... almost faint. Can we find somewhere to sit down for a minute?'

Fortunately, we were only a few hundred yards from a small café, where we were able to sit for a while. After a rest and a mineral water, Anna perked up considerably.

'I hope you're not sickening for something,' I said trying to sound concerned, although really I was just worried that if she were ill, I wouldn't be able to show her off at Maggie's. That sounds terribly selfish, but tonight meant a lot to me. I suppose in a way it was the first time Anna and I would go out together publicly, as a couple. Yes, that's why. It was a very significant step in our relationship. As the pottery shop was at the top of the hill, we gave up on the idea and bought some flowers instead.

However, by the time we arrived home, Anna was wilting again. We were due round at Maggie's at four. She liked a long session with guests. 'Look,' said Anna, her eyes closing as she spoke, 'why don't you go on without me?'
'Go alone?'

'I'll join you later. If I have a good sleep now, I'm sure I'll wake up feeling all right to come round to dinner. You've pointed out the house before: the one just up from the bar - with the dark claret-coloured door, and the crazy metal 'sculpture' dangling about, bing-bonging night and day in the fig tree.'

'Not a fan of 'The Unpredictability of Frogs?' I queried with a wry smile.
'The 'what?'

Feeling a slight pang of disloyalty, I repeated the title of the piece with greater gravitas and added, 'Like a lot of modern art it only makes sense when you understand the thought behind it.'

Anna looked unconvinced.

'The thought behind it? Sorry, I must be really thick. What is so unpredictable about frogs that it is to be celebrated in sculpture?'

'Possibly everything: possibly nothing. I have never really made a study of them. But when and which way will they jump? Which one will croak next? I guess that's unpredictable. I mean, you never know which way Maggie's frogs will move in an unexpected breeze or the sound they'll make.'

'That's the 'thought,' is it? Frogs are as random and meaningless as everything else? Very enchanting at three in the morning: the clanging erratic frog chorus.'

I was feeling slightly irritated by Anna's attitude, and told her that to be fair the frogs were rarely that loud, more of a chiming, and Maggie's paintings were actually pretty good and far more accessible to the untrained eye. I immediately knew that last phrase was a mistake. Her mouth set a little harder.

'Don't be patronising, Alistair. You don't have to pretend to know everything – and I am entitled to my own opinion.'

'True. But frogs apart, I'm sure you'll be fascinated by her work and love Maggie...she makes a lot of money,' I added.

'It's not Maggie, frogs or whether or not I'll like her paintings at issue here... I simply don't feel up to it.'

'But Anna, I don't want to go without you,' I protested, attempting to stroke the side of her face tenderly.

'Please come. You've only got to sit there.'

'I don't want to 'just sit there' like a thing on show.'

'You know I didn't mean that.'

'Look, I'm just so tired. I'm sorry, Alistair. I'll come up later - seven-thirtyish?'

I knew she was fairly strong-minded, so I didn't argue further, but I still felt bitterly disappointed as I trudged up the hill toward the bar, alone.

If Duncan had impressively lost two stone since I last saw him, Maggie had obviously found it and put it to good use. On opening the door, she flung her arms wide then clenched my body against her enormous bosom-bottom. The double zeppelins, whose inflation had now reached a critical point, were still surprisingly giving; as I disappeared into those two enormous pillows of flesh, I had a fleeting mental image that my body would leave a permanent indent there.

'Alistair! Alistair! My dear boy!' she gushed, holding my face in her podgy hands, while kissing me on alternate cheeks, no less than three times...still the same evocative aura of Ambre Solaire and alcohol; the burnished patina of her face a little darker; the wrinkles a little deeper.

'How well you look!' she exclaimed, holding both my hands in hers and stepping back to view me. 'Love has taken years off you, my dear. Now, you *really* are a boy.' Her small eyes glittered with delight. 'You look about seventeen again.'

'Maggie,' I chided, 'ever prone to hyperbole.'

'Ah well, eighteen then - and that's the truth.' She began to peer over my shoulder. 'And where is this little miracle worker? She who can rejuvenate with her elixir? Not shy I hope?'

'No, definitely not shy, but not too well I'm afraid, but she'll join us later.'

'Mmm… thank God, not shy. Can't be doing with shy. Life's too short, without wasting time cowering in corners. She's ill? Mmm…why ill? One should strive for robustness, don't you think?' She rolled the 'r' of 'robustness' for all she was worth, followed by heavily stressing the second syllable. We were walking across the stone floor of the kitchen now - at the far end a young girl was already busy preparing tonight's meal.

'Now Alistair, look here, every home should have one: A 'Nina.' On hearing her name, the petite doe-eyed girl smiled and nodded in my direction. 'Wonderful little girl, been working for me for the past year or so. She's just a gem. Cooks, cleans, does laundry, gardens…just about everything.' She beamed while counting Nina's many accomplishments on her fat digits. 'She's like a little wife really – does all the boring stuff so I can get on with my work. Yes, my little wife!' She laughed heartily, let the laugh die away and then spoke rapidly to Nina in Italian. Nina's hand flew to her mouth and she let out a small sound of surprise, glancing at me from beneath her long fringe.

'What did you say?' I said uncertainly.

'That you may look familiar to her because you are the action stunt-double for a famous actor.'

'Surely, she didn't believe you? 'Nina was now staring directly into a bowl of eggs, which she was vigorously beating, but I could see her cheeks redden.

'Of course not! Pulling your leg, my dear,' gurgled Maggie. 'Pulling your leg, you're still so awfully gullible, such an endearing quality in a man. All I said was your girlfriend was about her age.'

She beckoned me to follow her.

'To the garden,' she said, thrusting herself forward, 'where I think you'll find Sally and Duncan are already several gins ahead of you.'

In the shade of an enormous walnut tree, were indeed Duncan and Sally, sitting by a wrought iron table, strewn with bottles and glasses. As they saw us approach, they stood up, smilingly warmly. Confidently, Duncan strode across the grass to greet me, closely followed by Sally, whose tall, gawky frame moved even more inelegantly than ever under the influence of several afternoon gins. We shook hands and Sally and I exchanged an awkward embrace.

Indeed, Duncan had lost weight, but as I regarded his wrinkled, slightly jowlier face, it looked more as if he'd mislaid it, and his body was all ready and waiting to put it back in its place when he recovered it. In fact, the more I looked at Duncan, the more he looked like a walking, talking, empty scrotum. His erstwhile full, portly face, with plump cheeks, like two puce coloured pheasant's breasts, was - deflated. The skin, which was once deceptively taut over subcutaneous fat, now drooped in pleats, like a turkey's wattle. But, as you know, Marion had often impressed upon me that good social relations often demand lies - artful concealment; so, I wisely said nothing referring to scrotums or turkeys, and instead shook his hand enthusiastically once more while telling him his weight loss made him look 'quite distinguished.'

'And what about the new 'tash'!' said Sally proudly, placing her own finger length ways under her nose – just in case I wasn't sure where a moustache should be.

'Well, well,' I said, 'weight loss for Duncan, and a moustache for you, Sally - my, I've been away a long time!' At this, Sally fell around in such a paroxysm of laughter that she induced a coughing fit, which sent her staggering back to the table for her drink.

'Lorks, Alistair,' she snorted, 'you're still such a tease.'

The question of the misplaced weight began to preoccupy me somewhat. People don't really lose weight, do they? They absorb it, don't they? Eat themselves effectively. I think I should start a campaign to stop the misleading use of the term, 'You've lost a lot of weight' and change it to 'You've absorbed a lot of weight.' Well, it's more accurate. I think that's what happens anyway. Do fat cells just expand and contract as weight goes up and down, or does the number of actual cells increase and decrease? Really, I didn't know. There were some huge gaps in my understanding of human biology.

One can pay a high price for ignorance - no, seriously - a very high price.

So, there I was - lost in some stupid contemplation of fat cells and the extraordinary capacity for human beings to change shape - to almost metamorphosis from porcine to turkine; sipping gin served with ice balls and lemon slivers; and doing my best to be entertaining, which I always felt was my duty on these occasions. As I've told you before, Maggie found me highly amusing and Sally was easily pleased too.

If Duncan had seamlessly changed from piggy to turkey, there was no similar alteration in Sally, who stuck firmly to her original gene pool, which she shared with our equine friends. Her thin narrow face was framed with a cropped mane of wispy chestnut and grey hair and her pink gummy smile, including really elongated teeth, completed the picture. It was a pity she laughed so much really. Another strange feature was her amazingly mobile nostrils. They could move quite independently of one another in a most intriguing fashion. I had to consciously remind myself not to stare at them.

During another bout of hilarity, Sally threw her head back so forcefully with an explosive 'Ha!', that she hit her head on the trunk of the walnut tree, with a loud thud. Nina had just appeared with some freshly baked grissini, and was so taken by surprise at the sudden violence of Sally's merriment that she nearly dropped the tray. Meanwhile, Duncan leapt to his feet, thrust his fingers into Sally's gin, and proceeded to rub the back of Sally's head with an ice ball he'd retrieved from her glass. Sally, however, continued to smile at us all, waving away our concern with a flap of her long fingers, assuring everyone she was quite unharmed.

'Cracking good joke, Alistair!' said Duncan, still attending to his wife.

'Head-splittingly funny,' added Sally, her eyes rolling like a dazed cartoon character. At this moment her nostrils did a complete 'Kenneth Williams' and I fancied she could have easily held an ice ball in each one as a party piece.

'You've quite an egg coming here, darling.'

'Oh, nonsense,' chortled Sally, 'sweetie, you do fuss rather. Sit down now.' Nina hovered awkwardly with the grissini.

'Thank you, darling, I'll take those now,' said Maggie with a wink.

Perhaps purely to divert attention away from Sally's self-inflicted injury, we all began to chomp enthusiastically on the breadsticks, and make various complementary noises about their deliciousness.

'Absolutely superb breadsticks,' Sally brayed, returning the ice ball to her gin. (A long strand of hair was attached to it, but I let this remain unnoticed.) The conversation turned towards the lovely and indispensable Nina, and another twenty minutes crept stealthily past me.

It transpired that Maggie, I am pleased to say, was doing very well with her artistic pursuits. She had several contacts with local galleries now, and as her work seemed popular with the many English *visitors* ('Don't refer to them as tourists my dear, they're far too middle-class for that.') She was 'raking it in.' Hence, Nina.

'Postcards too, and even a tea-towel in the pipe-line, no less!' she announced proudly, clapping her hands together. 'Can you imagine, darling? My work depicting this wonderful landscape travels around the globe to be admired or despised by thousands.'

'Or used to dry beer glasses with,' quipped Duncan. Maggie gave him a long-suffering smile, and raised her glass to us all; the sunlight piercing through its translucent blueness and fragmenting over Sally's face, briefly making her a piebald carousel horse.

'To the prostitution of one's art,' Maggie drunkenly pronounced.

We all toasted in agreement; glasses were chinked, the conversation danced on; a game of boules was proposed and eventually played, with Duncan emerging as supreme champion, and the hours, well, the hours slipped by unnoticed...

At seven- thirty, there was still no sign of Anna.

'We're in no rush, my dear,' assured Maggie patting my knee. 'This is Italy after all. Give her another twenty minutes or so, then ring if you like.'

I did ring. On my third attempt, she came to the phone. She had been in the shower. Sorry, she would be a little late. She felt a lot better, would be up straight away. And yes, she'd bring the flowers, I'd forgotten, with her.

Maggie saw her first. I knew the precise moment when she set eyes on her. She stopped mid-sentence, her mouth dropped open a little, her tiny eyes, which were usually in constant motion like two iridescent beetles, froze.

'Oh, Alistair,' she breathed quietly; I barely heard her.

In an instant all were rising to welcome Anna. With my back to the house, I was the last to turn, and see her almost gliding across the lawn. Even I was taken aback. She was wearing a red dress I'd never seen her wear before, which was tapered into her waist. The neckline was low and somehow her breasts looked fuller. She was completely radiant. The evening sun quivered around her like a full body halo, and for the first time ever, I saw the woman she would become - when she finally kissed all vestiges of girlhood goodbye. Across her arms were laid the lilies she had chosen in town that morning, while her hair, still slightly damp, clung to her golden flesh. *'Your arms full, and your hair wet, I could not speak, and my eyes failed... and I knew nothing.'*

The reaction of my peers to the entrance of this goddess amongst us should have spoken volumes to me. But at the time, I was deaf as well as blind.

Now I return to that evening, I know I subconsciously sensed the initial awkwardness of the assembled company, to the incarnation of beauty in their ugly midst. Even Maggie, who had spent a lifetime modelling her sexual self-confidence on the popularity of the Venus of Willendorf, seemed to shrink within herself. However, Sally, who had never listed sexual allure amongst her strong points, and was therefore used to feeling overshadowed by other women, was the first to recover herself. With both nostrils flaring widely, as if to capture Anna scent, she strode forward hand outstretched, 'Anna, how simply lovely to meet you. We were all growing rather worried you wouldn't make it. Are you quite recovered?'

'I'm feeling much better thank you. Sometimes the heat just gets to you, doesn't it?'

'Oh, doesn't it just!' Sally puffed out her cheeks. 'But we're becoming used to it. Duncan, my husband...' she cocked her head in the deflated scrotum's direction, who responded by pointing idiotically at himself, and giving a small wave, 'and I have been here six years or so, and I wouldn't swap it for the foggy, dismal weather in Old Blighty for anything.'

Soon we were all standing in a semi-circle on the grass, continuing staggering attempts at introductions. Once these were over, I took Anna's hand. 'You're really okay now?' I said brushing a kiss across her face. 'You look stunning,' I whispered into her ear. Exhilaration pounded through me, fuelled by the intimacy I was now demonstrating.

'Mmm, never better.' She smiled in that sexy way I loved so much, and returned my kiss.

Just look at me! LOOK AT ME!

(The man standing on brimstone did a little dance, and didn't even feel his feet burning.)

Nina called to Maggie from the terrace and we all processed up to the house, where we found the dining room table beautifully laid for dinner. The double doors were opened onto the view, still simmering like an orange infusion. While we ate the first course of Zuppa di borlotti, a sort of bean soup really, Nina paced delicately about the garden, lighting candles and tea lights, which burned with growing strength as the sun sank. As the evening wore on, once or twice it seemed as if the candles had taken off, and were now spinning magically through the night air – *fireflies* - how completely breath-taking they were.

The copious amounts of alcohol consumed helped the party move beyond Anna's devastating beauty, and shortly we were all laughing and chatting again as before. Although, I did momentarily catch each of them holding lingering looks in Anna's direction. Duncan's face was a picture – more than once I caught him, with his sunken eyes poleaxed with longing…in another life…in another life…he says to himself. However, in spite of this he very gallantly paid his wife more attention than usual that evening. I found that quite touching. Maggie spent as much time surreptitiously studying me, as she did Anna…as if trying to work something out.

Courses came and went, each one brought in by Nina, occasionally assisted by Maggie, who'd disappear from time to time into the kitchen. Nina didn't join us for dinner. Her English conversation is still in its infancy explained Maggie, once we've exhausted the weather she's lost. The food she'd produced though was wonderful, and the conversation for the rest of us, easy, if not a little slurred. Anna was somewhat quiet tonight, but then she was with a roomful of people she'd never met before, and who were, I have to admit, all a generation apart. But age is immaterial, isn't it?

Finally, Nina came in with espressos and Maggie told us Nina was off to bed now so would we like to thank her for her unsurpassable meal and attentions. We all did so profusely. Then Nina kissed Maggie goodnight, and I watched fascinated as Maggie's hand grasped the girl's fleetingly and brushed a kiss across her fingers. Nina followed this by performing an exaggerated curtsy to us all, before backing graciously out of the room. We all laughed and applauded.

'Such a sweet little girl,' mused Maggie as Nina left the room. 'Barely twenty, you know…' she stared with longing into the empty doorway through which Nina had just disappeared. 'I don't think I could bear to be without her now,' she added, emotion rising in her voice, 'another year maybe…and then she'll be off. The wide world beckons us all to fly, eventually.'

I don't think anyone else saw the flickering struggle in Anna's facial muscles. I did.

'Ah, well,' said Maggie recovering herself, 'there'll be no more home-made ravioli for me then. Perhaps I'll lose some of my pasta belly!' We all laughed again, but when a mask slips, it is sometimes impossible to fix it back on straight. Besides, everyone has seen your face now. What's the point? My heart reached out to Maggie. You silly old fool, Maggie.

Suddenly I longed to be back in bed in England, alone with Anna, safe under the covers.

As the laughter subsided, and further praise for the meal petered out, Sally began to fold her napkin purposefully. Her exit was interrupted however by a ridiculously large moth, the size of a small owl, which after flying clumsily in through the open windows, began a disorientated circuit of the room. Within seconds, it had entrapped itself in the large paper lantern, which hung above the table.

'Goodness!' cried Sally 'Did you see the size of that!'
The moth bashed frantically against the sides of the lantern, its wing beats purring like a soft drum roll. 'Are you sure that isn't a tiny bat?' said Duncan trying to squint under the lantern to see inside it.

'Can't you get the poor thing out?' pleaded Sally, her right nostril rising in enquiry.
All of a sudden, the light went out. Maggie's voice came from the other side of the room.

'It'll find its own way out. They mistake lamps for the moon, puts their head in a spin.'
She paused; there was silence from the lantern.

'See. All calm now. They follow false gods and don't know where they're going.'
She put the light back on. The moth began to fling itself back and forth across the inside of the lantern once more.

'Now my dears, let's leave this room and I'll turn the light off for good. Give that poor creature a chance to escape; which he will... I guarantee it.' We left the dining room to the sound of burring wings and the donk, donk sound of furry moth thrown against paper. The light went out. It stopped. Under her breath Anna whispered, 'Ah, what now? The Predictability of Moths?'

After all the consternation caused by the moth, we all stumbled into the lounge, where we sat for another hour or so. Maggie's lounge was luxuriant to say the least, being dominated by a large burgundy Knole settee with tie back sides, which was littered with wine-coloured, plush velvet cushions. Various large canvases of Maggie's work hung on several walls, and covering every possible surface was an array of fabulous pottery, erotic sculptures, and the most eclectic *objets d'art* imaginable, including a multitude of religious artefacts. Here, cultural effects of countries as disparate as Italy, China, Africa and India snuggled happily into bed with one another. Where else would one find a tasteful reproduction of the *Pieta* reposed quietly just a stone's throw from a golden *Medicine Buddha*, holding a blooming myrobalan plant? This particular type of Buddha can apparently cure the suffering of this worldly existence with his foliage. (Looking at his neighbour- lain limply across his mother's lap - waving a leaf about seems a far more preferable option to crucifixion.) There's also a sort of 'Hindu thing' going on upon the large stone mantelpiece, where a whole herd of Ganesh statues are parading themselves, including two lively dancing Ganesh and a supremely stately sitting Ganesh, brandishing his trident and noose.

Unfortunately, although Duncan recognised Jesus, and even Ganesh, he was unfamiliar with the marble representation of the *Lingam of Shiva*, which sat proudly in the centre of the coffee table, and Maggie only just managed to prevent Duncan from knocking the ash from his Panatela into its round bowl. (If you're also unenlightened about the *Lingam* it's a shrine to the god Shiva representing his creative energy. *Lingam* translates as 'wand of light' – yes, it is basically a 'creative' glowing erection.) While providing Duncan with a genuine ashtray, Maggie chided him for viewing this as purely eroticism - Shiva apparently controls his sexual energies and turns them into creative power by generating intense heat. 'Without procreative energy we're all done for,' she cried as if rallying an army. Next, she passed the *Lingam* around for all to view. Offerings *are* placed in the bowl, yes, but they're more usually flower petals, or milk' … at this last word Sally pulled a face, and in the corner of my eye I could see Anna was secretly amused by the whole episode.

The focus was now firmly on Maggie's varied collection of religious merchandise, which she expounded on at some length as being a witness to her belief in all faiths and none. Whilst I admired her open-mindedness, I dared to suggest that it was a contradiction in terms on every count, and showed no real commitment to anything. I suggested that she was in danger of 'sitting on the fence', and such lack of loyalty, such failure to choose, might just find her wandering ceaselessly in Dante's vestibule. (The equivalent of milling about in the cinema foyer for the rest of eternity, without a ticket for either of the main features or the purgatory of a seemingly endless spool of pa-pa pa-pa pa-pa pa-pa –pa-pa PA! Advertising.)

> *Questi non hanno speranza di morte*
> *These have no longer any hope of death;*
> *e la lor cieca vita è tanto bassa,*
> *And this blind life of theirs is so debased*
> *che 'nvidiosi son d'ogne altra sorte*
> *They envious are of every other fate*

She just laughed and said, 'Piffle!' and that she'd be more likely find herself in the wonderfully named circles of The Sins of Incontinence… where no doubt I too will be residing. 'The sins of lust and gluttony weigh heavily, I'm afraid,' she chuckled. 'Although, I could endure the punishment of the former, more easily than the latter…which I believe is lying face down in the mud eating one's own…' She broke off with a shudder, 'Best not think about it…now who's for a liqueur?' she announced, opening the glass-fronted doors of a well-stocked drinks cabinet. Duncan declared he hadn't the foggiest as to what on earth Maggie and I were on about. 'Surely not?' I said surprised that he was not acquainted with Italy's most famous poet's supreme work, *Dante's 'Divine Comedy*. I sang, with that horrible *'obviously!'* tone to my voice. 'You've never…?'

Duncan shrugged, none the wiser.

'Not my field old chap. Anyway, doesn't sound the least bit amusing to me - always found the thought of death and damnation damned depressing.'

He grinned at Maggie, who was poised in front of her apothecary, dangling a bottle of green fluid.

'Oh, not for me thank you, Maggie. But a brandy would be very welcome if you've got some, thanks.'

While Maggie was pouring the drinks, a sluggish, gloopy silence descended.

Through half-closed eyes I continued studying the strange incongruity of her room; indeed no one else could have made a room like this work, but Maggie could. Several enormous candles sent a flickering glowing light, guttering around the room, while from an oblong wooden incense burner a heady sensuous aroma, (possibly patchouli) drifted like a smoke signal. And whilst we sipped our slightly syrupy drinks, we were overcome with an air of overwhelming lassitude. Maggie selected a record and placed it on her stereo, whereupon the air became thick, almost viscous with the blues.

Having obviously given up on the idea of going home, Sally hummed along nasally to the lugubrious lyrics; her face in repose a study by Modigliani. But the moment of tranquillity was short-lived. Eventually, something in the song triggered a memory of her past life, particularly a time spent with a catering company in Surrey, before she and Duncan left 'the dismal shores' for Italy, and as everyone else was half-asleep, she took the opportunity to perform a one woman show, regaling us all with amusing anecdotes. My favourite was the one when she was in the middle of icing an extremely elaborate chocolate cake, complete with white coat and one-use rubber gloves, when the doorbell rang. On opening the door, she realized it was a Jehovah's Witness. 'Well, obviously I didn't want to get trapped on the front doorstep, discussing Jehovah or whatever for the afternoon, so I thought of a very wicked lie. I held my smudgy brown surgically gloved hands in front of me, and said - with as much gravity as I could muster - 'Terribly sorry, I'm with a patient.' Sally threw her head back with slightly more caution than earlier, 'Ha!' she exploded, 'This young man took one look at my skin tight rubber gloves - one look at my face - which I can tell you I'd composed into a study of agonized embarrassment, shut up his book and scuttled down the drive!'

A tired, but warm laugh vibrated around the room. Maggie's vacuum cleaner laugh died away and started up several times over before she was done. Encouraged by this Sally led herself onto a further entertaining episode.

Meanwhile, Duncan's head was beginning to loll around and eventually came to rest on his chest, where the many folds of his turkey wattle cushioned it on their fleshy concertina. Sally gave her husband a long admiring glance.

'Better take the poor chap home,' she said in a well-humoured stage-whisper, 'he's obviously had all the excitement he can take in one evening.'

In a few short moments, Duncan was fully aroused and ready to go. After, smoothing a few non-existent creases from his slacks, he pulled himself from the sofa. As he did so, something quite dreadful happened - he broke wind - in the most unexpected and spectacularly loud, extended fashion. The most appalling noise reverberated around the room, like a low sliding note from a trombone played by flabby-lipped fish.

For a few seconds an astounded silence gripped our throats. 'Duncan!' exclaimed Sally.

'Sorry, everyone,' he said, his drooping cheeks flushing crimson. 'Never feed a man over sixty bean soup!' He fanned his hand over his posterior.

'Oh, Duncan, please don't!' implored Sally, both nostrils quivering in anticipation. Suddenly, Anna couldn't contain herself any longer and disintegrated into a fit of uncontrollable schoolgirl giggles. Well, it had been the trump to end all trumps. Without further licence, the entire room immediately erupted into a complete disarray of hysterics. Maggie did the dislocated jaw laugh; Duncan fell backwards onto the sofa, his wattle undulating with pleasure like a plate of over-cooked tripe; Sally laughed so much she began to weep and so did I. I hadn't laughed so much at something so stupid, since I was a child. Eventually, we all got a grip on ourselves; our adult selves resumed control and we were old again.

The Blythes insisted they would like to take us all out to dinner at their favourite restaurant sometime in the next few weeks. And the inevitable joke about 'no bean soup' was bantered around. They kissed everyone with exaggerated 'mwahs!' on the cheek, then departed, arm in arm.

Before we left, however, Maggie insisted on taking Anna and me upstairs to the attic to show us her new studio. Thanks to her newly discovered marketability, the attic had been recently converted, complete with several huge sky light windows. There was also an impressive arched gable end window, which apparently afforded the most beautiful vista over the surrounding rooftops to the countryside beyond. There were no blinds; we could see reflections of ourselves everywhere. In the centre of the attic was one huge, tatty, sunken chaise longue but no other furniture; lots of paint - everywhere; tins and tubes of it all over the place. Against the walls were several large notice boards, which were a patchwork of postcards of artwork she loved, her own sketches, and masses of photographs of the surrounding countryside and its people. Two large canvases, works in progress, were propped upright in the far end of the room: one, a Tuscan scene, Impasto style: blue, blue skies, terracotta buildings thickly palleted into place between sweeping rolling hill-sides, a verdant green, broken by stabs of yellows and oranges.

The second: a very obviously male nude.

'That's a change of direction for you, Maggie, isn't it?' I said tilting my head to one side to take in the full wonder of the body in front of me. 'I thought you were landscapes only.'

The style of painting was quite different here. More brush work, than pallet knife, more detailed. Much more detailed.

'Well, as you see Alistair, I find I have a talent for life studies too.'

'Anyone we know?' I asked jokingly, pointing airily toward the supine figure.

'Local lad - it is a *real* life-study. Rather successful I feel. He is wonderfully, palpably real, isn't he?' She picked up a few abandoned paint tubes, looked at them disagreeably, and threw them into the bin.

'They get all dried up eventually... He needed the cash...' I looked at her quizzically. 'Of which I seem to have a lot these days, an embarrassment of riches some might say, so he was only too happy to co-operate ...,' she added with the familiar rich fruity tones of yesteryear. 'Don't look at me like *that* Alistair.' She wagged her finger at me. 'He's twenty-two – for goodness sake! And besides, I don't have *that* much cash!'

Still on the downward slide of her laugh, she turned her attentions to Anna. 'You're very quiet, my dear. You're allowed to say if you don't like my art. Really, anything is acceptable, bar indifference. Indifference is pure death to life and to art.' I glanced nervously at Anna. 'The landscapes are not to everyone's taste,' Maggie continued, 'but I try not to be too chocolate boxy.'

'No, no, 'replied Anna blushing, 'I think they're wonderful, the real essence of the place, not just a photographic representation.' I guess she was saying what she thought Maggie wanted to hear. She was right of course.

'Ah,' breathed Maggie, sharp as ever, 'I can see your eye keeps drifting back to my young man. He is deliciously fine, isn't he? Unfortunately, my life studies don't sell as well as yet. He wouldn't let me show his face, so I let him look the other way - eventually. Bit of a cheat! It loses some of its raw honesty I feel...but what can one do when faced with such bashful beauty?'

I watched somewhat surprised to see Anna's blush deepen a little. She nodded silently.

'If you like ignudi' said Maggie hauling a blanket from a pile of canvases leaning up against the wall, 'take a look at these.'

I recognised this face straight away.

'Nina!'

'I pay her extra for the modelling of course.' All three of us regarded Nina's sprawling naked form. 'She's rather lovely too, don't you think?'

Nina, naked, lost something of her innocent childlike demeanour; a feeling of uncomfortable voyeurism seeped and tingled around my body. Maggie continued to place canvases around the room all featuring Nina in some form of semi- or complete undress. We were surrounded by images of her.

'As you can see, at the moment, she's my favourite study.' She gently traced her plump finger around the curve of Nina's back. 'Such a delicate form...young women are far harder to paint than old, fat, voluptuous ones like me.' She gave a short laugh. 'Really, my self-portraits are much better, but I fear not suitable for decent public taste.'

'These are amazing though,' said Anna, who didn't seem the least bit phased by viewing Nina nude from every possible angle. 'She's really quite beautiful.'

Maggie looked up pleasantly surprised. 'Do you paint yourself, my dear?'

'Well, I like to, but nothing like this.'

Maggie's face became a picture of satisfaction. 'I knew you did! I could sense the artist within the moment I set eyes on you.' She was now beaming at Anna like a proud mother, whose daughter had just been chosen for the lead part in this year's Nativity play.

'You must feel free to come and use my studio while you're here,' Maggie enthused grabbing both Anna's hands. 'Really, you will find life here such an inspiration, the art will flow out of you, won't it, Alistair?'

To be honest, I've never felt 'art' flow in any direction around my body. I could hardly draw, let alone paint or sculpt, but I nodded encouragingly. I guess my poetry, which Marion was so disparaging about, was my art. However, like Maggie's self-study, I suspected, (and here Marion would be in total agreement) - 'it is not suitable for decent public taste.'

By the time we finally extracted ourselves from Maggie's bosom, it was gone one o'clock in the morning. A soft, dark, peace enveloped the village, interrupted only by the fireflies whirring past like fairy helicopters and an unsettling discordant chime from the Verdigris frogs awakened by Anna tweaking a branch of the fig tree. *Brekekekéx koáx koáx!* In the moonlight several of them spun and dipped agitatedly on their wires – a strange triumphant smile passed across her face.

Above, the night sky - where thousands upon thousands of suns burn so distantly, they are but specks of light. In the further distance still, the Milky Way; just a mist of luminescence. And in between, darkness; billions and billions of miles of blinding blackness, broken by tiny chinks of light – massive suns – but all the darkness in between. Darkness... is it a property in itself or just what is, in the absence of light?

I wanted to engage Anna in this line of thought, but she seemed strangely remote, perhaps just a little tired. I was feeling quite excited now as in my mind neurons screamed down neural pathways, like forked lightning. Yes, I definitely had something here. Darkness is the eternal truth. Think about it. It exists always, because in the absence of anything else, *it still is*. Light relies on a source, on something positive being there. Something with energy, which is by its very nature, is constantly changing, transferring. Only darkness is self-perpetuating - existing quietly, silently, eternally, without effort or will - just being. God should be the eternal darkness, not light. There was no logic to light reflecting the properties of an eternal being. How could Christianity have got its symbolism so back to front? The Anglo-Saxons had it right, with the image of the sparrow flying in from a dark timeless night, into the window of a mead hall; briefly knowing light, laughter, warmth, life, then out the window the other end into the never-ending dark night. From the darkness of my mother's womb to the endless night of the grave...it is here where God is waiting. I knew you before you were conceived in your mother's womb. He is there in that blackness, I tell you.

An unusually cool breeze shifted through the fabric of my shirt, and my skin shuddered. I wondered vaguely if my theory would seem quite so convincing in the sober light of day. I hoped so, at the present time I thought I was about to reveal a theological insight of world changing proportions. Sleep on it, Alistair, I told myself. Sleep on it.

We were now descending the narrow lane which led down to the villa. Giving Anna's hand a gentle squeeze, I whispered, 'Love you,' in that tone of voice, which really means, 'Love me?' She squeezed my hand in reply, but didn't speak.

Anna remained subdued as we entered the house.

'Well?' I asked trying to break the silence. 'Did you have a good time?'

'You're very quiet.'

'Just tired. But yeah, it was fun. Really interesting.'

'So, you enjoyed yourself then?'

'Yeah…great food.'

'Yes, it was…Sally's a bit much, but....'

'No, I liked her. She's a real laugh.'

'Will you take up Maggie's offer of the studio?'

In the stark kitchen light, I saw that same strange little smile play around her lips, 'Yes…yes, I think I might.'

Wearily I climbed the stairs. I brushed my teeth thoroughly, as I always do, no matter how tired I am, and even gave the basin a good swill round. There was an odd film of pinkish dust around the taps. 'What's all this?' I asked.

'What?'

'This pink stuff…looks like…' I rubbed some between my fingers, 'plaster dust?'

She didn't miss a beat.

'Oh, I got one of the guys to fix the tap this afternoon. You know, Fabrizio.'

'I thought he was a plasterer.'

'It was only replacing a washer.'

'I guess so... that was good of him.'

****

I never gave it a second thought – at the time. Hindsight is a wonderful thing, but totally useless. Yes, now I look back and see…but at the time, I can only say in my defence, I was in the dark. Bang goes my theory.

Chapter Thirty-three: Speak to me

When I awoke the next morning, Anna wasn't in her usual place at the window. For a few moments I listened intently expecting to hear some sound of her in the bathroom, shower running, even the gentle shushing sound of her peeing. Nothing. Strange? Rolling onto my side, I looked at the alarm clock, which surprised me by informing me that the time was 11.25 am. No wonder Anna was already up and about. My head was thumping, and the phrases 'Chinese wrestler', 'mouth like', and 'laundry basket' bubbled up like effluent in my mind. I hadn't felt that drunk last night at all, but I guess I'd consumed an awful lot of alcohol, even if it was over a fairly long period of time. I knew the routine so well now: a shower, breakfast, plenty of fluids, vitamin C... soon be fine.

Anna wasn't anywhere to be found. I asked Sergio if he'd seen her. The most I could get out of him was she'd opened the door to them this morning, which was mimed, and that, 'Anna go.'

'Where?' I asked anxiously. '*Dove*?'

'*Non lo so.*' He shrugged.

Fat lot of good that was. I noticed it seemed very quiet.

'Marco? Dino? Fabrizio?'

Marco, it transpired, was working outside, sawing something in the garden; Dino I gathered was sick –vomiting... and ... (no wait for it...) vomiting *and* diarrhoea... while Fabrizio, *lovely dark-eyed Fabrizio*, was getting supplies. All this I learnt through the wonderful art of mime. Sergio was truly gifted.

Anyway, a breakfast of orange juice and bread spread thickly with butter and sweet chestnut jam revived me, and I took my second cup of coffee into the garden to sit in the shade of the vine by the pool. God, I fancied a cigarette. I'd lasted three months, but sometimes...oh, just to hold one between my fingers, the burning hiss as you light up, the first drag, to blow smoke distractedly with a long enigmatic sigh...no, I'd promised Anna. It was a terrible habit: smelly breath and fatal lung cancer just two of the drawbacks. Plus, if I didn't smoke, Anna would be less likely to take it up - and that was worth stopping for.

I took another sip of my coffee and squinted upward at my favourite burgeoning grapes. Perhaps she'd gone to see Maggie again? Maybe the allure of the studio proved too tempting? Suddenly, a wonderful thought struck me...would I be able to persuade Anna to let Maggie *paint* her? (Tastefully in the nude of course) My God, that would be something! Ten minutes or so passed whilst I indulged this thought, with all its exciting scenarios and permutations.

My glorious fantasy was disturbed by Marco, whom I observed through the trees, sauntering across the grass with his guitar. Oblivious to my presence, his gentle song drifted towards me. I couldn't understand the words, but I guessed it was a love song. Lying back in the dappled shade, I closed my eyes and relaxed. The words *'T'amerò per il resto della vita'* featured heavily in the chorus. Even I could work out it was something to do with love and life. Thinking back to the autumn, when Tom had first suggested I come here for the summer; how like a dream it had all seemed. Now I was here with Anna, dozing quietly to a soft Italian love song in my garden of earthly delights. Life was truly wonderful.

Splash!

The sound and the shower of water hit me simultaneously.

'What the!' Even under the water, I knew the shape of her body. She swam the entire length of the pool, completed a racing turn, and burst through the surface of the water, her face alive and gleaming.

'Where have you been?' Not answering immediately, she swam towards me with a bobbing breaststroke; her face disappearing and appearing from beneath the surface. She came to rest by my feet and folded her elbows on the side of the pool.

'Where have you been?' I repeated.

Before replying, she flung herself backwards and began a slow backstroke down the pool. I was now following her progress, teetering along the edge.

'Anna. Where did you go this morning?'

'For a walk,' she announced to the sky. Her arms swept elegantly passed the side of her face... 'up to the top of the hill.'

'There are snakes and scorpions around here, you know.'

'I didn't see any.'

'You might have woken me up.'

'Alistair,' she said, now poised at the bottom of the steps, 'you were in no fit state. Don't worry. I like to spend some time on my own occasionally.' She was rising out of the pool now, the water cascading in silvery rivulets down her body.

'Do you?'

'Doesn't everyone?'

Quickly handing her a towel, which was draped over the back of a lounger, I said, 'I think you should wear both bits of your bikini while these workmen are around.'

'If you say so,' she grinned.

'And just let someone know where you're going. Anything could've happened to you.'

Other people might have noticed a silly, challenging flash in her eye, but I didn't.

By that very same evening the gods had conspired to ensure my tragedy would reach its destined conclusion - I went down with Dino's bug. I must admit in the morning I suspected Dino's illness had been a ruse, one of those things young boys might claim in order to spend a day fishing or whatever. But no, this bug was very real. Apparently, Maggie's friend, Matteo, at the local art gallery was a victim too and Maggie telephoned through to say she and Nina would be filling in for him over the next few days. She very generously said she'd come round with a spare set of keys, so that Anna could use the studio whenever she liked.

Anna seemed almost overly enthusiastic about the idea, but I was certainly not going to be good company for a day or two and I had to agree that after a week of lounging by the pool, she wanted a different diversion. She certainly found one.

Now, I'm not going to put myself through the agony of explaining in detail what went on in that studio over the next few days, but suffice to say Fabrizio was often notable by his absence when I struggled weakly downstairs for more boiled water, and that Anna's output of artwork was not prolific. But as far as I knew at the time, he was 'getting supplies', and she was very measured in her painting.

    I trusted her.

    I loved her.

Why should I have thought anything different?

By the end of the week, I was able to eat a little boiled rice and dry bread. Sergio gave me a letter from the architect, who'd apparently been around to inspect work done thus far. All seemed well, and they were scheduled to return in four weeks' time to do some final touches and the one or two outstanding plumbing jobs. I managed to ascertain from Sergio they were all going to a development near the coast, which seemed to agree with him. As the afternoon drew to a close, the truck clanked its way up the cobbled road and disappeared in a haze of dust. Thank goodness for that I thought, shutting the door on the once more private villa. I went back to bed and slept for an hour or two.

It was gone six o'clock when I woke, sweating and uncomfortable. Perhaps after a shower, a little more boiled rice - perhaps I'd risk a poached egg - I'd be on the mend by tomorrow. Pushing open the shutters, I breathed in deeply; the view before me bathed in warm, soft, tangerine-blue light. And there, sitting on the edge of the terrace, with her knees pulled up close to her face and her arms encircling them tightly, was Anna. She was motionless, just staring, staring, into the vast space of the valley. I was about to call her name, but somehow it lodged in my throat. For a few moments I watched her. What was this strange uneasy feeling, which made my skin rise to goose-flesh? Shuddering, I turned and went to take that much-needed shower. Sometime later, in clean clothes, with my hair still damp, I walked gingerly into the garden. She was still sat in exactly the same position.

'Hello,' I ventured, 'beautiful evening, isn't it?' She didn't look up at me, but nodded slowly.

'I'm feeling much better. I was thinking, I wonder if you had a touch of this bug earlier in the week, you know, when we were in town.'

'Maybe.'

I sat down next to her, and pulled up a piece of tufted grass, which I began to rub between my fingers. 'I think I'm over it now. You could come back to the virgin's bed tonight?' (She had been sleeping in another room as a precaution these last few nights.) I reached out to touch her hair, but somehow all I could do was let my hand hover, then withdraw it. It was almost as if we were two magnets with like poles. I know I hadn't been the most alluring prospect in the past few days - vomiting and diarrhoea are no one's idea of an aphrodisiac - however, she was supposed to love me. Even Marion and I had soldiered on through sickness and health (all right, that's a bit of a lie, but we did try to remain civil.) But Anna had been distant all week. In fact, I'd hardly seen her, apart from at the beginning and end of the day, when she'd bring a fresh jug of boiled water, stand in the doorway and say, 'Best not get too close; no point in both of us chucking up.' Okay, so she wasn't Florence Nightingale; I could live with that. Besides, I didn't really want her to see me being that ill anyway. It had been pretty grim.

'I'm sorry I've been unwell and left you on your own so long.' She gave a little humph. *(Gosh, this was hard work.)* 'How's Maggie's friend from the gallery, by the way?'

'Back at work tomorrow.'

'So, you won't be going to the studio?' This got a response.

'Why ever not? I love it up there - the light's gorgeous, the freedom to paint - it's just wonderful.'

'Oh. I thought perhaps you were cross, because you'd been bored, or too lonely.' She scuffed at the dry earth with her bare heel. '...Maybe missing me?' I suggested. 'Have you been too lonely? I'll make it up to you next week. I couldn't help being ill.'

She turned to me, and I saw a sad, almost pitying, smile, 'Oh, Alistair,' she said putting her hand on mine, 'I'm not blaming you for being ill… I just…just…oh, I don't know. I feel sort of restless. Maybe I'm just homesick, perhaps?'

'Homesick?' (I couldn't imagine what for.) 'Florence,' I said confidently, as if it were cure-all remedy, 'that's what we need. - a few romantic days in Florence. We can even see the statue of David. How about it?'

'Yeh, okay.'

Not quite the excited reaction I'd expected.

We sat together looking outward, side-by-side. Once or twice, she gave a very heavy sigh - but then again, it was a very breath-taking view.

Chapter Thirty-four: Wo weilest du?

Florence. Now, how to take myself back to summer, in one of the most beautiful cities on earth, whilst looking out at my grim backyard on a dreary November afternoon? Here, life itself has been shrouded in a foggy dampness, and unfortunately, today, I found myself side-tracked by writing a poem. (Sorry, Marion.).

> November arrived across the city,
> creeping in from the hills,
> shrouded and sly,
> whispering to every form of life
> to weaken fall and die-
> And when wet November came to rest upon the world,
> sapping autumn's colours in its wake,
> we shuddered in the darkness of the damp and
> could not see beyond the white grey walls of loss
> and blank despair.
> Godless it felt.
> We had no hope of returning warmth or light.
> We lived like gravestones,
> cold, grey memories of a life that was…

The poem goes on a bit, but that's the gist of it. We lived like gravestones…. cold grey memories of a life that was. I know all about that. How can I crawl out from beneath the suffocating, heavy-greyness of my gravestone?

Tom suggests I seek medical help - antidepressants. I've told him if I feel no better after Christmas, I'll definitely make an appointment. Why Christmas should have anything to do with it, God only knows. It's the one time of year almost guaranteed to push one completely over the edge. Mine will no doubt be spent visiting Mother, who now resides at a home for the bewildered, the confused, and the just plain cuckoo. Mother is rapidly descending the stairs of degeneration; to be honest, some days I think she has a fast pass and is taking the express lift straight to the basement. The home smells of wilted hyacinths, lamb fat and incontinence, but the staff are amicable and I believe Mother is well looked after.

Last time I visited, she was sitting stiffly in a high-backed chair, wearing a pastel pink cardigan, embroidered with daisies (That nearly made me cry actually - the mother I grew up with would never have given such a garment house room, let alone worn it.) Anyway, she was watching the television, when the adverts came on: a young housewife was busy nourishing her nearest and dearest with savoury crispy pancakes. Mother gave a loud' Tut!', and looked at me with great annoyance. At first, I thought she was going to launch in with an attack on the evils of convenience foods so prevalent in the kitchens of the so-called modern housewife, but no.

'There are *so* many repeats on these days. I've definitely seen this programme before!' - I opened my mouth to speak; then shut it again - at least her memory hadn't totally failed her.

We played cards for a while, an equally frustrating venture. 'No, mother,' I said gently, 'a run has to be all in same suit; see, all hearts, all spades...' I showed her an example from my hand, '...look yours are all different suits: three of diamonds, four of hearts, five of clubs.' I picked up her cards and gave them back to her. She looked thoughtful. I took my turn.

'Now it's your go, mother.' She picked from the pile, rearranged the fan tightly gripped in her bony fingers, discarded, and with a flourish of triumph, she lay down exactly the same set of cards as before – a run of completely muddled suits.

'I've won again!' She chuckled darkly.

I sighed inwardly.

'Well done, Mother. Would you like to play another hand?' Naturally, she did.

'Your mother does enjoy a game of cards, Mr Johnson, doesn't she?'

I did my best to smile at the jolly care assistant proffering tea and a plate of Viennese whirls.

'Keeps their minds active,' she whispered to me, as if she were sharing a dangerous conspiracy theory.

The morsel of Viennese whirl seemed to disintegrate and dissolve into nothingness in my mouth, soft and powdery as ashes. What a simply perfect food for a care home.

I glanced up at Mother, to see how she was enjoying her afternoon tea; how she savoured the ashes in her mouth. Her papery cheeks were drawn in and on her pale thin lips a few fine crumbs lay like dust. She looked so lost. I realised she was drifting further away from me than she had ever been… how I stopped myself climbing onto her lap, longing to be cuddled, before her arms were folded forever in an eternal self-embrace, I'll never know.

So, to be realistic, what kind of a Christmas could we share? The two of us, shamefully compliant with the enforced jollity of paper-hat wearing, and me pulling both ends of a cracker, because 'Poor old Mrs Johnson is not as strong as she once was.'…crumbling as she was now, around the edges, like the dried pastry crust on a stale ubiquitous mince pie. Yes…as you can imagine, I looked forward to Christmas this year as much as one who'd be throttled just below the wattle, drawn, scalded, plucked, stuffed, basted and eaten in an atmosphere of cracker-joke hilarity…well, actually not quite that bad, but it was a fairly dismal prospect. Perhaps, I should get the happy pills before the festivities begin…

On a more cheerful note, Gary finally succeeded in finding a job at a new outlet park on the edge of town, and Mary still pops in from time to time. She often nods towards the typewriter, which sits on a small table facing the window overlooking the backyard.

'Well? Are you there yet?'

'Nearly,' I always reply.

Then she says, 'Well, you keep at it.'

Mine, has become a very small life: I live in a shrunken house with withered rooms; I eat small portions of boil-in-the- bag grey-flecked fish, swimming in its own thin, salty, off-white glue; I speak with restrained economy when spoken to, but Thaddeus doesn't initiate conversation very often. More than a year has passed since my life began to fragment and fall apart. All of humanity knows time is a great healer… But some times are longer than others.

Prometheus, I salute you. Your tortured cries echo down the centuries, screaming through the labyrinth of my mind. But let me comfort you in the sure knowledge that even your liverish torments will cease.

I miss my job, my colleagues, my old house, I even miss Marion, but most of all I miss, Anna. It's like watching a house of cards collapsing in on itself;

everything one had so carefully built, that formed part of one's life, one's existence, now gone. Bit by bit, it falls.

Mary's promised me a bottle of champagne if the answer ever changes from 'nearly finished,' to 'yes.' Her money is safe for a good while yet; most days I think if I live to be a hundred this will never be finished business. But one day, I trust I will look up into the evening sky and not have my view of it obscured by the ominous shadow of an eagle – *This,* is hope.

Ah, now in the image of Prometheus I find my doorway into Florence. Here, in the agony of his body bound to a rock in the crisping blaze of the sun, figure upon figure superimpose themselves - each locked in a battle to be free - *The Captives*.

Of every building, painting or sculpture we saw together in Florence, it was *The Captives* who gripped my imagination like nothing else; held as they were, in their struggle to be born. Just the sheer weight of stone bearing down on their shoulders; the mass of marble enclosing their hands; the heads immovably bound. No effort of will could release them. Theirs is the agony of inertia. Hours passed in the Academy as we wandered through its galleries, amazed by the wealth of art flowing like a river all around us, but in the back of my mind always an image of never-ending struggle. They called to me in voices half-formed, muffled, weary. What did they say? I strained my ears to hear.

Now, I know it is a popular school of thought to interpret them as Platonic images of the human soul imprisoned in the body and longing to escape, but they didn't whisper that to me. They were more concrete than that. They were every man that ever lived, who has yearned to be something more than the lumpened individual he realises he is; weighed down by the burdens of life, tortured by his limitations. Life races past me - if only I could free myself from every constraint of self-doubt; of fear; of failure; of the dark, heavy shadows of my past – then I could live. Then I could be the man I have the vision to be. How can I crawl out from beneath the heavy greyness of my gravestone?

(Strangely, a slow smile has just formed in my face, and I make a mental note, that tomorrow I will show Mary a picture of The Captives in a book I have upstairs. At last, I have found the one thing that is better for being unfinished. An unfamiliar thrill rises within me. How much less would these sculptures be if Michelangelo had 'finished' them, and they had stood alone without their prison of stone? Their imperfection and their suffering were the source of all their beautiful, stoic grandeur. All the stone stripped away, they would mean less, not more. The mystery of the sculptor's vision would be so exposed – naked - and all the agony of the human condition lost. They would not haunt me with their wearied voices, grown weak and hoarse from exertion; those voices I have come to love as my constant companion.

I pictured Mary's ruddy face, with the tip of her tongue poking through her lips as it always did when she concentrated. 'Well, I'll be damned, but I guess you're right with this one.')

Florence was searingly hot. At least in the Tuscan hills there was the occasional breeze, and a sense of green openness, but in Florence, everything baked. The whole city is like being in a kiln of recently fired terracotta pots. The walls and roofs of buildings absorbed, retained and reflected the sun's heat. We tried to dash quickly between the shadows and the bright patches of intense sunlight, but it was futile. Moving at speed drained us of all energy, and the shade offered little cool relief anyway.

Anna seemed to be evaporating before my eyes; the heat sucking every drop of vitality out of her. She often had to rest, leaning against one of the dry crumbling walls, as we wandered from gallery to gallery, church to church. I suggested to her she might be harbouring a low-grade version of the bug I'd had last week, especially as she was prone to feelings of faintness and queasiness.

In fact, only yesterday, the sight of a tiny octopus which turned up in a bowl of seafood risotto, nearly made her heave on the spot; all the colour drained from her face and she retched - just like Thaddeus with a particularly large hairball. It's almost laughable when I think of my reaction - I actually whisked my plate of guinea fowl with pancetta out of the way so it wouldn't get vomit on it. Not very gallant, but it's a favourite of mine, and not often on the menu in England. Anyway, thankfully, she wasn't actually sick - only felt ill.

She even apologised to me saying she was sorry for choosing the risotto, but had no idea that such a creature would emerge as she dug her fork into the rice. She had honestly thought seafood risotto would be a mixture of fish, with perhaps the odd mussel.

'Do people actually eat those little, slimy, spidery… ugh…the way all its legs were twisted in different directions - all fried and crispy - Oh, God – and the smell!'

I offered to order her an omelette instead, but she declined. A very affronted waiter took the offending cephalopod back to the kitchens. However, I have to say the meal wasn't a total disaster; my guinea fowl was, as I'd hoped, superb.

I suggested as soon as we got back to the village, she should go and see a local doctor.

'I'm sure it's just the heat. I'm not usually like this. It must be in the late nineties, if not a hundred.'

If only it had been 'just the heat.' How differently life would have unfolded.

Chapter Thirty-five: Summer surprised us

When we returned to the Tuscan hills Anna's health and mood seemed to improve. Our trip to Florence seemed to have had just the desired effect, in spite of those odd moments of nausea brought on by the heat; we did have a wonderful time. To share such a fabulous city together made my heart soar and I knew she loved me all the more for showing her such wonderful things.

In our hotel bed one night, we talked about the power of the sculptures we'd seen. *The Captives*, as I have already told you held a special significance for me, *(even more so now,)* but I was equally drawn to the Medici's tombs, with the reclining figures of Dawn and Dusk, Day and Night. Mine was a double joy. Firstly, my heart was gripped by the overwhelming magnificence of these pieces, and secondly, I gained a deep and lasting pleasure in watching Anna as she came face to face with such masterpieces for the first time. *In situ* these works take on a metaphysical grandeur. They were frightening in their true perception of the human condition.

Later in the darkness she whispered to me. 'I remember now where I've heard of the tombs before...it's been hovering in the back of my mind all day.'

'Where?'

'In a novel – *Antic Hay*.

'Huxley.'

'Well, yes. Something Coleman says about some people 'getting off' on sliding down slopes.'

Even in the thickness of the night I knew her exact expression at this moment - above her nose two vertical parallel lines would have appeared as she furrowed her brow in thought, and any moment now she'd make a funny clicking noise with her tongue until the answer formed in her mind. I couldn't recall what she was talking about at all.

'Oh, come on Alistair. You should know this. It's that godforsaken bit where they're dancing to that song, 'What's he to Hecuba?' and watching that dire play about the monster. It's so funny – you must remember it.'

However, before I could trawl through my memory bank, *(It must be twenty years at least since I read that novel in entirety)* the lines had popped into her head, and she told me. Not exactly of course, but very close to the actual quote, which I've written here for you:

'And some like sliding down slopes and cannot look at Michelangelo's 'Night' on the Medici Tombs without dying the little death, because the statue seems to be sliding.'

'What a good memory you have,' I congratulated her. 'Of course, on closer reading you'll be able to find many parallels between *Antic Hay* and *The Waste Land* which...'

'I have managed to work that out for myself, thank you, Professor Pedagogue.'

She gave me a playful dig in the ribs.

'Ow!'

I stretched out my hands and pulled her towards me.

We continued to spend some time engaged in intimate discourse on the nature of night, sliding, and the little death.

Yes - I think Florence had fulfilled its purpose. Our relationship felt completely back on track.

And although it sounds as though Coleman, and even myself, are making light of Medici tombs, really there is a serious point to be found here. Take a look at those statues – and you'll see it's true. Part of the uncomfortable feeling of insecurity these figures arouse in one may be due to the very fact that they do appear to be sliding; centuries of precariously static tobogganing. Of all of them only Day seems to actively try to hold on; trying to pull himself back from the inevitable edge. The rest are too languid; almost accepting, with a weary lassitude of knowing the truth. What is that truth?

(Consider this: What actually prevents them all from slipping is the fact they are completely fused to a tomb. What does this mean I ask myself?

My interpretation is that if you accept that every moment of your life is underpinned by your certain, and inevitable death, then you can hold on. Look at the face of Dawn. Just as she begins to rise, she glances back to see from where she has risen, and from where she will return. There's a sense of sorrowful recognition in her face. Now, look at Dusk, a more accepting 'Oh, still there. Never mind'. And Night, haunted by the dreams of a life lived...so quickly - over now. Was I ever really there? Only Day, at the peak of life thinks he can escape - but the rest know. Hate it as they do, they know what gives life its meaning. Knowing your life comes with a guaranteed grave stuck to your bony spine, you can lay back and relax - 'enjoy' the ride. Fight it, deny it and it's crash, bang, wallop to the floor for you.

'Who is the third who walks always beside you?'

Yes - hold my hand. Yes, you. Walk with me. Walk where I can keep an eye on you. No, not too close. That's close enough. Too close and your breath chills me.)

****

It's one of those nights when the wind is screeching and howling like a thing on fire, and a sudden, violent burst of rain catches Thaddeus unawares. He shoots through the cat flap with a clatter, circumnavigates the living room helter-skelter, then stands shuddering, with his ginger fur almost chestnut brown, he's so drenched. I wrap him in an old white towel to dry him off. Marion and I used to joke that his little face peering through the swaddling of the towel made him look like he was auditioning for the part of the baby Jesus in the local Nativity play. After a few moments of swaddling, Thaddeus struggles and I disentangle him from the towel and attempt to rub him down further while he lies like a lion on the carpet. But that's it. He's had enough, and with a flick of his tail and a very impolite spit, leaps to the top of the sofa, where he spends the next half an hour cleaning himself. 'Horrible night, eh Thads?' He agrees, and at his suggestion I draw the curtains and put the gas fire on.

But really, I digress - again. Back in the village, I was living: pure and simple. I was happy once more...

During the week following the Florence trip, we attended the event of the year: the royal wedding of Prince Charles and Lady Diana Spencer. Maggie was hosting a day of celebration, and requested the company of many of her wide circle of eclectic friends, plus a good number of ex-pats with whom she was acquainted, to join with her in witnessing the joyful nuptials on her television. With the wedding taking place at 11.20 am English time, we were invited to her house from midday onwards for an all-day jamboree. Her lounge was already over-flowing with the excitable throng of wedding guests, many dressed for the occasion. Even at this early hour, Maggie was already well into the Prosecco, sipping from a fluted glass while reclining opulently like a fully-fleshed Rubens on a garden lounger she had set up for the occasion. Her wedding attire amounted to a sleeveless sundress of some dangerously unsuitable diaphanous material, which only perilously draped about her. She spotted us from her day bed and twirled her hand regally in our direction. 'My dears, my dears, welcome! How wonderful to see you. Do come and help yourselves to whatever refreshment you require to get you through this noble ceremony of 'marry-arge'. Come, Anna, darling,' she said, her arm wobbling as she patted a large cushion which lay to the side of her, 'you must sit by me...a ring-side seat!' And like an obedient little lap dog, Anna picked her way through the chairs, then curled her legs beneath her and nestled next to Nina, who had obviously been allowed time off to watch the historic event. By contrast, I had to make do with sitting on an uncomfortable plank of wood balanced between two stools, positioned behind the sofa with Duncan, Matteo, from the gallery, and a man who looked like Uncle Fester.

'Such crowds!' he quipped jovially, shuffling along the plank. 'Here one can hardly stand, lie or sit! Allow me to introduce myself,' Uncle Fester said extending his hand. 'Arthur's the name, George Arthur.' I shook his hand and volunteered my name, as one does. 'And your lovely daughter?' he asked throwing a glance towards Anna. 'Ha!' exclaimed Duncan. '*Not* his daughter, old chap,' and accompanied this with an exaggerated wink.

'Goodness,' Uncle Fester burbled all of a fluster, 'the brides keep getting younger and younger.' With eyes bulging, he stared fixedly at the television, gripping the back of the sofa with blotchy thick liver-spotted hands. For the rest of the ceremony, we four all peered over the row of heads in front of us, at the television. Glimpses of the happy bride-to-be (overwhelmed by a froth of fabric), and her beaming father seated in a fairy-tale glass coach, were obscured by the Italian presenters who took up centre screen. They gabbled away in a most animated fashion. 'il matrimonia Carlo e Diana...'

'When are we going to see the dress properly?' wailed a dumpy woman who was perched on a wooden bar stool. With her pale silvery grey dress, yellow feathery hat and orange cheeks she looked just like a plump cockatiel, and I half expected her to bob up and down and ring a little bell any moment.

'Shhh, Barbara, when she gets out, of course.'

'We'll be lucky to see it at all if these two jokers don't bugger off,' grumbled another disgruntled guest. A plate of very English sausage rolls took a turn about the room, which had a calming effect on the agitated company, until they had the satisfaction of seeing the acres of crumpled ivory taffeta tumble from the coach. 'Oh, just like a fairy-tale Princess!' chorused some of the ladies.

'Looks like it needs a damn good ironing to me,' Duncan dared to whisper out the corner of his mouth. I had to agree; for one awful moment the long-awaited dress looked more like crumpled packaging than a garment.

'Ah, just listen to the cheers of the loyal serfs and the dazzling trumpet fanfare, all to hail the sacrificial virgin!' Maggie proclaimed raising her glass, slopping a little wave of Prosecco into her lap.

'Don't spoil it, Maggie,' squawked Barbara, from her perch, as she threw Maggie a surprisingly aggressive look. Maggie smiled serenely.

We watched them stumble over their vows and listened as the Archbishop announced that all wedding couples were as husband and wife: 'Kings and Queens of creation.' (It wasn't an image that came to mind from my own experience of wedded bliss.) As they processed to sign the register, I thought how like a giant serpent the train was as it slithered along the floor, following them both.

Above the sound of the bells of St Paul's, I just managed to overhear Anna say breathlessly to Maggie, 'Just imagine what her life is going to be like...'

'For as a lamb is brought to slaughter, so she stands, this innocent, before the king.'(Man of Law's Tale, 1386). I didn't say those prophetic words out loud, of course.

A little later we were all summoned to the garden, into the torrid heat of the early afternoon sun, where under the walnut tree a long trellis table, draped with union jack bunting, had been erected. 'Self servitzio, one and all,' pronounced Maggie with an exaggerated sweeping gesture towards the abundance of food. Then, with all the precision of a concussed sheepdog, she attempted to herd several guests in the direction of the table. 'Self servizio! Cominciare!'

It was the usual circulatory buffet format, pick up a plate one end and trail around the table picking up bits and pieces, which were sweating fatly in the sun, until your plate was full of all manner of British fare. It was heavily pig-based: pinky but not so perky. Chunky gammon; dense pork pies encased in thick jelly and substantial pastry; mouth-wizening scotch eggs; yet another plate of damp sausage rolls; some tired salads; cheddar cheese cubes and pineapple on sticks; Maggie's homemade pickled onions; along with other ubiquitous offerings such as bandy chicken legs; and salt and vinegar crisps.

'Have you partaken of some mushroom quiche?' Barbara chirped into my ear. 'I made it – it's very nice.' I smiled, and, not wishing to offend, helped myself to a slice of the watery yellow and blackish-grey offering. Anna and I joined Duncan and Sally who were sitting awkwardly on a plaid rug. With some effort, Duncan, toad-like, gulped down a flabby slice of gammon, coughed slightly, and announced that he could hardly wait for Sally's speciality, Eton Mess. 'You're such a pudding-face, Duncan,' she chided. 'Anyone would think he was deprived; the truth is he still gets it at least twice a week.' Uncle Fester, whose large backside had claimed a fold-up garden seat nearby, gave an 'ooh err missus' look in our direction, but I managed to avoid meeting his eye. Deflated, he returned to the sinewy business of the chicken leg in his purple fist.

It was dawning on me, somewhat embarrassingly, that everyone seemed to have contributed to the lunchtime feast but us. Somehow, I must've have missed the missive requesting our finest donations to the patriotic marriage breakfast. In the meantime, I was discovering the mushrooms in the quiche had the curious texture (and possibly taste) of slowly simmered slugs. But I ate them anyway... watching the crowds of people, walking round in a ring.

Anna had returned to spending days by the pool, still often drifting up to Maggie's to paint. It was August now, and conscious of the impending return to university in the autumn, Anna had begun to attack the reading list. Gently swinging in a hammock slung between two almond trees, she spent hours with Dickens, Shakespeare and Marlow, and a whole raft of poets. Occasionally, we discussed various points and I'd offer my interpretations, but I was cautious to avoid blurring the lines between us. I wanted to keep the two spheres in which we had to operate as separate as possible. And besides any whiff of me assuming a high and mighty stance from my superior knowledge resulted in Anna distancing herself from me in a way I could not bear. So, I began to take up a distraction of my own – gardening of all things. It's amazing how much time one can fill pottering and pruning, weeding and watching plants growing and fading. Marion would have found it very amusing to see me with my wide-brimmed hat, secateurs in hand, trimming the foliage. But it was strangely therapeutic. I was also fascinated by the tiny lizards, seemingly so torpid, until disturbed, then scuttling with great speed into cracks and crevices, scaling walls and suddenly still once more. Several weeks slipped by, slowly, effortlessly, as if the air were perfumed with some strange dreamlike narcotic. For the first time in my life I was truly relaxed, lulled into a state of warm indolent bliss. And every day and night I stole glimpses of her complete beauty and marvelled. Everything I had ever wanted was there, at that moment. *She's all states, and all princes, I, Nothing else is.*

'I'd love to see this masterpiece,' I mentioned one afternoon as she left the house.

'I'd prefer to show you when it's finished – I'm not that confident about it yet.'

'Fair enough,' I responded without a care. 'Don't be too late back though; I thought we'd go out for dinner tonight.'

She had only been gone half an hour when I heard the phone ringing. Bother, I thought. There was I, nicely ensconced on my favourite lounger under the vine, reading an English newspaper, which I'd bought myself as a treat in town that morning; a cold bottled beer to my left – and the phone rings. Damn. It took me a good couple of minutes to reach it.

'It's Maggie, Alistair. I think you'd better come and collect Anna; she's had a funny turn...bit of an episode.

'What do you mean?' I said with an obvious note of panic rising in my voice.

'Oh, nothing to alarm yourself about. Arrived here, was promptly poorly, little sick, little faint - just needs to come home. Bring the car, dear – still rather wobbly.'

I did as I was told, pulling up in front of Maggie's house only minutes later. Maggie opened the door wearing a sizeable purple sarong, and some golden flip-flops. 'What a pity,' she began, 'today of all days. I was going to ask Anna if she'd like to join me in a life session with Nina. It's her afternoon off, but she's saving up for driving lessons, so I offered her a little extra work.'

'Where's Anna?'

'On the sofa, do go…through,' she said as I disappeared down the hallway. She was reclining against one of the plush velvet cushions, resting a glass of water against her chest. 'Oh, Alistair' she sighed, 'you really needn't have come. I'd have been alright in a minute, but Maggie…'

'Insisted,' said Maggie entering the room. 'Looked decidedly peaky when she arrived,' she confided in a stage whisper; then leaning to Anna added,

'Didn't you, my dear? Shall I offer Alistair some refreshment before you both head home?'

Anna said she felt fine now, and that I could stay or go or whatever suited me best. Maggie hollered at the bottom of the stairs for Nina to come and say hello to Anna. There was no reply. 'Perhaps she's slipped out?' said Maggie, looking bemused. 'She was here when Anna arrived; practising her flute. I could hear her upstairs. Oh, well.'

Maggie beckoned me with a hand heavy with rings and I followed her into the kitchen. She took a jug of Pimm's from the fridge and poured two large glassfuls, ice and chunks of fruit plopping and splashing cheerfully.

'Well, I am still an English gal at heart. Chin! Chin!' she said sucking spilt Pimm's from her finger. She suggested that I went to sit beneath the walnut tree in the garden; she was going to have a quick hunt for Nina and would join me shortly. I checked once more on Anna, who had her eyes shut now, so I wandered out into the singing heat of the afternoon. The contrast between being inside the cool dark stone interior of Maggie's villa and the outside, where the sun had been beating down all day was remarkable. It was like walking into a pyroclastic cloud.

Ah! I could taste it just from the smell, so sweet, fruity and zestfully minty. As I strolled towards the shade of the walnut, I took several small sips. I hadn't had a Pimm's in ages. It always took me right back to a picnic I shared with an old school-friend of mine, Christopher Dawson, who'd been lucky enough, (well, clever enough,) to go to Cambridge.

Imagine if you will the quintessential summer's afternoon on the river – every cliché enjoying an unashamed day out: Pimm's, a raised game pie, strawberries, and a weathered punt, made comfortable with cushions glossy from use – and two young men, bent on capturing the hedonistic languor of a scene from Brideshead.

The cow parsley drifted past, nodding lazily in a gentle breeze and willows dipped their elegant branches into the water. Here, in the top section of the Cam, the river was verdant and mysterious. Very few people seemed to have bothered to attempt the punt to Grantchester today, and often we were quite alone; slipping through the water, almost soundlessly. Occasionally, groups of heifers stood wondering, staring at us; trails of spittle hanging like molten glass from their mouths.

Once or twice a group of students pushed vigorously passed us, all laughing loudly, high-jinks – a boatful of banter – none of them feeling they would have had a good day out until someone had fallen in. One puntful of young bucks tried to engage us in a splashing contest, but Christopher refused to respond. We exchanged world-weary looks, while Christopher slowed the punt right down until their jamboree faded into the distance. They shouted, what sounded like several disparaging remarks, as they disappeared round the bend.

'What did they say?' I asked, as I'd been unable to hear exactly.
'Nothing,' said Christopher, 'nothing at all.' Then he added irritably, 'I can't abide that sort of childish nonsense.'

'No, me neither,' I agreed, but followed this comment by scooping up a large handful of water and dousing him with it.

'Just you wait, Johnson!' he laughed, pushing his tousled damp hair back from his forehead.

He was wearing a white collarless shirt, with the top two buttons undone, and his sleeves were rolled up tight, so his biceps looked almost bound as he pulled the pole upwards from the thick mud of the river bed. Idly, I lay, watching him. The sun threw a dappled light through the trees, and in the pools of light his skin gleamed with sweat. Lazily, lowering my hand into the cool dark waters, I let my fingers trail like loose ribbons of weed.

'I've heard there are pike in this stretch…' Christopher remarked casually. I withdrew my hand rapidly, dripping water all over my shorts. He smiled down at me, laughing again, and then said, quite affectionately, 'Oh, Alistair, you're so gullible.' Still grinning, I turned my attention to a family of ducks bobbing gently in our wake. Out of the corner of my eye I was aware that Christopher was still gazing at me – a strange excited tremor ran down my spine.

We punted on for another half an hour or so, when Christopher declared he was too exhausted to punt any further, was 'exceedingly ravenous' and wanted to stop for a picnic right now.

'I say old chap!' Christopher said, clambering onto the bank, 'Isn't this a perfectly spiffing spot for a picnic.' (This wasn't Christopher's natural mode of speech, but a hang-over from our school days when we tried to talk like Lord Snooty from The Beano.)

'Topping!' I replied, 'Absolutely topping!'

Christopher threw a large tartan rug onto the grass, but because the grass was so long and stiff, the rug looked like an enormous pillow, all plumped up. He fell on it and rolled from side to side to flatten it, then lay, propped on one elbow, his eyes squinting up in the sunlight. Patting the rug, he said, 'This is as soft as a mattress.'

For some reason, I felt flustered, unable to respond as I knelt down by the wicker basket I'd carried from the punt. 'What's in this picnic, then?' finally escaped from my lips.

'Every kind of goodie imaginable,' he said springing up from the rug and taking over the unpacking of the picnic, producing each item with such a flourish that I felt compelled to 'ooh' and 'ahh' excitedly, and even to applaud the raised game pie. Christopher had certainly gone to great pains to prepare such a wonderful picnic. He'd been out early that morning, purchased the pie from the butchers, bought two custard tarts from the bakers, strawberries from the market, made the cucumber sandwiches himself, and even picked mint from someone's front garden when no one was looking – and he'd gone to the trouble of pouring the Pimm's into two large flasks to keep it perfectly chilled. He handed me a Pimm's in a pint glass; its beautiful amber colour, making it look as innocuous as cold tea.

'Now, now old bean, this just won't do…aren't you supposed to chop the mint up a bit. What, what?' I complained, pulling a long string of wilted mint from my glass. 'This looks like some straggly weed from the bottom of the river.' And I threw the unsightly piece of withered mint at him. It landed like a wet, green scar across his cheek. Making a thunderous face, he slowly peeled the strand from his cheek, and seethed, 'Down with your glass, sir, and run for your life.' And he was after me like a greyhound after a hare.

He caught me easily, wrestled me to the ground then held my body in a lock, face-down against the scratchy grass. I struggled, but he was always stronger than me. With his weight pinning me to the earth, I became intensely aware of the sweet hay aroma of the grass; the cacophony of crickets singing; the distant high-pitched shriek of a girl larking about on the river, and of the sound of Christopher breathing heavily against my ear. His body was pressing closely against mine – I tried to throw him off - but he pushed down onto me even harder. His face was against mine; the heady scent of Pimm's on his breath. He felt so heavy. It was as if I were trapped under the weight of a sarcophagus - I could barely breathe.

His mouth moved against my cheek, 'Give up, yet?' he panted. We'd been through this scenario so many times before, but something felt different...

'Fainites,' my strangled voice whispered, still using the language of our childhood. Slowly he rolled from my body, leaving me feeling strangely vulnerable, exposed, like an animal that had lost its shell. With a light tap of his foot against the back of my thigh he told me I was utterly feeble, that he could take me any time he wanted. He offered his hand to pull me to my feet. Hot and out of breath, we ambled back across the meadow pushing and shoving one another as we went, and finally resumed the picnic, which was as delicious as I'd anticipated.

'I know it's two lots of pastry,' he said apologetically offering me a custard tart, 'but I remembered how they were always your favourites when you came to tea at our house.'

I sank my teeth into the soft, gelatinous custard, my mouth filling with the sweet goo, fragrant with nutmeg. He was watching me eat.

'Good?'

'Mmm!' I nodded, with a tight-lipped smiled.

After lunch, Christopher took off his shirt and lay on his back in the sun, chewing a long strand of grass. His bare stomach looked muscular and taut; his slim hips which tapered into the waistband of his shorts were strangely compelling. 'Aren't you hot, too?' he asked me, his hand lighting on mine briefly. 'Why don't you take your shirt off?'

'I'm too fair- skinned. I always used to burn in the summer- remember?'

'Half an hour wouldn't hurt.'

'I'm fine.'

'Yes - you certainly are.' He smiled with an unnerving intensity into my eyes.

I laughed, taking this as a joke, a little fun word-play. Christopher flushed slightly, and then flipped onto his front, with his face buried in the crock of his arm. A criss-cross of red lines were slashed across his back: imprints from the rug. He looked like he had been whipped.

We never did make it to Grantchester. I couldn't get the hang of punting and we were both too tired and drunk by two o'clock to bother.

Later that evening, Christopher took me to formal hall. Everything was all so beautiful, rarefied and privileged. Christopher looked splendid in his gown, refined and intellectual; he even smelt sophisticated, having slapped an expensive aftershave about his face after his bath. As he talked and laughed so easily with other students and fellows alike, I felt proud to be his friend. With a warm and generous tone, he introduced me as his 'oldest and closest friend', while placing his hand comfortingly on my shoulder. My flesh sang beneath his touch.

After several sherries, we took our places at the grand lengthy table resplendent with fine cutlery and candelabra. Sitting opposite us was another of Christopher's friends, Susan. 'Susan…' she said, 'Geographer,' as I shook her hand across the table.

'Oh, right…Alistair…English.' I replied. She coincidently had a friend staying with her this weekend as well. Susan's friend was named 'Marion.' (There, I bet that surprised you.)

'Marion…' she said, shaking my hand confidently, and then added with a glint in her eye, 'Plummer.' I nodded sagely, wondering how on earth this woman studying plumbing was feasting with us at formal hall.

'How unusual,' I stuttered, 'not many women keen to cope with burst pipes and blocked drains!'

She leant across the table and with pained deliberation, whispered, 'It's my surname.'

'Ha!' I gave a nervous laugh. 'I see.' (God, she must think I'm slow.)

Benedic, Domine, nos et dona tua, quae de largitate tua sumus sumpturi…Christum Dominum nostrum.

Across the table in the candlelight, Marion looked surprisingly engaging, with her large heavily lidded blue eyes and high well-defined eyebrows, swept-back brunette hair and lips so perfectly even, they looked almost unnatural. She had a look of Bette Davis – which later she did her best to disguise, especially after the movie, *Whatever Happened to Baby Jane?*

It turned out that Marion was also visiting from a… *Hush! Pas devoir les enfants!* … from a red brick university. Maybe it was my imagination, maybe my paranoia, but every time someone asked which college I was at, and my reply rang no bells with either esteemed seat of learning, there was a little struggle to compose the face - trying not to look condescending, but failing miserably, the little downward cadence 'Oh, really?...and you're reading?'

So, Marion and I shared an immediate bond: glued together by our social and academic inferiority complex. We were united against the rest of the world.

Although much later that evening, I was to discover this had all been in my imagination. Marion didn't give a monkey's about what university anyone had been to. 'It's academic snobbery of the worst sort – surely you're not taken in by it?' Turned out Marion had had an offer from the other ancient university, but had preferred to go to Manchester. 'My father insisted I apply, but when it came to it, I just couldn't bear the thought of it. I was quite influenced by my boyfriend of the time, fairly socialist in his thinking. All that privileged pomposity, it just stuck in his craw– didn't appeal to me either...' (Many years later, Marion confessed she regretted her lack of resolution in this choice, torn between pleasing the boyfriend and annoying her father or vice-versa. It was my 'great refusal,' she declared. 'But just think Marion, if you had gone to Oxford, we may never have met.' She replied after a few moments with a cock of her head and a raised eyebrow, and sighing said, 'Yes...that's probably true, Alec.')

'Oh, I can understand why,' I lied, rolling my eyes around at the wanton display of privilege on show.

'May I call you Alec by the way? Alistair sounds such a poncey name.'

'Be my guest.' (When I think of the things Marion would come to call me in the subsequent years this was a mild transgression from my birth name.)

I have to say, Marion was quite striking in those days, feisty, with a strong healthy physique. The sort of girl you'd expect to see strutting about the hockey pitch in the winter, lobbing javelins around the university playing fields in the summer, while simultaneously running a successful campaign to be president of the students' union; notwithstanding directing, and taking the lead in an avant-garde, all-female, production of *Macbeth*; and still finding time to put in three hours self-directed study every evening - without breaking into a sweat. She was a powerful girl. What *did* she see in me? I have often wondered.

From what I can recall, I think she arranged to see me the next day for tea at The Copper Kettle, and we took it from there. However hard I tried, I couldn't persuade Christopher to come along. Strangely, he suddenly had some very pressing work which he had to complete for the next day. He came with me to the station at six, but, after waving me off, I never saw him again. I wrote several times. He never returned my letters, his parents moved house; we lost touch… I wonder what he's up to these days.

'Alistair.' Maggie awoke me abruptly from my reverie.

'Sorry Maggie, miles away.'

'I didn't mean to leave you so long, Alistair, but I had a phone call from England. Would you like to take a turn about the garden?'

'How could I resist such an offer - you're not reading Jane Austen at the moment, by any chance, are you?'

'No, Alistair I'm not. Should I be?'

'No, it's nothing.'

'Goodness, it's still rather warm, isn't? 'Maggie sighed, her voice a gloopy golden syrup. She refilled our glasses from the jug of Pimm's she was carrying and indicated to follow a small pathway, which led down to a second terrace. Here, was a small pergola festooned with trailing scented white flowers, under which two slightly rusty, wrought iron chairs sat, staring out across the valley. 'Henry's favourite spot,' she sighed. 'Still is...' Shielding her eyes against the fierce sun, Maggie peered into the quivering heat haze. 'He promised a new start...he was never more right, of course.' We fell into quiet contemplation; it was unreal, almost eerie. The earth beneath our feet was dry and dusty, almost bare. I realised Maggie must spend many hours, in this very spot, scraping the cracked soles of her feet against the parched gritty soil, watching the simmering landscape, longing for rain.

Eventually, sensing there must be something difficult she wished to discuss, I broke the silence. 'Penny for them, Maggie?' Normally, she was so verbose, only a really sensitive subject would cause her to pause so cautiously with her words. Perhaps she wanted to withdraw the offer of the use of her studio? Or better still, maybe she wanted to share with me the true nature of her relationship with Nina, which I must admit intrigued me.

'It's about Anna,' she began…ah, I thought, I was right - studio getting a little too overcrowded. 'There's no easy way for me to say this, and please forgive me if I'm speaking out of turn…' she was fiddling anxiously with one of her enormous rings, 'but have either of you considered the possibility that all this fatigue and nausea might not be the result of a latent bug, or heat intolerance, but that she just might, in fact, be pregnant.'

'Pregnant ?'

'Yes. Pregnant.'

'Pregnant ?'

'Well, I wouldn't have suggested it if I didn't think it was a possibility - it is a possibility, isn't it, Alistair? You haven't had the ole 'snip-snip' have you?' And she hung some invisible testicles between her finger and thumb and chopped through them with a scissoring motion of her other fingers.

I gulped hard. 'No.' (Although if I include Marion's frequent verbal castrations, the answer was probably about once or twice a week.)

'Do say if I'm speaking out of turn, but if Anna was… you'd want to make sure she was alright, wouldn't you?' I nodded – speechless. 'Alistair dear, do shut your mouth; you look like a fish flapping about at the bottom of a boat.'

I shut my mouth, my lips feeling dry as they met. Through the empty arid air, the haunting cry of a buzzard tore through the skies. Upon the fractured surface of the stone wall a green-brown lizard darted – disappearing into the dusty cracks.

The word 'pregnant' fell into my mind like pattering rain drops, then faster and faster the word crashed down – a deluge, a flood of words – each one the same – Pregnant. Pregnant. Pregnant – big fat raindrops pounding, bouncing off flagstones.

Sometimes, seconds last for hours. Between a 'tick', and a 'tock', a whole world can change.

Have you ever seen the Severn bore? Think of that tidal surge now. Imagine it starting at the tips of your toes and rising; rushing through your arteries, forcing, gushing through every capillary; up your body, bursting in your heart and its unstoppable power driving onwards into your brain – flood upon flood.

'It might be best if you didn't say I'd put this idea in your head, Alistair. Let it come from you.' Maggie patted my hand. 'I might be wrong of course,' she continued, a light-hearted tone creeping into her voice, 'let's hope so, eh? I mean, I presume it would all be a bit awkward, wouldn't it?'

I looked up staring into the middle distance. Maggie began flinging the fruit from her Pimm's about the grass. 'I like to think birds will eat them. Some creatures actively seek out fermented fruit, you know.' She smiled at the thought of these kindred spirits, and attempted to fold her arms across her chest. Her unfettered bounteous bosom hung like two lolloping sacks of flour beneath her sarong. I wondered if her nipples reached down to her navel and watched fascinated as the skin in her cleavage puckered up into crinkly ruched folds.

'There's a chemist just down the road from the gallery,' she offered. 'These new tests work in minutes – apparently. Well, I know they do actually…' My eyes widened in disbelief. She slapped my hand playfully, and with a gurgle said, 'Not me you fool! Had a bit of a crisis with Nina a few months ago - negative - thank God!'

I must practise concealing my emotions better, for before I could stop myself, my next thought was out on the air, spinning around in excited confusion like sycamore key in a brisk wind. 'She has a boyfriend? But I thought you and ehm…Nina were…' (Oh, God, what to say?) 'close.''

'Close?' There was an interminable pause, while she tried to assimilate what I'd just implied. Suddenly, 'the penny dropped'. 'Ooh, really Alistair! Surely you didn't think?!' Clapping her hands to her face, she laughed her fulsome undulating laugh; the golden molars gleaming in the sunlight.

Stumbling on, I said, 'But you seem… so fond of her.'

'*Fond* of her? I *lov*e her Alistair – but, she's like a daughter to me…Goodness, to think you got the impression that I had anything other than maternal feelings…' And she looked quite perplexed for a moment; then reminded me of the perils of judging others by my own standards. 'Oh,' she added, as a thought came to her, 'don't mention the boyfriend to Nina. Things have been more on-and-off recently, more off than on. But it's certainly nothing to do with me!'

With my florid cheeks betraying my embarrassment, I stammered something about the paintings.

'I am an artist, my dear, not an ageing, predatory lesbian. I mean *look* at me Alistair. Look at me! Really, as if! You do have an extraordinarily overactive imagination.' She chuckled deeply.

Maggie indicated that I drink up my Pimm's, and then she took my arm and we took another turn about the garden. 'My days of Eros are long gone, sadly. Since Henry's passing there's been no one. Are you amazed, Alistair? I certainly am. Never thought I'd end up living like a nun.' She stopped and pulled the dried leathery petals from an overblown rose, and scattered them over the soil. 'Such simple symbolism,' she sighed. 'What is so laughably ironic is that when Henry was alive, all through our marriage really, we each indulged in a series of love affairs, including I must confess…' (and here her fruity voice oozed with over-ripeness,) '…on my part, one or two memorable rather special Sapphic encounters – so you weren't completely wide of the mark. But now he's dead and incapable of it, so am I.' She gave a hauntingly hollow laugh. 'Do you know my dear, I now wonder if I only ever had lovers to annoy Henry, to make him jealous, make him notice me.'

'Who knows why we do what we do?' I said vaguely, for obviously my mind was in a very different place.

'But you Alistair – lucky man' she paused and gave my arm a squeeze… 'love still lives and breathes in your loins.' I felt my face flush.

'Oh, and if I were twenty years younger my dear, Henry would be watching me like a hawk in your presence.' I smiled at this last comment. 'Next time round, Maggie?'

'Oh, I do hope so Alistair, I really do.'

Walking back into the villa my eyes struggled to adjust to the apparent darkness; patches of black-yellow sunlight clouded my vision. And then, as I entered the hallway, there she was, walking towards me. She said she was on her way to find me; where had I been all this time? My eyes immediately lighted upon her stomach, which I have to say did appear to be a little rounder.

'Alistair, I just asked you a question.'

'Oh, um, the edge of the garden.' I rubbed my eyes. 'It's all gone blotchy. How do you feel now?' I said trembling slightly.

'Fine, absolutely fine now, but I'll come home with you now. I fancy a swim before we go out, not in the mood to paint now, sorry,' she said to Maggie, who was now behind me, a hand resting on my shoulder.

'I don't think anyone has taken so long to produce a piece of work my dear since John Singer Sargent painted, *Carnation, Lily, Lily, Rose*. He painted just a few moments each evening as dusk fell – for months, I believe. Extraordinary.'

'Or are you our very own Michelangelo, recreating the Sistine chapel,' I added. 'You know Maggie, I still haven't been privileged to a viewing of this masterpiece.'

'I told you earlier, I want it to be finished. There's not much to see at all at the moment.'

'But you've been up in that studio for hours.' I smiled teasing her.

'I had to make an awful lot of preliminary sketches.'

'Ah,' I said sagely, 'now make sure you gather them all up before we leave – they can be worth almost as much as the finished article you know.'

Anna gave me a rueful look. 'If you carry on like this,' she said, 'I'll destroy everything even before you've laid eyes on it.'

'So temperamental! Alistair, what is one to do with these artistic types?' A light flurry of laughter, and we climbed into the Morris, where the leather seats scorched the backs of our legs. Definitely a gentle swelling of her stomach. How had I not noticed before? Tick…tock.

At dinner that evening, I winced as she drank a second glass of wine. How to broach this? And to broach it soon. I could hardly eat a thing over dinner. I still had the Severn tide surging through me. This was nothing short of a miracle. Maggie did not know why the possibility of Anna being pregnant had not occurred to me, but you know why, don't you? And I knew why. The problem is one doesn't really expect miracles, so when they happen, we often miss them.

I couldn't concentrate on Anna's conversation; I looked at her, but couldn't listen. Images pulsed through my head. I would have a child. We would be a real family. I saw myself cradling the fragile, fluffy head of a new born; Anna is smiling adoringly at us both. 'This is everything I've ever wanted,' she sighs. Marion! Gosh, yes, Marion, almost choking on her own tongue, as she bumps into us in town – out with the pushchair. I picture her face as I tell her. God! A photo of my mother … proud at last, holding a longed-for grandchild… and Tom and me in the park, kids riding on our shoulders. I'll give him – or her – the best start in life; I really will. I've stopped smoking already and I'll cut down on drinking. I'll be nearly sixty when they're ten; close to seventy when they're twenty. That's OK if you keep young and healthy. Just think, Anna will be forty then. A little voice says, 'Daddy' I'm actually grinning broadly. The tide burst through me.

'You seem to be enjoying some sort of private joke?' Anna said, between mouthfuls of her favourite pistachio nut ice cream. 'You've been away with the fairies half the evening in some kind of dreamy trance.' She pointed her long ice cream spoon across the table at me. 'What were you and Maggie talking about in the garden today? You were arm in arm; I saw you through the window. She fancies you, you know. You can tell me if you're having an affair.'

I told her there was never any possibility of me ever loving anyone but her for the rest of my entire life. And added, rather unfairly, that whilst being a good friend, Maggie could be the last woman on earth and I still wouldn't. She looked quietly pleased and scrapped the last spoonful of melted ice cream from the bottom of the glass.

When she got up to visit the loo, I couldn't help holding a lingering glance at her belly again.

'You keep doing that,' she said, a little irritated. 'I know I've put on a bit of weight – it's all this eating out, and Italian food. Leave home an English rose come back an Italian Mama!' I was speechless with the unintentional dramatic irony of this comment. 'I'll lose it again!'

'No, no, I like it, 'I murmured.

'Well maybe you *should* be going out with Maggie; you obviously have a preference for the bigger woman.'

Chapter Thirty-six: And I Tiresias have foresuffered all...

That night in bed, in the quiet darkness, I eventually asked her. She had been doing her best to arouse me – well, had succeeded in arousing me – but uncharacteristically for me I was making excuses (I just couldn't). Anna, was not used to being turned down – ever – and was in danger of descending into one of her 'oncoming underground-train' moments if I wasn't careful. Trying to diffuse the situation, I said, 'There's a very good reason why I feel I shouldn't.'

'I can't imagine what it is?' There were a few seconds of silence, while she sulked, then determined to still get what she wanted she changed tack and went into 'Matron' à la Hattie Jacques mode'...oh dear, this is always such a favourite of mine. (Please, don't ask me how this particular fetish for playing 'Carry on Doctor' came about; I can't even remember. From sheer embarrassment I'd prefer not to include it, but without it, you wouldn't understand the context of the moment...I wonder if I do subconsciously have a thing about big women?)

'Now, lie nice and still. I'm just going to examine you one last time.' Anna's voice slid into the rich buttery tones of Matron. 'This shouldn't be at all painful. In fact, some people say it's quite *pleasurable...*' She whispered this with relish as her fingers curled in a tighter grip. 'Oh, goodness! This is magnificent for a man of your age, Mr Johnson...' she said with all the essential bottom-slapping naughtiness, '...wouldn't want to waste it, now would we? Doctor Tinkle will be so pleased with your progress.' God, this took some self-control.

'Really,' I said turning away from her, 'I don't think we should.'

'Oh, for God's sake Alistair! What more do you want? ... I *was* joking about you and Maggie earlier, you know. Should I be worried?

This was not quite the romantic setting I had envisaged for revealing the wondrous possibility of her carrying our child.

'I've told you there is absolutely no chance of me ever even looking at another woman, while I have you. But it is something Maggie said today, though.'

'What? What has she said? You seemed so happy tonight, and now this. What's got into you?'

'She thinks, and now I think about it, I think...'

'Yes?'

I took a very deep breath. There are some sentences in life that you never thought in your wildest dreams could leave your mouth… 'that you might be pregnant.' Likewise, I guess there are some sentences you never expect to hear in your wildest dreams, that reach your ears. The silence was all pervading. Had I been the last person, the last living creature on earth, I don't think the silence I heard could have been louder.

'Well?' I ventured eventually into the blackness, 'Do you think you are?'

'For God's sake! No.' Immediately, the silence fractured, shattered by the abrupt thunderous explosion. 'Definitely, no! How can you be so stupid? How could I be pregnant? I'm on the pill. I haven't missed any. It's impossible.' My heart lurched.

'But Maggie said…'

'I don't care what Maggie said. It's none of her fucking business! Whatever made her come up with such an idea? I think *I* might bloody know before Maggie! What the fuck has she been saying to you?'

'Whoa,' I reached out for the light. 'Calm down. She's just concerned for you. All this feeling sick and faint isn't normal, is it?' She was sat up in bed now, arms folded defiantly.

'Oh, God, now I get it!' she said, turning on me, like a spitting cobra. 'That's why you kept looking at my stomach tonight. Alistair, if I was pregnant, I'd be two weeks pregnant. I had a period a month ago. Did you miss out on all your biology lessons? It would be a cluster of cells,
less than a baked bean.'

I was not going to give up on this dream so easily.

'Maggie said there's a pregnancy test you can buy in the chemist. Let's just check eh? If you're not, then perhaps you should see a doctor about these episodes anyway.'

'It'll be a complete waste of money. I can tell you now, categorically, I am not pregnant… and neither do I want to be.'

Inside I was in a state of complete agony. I had convinced myself that she would be as overjoyed at the prospect as much as I was. How wrong I was. Beneath her veiled shroud of the lacy bra, the virgin wept.

Later the next day, after a reluctant trip to the chemist, Anna ushered me out of the bathroom. 'I can pee by myself you know.' She emerged after several minutes.

'Well?' I said crazy with anticipation.

'I didn't do it.' She held the instruction sheet up to my face. 'It says first thing in the morning.'

'Oh,' I said.

The rest of the day passed in a series of awkward silences. She wandered about grumpily, glaring at me if I so much as looked at her. For several hours in the afternoon, she disappeared; I've no idea where she went. At dinner, she poked about at a very nice Salad Niçoise I'd prepared for her, and in the end tipped most of it in the bin. Later, as the sun slid beneath the horizon, I watched her from the bedroom window, drifting aimlessly about the garden, often stopping and standing still, so lost in thought. 'Let me in,' I whispered, 'Let me in.' I just didn't know what was going on in her mind. What are you thinking? I never know what you are thinking. Surely being pregnant with our child, was not such an awful thought, even though she was young? She knew I adored her, would always love her; always take care of her. Funny, I remember her being like this the evening the builders left, before I suggested that trip to Florence, when she had also pulled an invisible shield around herself. I couldn't bear the distance between us.

At night, we lay side by side, rigid, like a Knight and his Lady sealed forever in our separate tombs.

When I was a child, those tombs with the stone effigies on top held a grim fascination for me. I really believed that they were the actual bodies encased in stone, somehow petrified. Once upon a time, a long, long time ago, in dark corner of our local church, my friend and I squatted side by side, each daring the other to just touch Sir Oliver Thingy's foot. Our mothers were arranging flowers for Easter Sunday and were lost in contemplation of spring flora. There seemed to be some disagreement over whether or not to cut the stamens from the lilies. Mother was all for it, as last year the Vicar had somehow brushed his newly laundered surplice against the altar display, and given himself an unsightly, rich-auburn dusting of staining pollen. Others despised such pragmatism in the face of such beauty. 'He'll just have to learn to stop waving his arms about so much,' said an emphatic voice. While the women gnarled over this quandary, Stephen and I lurked, with our backs against the dusty casing of the organ. Stephen picked nervously at a thick crusty scab on his knee, which was hinged like a cellar trap door. Underneath, his skin was the raw shiny pink of the inside of a strawberry.

As the odorous perfume of the lilies wafted like incense around the church, Stephen pulled his jumper up over his face.

'Phwoar!' his muffled voice gasped, 'what's that stink?'
'It's them big white flowers.'
'Flowers? Smells like old ladies' wee-wee.'
Giggling, I copied him, dragging my pullover upwards and burying my nose in it. We both sniggered to our hearts content, while alternating between breathing in the heady fragrance accompanied by exaggerated nose wrinkling and disappearing back into our itchy sweaters. Eventually, even this supreme joy paled, and we got back to the serious business of the stone body.
'You're the oldest,' he whispered, flicking the bit of trap-door scab across the stone tiles.
'Yeah, but it was your idea.'
'But what if there's some kind of curse?' His eyes widened; the raw skin on his knee bloomed wet and shiny.
'What? Just for touching a foot?'
'Could be.' Stephen dabbed his sticky knee with the corner of his shirt sleeve. 'Imagine waking up in the middle of the night… and he's there; at the end of your bed – all stony and cold.'
I shuddered, then said, ''s'alright for you then. You got your older brother there. He's big.'

Stephen thought about this for a bit. 'Okay. If you do it, I'll do it.'
'Why don't we do it together?'

So, we did. On the count of three, our six-year-old fingers stretching towards the pointed, gritty, six-hundred-year-old boots …the briefest of touches. Then terror ran alive in our veins and we fled down the aisle of the church with Sir Oliver Thingammy pacing after us, his stone sword raised, his pounding footfalls shattering the tiles as he ran…

How still one is as an effigy; even your voice box is paralysed. Noises drift in from the world outside, but we don't react. We just wait, silently, for the morning. So cold. So alone. Speak to me. Why do you never speak? Speak.

286

What that knight needed was for us little boys to fall prostrate upon his body, hold him to our warm living flesh; tell him we loved him; being dead was just too bad – it really was.

I still cannot bring myself to touch those tombs.

Chapter Thirty-seven: The shouting and the crying

'It's positive. Though God knows how. Happy now?' My eyes blinked open. Anna sat on the bed by the side of me, a stick of plastic in her hand. 'Look. See, 'daddy'- positive.'

Tidal wave of joy is an understatement. A desert overwhelmed by the sea. Oh, my God. I pulled her toward me and held with a force that could crush a rib cage. 'Oh Anna! This is the most amazing ...When did you do the test?'

Her body seemed so small and soft, pliable. It was as if all the fight had left her, and an acknowledgement of the truth had left her submissive. Christ accepting without resistance; she was the vessel of my redemption.

'At about five this morning, I couldn't sleep. I did the test twice. It could still be wrong of course, almost too early on to register.'

Over her shoulder I glanced at the clock, it was already nine o'clock. She pulled back from me, her eyes full, her skin flushed.

'But now you know for certain, you're OK about this, aren't you? Yesterday, you seemed so...angry, so unhappy...I've never wanted anything more than this in my whole life. But you...Well, I know it's not ideal timing, but I'll support you. You can still finish your degree. Oh, say you're happy.'

'I'd be lying to say I was happy, but the truth is, I don't agree with abortion.' (A chill ran through me - I hadn't even given such an option a thought.) She continued with heaviness in her voice, 'So I have no other choice, but to accept the situation... and that may take some time.'

She seemed awfully serious, almost grave. She left the bed and walked over to the window, where she stood silently for a moment. 'God, Alistair, what on earth am I going to tell my parents?'

I was standing behind her now, and pressed my body into hers, enveloping her in my embrace. I kissed her softly on the shoulder. Her body stiffened under my touch. Of course, she was anxious...

'It'll all be fine, don't worry. I'll look after you. Oh, Anna, this is more than I could have ever hoped for. Trust me, everything will be fine.'

The mist was burning off from the valley and the air already alive with the heavy drone of bees. I placed my hands upon hers. From deep within her an unfathomable sigh escaped. Our circle was complete.

Hold on to that moment. For me, it was one of the best.

Later that day, I phoned Marion, and told her. Hold on to *that* moment. It was also one of the best. I tried to be sensitive; after all nobody knew what Marion had been through in our hopeful years. No one but me knew the depth of her agony of loss and disappointment. However, a lifetime of emasculation rose up and roared in defiance, 'Anna's pregnant, Marion. I thought I should let you know before you heard it from someone else.'

Oh, the sharp intake of breath. I knew she'd be seething, writhing with indignant fury, jealousy and shame. Then the pause…the taking a grip of oneself…then the response. Controlled, dignified. I knew immediately Edward must be within earshot.

'Thank you, Alec. That's very thoughtful of you. You sound pleased, so I'll presume congratulations are in order.'

I wish that hadn't felt so good, but God, it did. When I later told Anna, she was furious. It was, she had said, ridiculously early to be telling other people. The pregnancy hadn't even been confirmed by a doctor, she might even lose it at such an early stage. Had I even thought of that? She made me ring Marion again and swear her to secrecy for at least two months.

Maggie, not surprisingly, was delighted. I think she seemed more thrilled at being proved right than in the actual news itself. She claimed to have a sixth sense about such matters. 'I knew, the first time I laid eyes upon Anna, as she walked across the lawn. I could see it in her complexion.' The fact it was impossible that she'd have been pregnant then seemed to have escaped her. 'Why didn't you say something?' was my only response. 'One can hardly greet people with speculations about the state of their womb, Alistair!' (I had to agree with her there.)

We made an appointment to see the doctor on Friday of the following week, after which I suggested we could return to England early, in order that we could go and tell her parents face-to-face rather than just over the phone. Anna could obviously move into my house. Marion's old room could become a nursery. I wasn't suggesting this to be cruel; it just happens to be the best room for the job. Tom's wife, Eve, has had four babies; you must meet her I said to Anna, I'm sure she'll tell you all about it. You'll like Eve. She's not a bit like academic's wife, but then I suppose Tom isn't much like an academic. I wondered out loud if it would be a boy or a girl, and voiced my ideas for favourite names.

The fact that Anna wasn't sharing my enthusiasm didn't dampen my spirits. She was just taking time to get used to the idea. I knew she'd come round to it in the end. She didn't seem angry anymore, just lost in thought. Anyway, I had enough enthusiasm for both of us at this point.

During these few days, Anna wanted for nothing. In the mornings, I brought her breakfast in bed; took her out to dinner wherever she fancied; and told her how beautiful she was and how much I loved her every moment of the day and night. Constantly, I reassured her that I would take care of her and our baby. 'I know you will, Alistair.' (Of course, I didn't know then that she had made a choice: a very mercenary, but pragmatic choice. And every time I assured her of her future security, I was simply reinforcing the fact that she had made the right choice. Confused? All will become clear - just bear with me.)

I was six days into the living the dream of a lifetime, when I woke up – and it was all over. This is not a clichéd metaphor. It is what actually happened.

We had been out on a dinner date with Maggie and the Blythes. They too had been delighted to hear our news. It's not confirmed yet, was all that Anna would say. To which Sally responded with a smiling nod towards Anna's belly, 'O, I think it is...don't worry, you'll make a wonderful mother.'

Shaking my hand, Duncan chipped in with, 'Well played, Alistair!' which won him a withering glance from his wife. But in a funny kind of way, his comment filled me with pride. I felt a shared camaraderie with other men that had so far eluded me.

Anyway, the dinner had ended pretty late and we'd gone back to theirs for coffee, so subsequently we weren't home until gone two o'clock. Maggie had been in full flow, all evening; having such strong affinity to a number of fertility goddesses, I suppose pregnancy and all related subjects got her juices going more than most things. Breast-feeding was high on her agenda, as was squatting. There was a whole lot more to this pregnancy thing than met the eye.

However, I was very concerned for Anna that she should be getting home to bed. She seemed excessively tired all the time as it was.

'Don't be such an old woman, Alistair,' protested Sally, pausing in the doorway as she set off to the kitchen to fetch a further pot of coffee, 'Anna can say for herself when she's tired, can't you? Goodness me! Let the girl enjoy a social life while she's got the chance.'

As I looked around at the assembled company, even I had to allow myself an ironic inward smile, at that last remark.

And that's how we happened to both be sound asleep at eleven o'clock the next morning. We'd been out enjoying our dazzling social life. And here we lay, naked, dead to the world, under a single white sheet; it had been a very sultry night...

I was six days into the living the dream of a lifetime – when I woke up – and it was all over. This is not a clichéd metaphor. It is what actually happened.

It is hard to remember the order of events; it's all so confusing. Like trying to recall the detail of a crime one had just witnessed. What *was* I aware of first, as I came to consciousness?
Was it the sound of his voice shouting, '*Il mio dio! Voi bastardi! Voi bastardi*' or the sensation of the sheet sliding from me as he attempted to pull Anna to her feet from the bed?
Or was it the sight of the bunch of flowers he'd bought for her, tumbling through the air like a bride's bouquet tossed heaven-ward at a wedding?
Or did all that happen in one single moment of intolerable bewilderment?

'What? What the ...!' '*floundering like a man in fire or lime,*' a strange semi-conscious writhing on this same divan or bed, raw and flayed, exposed.

My immediate fear that we were being attacked by some psychotic homicidal maniac was slightly allayed when I recognised him as one of the builders. 'Fabrizio? What... what the fuck are you doing?' Surely, he'd understand that question. He pulled Anna closer to him. She was dragging the sheet with her, as if it were a toga. It looked like some bizarre hostage rescue attempt; he was edging towards the door; an insanely wild look on his face, holding her half behind him, as if I were a dangerous madman pointing a gun or something. 'Let Anna go!' I shouted very firmly.
Grabbing a pillow to cover my nakedness, I stood up and started towards the pair of them.

It was then for the first time I took my eyes from him and noticed Anna's face. It was not the face of terror or alarm of someone in the arms of a violent stranger, but a look of guilt – almost to the point of sickness. But still I didn't see. Here in front of my very eyes; and still I didn't see… I did not want to see, did I?

I repeated my command, 'Let Anna go!' This time he did let go, but then used his available arms to push me with all his force across the bedroom. I flailed backwards losing the pillow and my last shred of dignity with it. Hitting the bed with the back of my legs, I lost my balance, and landed in an awkward slump on the cold stone tiles.

Fabrizio launched into a tirade of Italian. I had very little idea what he was saying, but he was very passionate about it. A few odd words I grasped, Maggie was mentioned more than once, but he was gabbling furiously. Then, he turned to Anna, and then, this grand illusionist whose sleight of hand had kept me in the dark for so long, simply dangled my beautiful, dazzling, golden possession in front of me… See what I have taken when you weren't looking; see what I have slipped out from beneath your very skin, from between the bones of your ribs, and stolen…Didn't even feel me there, did you? Slithering closer to you than the very sweat, which now pricks uncomfortably in every crease of your flesh…He held her face in his hands and kissed her – full on the lips.

And in an instant, I saw. My God I saw. My eyes were not covered and closed, but peeled back, lidless eyes, staring as the incomprehensible took shape before my eyes, a heap of broken images - fragments of a puzzle – slotted together seamlessly. A picture formed.

I knew the words for 'father' and 'sex'. And 'disgustoso' was not so difficult to translate. The look on his face of confusion and growing horror, as understanding crept its stealthy path into his brain, must've have been equally matched by my own; as through her tears Anna said in a stuttering barely audible voice, 'He's not my father. I lied to you. He's my lover, *la verità - il mio amante*'

Imagine the faces of us three. Anna: a captive bird, snared, wings beating in panic, watching a net falling in slow motion, knowing there's no escape; Fabrizio: punch drunk with confusion – he comes to find his 'girl' to resume his summer fling – comes to surprise her, wake her like some sleeping beauty, only to find her in bed with a man he had been led to believe was her father. And now, in a state of outrage and disgust, he discovers what seems an even worse truth: this 'father' is in fact his princess's lover. And he had been lied to all along. And me... Oh, God me. Who am I in this 'ménage à trois'? I really cannot bear to look.

Remember Prometheus…this was the first time…oh, howl, howl, howl!

For a few terrible moments, we were trapped in this ghastly freeze-frame - staring each one to the other – transfixed.

Fabrizio woke up first. He released his grip on Anna. His hands falling limply by his sides and for a few moments his head dropped to his chest. I heard Anna whisper in an imploring tone, 'Fabrizio, I'm sorry.' And she raised her hand to touch him. He backed away, took one last stare at us both, still unable to believe his eyes, and turned and ran. His footfalls leaped down the stairs three at a time, all the time shouting Anna's name, again, again. The door slammed with a shudder.

Second freeze-frame: Anna and I, now alone in the bedroom. She is still motionless, a white sheet loosely held against her, pale and crumpled. I am still hunched, naked, on the cold stone tiles.

I cannot speak. Words fail me completely. My tongue weighs like lead against the floor of my mouth. Images flash through my head. Pictures without words. It is as if I have slipped through time and find myself in a pre-language state. There are no words to describe how I feel. No metaphors to help me cross the bridge between my inner self and you. Sometimes in life we find ourselves in a very lonely place, where no one else can follow. This place is somewhere on the outer edges of the universe. Where in amongst the darkness and the silence things are born and die in an agony of violence. I sit on the very outer reaches of space and time and watch a supernova expand, collapse, and then rush away from its own death searing across the blackness. And I see two dark eyes staring right through me, a pinkish film in a basin, a woman in a red dress, and a blue line on a white stick of plastic.

She said nothing, but did eventually hoist up her sheet-toga, and shuffle across the room towards me. In an appeasing gesture, she placed her fingertips upon my head, and suddenly, without any warning, I began to shudder violently. Pulling my knees up to my head, I buried my face in my hands, and felt the fierce tremors of an earthquake rock my body. The man who'd been dancing on brimstone tripped and fell, and from deep, deep inside his soul, a scream of anguish ripped through his body and flew, like a demon escaping from the very gates of hell, out of his mouth.

'Please, Alistair don't'. She'd grabbed a bathrobe, and was trying to swaddle me in it – as if that would provide some comfort. Next, Anna attempted to hold me, but her embrace, once like a warm balm, felt like a chemical burn on my flesh. I flinched. She withdrew her hand. A word, several words, finally found their way into my mouth.

'Leave me alone – please.'

'But... we need to talk. Oh, Alistair, I'm sorry. It was just...it wasn't serious or anything...you know how it is.'

My eyes lifted and met hers. *Yes*, they said, *I know how it is*. I think the truth she met in my eyes frightened her. She took her clothes into the bathroom, dressed in silence, and then did as requested and left me alone.

I don't know where she went. And something in me didn't even care. My heart was torn out of me - all feeling fled.

I felt as lonely as the day that I was born. Let's get right to the heart of it now – I was unwanted. Sometimes I think I felt this disconnect from the world right from the start, deep within the womb; apologising for my parasitical nature all the days of my life: the unwanted child bringing itself into being inside an unmarried, unwilling host. Mother was no girl – she was thirty-three when I was conceived. I have no idea why she kept me. She tried to love me, and perhaps did in her own way, but I always felt my existence was slightly resented: a living, walking, talking advertisement to her shame. Was I God's way of smiting her for making 'time for love,' or something far more evil? I never knew who my father was. 'He died abroad when you were a baby,' had been the stock answer. There weren't even any photographs. Mother said they had been kept in a shoebox under the bed, which had most tragically, and mysteriously, disappeared in a burglary. Even the image of my father had been stolen from me.

She forgot that when I eventually needed a copy, my birth certificate would say: 'father unknown.' It was a mystery, a dark secret. (90% of the universe is dark matter. My father is 10 to minus a trillion part of that dark matter.) She took this dark matter into herself, like a precious pearl from a parallel universe shrouded it with layer upon layer of tar-like conglomerate, and swallowed it. This secret stone lay within her body never to be passed out.

What was the truth surrounding my conception? At best a cad or in my bleaker times I wondered had she been raped, abused? Was I the result of some dreadful assault upon her? I would never know. She belonged to that generation that swallowed secrets whole and let them grow like kidney stones – too excruciating to pass out of the body. I'll never know who he was, or how I came to be. She will die with a bellyful of blackened heavy stones like the fox in *The Little Red Hen*.

Draped in a white towelling dressing gown, with the cold tiles against my backside, never more utterly wretched in my entire life, I sat immovable. Utterly broken. Disgust is a very powerful human emotion. It slides so easily, so willingly, into bed with shame. And their lovemaking is deep, dark and abusive. Their offspring develops in your very soul. And their hunger is insatiable.

'As Gegor Samsa awoke one morning from uneasy dreams he found himself transformed in his bed into a gigantic insect.'

But even I could not remain there forever, nausea rising in my throat, arms embracing a body I despised. Shower before dressing. *'What shall I do now? What shall I do? I shall rush out as I am, and walk the street with my hair down, so. What shall we do tomorrow? What shall we ever do?'*

Dressing and descending the stairs seems fitting, so that's what I do. Sergio doffs an imaginary cap to me as he enters the kitchen, to find me heating some water for coffee. He is already working, as according to our prior arrangement he was to collect the keys from under the millstone if there was no answer. We could have so easily have been away you see. He smiles and says, 'Anna, she go!' (he's so delighted to show off the little English he has learnt) and does a 'poof!' gesture with his fingers to his mouth as if to indicate a magic trick. I nod. I even return his smile. Does he know? The inability to speak afflicts me once again.

The phrase 'Take me now' pops into my head from nowhere. I realise I am importuning God for a heart attack, a fatal embolism – anything. A true *me transmitte sursum caledoni!* moment – I just don't want any more. But there is more… And as I stood in the kitchen wondering whether to drink this shit-awful cup of coffee I'd just made myself, or try to drown in it, I could never have anticipated just how much more there was to come.

Chapter Thirty-eight: After the agony

Before I had finished my coffee, a plumber who I had not seen before arrived. He was obviously a good friend of Sergio's, sharing a similar taste in pullovers, and after much back slapping and warm exchanges, Sergio turned to me and introduced us. Christ knows what his name was... I could hardly remember my own.

It was obvious I would be unable to bear spending the day in this house. My needs were for isolation, alcohol, solace somewhere. For some reason, I felt I had to explain my evacuation from the house to Sergio, and told him I was going to visit Maggie, who lived behind the bar.

'Oh, Maggie! Maggie,' he nodded knowingly, and looking from me to the plumber, gestured the cupping of two enormous watermelons to his chest. I suppose anyone who'd visited the bar would have a fighting chance of having met Maggie. The plumber laughed, loosening some thick catarrh in his throat as he did so, and then copied Sergio, lightly tossing his melons in his gnarled palms. 'Yes.' I said, stony-faced, '*that* Maggie.'

So lost were they in mutual admiration of each other's mammaries, they were oblivious to my reaction. I left them both dancing noisily round the room, singing the Italian equivalent of *I've got a luverly bunch of coconuts* with their respective breasts, now apparently the size and weight of Halloween pumpkins, bouncing freely. Until that moment, I had quite liked Sergio.

To get to Maggie's house I would have had to have turned right as I left the house and then proceeded up the hill, towards the centre of the village. I turned left. Here, one skirted round the bottom of the village, until meeting up with a dirt track, which zigzagged, between the vines, up and around the hillside. The ground was baked to a light, smooth beige-cream crust, and at first, I paced along quickly, with my feet pounding the earth heavily. Initially, the incline was quite gradual, but as it increased, a fiery sense of rage and anger spurred me on, pumping my blood into my aching muscles. Self-loathing, mingled with wrath is a rocket-fuel cocktail. Sweat ran down my brow in rivulets, until my eyelashes were blinking with sweated tears. Upon my upper lip my pores opened and salty water seeped down the cracks in my lips into my mouth. Even the fabric of my cotton trousers stuck uncomfortably to my flesh. Still I surged forward, thudding along the path like a fairy-tale ogre, with my face ugly, ruddy, contorted, from heat and emotion. As I broke into a run, I could actually hear my own blood rushing in my ears. The path turned sharply, beginning to rise even more steeply. Desperately, gasping at the dry air, my lungs clawed their way out of me. Higher and higher they rose, compacting very tightly to squeeze up the windpipe. They for one were not prepared to die for want of breath, even if it meant turning inside out to do so. My run was, without me realising it, slowing to a stagger. Blinded by sweat, I went off the path, stumbled on a clod of earth, and fell with a thud. Not a moment too soon. My heart and lungs were already in my mouth and making a hasty exist through that orifice.

I lay, a heaving, gasping mound. My face was pressed into the dry soil. I could feel the dust suckering itself to my wet skin. Through bleary eyes I peered down endless rows of twisted vine trunks, each anchored into the baked stony earth, clutching with arthritic fingers, clutching, holding on.

I stuck out my tongue, and licked the earth. The dry dust leapt. Can I detect a *gout de terroir*? So dry, with a burst of violets in the mouth... now, a subtle lingering after-taste – but what? What is that familiar taste? It lingers long after I have wiped my tongue with the back of my hand. Death? Is that you? Only the crickets reply. A shadow slips between the rows of vines – and is gone. I didn't lick the soil a second time.

Eventually, I rolled onto my back, shutting my eyes to the fierce sunlight. A pain radiated from my hip; I guess I must've fallen on a jagged rock. Now pulling myself to a sitting position, I rolled down the tops of my trousers, and sure enough, over my hip bone, a large purple and red graze pulsated and oozed. What could I do? I couldn't go home like this. What if Anna was there? I didn't want her to see me like this. I could continue up this path then at the very top of the vineyard take the path that led back into the top of the village; go and see Maggie as I'd first intended. It was a long walk. But walking would clear my head. She would tell me what to do. I just didn't know what to do. It was a much longer walk than I remembered...

'Alistair! For heaven's sake! What on earth has happened to you?' Maggie's face became three round 'O's of disbelief. My shoulders slumped; my face crumpled. I almost fell into her. She propped me up, half leaning against her, half against the doorway. 'Heavens, Alistair! Let's get you inside.' Maggie dragged me along the corridor into the living room where I collapsed on the sofa. She found some antiseptic and a few balls of cotton wool, and with a sharp stinging sensation I cleaned up the graze on my hip. Seconds later she returned with a tall glass of cold water. Clear. Pure. Water.

Maggie was uncharacteristically silent, when I was at last able to recount the events of that morning, which now seemed so impossible, it was as if I were fabricating an elaborate story. 'I can only think they met here, Maggie. That week when I was ill, and you and Nina were working at the gallery. Anna had the keys...' She shifted uncomfortably in her seat, and nodded towards the empty glass, still in my hand,

'Something stronger?'

I really meant to say, 'No. Just more water, please.' I knew I was already dehydrated enough, but instead the words, 'I think I'm going to need it,' came out, and moments later there was a large bottle of gin, some tonic, and a metal tray of ice cubes sat enticingly on the coffee table. While Maggie had been out of the room, I had brushed my hand against the nap of the soft dark velvet, wondering if Anna's bare back had lain against it ... The sculptures in the room knew the answer, but they just stared at me – 'old fool' one of them says, 'Cuckold,' sneers Ganesh.

The first gin goes down in one. On an empty stomach and in an already dehydrated system it gets to work straight away, and the jagged serrations of the day blunt a little. I breathe out. Maggie refills my glass saying nothing.

'Now, Maggie. I have to ask you this. Was there anything to suggest she met this... this plasterer, here? I have to know.'

She took a large gulp of her drink, looked rather pained, and twisted her mouth. 'This is the *plasterer*, you're asking me about?' I nodded patiently; surely it wasn't that difficult a question? She added slowly, '...the one with the very dark eyes?'

'Yes...dark eyes. Part of the Sergio and company brigade. Sergio always wears a moth-eaten pullover. Do you know them? Sergio seems to know you. But was he here? The plasterer.'

She nodded. 'Yes...' Her eyes were flickering around the room. 'I know Fabrizio.'

'So, he was here?'

'Oh dear,' she shook her head sadly. 'This isn't going to get any easier, I'm afraid. Sergio's lot were my builders too, last year, when I had the attic converted. They do most of the local work around here. Fabrizio stuck up a relationship with Nina. They seemed quite close. Lasted until a few months ago...' She took a deep breath, 'I don't know what went wrong. Well, I suspect it was that pregnancy scare I told you about.' (My soul shrank within me. Recoiling.) She continued musing, 'There was one occasion...yes...when late one afternoon – to my great surprise – I caught him leaving as I returned from town, rushing down from the attic; I presumed he was looking for Nina – was trying to patch things up with her...' Before Maggie had finished, I was out of the room and rushing up the stairs. As I burst into the attic, sun flooded the room with dazzling yellow light. Hungrily, my eyes scanned the room, monstrously eager for evidence: an altar on which to impale myself. Everything looked as it had before, the sunken chaise, the paints, paintbrushes, dried pallets of paints, paintings stacked under blankets. Where was Anna's painting?

Panting, Maggie stumbled through the doorway.

'Alistair. Why do you want to torture yourself? Who knows what was going on? I certainly don't. Come downstairs. Come on my dear, down.'
I swung round, dizzy with hunger and exhaustion. 'Where's her painting? I want to see her bloody painting.'

Maggie, raised her eyes heaven-ward, 'Really, I don't think...'
'Just show me her fucking painting!'
Reluctantly, she moved over to a pile of paintings to my left, and gently pulled back some sacking to reveal... what? A mass of swirling lines, splodges intersected by deep gouges made with a palette knife. After lifting it onto an empty easel, Maggie stood back, still breathing heavily, for once looking every bit her age. For several moments we regarded the painting, in this breathy silence.

Eventually, I said, 'What the heck is it?' somewhat taken aback.
'I haven't a clue,' Maggie replied. 'While I'm all for impasto, I don't think I've ever seen anyone manage to adhere quite so much paint to a single canvas ever...is it purely abstract or are these two figures? Two figures perhaps, women, maybe?' For a minute, I was almost relieved. Almost at the point of feeling a moment of lightness creeping in, almost a laugh rising, as we regarded Anna's artistic labours, but then I noticed the painting against which Anna's had been propped. It was the life-study we had seen the first night we'd been to Maggie's. I looked again. Only this time I didn't just look... I saw. 'It's him, isn't it?'

'Oh, Alistair, really; come on. Leave it. There are more important issues to discuss. Come along now.' I saw now his beautiful form. The strong muscular definition of his lean brown arms; his thick black hair in twisted coils; the taut ripple of muscle stretched across his belly; the fine line of dark hair leading down from his navel, blossoming like a sea anemone...

'Alistair!' Maggie sounded quite abrupt. 'I live to exaggerate, my dear. Enough of this,' and she threw the sacking back over Fabrizio's beautiful body. He was gone.

As I descended the stairs, I imagined him rushing down them, with his body still hot and trembling, the lingering scent of Anna's body mixing with his own. His lips slightly bloomed from the passion of her rising kisses; her fingernails still leaving an indent in his backside. What did she say to him? What did she need to say to him? What use were words to either of them? Speak. Why do you never speak?

In silence, Maggie poured us both another drink. I'd never noticed how sour gin can taste, or is it bitter? I never did understand the difference.

'It's not just the betrayal, Maggie, or the passing me off as her father, it's the fact I don't know now…if…well, it's unlikely…' No, try as I might, I just couldn't say it.

'My poor love. I understand.' Maggie struggled from her seat, and repositioned herself heavily against me on the sofa. Placing her weighty arm around the back of my neck, she drew me to her soft bosom. She held my head there, rocking slightly as if comforting a child, and finally – finally – I wept. There was nothing more to say. I could hold my broken dream up for examination, but not even Maggie knew how to glue it back together.

After what seemed like hours, I rose, and with a final hug she just said, 'Do your best, Alistair – there's still a fifty-fifty chance, you know.' I still hadn't told her the truth.

It was some time after seven when Anna returned, looking shamefaced and weary, eyes reddened and dark from crying. I was lying on the sofa, where I had been since returning from Maggie's. She glanced at the empty bottle by the side of me and the second, opened, nearly drunk on the coffee table.

'Now let me guess where you have been,' I slurred, dragging myself up into a half-sitting position, 'walking in the hillsides? Or tell me, Michelangelo, have you been hard at work on your painting… the light in that studio is so fucking wonderful, isn't? Illuminating, I've heard. Inspirational. So, what was it today? Some help with your fresco? Painting on wet plaster. So exciting, such a sense of urgency. You have to work quickly you know, it's got to be wet, or it doesn't work.'

'Stop being so bloody crude.'

'Me? Crude? I'm sorry. Am I offending your sensibilities? Let me try to be more sensitive about this; I mean goodness knows you deserve to be treated like a lady. I've had all day to think about this, work it out. It was while I was ill, wasn't it? What an opportunity! He was hardly ever here, and neither were you.'

'Alistair, it's finished. It was as good as over with him when he left weeks ago. Does any of it matter now?'

'Oh, it's over now, is it? Oh, well that's alright then, isn't it? You fuck who you like, Anna, 'cos I'll always be here for you. Good ol' Daddy.'

'That was his notion, his presumption. I just didn't correct him.'

'How convenient: innocent by omission.' The sneer on my face was quivering; a dangerous emotion threatened to bubble through the surface. 'You have no idea how you've destroyed me, do you?'

I was sitting upright now feeling sicker, drunker, than I ever had.

'How could you?' I shouted at her. 'You must've hardly exchanged two sentences with him, and yet you… you let him fucking fuck you!'

'If you're going to be like this, I'm going out again.' Anna turned to leave. 'I'll come back when you're sober.' I was up like a shot.

'No, please, I'm sorry. Don't go.'

She swung round in the doorway, almost a silhouette in the twilight. Her voice was strong, almost defiant, 'It was a mistake, all right? He's young, good-looking. Sorry, but even you could've seen that. It was just lust. You're right, I didn't know anything about him, apart from everything I could see on the surface, and that was enough; it felt good enough at the time.'

'Oh, I'm so glad about that. I've no doubt he was *il miglior fabbro* in the bedroom, so I'm not going to humiliate myself further by asking, but whatever the level of your sexual satisfaction – I have to know …do you love him at all? As you seem to be so conveniently forgetting that's how I feel about you.'

She contemplated this question longer than I thought she needed to, and finally said, 'I assumed I'd just told you that. What do you mean by 'love' anyway?'

A chilling shadow fell across my heart. 'Surely you know? I would have thought,' I staggered on, 'that your feelings for me might have given you pause for thought. Didn't you think for one moment that if you love someone, you'd do anything to avoid causing them the kind of pain you've inflicted on me?'

'Look, if it makes you feel any better, it just happened – it didn't mean anything. You of all people should know what I'm talking about.'

'Of course, it fucking 'means something'! Things don't 'just happen'. You made it happen. Choosing whether to have tea or coffee in the morning 'doesn't matter'. Believe me: this fucking matters.'

Perhaps shaken by the anger in my voice, Anna simply turned her head away and stared at the floor tiles. Her chest was rising and falling rapidly; she swallowed hard. Fervently, I hoped she was about to cry. For a moment, a silence hung between us. A gaping hole was opening up in front of me, and like a fool I could not resist leaning further and further forward to see what lay at the bottom of it.

The one question, which turned the knife in me more than any other, had to be asked. I posed it, the words slowly forming in my mouth, presuming the worst. 'You see the real problem is Anna, now, I don't know if you're pregnant, with my baby, or his.'

'It's yours,' she said emphatically, looking towards me with eyes glazed, but no tears.

'How can you be sure?'

'I just know.'

A deep, ancient, weary sorrow rattled its dry bones and rose uncertainly within me. Its voice silent for so long, sounded like a hoarse whisper. 'Anna, you know Marion and I never had children…it wasn't through choice.' (tick-tock) How the wheels within her mind turned. 'So, you see, you're being pregnant was always a miracle for me, Anna. And like most apparent miracles there is usually a rational explanation – sadly.'

'But it has to be your baby, Alistair. I know it is.'

'I doubt that very much. I am afraid like the king in *The King's New Clothes* my ego made me agree to believe in something I should've seen was impossible. I so wanted to believe, Anna. And now I am exposed for the fool that I am.'

'*Impossible*? Have you ever had any tests?' She fixed a stare straight at me. For all the world I wanted to lie, as I always had done, allowing the mystery finger of blame to hover uncertainly between Marion and me, (although always weighted towards Marion.) I couldn't lie to Anna. The answer was 'yes', and the test result was 'low sperm count and what few sperm there are, are immotile. I'm sorry conceptions are very rare in such cases.'

'Immotile?'

'Can't swim,' I explained. These two fascinating facts about the paucity and lack of cross-channel swimming potential of my sperm were known only to the urologist, me, Marion, and now Anna.

'There's still a chance then! Look it *is* your baby. I know it's yours.'

Confused, another thought struck me.

'Does he even know you're pregnant?' She looked away, staring out of the window. I waited. She redirected her gaze to the floor. I waited. 'You did tell him, Anna, didn't you?'

'It's your baby, Alistair.'

'Just *saying* something doesn't make it true, Anna. You want it to be, because you know I'll look after you. That's what you've been accepting; adjusting to these last few days isn't it? Not just having a baby, but accepting you've got to be with me for the foreseeable future – just until you're back on your feet.'

'That's not true. I want us to be together. I love you.'

'Do you? Did you ever really love me?'

'Of course, I love you.' To my ears, it sounded as though she was trying to convince herself, not me.

Humiliated and angry, I muttered,' You've a bloody funny way of showing it.' I attempted to stand up, but failed. Anna strode across the room and picked up the bottle from the coffee table. 'You really shouldn't drink so much. How much have you had?'

'Not nearly enough.' I made a lurching grab for the bottle.

'Do you think this is the way to win me back?' Tears were falling now, but I couldn't tell if she was upset, ashamed or just overcome with fury.

I shrugged my shoulders. 'From what you've just said, I didn't realise I had to *win* you back.'

Then she noticed the pack of cigarettes besides me and the ashtray.

'And God, no wonder it stinks in here; you've been smoking! You promised you'd given up.'

'I had, until today. I would have given up anything for you Anna; everything, if it meant I could have you. But I don't, do I? Not any more, maybe I never did.' I drained my glass and stared defiantly at her. The alcohol seemed to sluice into my brain almost instantly, empowering and inflaming. 'Perhaps you're right, none of it really matters – smoking, drinking, fucking, swearing, living, loving, dying. Who cares? So, off you go to fuck the plasterer, and while you're at it, give the carpenter a good shagging, and if you feel inclined, brighten up Sergio and Dino's day too, and I'll sit here and drink and smoke myself into oblivion, and we're all be happy as pigs in shit and declare that it's all alright because none of it really means anything. None of it fucking matters. OK?'

She stormed out of the room, slamming the door behind her.

'You should tell him, Anna,' I shouted after her. 'He's got a fucking right to know he's going to be father, hasn't he? I mean, I took my responsibilities of fatherhood seriously when I was a father, didn't I? All bloody six days of it.' Seconds later I only just made it to the toilet before being horribly sick.

Well, you made a real good job of that Alistair. The mirror reflected an image I could not bear to see ... me. What happened there? She's the one in the wrong, but I feel like I'm the one who should be grovelling? Fuck up. What a complete fuck up.

Later that night, she must've crept back and gone to sleep in the spare room alone, while I slept beneath the virgin – alone – for the second time since coming to Italy. The more I sobered up, the worse I felt. At three-ish in the morning I gave up on the idea of getting any sleep. After checking where Anna was and feeling sick with the turmoil of emotions raging within, I went down to the kitchen to make some coffee. Was there any way back? I couldn't see it.

Chapter Thirty-nine: bats with baby faces

Now of course I see so easily what I should have done. It was so simple really. I should have accepted her with open arms, forgiven every misdemeanour, brushed aside all transgressions, all sense of betrayal, all ideas of ridicule, humiliation, held my hands up in appeasement, let pride shoot me in the stomach. I should have promised to bring up that child as my own, whether it was mine or Fabrizio's. Then perhaps I would still have her now. But in life there's no rewind button; let me do that 'take' again; rewrite that scene. No, life is forwards only. Commit it to the paper and it's there, forever. No time for revision, correction, no proofreading; tinkering, tampering; altering the order of events. One cannot scrape the paint from the canvas into a multicoloured ball of slime; no, this paint sticks like shit. These are hard lessons to learn. I wish with my very soul I could change what took place over the next few days, but now I can't. I played these following scenes like an idiot. I wish I could change things – but I can't.

What follows is so painful to me that I do not think I can write about it without being hideously drunk. However, in part, I know it was alcohol which was my downfall; it helped to get me into this mess. I should know this duplicitous friend better than to expect it to help me out of the mire. So, for the moment, I resist. I'll write this during the day when my friend's seductive voice is more of a whisper. I feel I owe it to Anna to at least record this sober.

What happened next is this...

At some point during the night, I must've wandered into the living room again and fallen asleep on the sofa, for as I came to consciousness, I realised my neck was stiff, and my back ached. Anna was sitting opposite me on the other sofa, waiting for me to open my eyes.

'I was just about to wake you up, Alistair. I think something's wrong.' Rubbing my aching neck, I pulled myself up, staring at her slightly dumbfounded. 'Well, yes,' I said with a slow sarcasm, 'I think we worked that out yesterday.' She bit her bottom lip, and closed her eyes as if wincing in pain. 'No. I think something's wrong with me – with the baby.'

'What?'

'I don't know. I've got this cramping pain, here, and there was some sort of blood this morning.

'Sounds like a period to me. Women get them all the time apparently. Maybe you're not pregnant after all.' I said this with such a casual air – oh Alistair, how could you be so cruel? 'Those little stick things can be wrong,' I continued. 'Maybe this whole episode was all a figment of our collective imaginations.'

'I think I ought to see a doctor.'

'You're welcome to take the car if that's what you're wondering. Surprisingly, I have no plans for today.' She looked really hurt. And, God forgive me, I'm ashamed to say, I was pleased.

'Would you take me, Alistair? I don't feel up to driving, and…well, and I need you to be with me. It could be a miscarriage. Please.'

I thought, but thank God did not say, 'Miscarriage? Of what? Justice?'

For a few seconds I studied her face, and had to acknowledge that she did look pallid, drawn, tearful. I had also been about to make some spiked comment such as: 'Doesn't your friend Fabrizio drive?', but my heart began to soften a little. Glancing up at the clock, I struggled from the sofa, 'Give me ten minutes for a shower.' And without so much as brushing my hand affectionately across her shoulder, I left the room.

It was at least an hour or so later that we set off, in a stony silence, up the thin winding lane. Already, the metal shell of the Morris, radiated heat like a barbeque, filled with white coals, while inside a rich leathery smell rose, mingling with the scent of a small bunch of lavender, Anna had left on the dashboard. Once or twice I risked glancing at Anna, hoping we would find some way of speaking, but each time she was just staring out of the passenger window.

As I drove on, it occurred to me that I didn't actually know where the doctor's surgery was. I knew it was somewhere in town but I didn't know exactly where. 'Do you know where the doctor's is, Anna?'

'I thought you'd know.'

'Well, I got Maggie to ring last week to book you in, but no, I don't know where to go yet.'

Under her breath she muttered, 'Oh, God.'

What happened next is the only piece of good fortune in this whole sorry tale. I saw a sign for the hospital.

'Look. I'll take you to casualty. They'll give us directions, or perhaps even see you if we're lucky.'

Thankfully, the casualty department of this slightly antiquated hospital was almost devoid of injured parties. Only two people were there: one, an elderly man, with his hand in blood-soaked tea towel; and the other, a young vexed-looking mother, with a little girl of about six, who was whimpering, while cradling her wrist, which was so thin it looked like a bird's leg. Indicating to Anna to take a seat, I approached the reception, took a deep breath and wondered how on earth I was going to explain Anna's predicament. '*Buon giorno.*' I said. Often this had been enough for people to immediately realise I was someone who could not speak a word of Italian and they would, if able, answer me in English – naturally, this was not one of those times.

'*Il, buon giorno come posso li aiuta?*' came the rapid reply.

'*Parla l'inglese?*'

'*Sono davvero spiacente* – No.' She smiled pleasantly, and tapped the tips of her exquisitely manicured nails together, waiting for my next move.

Hoping to gather reinforcements, I turned round to Anna saying, 'Have you remembered the phrase book?' However, she just shook her head, looking pasty. It could be that this bug had finally taken hold, broken through her defences at last? A second, stronger wave of pestilence, that had lurked for weeks in the smelly drains, multiplying, and then rising like a putrid incense into warm air. Perhaps this had coincided with her normal period, which was just a bit erratic this month. If it was a miscarriage –Fabrizio's aborted offspring – I found it hard not to feel a small sense of relief. *Miserie nobis.* I began to reconsider if it was going to be worth the effort of getting the receptionist to understand me. Meanwhile, the receptionist leaned across her counter and peered at Anna.

'She,' I began, pointing at Anna, 'is sick. Nausea.' The receptionist was nodding excitedly, '*nausea, vomitare.*'

'And pain.' Not a flicker of recognition there. I held my stomach, and grimaced. All eyes were on me now, even the whimpering little girl was staring in a doleful silence.

'*Dolore,*' the receptionist intoned mournfully. Tapping my skull, with what I hoped was a universal sign, 'I think,' (Here goes. I steeled myself.) 'She's pregnant.' Which I accompanied by what I thought would also be the universal mime. The reception cocked her head on one side, 'Ahh.' And she gave Anna a little wave,

'*Incinta.*'

'Well, maybe, yes.'

The receptionist poised her fingertips together once more, considering her next question. Slowly, deliberately she asked '*Siete - il - padre?*' Oh, God here I go again. '*Padre? Papa?*' she repeated. There was no way I was going to confess here and now, that I did not know. I could almost hear Anna's tense breathing from across the other side of the room. I heard the word 'No,' escape from my lips.

Slightly more confused she asked, '*Siete il suo padre? Lo zio, l' amico?*' She was looking from me to Anna and back again. '*Dove e il padre del bambino?*' She addressed this question to Anna, whose eyes were glassy with tears. With a self-defeating gesture, the receptionist rang a bell on the counter, and within seconds a tall, distinguished looking man with steel grey hair appeared, his stethoscope dangling like a medal round his neck. He marched up to the receptionist who obviously very quickly filled him in on the details.

He turned to me, a thin smile on his lips, 'Hello, I am Dr Vitale; I speak a little English. Come with me.'

He gestured to Anna to follow, so I immediately went over to offer her support. She looked fairly ghastly now, almost a greyish-green tinge to her skin. As we staggered into a small consulting room just beyond the reception area, it was almost comforting to have her hanging on to me. Once seated, she explained to the doctor, where she felt the pain, her general sense of malaise, feeling sick, faint, and the spotting of the watery blood. The doctor's face darkened. 'Anna, how many weeks pregnant?'

'It's hard to say.' I interjected. Dr Vitale didn't seem to understand what I'd said.

'I don't know.' Anna's voice was little more than a whisper.

He turned his handsome wise face in my direction, 'You're not the father of the baby?' Anna put her face in her hands. 'You're not Anna's father?' Involuntarily, I found myself shifting forward in my seat. 'Are you family friend? Is there a father we can telephone?'

All of a sudden, I stood up, surprising Anna, Dr Vitale, and myself. The word 'Yes,' struggled out of me. Already leaving the room, I said, 'I'll find him. Get him here.'

And I was gone. I heard Anna and the doctor calling me back, but I just kept running. I would find that little bastard and make him face up to his responsibilities. Anna was in safe hands now. I was still sure she was just heading for a bout of sickness and diarrhoea *a la* Dino, but I'd like to scare the pants off Fabrizio. I was sure Anna hadn't told him she was pregnant. I'd bloody make sure he knew.

It is quite difficult to drive like a madman in a Morris, but on this occasion, I managed it. Before going home, however, I stopped by at Maggie's, whom I thought might know where this creature's lair was. Hammering and even kicking my toe furiously at the door brought no attention. Such a fury was rising inside of me now; I think had I met the bastard, I would have thumped him, and thumped him hard. I'd never really hit anyone in my life - although, I'd often had terribly violent dreams. Here, for the first time ever, I was searching out another human being to cause them physical and emotional pain. Suddenly without thinking, I strode up to the fig tree and gave one of the frogs a massive whack and watched it twirl frantically and dangerously, bashing and clanging into the other frogs. It finally came to rest wrapping its wire around the branch. 'Get out of that one,' I whispered.

As I slid around the side of the house towards the garden, my usual stride developed into a distinct prowl. Under my breath I realised I was actually growling. This slightly alarmed me. I have often feared I could so easily slither into madness; my grip on reality eluding me, as slippery as the shadow of a snake. Muscles hardened. Adrenaline pumped. I could creep through the back door. Stealthily ascend the stairs. Find him there – perhaps waiting for Anna. I have devil's eyes. Blood red, shiny as garnets, my black, slitted pupils scan the garden. My body fell slightly forward as I rose on my newly-formed cloven feet, and how my head pulsated as two sharp horns wriggled their twisted pointed passage through my skull. Shhh! *The very stones prate of my whereabouts.* I paused to the side of the backdoor, my breath an ever-outward hiss. Suddenly, the door opened, and I was nearly knocked right off my cloven feet. 'Oh, my Lord!' gasped Maggie. 'You frightened the life out of me, Alistair!' Her bosom was heaving, like a pair of worn out leathery billows and her eyes were bulging as fiercely as if she had some alarming thyroid disorder. Looking at these bulbous eyes I realised they were more puffy than bulging...magenta swellings, blurred beneath streaks of coal dust. The devil costume fell embarrassed to the floor and slunk shamefully under a stone.

'Maggie? Have you been crying?' Her body heaved in one enormous shuddering sob, and for a moment it seemed as though she was an opera diva about to launch into the towering heights of an aria. In fact, so powerful was this image, when she opened her mouth to speak that's what I actually heard: all the human agony, grief and the profundity of hope against all hope of:

La Mama Morta.

'Porto sventura a chi bene mi vuole!	I bring misfortune to all who love me.
Fu in quel dolore	It was then, in my misery,
che a me venne l'amor!	that love came to me!
Voce piena d'armonia e dice:	And murmured in a sweet, melodius voice:
"Vivi ancora! Io son la vita!	"You must live! I am life itself!"
Ne' miei occhi è il tuo cielo!	Heaven is in my eyes!
Tu non sei sola!	You are not alone
Le lacrime tue io le raccolgo!	Let your tears fall on my breast!
Io sto sul tuo cammino e ti sorreggo!	I will walk with you and be your support!
Sorridi e spera! Io son l'amore!	Smile and hope! I am love!
Tutto intorno è sangue e fango?	Is all around you blood and mire?
Io son divino! Io son l'oblio!	I am divine! I can make you forget!
Io sono il dio che sovra il mondo scendo da l'empireo, fa della terra un ciel!	I am the God who descends to earth from the empyrean and makes this world Ah! paradise! Ah!
Io son l'amore, io son l'amor, l'amor"	I am love, love, love"
E l'angelo si accosta, bacia,	And the angel approaches, kisses me,
e vi bacia la morte!	and in that kiss is death!
Corpo di moribonda è il corpo mio.	The moribund body is my body.
Prendilo dunque.	Take it then!
Io son già morta cosa!	I am already dead like it!

The effect only lasts for a few magical seconds, during which I was transported; felt myself rushing, soaring into the summer sky, renting the blueness in two: part-Superman, part-angel-of-death. I rose like a rocket, only to descend slowly to earth with my gigantic blackened wings folded in a protective shroud around me. In reality this must've happened in a split second – a subliminal few frames in a movie, because Maggie, carried on as normal.

'It's Nina,' she said, sorrow snatching at her breath. 'She's gone; left early this morning. She wouldn't say why.' She nodded to confirm the question obvious in my eyes. 'Yes – with him, Fabrizio.' So that was it. We sat together in the kitchen, dissecting the misery of the last twenty-four hours, with an array of blunt, rusty surgical instruments. Apparently, Fabrizio turned up at Maggie's late the night before, confessing his undying love to Nina, who had surprisingly been only too happy to forgive his recent indiscretions and welcome him back with open arms, and legs. Together they decided to return to Fabrizio's hometown of Naples, where there were new work opportunities. Fabrizio could join his uncle's building firm, and Nina could probably get a job at his father's restaurant. Maggie had begged her not go, judging Fabrizio to be a Lothario out for what he could get in every sense of the word. But Nina would hear none of it. In desperation, she told Nina that there was a good chance that Anna's baby was Fabrizio's and he should face up to his responsibilities. Strangely, this had thrown them both into a complete rage. For reasons best known to Nina, she protested wildly that the chances of Fabrizio being the father were zero. Tears pressed out of Maggie's eyes as she relayed Nina's words, 'She said, how dare I try to manipulate the situation in such an evil underhand way. And that I was only saying this to keep her here, and that I had no idea, no idea at all. She said I was so self-centred that I saw nothing beyond my own needs, and I was a…a…oh, God…' Whatever Nina thought Maggie was I was never going to find out because she broke down into unspeakable, choking sobs, which racked her body most alarmingly.

Finally, surrounded by the bloody entrails of our morning's endeavours, we sat in a state of peculiarly, calm exhaustion. Maggie insisted I return immediately to the hospital. 'My dear Alistair, only *you* can salvage something from this mess. Anna needs you now, and goodness knows my boy, you certainly need her.'

In the subsequent days that followed, I found out that, against all her better judgement, this foolish lovesick old woman had departed for Naples that very afternoon. I also know now, what I did not know then, that Maggie had 'lost' her own daughter to heroin addiction nearly fifteen years before. Remember, her advice to me when she spoke of all her traumas? Nothing had been specific, all was oblique. Now I really knew the truth, much of who Maggie was fell into place. She told me during a heart-to-heart, many years later, when her guard slipped and her worst nightmare uncoiled itself and emerged briefly from the depths of the shadows.

When she recalled her loss, the pain in her eyes was so intense I could hardly bear to meet her gaze. So instead I listened; and as I listened, I watched this barbed fragment from Maggie's life twirl and spin before my eyes, and then pierce her right through the heart.

She had suffered years of repeatedly searching for her lost daughter, only to find her once again, caught in the moonlight, thin, white and wasted: a skeletal shadow reposing upon a low damp mattress. Here, in the most appalling inner-city squats and cockroach-ridden bedsits, Maggie found her little girl, residing amongst the lowest of the dead. Each time, she had tried to rescue her. But some people cannot be rescued until they want to be, with heroin addicts being top of the class in eschewing the lifebelt. And the once beautiful, Juliet, whose childhood had been a formulaic whirlwind adventure of ballet classes, pony club and flute lessons, clung to her new-found lover in a vehement never-ending embrace of *post- coital tristesse*; disappearing, locked in the arms of this smiling cadaver, into the cold, dark, unfathomable depths of the Mariana Trench. Expressionless eyes, pearly white. Her bone-white face sinking into the gloom, immovable, brittle - bleached as a cuttlefish shell. Falling, falling, downward. The expense of spirit in a waste of shame...

'Jools, as she likes to be called now,' said Maggie, with an indulgent smile, as if this 'renaming' were a passing teenage rebellion, 'has my number – all the local hospitals have my number. In all the years I've been here, not a single phone call, Alistair. I try to think of this as a blessing.' In one swift almost imperceptible movement, her mask was successfully back in place. I never saw her without it again.

If only I had taken Maggie's advice and returned immediately to the hospital, how different my life could have been. But I was very tired, so very tired. I would just pop into the house, for a while. By now, I was even angrier with Anna, as the knock-on consequences of her actions sank in. Poor, poor Maggie. And Nina, now feeling compelled to throw herself into Fabrizio's selfish arms. She would be let down again within the month. Me – a man whose heart is broken, who would have to face Marion's "You never learn, Alistair, do you?" speech'; face her unspoken triumph over my failures.

I wanted to take a hammer to the freshly plastered wall – its pale terracotta pinkness mocking me. I ran my fingertips over its cool, smooth surface, gouging just a slither of a line with my thumbnail. 'I should smash you to pieces.' However, a sense of propriety holds me back; this is after all Tom's house. Instead, I see a bottle of whiskey malingering by the fridge, and feel a fortifying shot would help me face the rest of the day. So darkly golden, almost bronze; what a warming, almost burning sensation, and as I relax a little to its smoky peatiness, I find an unexpected smile spreading across my face. I'm back at the Christmas party at David's. 'Splendid! Splendid choice!' I say out loud. Oh, to be back there now, before all of this. It seems like another life. If only Tom were with me, he'd help me through.

On the positive side, at least Fabrizio is well and truly out of the picture; perhaps we could get over this. I have another small splash of whiskey to toast the F- word's departure. Mmm, I like that. I might only refer to him as that from now on. Perhaps, in a few years' time when all of this miserable time is behind us, Anna and I will only hear the phrase 'the 'F' word,' to invoke a look of intimate understanding with one another; a mutual acknowledgement of a difficult period over which true love triumphed.

Another thought nagged away at me. Why was she so sure she couldn't have been made pregnant by Fabrizio? Maybe I had jumped to that conclusion. How long had we been away? An image of a snowy night flashed into my mind.... was she telling the truth about that idiot Gregg? I knew she was still 'friends' with him. A whole new line of anxiety opened up for examination...

I'd been in over a couple of hours and there was still no word from the hospital. Perhaps I should ring? But they were expecting 'the father' to turn up. If I ring and say Fabrizio disappeared to Naples, then she will only want me because she knows there's no hope of being with him. If I turn up at the hospital, I've got to go through all that 'Are you the father?' nonsense again. If I wait for her to ring me...I'll know it's me she wants. She can come back here, and slowly we can patch things up. Anyway, I think she needs to run after me this time.

If it wasn't Fabrizio's, could it really be Gregg's? Or maybe the whole idea of her being pregnant was illusory and this was a sequel entitled: 'The Return of Dino's Bug.' Surely the bug was the most logical explanation. Convincing myself that I wasn't even that worried about Anna anymore, I decided to do nothing. She'd ring wanting a lift home soon, or arrive in a taxi, running through the house headlong for the loo.

By now I was lying on the sofa in the lounge, with the golden, late-afternoon sun, just catching the whiskey, so it looked like a bottleful of runny honey. Feeling so desolately cold inside, I found the whiskey had a remarkably warming effect. And as you know, I was also a man with an unquenchable thirst: a timeless drink; 'A splendid choice, Alistair!'. And like a little fat drunken bee, I sipped and sipped my nectar, until I dozily drifted far away.

And so, I spent a second night on the sofa, well, at least the first half of it. Waking in the blackness of the dark rural night skies was alarming, disorientating. As I fumbled for the lamp switch, I felt a strange chill in the air, and as the room became illuminated once more, I noticed I'd left the window and shutters wide open; the air was horribly alive with mosquitoes and all other sorts of insects drifting with loosely connected, dangly legs across the ceiling. Oh God, what time was it? One-thirty? One-thirty! Shit.

Two things could have happened: either Anna had been kept in overnight for observation or something, or she had been declared able to return to civilian life, and in a fit of pique that I had not sent Fabrizio to her bedside, had booked herself into a hotel in town. Anyway, there wasn't much I could do about either of those scenarios at this time of night. My stomach was uncomfortably awash with alcohol, so I went down to the kitchen and ate a large quantity of over-ripe cheese, accompanied by some black coffee. Needless to say, I felt rather nauseous as a consequence.

She should ring me. She should say she is sorry for all she has put me through. And I still needed to know for sure about Greg. If I chase her now, after this, I'll be doing it for the rest of my life. If I'm patient.... wait it out, until she rings me, I'll have recovered a fig leaf of dignity. She will respect me more in the long run. And I will know she wants me as much as I want her.

So, calling on every ounce of stupid pride I possessed, I closed my heart to everything she meant to me. Resisted every urge to jump into the car and race back to the hospital, or scour the hotels until I found her. When I finally gave in and thought I should perhaps at least make an enquiry, I realised the phone had been left slightly off the hook. Replacing it, I lifted the receiver once more; it sang with inviolable voice, across the desert, a dull, dull monotonous drawl. Several times I began to dial the number, only to replace the receiver half way through. No voices spoke. Not mine; not the receptionist.

Twice I sat in the car, for at least half an hour. I even turned the engine over once. How loud, how rude it sounds in the cool still air, like a sudden burst of laughter in the catacombs. Shutting the car door with the quietest clunk I could, I decided to sit on the wall and observe the night sky. It was such an extraordinarily quiet night. The stars, scattered across the ink-black sky looked like a broken string of pearls falling through the dark depths of the ocean. *'Those are pearls that were his eyes.'* They are so far away; you cannot see them falling, falling. Falling away from the centre. *'The centre cannot hold, Things fall apart.'* (There is even a theory for this you know; it is called the Big Rip and basically means that eventually the expansion of the universe will become so rapid even the forces holding molecules together – even the molecules of living things – will be torn apart. The whole of creation tearing itself to shreds, unravelling chains of DNA spiralling across the expanse; I only wish I could be there to witness it.)

Once at scout camp, I remember we all had to lie on our backs, in the middle of a field looking up at the stars, while our aging scout master attempted to point out various constellations.

'Can you believe,' he whispered trying to engender a sense of wonder into the occasion, 'as far as we know the universe goes on forever – it never ends – on and on it goes into infinity.' We were polite boys in those days, and all gave a respectful, 'Wow!' Or 'Cor!' such as we thought would please him. One lad said, 'So, Akela, how far do you reckon *we* can see then?' Akela sucked air in through his teeth; I knew even back then, that this delaying tactic meant he didn't really know.

'Oooh, I should say, well… it's not the same for everyone of course, but about one and a half million miles.' Another round of 'wows' lit up our circle.

'So,' said the same boy 'what's that then? About halfway, d'you reckon?'

'Ooh, not even a tenth of the way,' the old man replied smiling. (I said nothing. But something nagged away at me all night, as I lay awake in the tent. How can you see halfway, a tenth of the way, any measurable way, into infinity? It just didn't make sense.)

After what might have been a whole hour of staring into space, I thought it seemed the sky was lightening. Certainly, one or two birds were breaking the silence. An early morning walk began to beckon ... a chance to see the sun raise its lazy head above the parapet once more, shimmering into the pale-blue blackness of another day. I set off down the path I knew led upwards to those fateful vineyards.

How strange, eerie, and desolate things were now. The cool dark shadows of a grey dawn, fingering my eyes. The blackened wizened shapes of the vines stretching into the distance, and beneath my feet the silent earth – hard, cracked ridges with dusty earth between. It was like walking up the wall of an ancient cathedral, where the once well-defined faces had become mere bumps and ridges, where the once sweeping arches now crumbled like sandcastles under my feet. With every fibre of my being I yearned to be home in England, where at this time of the dawn, the grass would be drenched in dew, and the air heavy with the scent of roses. I pictured myself barefoot in the garden, intensely aware of the silent bliss, that the world was mine, not yet possessed by anyone else ...how sweet it smells; an almost floating sensation of scent. But not here. Here an acrid smell fills my nostrils. Pungent, unpleasant. Something in the air bodes ill. I know not what.

In comparison to the other day, when I took this path in the full heat of the sun, the walking was easier. The vague nothingness of this time of day suited me: neither too light nor dark, neither too hot nor cold. Hovering between night and day: a pause between moments of real time. If I could walk fast enough, I thought, I could stay in this nothing time forever, always in the strange soft gloom before dawn. Day could chase me around the globe for an eternity, and yet, I would always be here... between states of being. But I could not run fast enough. And in triumph the sun rose behind me, its face glorious in victory, its golden glow forcing me to embrace the new day...

I arrived in the village at around eight. Shutters were already flung open, with bedding spilling out of windows; and morning greetings poked holes in the warm, sterile air. Already the little grocery shop had a fine display of fruit and vegetables perilously cascading from angled boxes: tomatoes gripping onto their vines for grim death; teetering piles of red and green peppers; torpedo shaped aubergines lined up for firing at unsuspecting passers-by; and some overly ambitious courgettes, which now resembled long party balloons.

It was far too early to drop into Maggie's as she was definitely not a morning person, and as I thought of her corpulent mound of flesh rising and falling beneath her sheets, I decided it was best to leave her be.

As I dropped down the lane leading to Tom's house, I realised the front door was wide open. My heart jolted. Had I shut it last night? I was sure I had. I'm so particular about security, even here, where the crime rate was probably zero. There were only two possibilities? One Sergio, unlikely as I thought they were finished now, and two – Anna.

My heart leapt like a salmon returning from the ocean as I quickened my pace. My plan had worked. She'd come back to me; now to graciously accept her apology and find a way out of this mess.

'Anna. Anna?' I called. No reply. 'Is that you Anna? I'm in the kitchen.'

No reply. But this time there was a movement from the upstairs lounge. I was just at the foot of the stairs when the broad silhouette of large man appeared at the top. I jumped back. Before I could recognise the man, I realised I knew the voice. 'Thank God you're all right,' it said.

Tom. Tom? Tom here? He continued down the stairs towards me. 'And where the fuck have you been? I've been here since six, worried sick.'

'I went for a walk,' I croaked, my voice sounding strained from not having spoken for a while. 'I thought you were Anna.' My hand ran over my chin, which felt coarse and bristly. 'We've had a bit of a falling out – well, more than that really. It's been bloody awful actually,' I added.

'What in God's name have you been doing, Alistair?'

'Oh, it wasn't me,' I protested. 'It was her.'

'No. I mean in the last twenty- four hours.'

'It's a long story. I'll make some coffee and tell you all about it. I mean, it's so weird,' I said walking back into the kitchen, 'I was only thinking how good it would be to have you here to help me through this – and here you are.' I shook my head with disbelief. 'What brings you here, so out of the blue, anyway?'

'Anna.'

'Anna?'

317

'Yes. She called home yesterday lunchtime, said she'd been trying to get hold of you, after you'd run out on her at the hospital. Fortunately, I was in Basel visiting an old friend. I came as soon as I got the message. Anna was worried for your safety. Said you'd had a terrible row. Thought you might have…done something stupid, committed suicide or something.'

'Suicide?'

'So, you came all the way here for me?'

'Not entirely. I'm here for Anna too. Why haven't you been back to see her?'

I shrugged; it seemed so difficult to explain.

'You should have gone back, Alistair.' His tone of voice was sending a chill through my heart. I looked intently at him waiting for his next sentence. 'She could've died yesterday.' His mouth trembled as he spoke those words, 'Don't you have any idea how serious this has been?'

'Died?'

'Yes. Died.'

Do you know those news reels of earthquake disasters, where buildings waver for a few seconds then crash to rubble on the ground, where roads and bridges bend and twist in contorted shapes then groaning break apart, where a great chasm opens up in the earth and swallows life itself into the gaping wound…? There in the centre of such a scene, I stood.

'I thought it was just a bug, or a … or a miscarriage. I mean some women have them without even noticing, don't they? What happened?' How feeble and distant my voice sounded.

'It wasn't a straightforward miscarriage- even if it had been, you should have been there, Alistair. What kind of row could have kept you from her?'

'So, it *was* a miscarriage? But, not straightforward?'

'No, it was ectopic. I spoke to Dr Vitale on the phone about an hour ago.'

'Ectopic?'

He glared at my ignorance, and answered in a slow unforgiving tone. 'It means the foetus grew in the fallopian tube, not in the womb, so it gets to a certain size and burst the tube.' He was gripping the back of the kitchen chair, his knuckles an unpleasant purple and white. 'Hence the severe pain and life-threatening blood loss, and the necessity of major surgery. What were you playing at? Leaving her on her own, like that?'

With my head in my hands, a cold fear spilled through my veins like acid. It seemed so pathetic now to talk about my anger, my disappointment, my own wretched feelings of inadequacy. I didn't want to say it, but somehow, I couldn't stop myself. 'It wasn't my baby. She'd been sleeping with someone else. I suppose that's why I wasn't there. Oh, God what am I going to do?'

(How could he understand the pain of having one's hopes dashed in this way? Tom, who could so easily fill his wife's belly with a child. Tom, whose houseful of infants screamed his fecundity, like whoops of victory to every damn passer-by. Tom, who had never once seen his wife emerge from the bathroom, shaking her head, with tears in her eyes, and then fall on his chest in uncontrollable sobs. Of course, that was a long time ago, but once, unbelievable though it seems, once, that was Marion. She of the high-powered career; she who scorned other people's children as snotty-nosed irritants; she who wanted a baby more than she wanted me in the end. I knew by the end of the second year of her desperate longing, and my desperate failing that we were at the beginning of the end. Some couples would have found a way through, but not us. Together we entered a gateway bearing the inscription: 'Abandon hope all ye who enter here,' and from then onwards, we were lost.

In bed at night, we slept turned away from one another. We were that most ironic of married creatures, not the beast with two backs, but its ugly mutant half-brother, the beast with two bellies.)

This snippet of information about Anna's holiday romance had taken some of the self-righteous wind out of his sails, because all he said was 'never,' and sank down into a chair. Anna had obviously carefully edited out some of the finer detail of the last few days, when she summoned Tom here.

'But, she just,' he began, 'she just, said she was worried about your state of mind – you'd been acting strangely, and she thought you'd taken the threatened loss of the baby very badly.'

'It's been a little more complicated than that.' I stared at him hard. Images of the scenes in the bedroom, the vineyard, Maggie's, the hospital, leapt around my head, burning like the flickering flames of a fire. Memories I did not want to share. Then suddenly in amongst this fire an image rose up searing a hole in my mind – Anna – close to death – she nearly died – what was I doing still sat here? My God, I must go to her!

'Tom - I have to leave right away.'

'Of course,' he said, as if also waking from a stupor, 'I'll drive.'

'No, I must take us.'

'You're in no fit state to drive.' I looked down at myself, realised than my whole body was trembling in shock. I handed over the keys to the Morris, a few moments later we were on our way to the hospital – about twenty hours too late.

Chapter Forty: Entering the whirlpool

The same receptionist sat poised, with her long, elegant hands pressed palm to palm, in front of her face, looking as if she were praying. Feeling somewhat awkward about interrupting, we approached the counter rather reverently, only to realise she was just checking that the length of each of her nails were equal to its opposite finger. She glanced up; a smile already fixed to her face – it dropped on seeing me. 'Mr Johnson. Please wait.' Her practised phrase trod the boards publicly for the first time.

When she indicated we sit in reception, I turned to Tom. 'This is ridiculous – just tell her we need to see Anna. You speak some Italian… I'm not waiting.' He held his hands up in appeasement, 'I don't think we'll be waiting long.'

'No?'

He nodded over my shoulder, I turned round, still half expecting to see Anna wandering towards me in one of those thin hospital gowns, pale, wan, but arms outstretched to hold me. However, striding towards us was a somewhat grimmer version of Dr Vitale than the one we'd seen yesterday. The thin smile was now just a thin set mouth, the handsome glittering eyes, steely and grey.

His professionalism overtook him and he extended his hand; 'Mr Johnson,' and turning to Tom shook his hand saying, 'and you are Tom Gower? Come.'

As we went into the same room in which we had sat yesterday, I realised I'd have felt less guilty entering a police interrogation room on a charge of rape and murder. If Dr Vitale thought me despicable, he never said so. Perhaps his English wasn't up to it, but he just stuck to the facts, reading from notes on a clipboard.

Anna had apparently become critically ill within a few hours of my departure, but had somehow managed to call Tom before she collapsed. Emergency surgery had been performed… severe blood loss – state of shock – large scar, unfortunately. The pregnancy was quite advanced; most ectopics would have caused problems before this. It was very bad – the position of the foetus, in the corneal portion of the fallopian tube – very rare site for ectopic.

At this point he turned the clipboard around and pointed his fine long surgeon's finger, his mohel's fingernail, to a diagram of a uterus, with a tiny baby clinging to life, just where the fallopian tube enters the womb. So close…and yet…

Tragically – necessitated – hysterectomy. Inevitably – loss of foetus.

'I'm so sorry,' Dr Vitali concluded.

A silence - blank, white - like a November fog enveloped us all.

Eventually Dr Vitale spoke again.

'You see Anna for a little time.' He touched my hand as if he understood there had been more to the events of yesterday than he knew. But I was beyond any kind of comfort.

I rose from my chair, a condemned man.

'I'll take you to her.'

Tom stood wearily to his feet. 'Dr Vitale,' he said slowly, uncertainly, 'exactly how far pregnant was Anna?'

Dr Vitale paused, and turned in the doorway.

Suddenly, I could not breathe.

'How many weeks pregnant?' Dr Vitale enquired, in order to establish he had understood the question correctly.

'Yes.'

'The foetus was about twelve weeks - very late for ectopic.'

Tick-tock.

At the end of the 11th week the foetus is easily recognisable as a small human baby...the eyes are completely formed...the limbs are growing rapidly...movements of the limbs and spine increase...the ovaries or testis have formed within the body...but the eventual sex cannot yet be distinguished...the heart is formed...the approximate length of the baby is 5.5cm (as long as a little finger) and its weight is 10g.

How to walk? How to breathe? How to force my heart to take another beat? Nobody speaks.

We followed Dr Vitale down a long corridor. Finally, reaching double doors marked *unita di maternita*.... As they flung open, a strange odour filled my nostrils: the smell of human life, with all its 'mewling and puking'.

My eyes scanned the beds of women as we processed like servers behind a priest. One woman was reading; another encircled her small baby nestled close to her breast; one was lying on her bed resembling a strange human hillock. And then a small side room alone: a side chapel. Dark, reverent, apart, - that none should enter but those with the most heinous of sins to confess.

'Mr Johnson, A few minutes only please. Anna is very tired. She must not be...made sad.'

322

I think he meant upset or distressed, well that was crying in the wind if ever I heard it. How could I make her sadder or more upset than she already was? I had brought her lower than anyone could. There was nothing more I could inflict upon her.

I heard Tom saying, 'I'll be just here, if you need me. Alistair, this morning, they didn't tell me everything... I'm so sorry.' And I pushed open the door - A rush of stale air, almost ranker than death.

This moment in time is always with me, like the corner of a frosted garden, where the sun is never quite strong enough to undo the bitter chill of the night, layer upon layer of cold ice – deeper and deeper – a little corner of perma-frost in my heart, if not my very soul.

There, upon the pillows, her face so ghastly white and immobile – it was as if she peered at me from inside a glacier. Her eyeballs themselves – frozen, static and lifeless. My beautiful Anna.

Horrified, my eyes glanced down to her arms lying pallid either side of her body. In the hand closest to me, a large needle plastered to the back of her hand bulged, lifting the skin. A bruise radiated outward like a reddish-purple storm cloud. I followed the drip back up its pipeline to a flaccid bag of clear fluid draining into her.

Everything was shades of white. An after-life vision of a ghost of a life; tinged faded-lace white, yellow soured-cream white, ivory dead white, pale funereal lily white, the dentine white of aging elongated teeth, the crumbling sage-white of deathly marble, the skull bone ash white of spent life. The white you see behind your eyelids when your eyes refuse to accept the blackness of the night.

When my aching eyes travelled back up Anna's body, her eyes were now glassy with tears. She shut her eyelids; some tears crept a silent path down her face. As if in slow motion her eyelids rolled back, like the unfurling wooden slats of an old bureau. Vaselined eyelashes. Then, for the first time since I had entered the room her eyes met mine. They didn't sparkle, they didn't dance; there was nothing there but a still, hollow, dullness.

'I thought you were dead.' Her voice was dry and scratchy from the anaesthetic. 'Really,' she whispered hoarsely, now shaking her head as if now amazed at the absurdity of the thought. 'I really believed, that only the fact you'd killed yourself would have kept you from me yesterday – all things considered.' She took in the full picture of me standing there, unshaven, unwashed, unbearable.

I looked downwards as shame slid through the tunnels of my veins, a cold, deathly serum from a fatal injection. My hands covering my face; I collapsed on the end of the bed.

What words are these? Grief? Despair? Desolation? Get behind me; you have no place here. Words have not yet been uttered to express the wretchedness of my soul.

'I thought I was going to die for certain.' She spoke deliberately, almost as if she had rehearsed this speech. 'I thought I am going to die… in some second-rate hospital in the middle of fucking nowhere. And in all the pain and all the fear I kept thinking he will come – in spite of everything he'll come because he loves me. And if he loves me, he'd be here at a time like this.' She was speaking through a kind of choking guttural sob now, but I could still understand every syllable. 'I knew I was going to lose our baby, Alistair. That was bad enough, and you may not believe me, but when I realised our baby was going to die, I suddenly wanted it more than anything else I've ever wanted in my life…even my own life, my fucking nineteen-year-old life, which may as well be over too.'

'It was 'ours', then? Definitely, 'ours'?'

She looked confused. 'I was three months pregnant – of course it was ours.'

(Greg sat grinning in the bedside chair. *'You can't even ask mate, can you?'*)

'I should've come…I just… I couldn't… It was…' I struggled to vocalize anything, then fell to clutching her feet underneath the covers. 'Oh, God I'm so sorry. Please Anna, forgive me. I meant to come… I just couldn't. *If* I'd known… Oh Anna.'

'Oh, Death where is thy sting?'

'You know very well my friend - I'm here,' he whispers softly, 'piercing you through the heart as you speak. Please, stay a little stiller- ahhhh. All done now. It hurts doesn't it? Don't try to mock me, deny me. There is no pain worse than death – believe me Alistair, I should know. But take comfort. *'Who is't can say 'I am the worst'?'* Trust me Alistair, it is not you yet – not by a long way.

Be ready… I am always here, walking beside you… a breath away… a heartbeat away.

I began half crawling up the bed, just wanting to hold her close, through the blindness of my tears. Then I felt her hand on my head.

'No Alistair. Don't – and mind my scar.'

Propping myself up awkwardly, I wiped my eyes, choked and afraid.

And then she spoke the unspeakable truth – pronounced the death sentence on us both.

'I'll never have children now.'

The death sentence which would last a lifetime; the death sentence which would last for eternity.

'I know. Oh, Anna I'm so sorry.'

'*You're* sorry? 'Sorry' isn't always enough, is it?'

The phrase seemed to find an echo in my mind, and I seemed unable to answer. Ironic, isn't it, don't you think?

Was my infertility some sort of contagious disease I had unknowingly passed on to her? My offspring, a sort of antithesis to life? Rewind the procreative clock backwards. Had I deliberately programmed my creation to settle down in the wrong place to cause such catastrophe? A subconscious master plan of luring her into my lonely, sterile world, *'solamen miseris socios habuisse dolris'*? It was ironic of course that the first time I actually managed in my entire existence to procreate, I actually decrease the world's potential population. My contribution to humankind, all in negative numbers.

Goodbye to all my children. Goodbye to all Anna's children. Goodbye to Anna. Goodbye to me. Goodbye to all that. Goodbye to forever.

Ever since my DNA had first crawled out of the slime it managed to reproduce, pass on some kind of copy of itself. Throughout every age it wove its precarious path. My ancestors' mineral, animal, human all found a way to pass on life. From the moment of the Big Bang to the formation of the stars, planets, life on earth, every damn one of them could pass on the baton. Not me. A billion years of smooth exchanges, then whoops – 'What a klutz!' – Sorry folks... dropped it. Oh, dear. Aeons of evolution wiped out in a second. You're the end of the line. It all dies with you.

Watch the cup, the elixir of life pass from your lips. Hear the dreams falling, crashing all around. See the stairway to heaven pulled upward, never to descend again. Stand alone, beyond the Garden of Eden, banished by God.

'Never – Alistair; I'll never have a child. They cleaned me out. Taken it all.' Her glazed eyes searched desperately around the room as if praying for escape. 'I'm nineteen,' she wailed. A gasping intake of stuttered breath. Her chest expands and pain creases her face.

Reaching out, with a dry, coarse palm I attempt to caress her wet cheek. Her left hand rises slowly enfolding mine, and purposefully she removes it from her skin.

'It's no good. I don't want this anymore.' She's staring at the foot of her bed, sounding as if she's regarding a disgusting half-eaten plate of hospital food, and at first, I really don't comprehend what she's talking about. 'It would never have lasted forever–' she continued, 'you'd be the first to admit to that, and somehow what's happened…draws a line under everything. It's over Alistair. Please leave now.'

These words are so totally unexpected that I truly cannot make sense of them.' Leave? What do you mean, leave?'

'Leave here – leave me. Go back to Tom's, back to England. I don't know where. It's finished between us; go wherever you like. Just don't come near me.'

'Don't say that, Anna, please. I'm sorry. I'm really sorry.'

There was a light tap on the door, around which the noble head of Dr Vitale appeared, looking almost as if it were floating, strangely detached. He smiled at Anna, conveying in his eyes a warm understanding. Don't worry; his eyes whispered reassuringly; I'll get rid of him for you.

He turned that steady gaze to me. 'Mr Johnson, Anna must rest now.'

I needed more time. *'HURRY UP PLEASE IT'S TIME'*. How dare he dismiss me as if my audience were over, thwarting my petition for forgiveness, denying my access to absolution. I appealed directly to Anna, believing she would usher this Vitale away, put him in his place. 'Anna?' She wouldn't even look at me, but stared at the back of her hand, where the needle seemed to have come loose from its plaster and now pirouetted awkwardly in an oozing pool of blood on the back of her hand.

Without a word Vitale swept into the room, and immediately set to work on Anna's hand. Whilst his elegant, intelligent hands held a clean dressing in place, he stared hard across the bed at me.

'Tomorrow,' he said. 'You come tomorrow.'

'But I think Anna needs to talk to me now. Don't you, Anna?'
She didn't even look at me, but just bit her bottom lip and slowly shook her head from side to side.

'Thank you, Mr Johnson. Tomorrow.' He flicked his head towards the doorway.

What power did he exert over me? His bloody white coat; the gravity of his manner; his array of magical objects enabling him to hear, to see, inside the human body. Even as we stand here on opposite sides of this hushed silence, can he hear the frantic, frightened beating of my heart? See the blackness of my soul, just as easily as he saw and removed the life I had created, which had threatened to kill Anna? Diminishing under the power of his gaze, I found myself backing through the doorway, withdrawing from their presence. Accepting 'tomorrow' was the best I could hope for.

Tomorrow and tomorrow and tomorrow…and every day was the same, apart from the fact that as Anna grew stronger so too did her resolve that she wanted nothing more to do with me. *Forgiveness. What about forgiveness?* One day I'll forgive you, she had said, but that won't change anything. Forgiveness can't turn back the clock. Forgiveness can't give us back what we've lost. Forgiveness is just gift wrapping a bag of shit. It changes nothing. It's just a way of trying to feel better about things. A sort of vent really, allowing the pain of the forgiver to seep out a little; the forgiven to assuage their guilt.

I had replied, wouldn't that be better than this bitterness? It would be a way forward. Then she had stared at me for several moments, until I had to look away at the floor. She was right I suppose – at this moment in time, there was no forward – only the present moment, creeping, creeping.

****

These were dark days indeed. I slunk about the house too despairing and lost to do anything, while Tom lived outdoors. Seeming to relish the silent solitude he found here, Tom spent hours quietly sitting on the edge of the terrace, a never-empty glass of wine in his hand, a never-empty head of thoughts. What was he thinking about all that time? He seemed almost as troubled as I was. In the evenings, he'd spend a good half hour on the phone to Eve, sometimes I'd overhear him saying goodnight to the children, and sometimes his voice was barely a whisper. Were they talking about me I wondered?

Neither of us ate very much, just the odd bit of dried bread and cheese, or the occasional apple, which we'd take a bite or two out of and then lob into the long grass. Chewing, swallowing; the pappy sensation of mastication - it was all too difficult.

On the third day, I returned from visiting Anna, inconsolable, as the reality of my situation began to sink in. She really meant it. All the excuses I'd comforted myself with up till now, that it was merely the shock of events, anger, tiredness, excess of drugs affecting the brain, began to retreat, and were replaced with the single stark truth - Anna was through with me.

However hard I tried to reach her; she was striding faster, away from me. I'm running, running after her, 'Don't leave me Anna!' Always several steps ahead of the game; inexorably she rushes away from me. Powerless I am, utterly impotent. Is this my just deserts? Are you behind this 'Cosmic sadist'? I'm sorry. All right. More sorry than I could ever be. I'm crawling, begging. Is that what you want? Was I so bad? If I blindly believe in you, will you let me off? But you don't bargain do you? Man is free and yet all around me are men in chains. It's just an illusion of freedom – *thy* will be done.

Tom wandered in from the garden to find me with my head in my hands; my face pressed against the smooth marble of the table.

'What am I going to do? What am I going to do?'

'You have to let her go.' He says this bluntly, as if it's a simple statement-of-fact. 'Let her put her life back together, somewhere else, with someone else. And you must try to do the same. That's the bottom line.' The very thought of it tears through me. 'You should be grateful for what you've shared,' he continues, draining the last drop of wine from his glass. 'You knew from the start it couldn't be forever.' He's been using the same glass for days and it has a series of dried, red wine stains encircling the bowl, like the ancient age-rings on an oak.

Lifting my head slowly from the table, I turned to face him. 'I should never have left her side, should I? What was I thinking?'

For a few moments Tom doesn't seem to know what to say and unfortunately clutches a quote the from the back of his mind, forgetting that it's Lady Macbeth's words to her bloodied husband: 'What's done is done,' he says with a grim finality. My grip on the dagger tightens welding me to my guilt.

Then, somehow, he sees this as the right moment to unburden himself of what has been really eating him these last few days.

'I know you won't see it now, but honestly, Alistair, perhaps it's for the best. Having kids in a relationship isn't always easy. Anna and you with a baby – it would have changed everything anyway. You'd be splitting up sooner or later.' I glared at him. 'Sorry mate, but it's the way things are. I don't suppose you want to hear anything like this, but at the moment Eve and I are on the brink of divorce…that's the real reason I got here so quickly the other day. Lucky for you, I couldn't bear being at home with them all. To be honest, that's the truth of why I was in Basel – escaping the menagerie. In spite of being totally pissed off with me, Eve was still good enough to ring me straight away after Anna called – knew I'd want to come and help.' With a slightly trembling hand, he was refilling the stained glass, 'I still love her…in a way. She's fun, kind…but I have to admit intellectually… we're poles apart. Jeez! Some of the things she comes out with, sometimes I just want to put a restraining order on her mouth. Yeah, I think I do still love her; love the kids to death, but the strain having them has put on our relationship… I need my space. You wouldn't understand if you've not…' He took a quick gulp, and let out a small strangled laugh. I could not believe what I was hearing. 'I mean, God, the bloody twins crying all through the night – always in our bed. Five nights out of seven I sleep on the ruddy sofa. And women, they're so fulfilled by babies. Honestly, once they've got that infant to their breast, you're surplus to requirements. It's not how you think it's going to be at all. They're always too bloody tired; your sex life dwindles to nothing. You begin to think, what's the point of going home at night…she's a wreck, the house a fucking pigpen… How we ever conceived Hermione…Lord only knows! Maybe we should've called her Jesus; she could've been an immaculate conception for all I remember.' He gave a harrumph. 'Look, all I'm trying to say Alistair is… that you've not lost what you think you've lost. Romantic idyll it ain't.'

In all the years I had known Tom I don't think he's ever had quite such a towering moment of profound crassness. Had nothing of the past few days permeated that thick hide of his? I had let down and lost the person I loved most in all the world and Anna had escaped death, only to be condemned to a childless, finite existence. A raw scar ripped across her belly. Emptied out.

'You have no idea how lucky you are,' I seethed. 'You have a wife; you have four lovely children. I have nothing. Nothing, God damn you. Anna will never have a child, Tom. Not with me, not with anyone. Never. You stupid prick!' My teeth and fists were clenched, 'How dare *you* talk to *me* about what I've lost. You bastard! You fucking ungrateful, self-centred bastard.'

For the second time in the last few days, I came seriously close to hitting another man. I surged towards Tom with my fist raised, senseless with grief and anger – but it was no good. He caught my arm mid-air, and after a few moments of futile struggle, I flailed weakly and fell weeping onto his chest. I couldn't even fight like a man.

Tom's big, strong arms wrapped around me; I could hear his deep voice resonating in his chest cavity. He was saying he was sorry; was saying he always said the wrong thing; was hopeless. Sorry. He really wanted to help; he just didn't know how. There was something so safe about being held there, protected for a brief moment. Slowly, we fell apart.

Embarrassed by our closeness, our sudden intimacy, Tom made that kind of comment, which was supposed to make us feel 'all manly' once again. 'We're a couple of stupid buggers, aren't we?' he said sort of laughing. *Yes, Tom we are. Absolute fuck-ups.* I was crying now, but without tears – just that awful chest-heaving sobbing as if some raging internal daemon is using your lungs as a punch bag. This sort of scared Tom, 'Steady, Alistair.' he said, placing his hand on my shoulder. Feebly, he tried to pull us back to normality, saying perhaps he should have let me hit him, would have got it out my system. Yes, hit someone else - punch out at my old friend - because I can't splinter my own jaw, close my own eye with a blackened swelling like a rotten plum, can't kick myself hard in the bollocks. What a good idea, hit my friend...except I know what I really need is someone to thump me.

The only thing I fought with at the moment was to control my own emotions, and the jagged rising and falling of my breath. Eventually, I triumphed. A miserable, quiet, nothingness descended, broken only by the gentle glug of wine pouring into an empty glass. As he left the room, Tom patted my arm, placed the glass in front of me, and softly said, 'It'll be all right.'

An hour or so later, he returned to find me still sitting on the same kitchen stool, catatonic – the wine, for once, untouched.

Chapter Forty-one: under the shadow of this red rock

As Anna grew stronger, she began to take control of the situation. I was free to go whenever I wished. Her brother was going to fly out to accompany her home at the end of next week. (Still, she hadn't told her parents.) Until James arrived, she would remain in the safe hands of Dr Vitale. There was no need for me to stay any longer; it had all been arranged. She then thanked me in oddly formal tones for organising the health insurance for the holiday. I begged her to let me stay; to look after her, to please give me one more chance, at least accompany her to the airport, but she wouldn't hear of it.

'Alistair, don't start on that again. It would help me enormously if you'd stop pressurising me in this way.' For a moment her composure slipped; a little snag in her voice, a glassy look in her eyes. Then her resolve dragged itself to its feet again – one more push soldier – ram the bastard.

'You have a long journey ahead of you; the drive back will take you a few days at least. I spoke to Tom on the phone last night, asked him if he'd travel back to England with you. He's been wonderful, hasn't he? But he needs to leave as soon as possible.'

This was news to me, although to be fair I hadn't seen Tom last night, having gone to bed just before ten, utterly drained.

As long as Anna inhabited this alien, organised, efficient persona, she seemed to hold things together. This 'back-to-work troops' attitude concealing all manner of unimaginable horrors, I knew lay beneath a fragile crust. For the rest of my life I will wonder if I should have taken up an ice pick, broken open the thin veneer, made her vulnerable – vulnerable enough to seek the comfort of my arms.

Instead I stood at the foot of her bed, gazing down at her, my heart twisting with grief, 'Where will you go?'

'I'm going to spend a week or two at my brother's flat in London.'

'And then?'

'I don't know.'

'You'll come back in October though, won't you? Term starts quite late this year.'

'I'm not sure what I'm going to do yet. But I won't be returning. How could I?' She anticipated my response adding that I shouldn't waste my breath trying to persuade her to do otherwise.

'Will you ring me though? Let me know how you're getting along.'
'Maybe.'
She lay back on her white pillow, with that exhausted frozen look overtaking her once more. Moments later, as I came through the double doors of the hospital, I was overwhelmed by the fierce intensity of the glare of the sun. It is only with hindsight I understood why I felt so cold.

When I returned to the villa, Tom was talking on the phone, rapidly scribbling notes on a pad of paper beside him. I looked quizzically at him, but he raised his hand to stop me interrupting him. After further nodding and scribbling, he replaced the phone. 'Well, that's been a good half hour's work. I've managed to book us a ferry for Wednesday 8.30pm. Not the best time probably, but it was a question of what's available…peak holiday season and all that.'

'You could've have asked me first. I feel railroaded into leaving.'

'Sorry Alistair, but you weren't around this morning, and Eve's insisting. I have to go back. I've my own battlefield to return to. We were lucky to get that ferry; if I'd left it any later in the day… and Anna's right; it's the best thing if I accompany you home. Just imagine that long drive alone. Anyway, I can't shirk my responsibilities any longer…' he trailed off sheepishly. I watched him, gathering up the scatterings of magazines, and books which radiated about his favourite chair. Purposefully, he tidied them away on the shelf. Over his shoulder he said, with an apologetic laugh in his voice, 'And bloody hell, Alistair, just being in the same room as you now – I feel so damn guilty. You were right: I'm an ungrateful lucky bastard; about time I grew up.'

'Hang about, Wednesday? Doesn't that mean we'll have to leave first thing tomorrow – to make the ferry?'
He knew exactly what *that* meant.

'Yes' he replied, and picking up the notepad, turned and walked towards the door, without even looking at me. He paused in the doorway, and said hesitantly, 'If you don't mind, I'd like to come and say goodbye later on as well – if that's alright with you? Well, I presume you'll go one last time, won't you?' If I had been capable, I would have answered in the affirmative, but I was buried beneath a choking mudslide of despair.

There were two cases to pack, mine and Anna's. The red dress hung silently in the wardrobe. How beautiful she had looked that night...all the radiant loveliness of her. Gently, I slipped the shoulders free of the wooden coat hanger, let the soft, silken fabric, drape over my bare arm...still, lingering, the scent of her; almost here, the shape of her. I knew now, it was quite possible that this dress was the next thing to touch her flesh, after the first time she had lain with Fabrizio. He quite possibly stood in the doorway, watching her sliding into it; kissed her before she came to join me – blind with longing to see her: a late entrance, so instantly forgivable.

I was torn as to which case to place the dress in - so beautiful - even in betrayal. Oh my God, never let me lose the memory of her walking towards us across the lawn. Never. As the years have gone by, occasionally I hold it against my skin, something of her fragrance remains even now...sometimes I lie on my bed with it draped across my face and body, breathing in and out through the shadowy red light.

Her underwear, bikini, all the baggy t-shirts, the jeans she hadn't worn because it had been too hot, those flowing, hippie cheesecloth trousers, the khaki army shorts, the one grey sweatshirt for cool nights, her sunglasses, her floppy hat, Roman-style sandals from Florence, and the lacy bra, which had veiled our lady, all now lay neatly in the case.

I was to drop it off at the hospital that evening when I went to say goodbye. When I went to say goodbye, I was to drop the case off at the hospital. At the hospital that evening, I was to drop the case off, as I said goodbye. Don't make me go there again. Please don't make me go there again...

As we sat, our faces white as ash,
My eyes still swollen from tears,
The phrase 'we are the dead', comes to my mind,
Again, and again,
'We are the dead.'
The withered stumps of time.
A sudden rush of hopelessness.
'You know my throat hurts as if I have been
shouting or screaming for days.'
Death comes slowly-
saps all moisture-
a dryness in the mouth.
Leaves sapped out-
dry, hollow, waste of despair,
where once rivers made floods,
(made my blood rush in my body
to feel your mouth on mine.)
Blindly, we stared into one another's failing eyes
and saw what little time we had
pass away.

Chapter Forty-two: each in his prison

Tom insists on driving my car. He drives steadily, persistently back to the borders between France and Italy. Unresponsive, subjugated to his will, I stare out of the window. Have I been drugged I wonder as I find myself passing along endless miles of autostrada? Why am I allowing this to happen? I really don't know, but it is. And I am drifting along at sixty miles an hour – not even at the speed of sound – and yet I say nothing – I allow myself to let the distance grow. And grow it does.

Before I know 'what's what' we are in France, and by late afternoon we enter a typical small French town, where Tom declares we are to stop to recharge the batteries and stock up on provisions. He's going to book us into a hotel so we can have a good night's sleep; a meal out, we ought to eat something; then tomorrow on our way – up to Calais through the day – a chance for a kip in the car and then the last push across the Channel, sailing at the violet hour, with gulls crying, reeling above our heads... bringing the sailors home from sea. Homeward.

Our hotel is a paltry affair, near the station, just for passing traffic; no self-respecting person would stay here for anything like a holiday. It's passing traffic only. Thankfully, Tom's French is pretty good, he's quite *au fait* with languages, so I don't have to say a thing at the reception, just smile weakly at the *Madame avec une moustache*. My ancient French phrase book contains such useful gems as *j'ai deux paires de chaussettes a raccomoder*. I don't think I'll need that tonight -or possibly ever. Is there anywhere in the world where one would utter that phrase? I repeat it, over and over in my mind, while Tom shows off – 'chatting'. Madame Moustache is impressed and hands over the keys with a twinkle in her eyes and a garbled torrent of French. I bet Tom is even lost at that speed, but he laughs as if he's understood some very funny joke, and points his finger to her saying, '*Sans blague!*' Even I smile and raise my eyebrows, as if 'in' on the joke. As we climb the stairs, I seriously wonder if any of us knows what we're really laughing at - if we *ever really know* why we're laughing. Are any of us *really* in on the joke? I don't think so.

The jollity dies quickly when we locate the room: a dismal twin-bedded room overlooking the railway line, with a shared bathroom at the end of the corridor, which stinks. 'It's certainly cheap,' admits Tom. 'It's only for one night.'

Later, we escaped the regular, rattling, rumble of our room to an unassuming restaurant just off the square, where we attempted to dine on a ragout of beef and a carafe of red, but I could barely touch it. Tough, chewy, indigestible – and that was just the wine; we both wished we'd gone elsewhere, ordered something different.

You know, now I think about it, grief is like that bloody awful casserole. Even now, sometimes my sadness overwhelms me, totally defeats me. I can feel it in my mouth, just like those ghastly gristly pieces of meat you simply can't get rid of. Round and round you chew it, sick, repulsed, almost horrified. You can't spit it out in company – too embarrassing – you're too polite, how awful for everyone else to suffer the appalling half-masticated contents of your mouth… so you chew and chew – disgusted, ashamed – unable to spit or swallow. Yes, grief was like that. Abruptly and without warning filling my mouth so that at times I could barely speak, even breathe.

Both Tom and I smoke several cigarettes after the meal. He doesn't usually smoke these days either, having given up shortly after Ray died, but at the moment both of us are at a crossroads, where a nod at self-destruction seems appropriate. We don't talk about Anna. We don't talk about Eve. We don't talk about the past, or even the future. We talk about cars. And both of us know fuck all about cars.

****

Later, in the shadowy world of the night, I lay awake for hours.

For many, many, long hours, I peered upward, from the bottom of the ocean floor, gazing blindly through this greenish-black haze of night. Nothing seemed the least bit real. Tediously long goods trains rumbled slowly through the bedroom; the haunting, eerie wail of a vixen's scream pierced my skull, and the clock tower knell marked my progression towards an uncertain dawn. Finally, with an unpromising thin slate-grey light, she slunk wearily in, rubbing her bony spine against the window pane. Welcome my love, she sighed, her breath still fusty from sleep: it's a new dawn, it's a new day...

Tom was still slumbering deeply, a snoring worthy of a walrus emanating from the embroidered eiderdown. *Is there nothing in your head?* I stare at over at his comatose bulk. *Do you remember nothing?*

And then, floundering through her sleepy greyness, I slipped, like a newborn apparition, pale-skinned with hollow eyes, stale from the shroud of bedcovers, dressed, and left the station boudoir. No other person was about at this time, save for a wretched little man beginning to assemble the breakfast room, with the requisite amount of hard crusted bread, mean portions of foil wrapped butter, a soupçon of jam; the bitter scent of roasted coffee already burning the air.

Out, out into the soft grey light, through a myriad of close streets, with walls hung with a dank, drain stench. Thin cats, sleek and skinny as weasels slide round corners; the buzzing drone of a 2CV whines away from me. Eventually, I found myself drifting towards the market square, where already the market traders were erecting their stalls: perfumed sheaves of blue-mauve lavender; fresh verdant and russet lettuces like mounds of miniature crinoline skirts; a chequered cloth barely visible beneath a mountain range of every size and shape of dried sausage; shiny rolls of plasticised prints for table cloths and an array of dresses, made from fairly similar prints to the table cloths.

Almost dizzy from lack of sleep and food, I'm tempted by a stall already selling strands of fried donut mixture. I lean up against the water fountain, its gentle splashing at my back, and unwrap the sugary, hot stick of batter; it smells better than it tastes, and after a couple bites, I discard it in a bin...recognising once more, that the gnawing ache within me is not hunger after all...

Just when we least expect it, we face our nemesis...and here, in a corner of a market square, in an obscure 'nowhere' town in the middle of rural France, was mine.

There was a tank full of them, meandering in desultory fashion upon a makeshift seabed, scuttling across the floor of their imagined seas, seemingly without a care in the world. But as I approached, my God, I saw something else, beside the aimless wanderings of a speckled bronzed crustacean.

'I'm doomed,' his eyes said to me. Eyes that could not cry, eyes that could not lie; out on stalks already wet – drenched in tears. His long face sombre...all those whispering legs, waving, floating, up and down, absolutely ineffectual.

All his life he'd carried his two formidable weapons. Great crushing claws that looked too heavy for him to carry. But all his life he'd manfully held them aloft: his lobster claws. Now two tightly bound rubber bands held them shut. They were a sheathed sword, an unloaded pistol – next to useless. I peered through the glass. It would not be me to take him home to a pot on a rolling boil, transforming his cool blue self to a blazing flamingo red ...but someone would. It's all over bar the shouting as they say. Those stalk-like eyes found mine once more, and I backed away. We exchanged a look of pity, and then I moved on through the market, haunted by his face.

Do I look like that lobster now, with searching, tormented eyes? Touching the glass, with my bound claws, knowing there's no escape. Am I so lost?

Have you really sealed my fate?

It's all over bar the shouting.

But the screaming's already begun.

'Take into the air my quiet breath…it's a quick death, God help us all. It is not.'

Chapter Forty-three: yet there the nightingale

Do you remember it was November when I began writing about the appalling events of last summer – when my beautiful dream exploded like a Pyrex bowl dropped on a cold, stone floor? Shards were scattered everywhere. Please do not walk around this area with bare feet. They take forever to sweep up. Such tiny slivers, hiding in dark corners, sharp as scorpion's stings. Deathly if swallowed. Sometimes a naked baby comes into the room. Crawling. Can you imagine? Crawling through such a minefield. Then the panic is frantic. I try, I try to pick it up, but I can never grasp it. You cannot possibly envisage how awful it is.

Anyway, we are now a long, long way from November; in fact, it is now June. It took me the best part of six months to write those few chapters. How often I wanted to give up, to walk away from it all, but I knew there had been some truth in Mary's ruminations on the preferred excellence of finished articles, and besides what else do I have to do?

Now I wait, wait with some anticipation – hoping to hear some distant cranking sound from above, and watch with almighty relief, as a lumbering, great wobbling *Deus ex Machina* descends upon me. Surely one will come? After all, both you and I sense the closing chapters are upon us. Where is my 'god from the machine'?

Well, the ensuing silence can mean only one thing – there is no rescue party to provide me with some improbable resolution. No; I am to provide the final soliloquy – a lone figure – to do all that last strutting and fretting business, without any miracles in attendance.

Although, I expect there are some unanswered questions I now know the answer to, that I can furnish you with to provide some sense of closure. What has happened to Marion? To Tom, Ruth, Mother, and Thaddeus?

First, Marion: Marion is still, surprisingly, with Edward. They plan to marry next month, and I have threatened to compose an epithalamium to celebrate the occasion, as my wedding gift to them both. In this strange modern world, we inhabit these days, I am invited to *their* wedding. But I don't think I'll attend; my presence would just seem to accentuate the farcical hollowness of the vows. I mean, we have *all* failed already – failed to forsake all others; failed to love and to cherish; failed till death do us part – failed the whole damn shooting match.

I suppose one could argue, if one takes 'death' in the metaphorical sense to mean the death of one's relationship, or one's love, and it is when *that* dies a death, we are free to move on, we might have got away with it, but I think that's rather stretching the point. I believe it was always intended to mean death in the literal 'six-feet under' sense. Besides, Marion as the 'mature bride'! God help me! The pastel coloured outfit I know she would choose, with matching shoes and handbag, would be enough to finish me off. Let alone, dear darling Hattie, lording it up as Daddy's little princess for the day! And Marion's relations looking quietly pleased, that Marion has at last been 'clothed in her rightful mind' and rejected me in favour of a partner worthy of her esteemed heritage. No, I think a telegram, and a well-chosen coffee table book will be the order of the day.

Tom – I don't see so much of Tom these days. He is really trying hard at his marriage. Things have not been easy. Turns out, Hermione is on the autistic spectrum– screams a lot – so things are even tougher at home than they were. To add to their joys, a student of Tom's discovered a long-forgotten copy of one of Eve's old videos. Remember, I said she was an 'actress'. She had very few lines to learn apparently (just had to articulate a series of grunts and noises really) but that didn't stop her gaining a loyal fan club of half the male students in the university. An impossibly tall second year, with a prison pallor complexion, who'd made the discovery, was caught and duly reprimanded for showing the video in his room in hall, for a small entrance fee. By the time we became aware of his enterprise, he'd earned enough to buy a small car.

If it had happened to anyone else, anyone other than Tom and Eve, I'd have thought it was a fairly amusing, if not somewhat embarrassing joke. But it didn't. It happened to them – and it made me sick.

And now to Ruth…dear Ruth. How is it that you are always right? Why is it you, always standing like the gatekeeper to everyone's dreams – even your own? When I recall the night of that staff party, when I had been so sure that you and David were having an affair, I still find it hard to believe the truth. You were having an affair of sorts, but not the kind which had played out in my head. In any event, I'm afraid the thought of some people engaged in any form of sexual activity is always more ridiculous than sensual, and the thought of your awkward fumblings and fingerings of one another had certainly fallen into that category. So why was I so devastated when I learnt the truth of your relationship?

It was shortly after I'd returned from Italy, when we happened to bump into one another in the park, late one September afternoon. Naturally, we fell into conversation, and after a few clichéd exchanges, Ruth said, 'If you don't mind me saying, Alistair, you look dreadful. Are you ill in some way? Please, let me buy you some tea or something.' We were standing right next to the café, where a few metal tables and chairs were scattered on the pavement, under some lime trees, hoping to create the illusion we were in the artist sector of Paris or something similarly unlikely.

Ruth ordered: tea - no milk, and a coffee for me. Anything to eat? No thank you. Eating is not really a priority these days.

Already, I suspected she knew about what had happened to Anna, and purely wanted to flesh out the bare bones with all the pain-filled detail. But I was wrong. She had no idea. It was me who volunteered to spill my heart to her. But only to shroud the bones with the first layer of sinew and the odd muscle, not the fully fleshed incarnation of the truth. Why I told her *anything* I'll never know. Perhaps it was the counselling training she'd had – gave off the same aura as a confessional box – making you leap in and splatter the contents of your heart upon the walls: 'Forgive me Father for I have sinned. It has been a lifetime since my last confession…' but she never uttered the words *'ego te absolvo a peccatis tuis in nominee Patris et Filii et Spiritus Sancti.'* and laid my soul to rest. But then, she wasn't a priest…and this wasn't a full confession. I didn't mention Fabrizio, or how useless I had been; I only told her about the lost pregnancy and all that followed; how Anna had fallen to pieces, didn't want to see me anymore and would not be returning here.

She could so easily have said, with her sagacious tones, 'I told you so.' I could see it written all over her face, but she remained silent. So, I said it for her, in so many words. 'Well, I guess you'd have every right to say, you warned me – that you saw this coming.'

'To say that would imply some sense of triumph, Alistair. Be assured I feel no sense of glory in your misery whatsoever. What's happened to Anna is a tragedy, an absolute tragedy. But even I had not foreseen such dire consequences. I don't think anyone could have. In spite of all my reservations, I am truly sorry…for both of you.' She looked up from her clear steaming beverage, which had been poised at her lips for a few moments– still she didn't sip it, but blew another ripple across its bronzed surface, misting her glasses, obscuring her eyes.

'Poor Anna, she must be devastated.' Her sympathy unnerved me, and I had to fight back the need to break down into inconsolable sobbing. Instead I gathered myself for a more diversionary attacking mode. '…Well, at least now you may, well,' I began, slightly surprised by my own forwardness, 'at least, I would surmise you understand more now… how all of us are sometimes guilty of blundering on regardless because we just can't help ourselves.'

'I'm sorry Alistair, I'm not with you.'

'You and David. Surely when that goes wrong, they'll be someone waiting in the wings to say 'I told you so.'

'Myself and David? How, Alistair? How on earth?' Her teacup clattered back into the saucer. 'How could you possibly know anything about that? Only David, Angela and myself have ever discussed… there's no way you could know.'

Her reaction made me feel uncomfortably anxious. I didn't think it was that big a deal considering what I'd just told her. Weren't we on the level now, just colleagues exchanging confidences?

'At the staff party, on numerous occasions…' I mumbled, 'it was obvious to me…how close you seemed, intimate, and Angela seemed quite hostile, in the only rather understated way she knows how. There was a distinct hostility, between you both.'

A knowing, sad smile spread across Ruth's face. 'Ah,' she said. 'I see. Yes, I can see why someone, like you, would jump to all the obvious conclusions. But you're wrong.'

Just at this moment, one of the staff from the café began a round of collecting used crockery from the table. 'Have you finished with these?' an effete young man said briskly, before adding to the growing pile on his tray, and giving the table a glancing wipe with a cloth.

'Do you think they want us to leave?' whispered Ruth, as he moved off.

I shrugged and glanced at my watch.

'Perhaps - they close at five.'

Following the interruption, there was a moment's quietness, while we each considered our next move. After a few seconds of studying one another's shadow, I ventured, 'How was I wrong, Ruth? I only ask because in the light of what you've said to me in the past, it all seems rather...hypocritical.'

She repeated the word 'hypocritical' as if searching her mind to remember what it meant... 'I hope not.' Ruth's face became a portrait of deep-seated pain. Feeling strangely afraid, I waited for my answer. 'Can I trust you, Alistair?' She gripped my hand across the table. 'Really trust you. That this would never go any further.'

'Of course.' My mind was running way ahead now – what secret was coming my way? What hidden truth was about to be revealed to me?

'That I have feelings for David is obvious I suppose. I love him, always have.' How soft her face became, with the mention of his name. 'It's that love which has kept me here over the years, when really I should have pursued career opportunities elsewhere. But, and it's a big 'but', Alistair – I never told him, until last year. I remember the moment so clearly; we were discussing, of all things, 'Henry James and the concept of the unreliable narrator', and it just somehow came out...the truth. Turns out after all this time, he's always felt the same...' a little satisfied smile fleeted across her face, then vanished, '...but David, also loves his wife, would never betray her. And I too respect the institution of marriage and all it entails. And besides...there could never have been anything more.' She paused and I realised there was something else to come: something even more insurmountable to their consummation than David's loyalty.

Ruth stared out across the lake, where once I had imagined ending my life beneath the ice. How different it looks now, in the September sunshine, with golden-green flecks glimmering, and two impossibly perfect Mandarin ducks bobbing in unison across its rippled surface.

'And, so you did nothing?'

She gave a half-hearted laugh and looked at me again. 'Yes, Alistair, you could say that. 'In your book' we did nothing. But believe me, inaction is sometimes every bit as painful as action.'

'But Angela is still jealous? Still presumes?'

'Well, she did...until...'

'Until?'

There was an interminable pause, ended by a weary sigh. 'I told them both the real truth. It was over the summer actually, while you were away. I couldn't

bear to be hated any longer, if you must know. I never wanted to play the other woman; it's not really my style is it, Alistair? And, I couldn't bear to see David so guilt-ridden and tortured by vain hope.'
She was rising now, pushing the metal chair against the tarmac, with a gritty, scrapping sound.

'What a summer!' she said shaking her head. 'I will never fathom out why or how I allowed myself to let my guard down.' I gave her a quizzical look, which she successfully ignored, and we began to stroll around the edge of the boating lake, the late afternoon sun filtering gently through the great oaks. From nowhere, a young boy on a skateboard scooted by with shiny beetle-black knees and elbows. 'The park's been full of them this summer.' Ruth watched the figure disappear around the bend. 'It looks such good fun, don't you think?'
I was not to be thrown so easily. 'The truth, Ruth, you said, you 'told them the truth.' What do you mean?'
'Oh, Alistair, I've already said far more than I intended....' She stopped and turned towards me, a desperate panic behind her eyes. I could see she was trying to make a momentous choice. I locked my gaze into hers.

'Can I trust you, Alistair? This is to go no further.' I nodded solemnly. 'You're only the third person I have ever told this to. I would like to make you the last.'

My heart was beating faster, something dangerous was in the air – a locked-up evil was about to take a gasping breath.

'Don't you owe me the truth?' (Looking back this was so presumptuous; she owed me nothing, least of all the baring of her soul.)
What happened next was the truth – the most unexpected truth. Even I had not foreseen, what truth was about to be born from the darkness within.

Without any further warning, a strange transformation overcame her; she seemed to collapse from within. Her words seemed to rise like unwelcome vomit in her throat, linger momentarily in her mouth; then slowly, spilt out over her lips…

'I was barely twelve…not much more than a little girl… my mistake was to take a short cut, alone, through the woods…' (Already sudden, urgent, tears were forming in her eyes, in my eyes) '…when it happened.' Her fingers, a whitish-yellow, were interlocked tightly like a woven web. 'He was strong…just too strong. So scared, I couldn't even scream.' In just those few sentences she'd uttered, I 'knew', and my heart broke for her. She hung her drooping head. Somewhere, I could vaguely hear something, murmuring with a faint imperfect sound. 'I told nobody. Couldn't. Couldn't tell. Still can't utter the word...didn't even know it at the time...said I'd fallen out of a tree into some brambles. Scratches, badly bruised.... all these years. He said that if I told anyone, he'd kill me while I slept. He didn't need to bother; I was already dead. All these years later. I can't...not just the telling - I simply can't. Do you see what I'm saying?' Suddenly, she raised her eyes heavenward, searching for the vast expanse of blue-sky dancing through the gaps between the boughs of the trees. Out in the vastness where one could disappear into nothingness. Where like a bird one could fly away – escape. Somewhere in the park a nightingale sang its inviolable song filling all the desert with its lament. Tortured, she met my frightened gaze. 'I was never really a threat... I couldn't be, you see.'

'Oh, Ruth, I'm so sorry.' She shrugged as if resigned to the inadequacy of those words.

We stood together, forlorn and hopeless, in speechless silence...and stared with unseeing eyes across the blackening lake.

No doubt, like me, your opinion of Ruth has altogether metamorphosed. I leave her there. I was truly sorry, but what more can be said? We never spoke about it again.

And now to Thaddeus and Mother, both of who seem to have been in cahoots over the spring, each achieving a similarly impossible feat: they both disappeared.

Thaddeus's disappearance is possibly temporal. He never returned one evening, and in spite of endless searching, sticking postcards on lamp-post alerting everyone as to who he was and where he belonged, I never heard a thing. Weeks later, gatherings of fluff, like ginger tumbleweed, still turned up in the most unexpected places...rolling through my empty life like lost whispers.

'He'll be back,' reassured Monica, after scouring the streets with me on a bitterly cold, windy day in March. 'I bet he's probably shacked up with some old lady somewhere, being fed roast chicken and prawns every day.'

'Maybe...' I turned my collar up and let the wind blow the tears from my eyes.

Mother, however, preferred to perform her disappearing act in the middle of the night. I went to bed that evening the proud possessor of a mother, and was awoken by a phone call in the early hours of the morning which informed me that she had escaped, and I was abandoned.

'I'm so sorry – your mother slipped away in the night. She went very suddenly. Was all safely tucked up at ten o'clock; when I went to check on her during the night, she'd gone I'm afraid,' whispered the consoling voice from the care home.

Mother – you rascal! Managed to evade security guards, cameras, pressure sensors, double Chubb locked doors, the lot! Nobody saw her go. She knew a secret exit – found it, and slipped out.

Silently. Unobtrusively. The ultimate disappearing act. Here one minute, gone the next. How was it possible? It all seems so real, this life. And whoosh– it is gone… and we are gone from it.

She left a few things to remind us that she'd passed this way: the embroidered daisy cardigan, of which she'd grown inordinately fond; her frail Viennese-whirl textured body… and me.

I sat with her for more than an hour, holding her cold waxen hand in mine. Where have you gone, Mother? At first, I wanted to gently peel the cardigan from her, and dress her in a starched blouse, such as she used to wear, but she looked too fragile to touch. And besides she seemed to suit it now, so I buttoned every button so she looked complete, neat and tidy. Plus, I concluded if she gone to bed wearing the embroidered cardigan, she must've really loved it.

My eyes fell upon a photograph on the bedside table of Marion and me. Smiling broadly, we were posing in front of some dull stately home we'd taken Mother to for the day, possibly ten years ago or more. She loved anything historical. Strangely, we'd been there all through the night as mother lay dying grinning above her, bright and breezy, from our photo frame. I picked it up and lay it on mother's chest, then placed her hand upon it. Kissing her softly, I said the things I'd always wanted to say to her when she was alive – not least that I had loved her; forgave her.

As I left the care home, a creeping sense of uncertainty descended upon me. For the first time in my life, I viewed the world without Mother in it: a world where Mother would never again move of her own volition; a world where she would never again 'win' at cards; a world where she would never again utter a single word. It was the most beautiful of sunny days and her pale bewildered eyes would never again open to see it. This, I decided, was indeed a profound moment in my life. Everyone else around me was living a normal day. But my mother had just died, and no one else had any idea.

I popped into the corner shop for a newspaper, whereupon I had a sudden, unexpected craving for ice-cream, specifically a Cornetto. Unwrapping the foil, revealing the rivulets of brittle chocolate sprinkled with crushed hazelnuts, I struggled to repress the desire to burst into song which seemed to have become obligatory when enjoying this particular frozen product. Quietly, under my breath, I murmured 'give it to me, delicious ice-cream of Italy.' As I wandered back to the car, the lingering smell of disinfectant and death fresh in my nostrils, my teeth sinking into the soft cold ice cream and my mouth full of sweetness and grief, I had never felt more in the long shadow of our old friend, The Emperor of Ice Cream.

****

I rang Marion when I got home and uttered the immortal lines: *'Mother died today. Or maybe yesterday, I don't know.'* You see, one could not really be completely sure of the time of her departure.

'*Alistair*, this is no time to be *clever*,' she said, obviously appalled.

'Sorry,' I replied, 'but it just so happens to be true.' (Furthermore, this was the only time in my life I would ever get the opportunity to put these famous opening lines from Camus' 'The Outsider' to such pertinent use. And I'm sure Mother would understand – if not be rather amused.)

Chapter Forty-four: September 1983: "a new start"

It is now three years since I first met Anna, about two years since I lost her, and still I think about her almost every moment of everyday. There's very little to keep me here any longer; I seem to have an extraordinary capacity to shed my loved ones, at the moment.

Furthermore, I'm running out of money too. At some point, I'm going to have to get a grip on things. Although Mother left me quite a few thousand in her will, the home had eaten into a large chunk of her savings, and there were various debts of my own to pay off too. I was staying here for only two reasons: one, in case Thaddeus should ever decide to come sauntering back into my life, and secondly, because this is the only address I believe Anna would contact me at. Not that she has made any attempt to contact me yet. But you never know.

On the very last day of September, early in the morning while I was making a cup of tea, there was a clatter as the letterbox snapped shut. A distinctive lavender-coloured envelope told me immediately it was a letter from Maggie, who had been good enough to correspond with me occasionally since that fateful visit two summers ago. Eagerly, I opened it – several cups of tea later, and after a long telephone conversation with Marion, I had made a decision.

Chapter Forty-five: the wisest woman in Europe

'Well, I have to ask one more time, don't I? Jus' for luck like.'

'If you must. Go on, ask away.'

She was hovering by the backdoor, her hands behind her back, concealing something. 'Well, you're only allowed what's behind me back if you can truly tell us that your writing's finished, Mr Johnson – before you're skipping off, leaving it all going off half–cocked.'

I smiled affectionately at her and beckoned her to come up the back steps into the kitchen.

'Am I to know then?' she persisted. 'Is it finished?'

'Oh God, Mary, I wish I could say 'yes'– I really do. But the best I can do for the moment is say, truthfully and honestly 'almost.'' I winced a little.

'Almost! Well that's no good to me, is it? What am I to be doing with this, then?' She pulled from behind her back, a bottle of champagne, which I guessed she'd been saving for many months now, in anticipation of conclusion: finality.

'Can't we accept *almost*?' I said hopefully.

'What? You're wanting *me* to accept the *unfinished* article, like those Captives you were so keen to show me? A lot of arty-farty nonsense that was! Ooo, you've a nerve and a half.'

Grinning broadly, at this wonderful, beautiful woman, I made my feeble excuses. 'I just feel there's a chapter or two to come, which… haven't happened yet.'

She wrinkled her brow. 'And there's me thinking this was all about *the past*?'

'It is.'

'There you go again! Half the time I haven't a bloody clue what you're on about. You're a strange one for sure. Well, I guess you give me no choice. I'm not prepared to pay to have this sent all the way to you in your new place, so you'll have to take it now, and promise me you don't drink it till you can finally declare: 'It is finished!''

She handed me the dark green-black bottle with its crumpled gold top.

'I promise.' I hugged her close to me – all eighteen stone plus of her. 'Thank you, Mary, not just for the champagne, but for everything.'

'It's been my pleasure. Take care now, won't you? I shall sure miss you.'

'Me too. You know, I couldn't have done it without you.'

'Now there's baloney for you.' As we fell apart, she looked redder than ever, and lumpy blotches were visibly rising beneath her skin.

''Tis warm in here.' Mary flapped her hand in front of her face. 'Am I turning beetroot red?'

'Not at all.'

'Oh, good.'

I made her promise to come and see me for a holiday, and she agreed she would, but we both knew that that was something that would never happen. As she stumbled back down the dark garden, she called through the gloom, reminding me I was not to forget that Monica would let me know the minute she had a sighting of Thaddeus…as if I could.

Later that evening, as I stood in my unlit bedroom, taking in the view of rooftops, frosted bathroom windows and streetlights for one last time, I saw her, stood at Monica's backdoor, cigarette glowing. *How far that little candle throws his beam! So shines a good deed in a naughty world.*

Goodbye, Mary. And thank you for everything.

Chapter Forty-six: among the mountains

It was the same journey, and I travelled at more or less the same speed, and yet, and yet, it seemed to take twice as long. 'Speed equals distance over time.' But some 'times' are longer than others. This we now know. (Surely, someone should tell the physicists that their equation is imperfect?)

Unable to help myself, I had taken exactly the same route, and booked into the same hotels as before– never one to bypass the opportunity for indulging in open and unadulterated nostalgia. But this was quite a different country now: winter can make both people and places almost unrecognisable. And I knew, deep in my heart, that nothing could ever remain the same. Sweeping fields of corn and dazzling acres of heavy-headed sunflowers now stood bare and stark, empty frozen earth, bereft of life, stared blankly into nothingness. The blue-blue sky, had turned a heavy leaden grey, causing it to collapse under its own weight, and now it lay, sunken and tired, only feet from the cold earth itself.

Furthermore, the painfully outdated hotel just outside of Dijon had changed hands and the Rococo bedroom suite (reminiscent of *Beauty and the Beast's* boudoir) was gone, and replaced with modern black ash veneer, already chipped on the edges revealing the plywood interior. I had so much been hoping to stare, and stare, into the gilded looking-glass, searching for a glimpse of a long-forgotten reflection... Anna standing in front of it, smoothing sun lotion over her brown, round, shoulders: the shadow of a shadow.

But the looking-glass, along with all the other hopelessly old-fashioned artefacts had gone, and in its place, all was new, clean, and phony... and totally without charm, or character. The smart young French couple running the establishment followed suit.

Bugger 'Heraclitus' and his smug: *'No man ever steps in the same river twice.'* But it does not stop me trying, and I wade deeper and deeper, searching for a way back.

Only Mont Blanc was instantly knowable, with its massive shape looming in the distance. It was perfectly white now, softer and more beautiful than it had ever been, and like a Tolkienesque dwarf I was yet again going to tunnel into the very depths of the mountain's heart. For seven long miles I plunged through this artery, imagining the weight of rock above me and the molten metal, deep, deep, below me. I hoped for dragons and evidence of secret doors, of runes and long forgotten lives, but there were none. And when finally, I emerged at the other end I was thrown out into yet another completely different country.

After several miles, I stopped at a café in a little village and sat on the veranda, drinking a cup of coffee, mesmerized by the lonely beauty of the mountain. There was no fiery sunset bathing it in a shower of warm apricot tones, but instead a slowly descending cloak of icy blue coldness. Distant, proud and stoical, Mont Blanc did not flinch once as this freezing shroud enveloped it.

What would it be like to be lost and alone in such a place? Imagine lying exhausted in the snow and ice, your mouth dry from dehydration, your lips cracked and bleeding, your extremities knife-sharp with pain. The creeping cold works from the outside in, penetrating to the core, until your very heart freezes and ceases to beat...

For a few moments, I took myself there, so that I might stare up at the darkening sky and marvel at the emerging stars, wonder at my place in all this immeasurable isolation. I had to acknowledge that the very fact human life existed at all in this vast, vastness amazed me. Were we not apparently only in existence in the last two minutes or so on a twenty-four-hour clock of creation? That my existence on earth had coincided with Anna's at all, could be seen as something of a miracle.

A sense of wild abandonment came over me; the coldness ceased to bother me. Time stretched behind and before me, unravelling implausibly into all that infinite space...

Vaguely, I am aware that there is no longer a third walking beside me, but only a dark shadow prostrate upon me. It's warm, like a comforting blanket, and I relax, strangely contented. I'm no longer afraid.

Behind the mountain, the sky turned from iron grey to granite black, and I pulled my new winter coat around myself, drained the last of my coffee and set off into the night-time, towards the south.

Chapter Forty-seven: The sea was calm

Threaded through 'The Unpredictability of Frogs' and the bare branches of the fig tree, were a string of tiny white fairy lights, illuminating the remaining immature figs as if they were beautiful teardrop-shaped decorations. A small gust of wind rattled the frogs' bones, and their voices, like fragmenting rust, croaked in response. At the window of the living room, a single candle burned, and behind it, the faint coppery glow of a room lit by a fire; the rest of the house in darkness. Through the crisp evening air, the smell of wood smoke drifted and swirled, and from the cattle stalls at the farm beyond the village, I could just make out the deep lowing of cattle. The church bell began to clang out through the gloom, calling the faithful to an evening Mass, and for the first time, in many months, even years – I felt happy. Not just that brief sense of well-being, but a deep, lasting contentment.

As I approached the door, this sense of happiness, this strange feeling of being more at one with the world, grew.

For some time, I stood quite still. Through the dimming sky, soaring through the dusk, a voice pure, and filled with a yearning to go beyond, beyond the confines, rose, and rose again.

Ave María, grátia plena, Dóminus tecum. Benedícta tu in muliéribus, et benedíctus fructus ventris tui, Jesus. Sancta María, Mater Dei, ora pro nobis peccatóribus, nunc et in hora mortis nostræ. Amen.

I could not tell if the voice, ascending from the church, were that of a young boy or a girl, but as it pierced the evening air so beautifully, and then rained down upon me like a sublime shower of silver arrows, I found myself caught somewhere between the agony of St Sebastian and the ecstasy of St Theresa. I hovered, uncertainly, my fist poised. Then I knocked at the door…

The moment she opened the door to me, the aroma of a rich casserole filled my nostrils, followed by the warm familiar scent of Maggie's fragrance as she held me close to her. She was wearing an enormously long, burgundy cardigan tied around her like a blanket, and her hair, now a shade of deep aubergine had grown into a wild array of medusa style curls. Her body, however, still had the same, familiar, consistency of well-risen bread dough. And oh, how that embrace seemed to envelop my very soul!

'Alistair, my dear boy, welcome home!'
Almost immediately, she insisted that I shut my eyes tightly and with a childlike excitement led me by the hand into the kitchen. When I opened them, I was standing by the range. 'For you,' she whispered, looking downward. Curled together in a basket, their soft bodies intertwined, were two small kittens, one tabby, one grey and white. 'As yet, unnamed,' murmured Maggie with obvious pleasure. 'Although, they have told me that they already know their own names but refuse point-blank to tell me. Such petulance! So, my dear...it's up to you...' We each scooped up one of the warm, tiny, purring felines and studied their faces closely. 'Maggie, what a wonderful present! They are beautiful. But the naming of cats is a difficult matter. Their names will be revealed soon I am sure.' As I looked into their round blue eyes, I was already in love... felt the cheese wire wrap around my heart once more.

Sometime later, we were seated at the kitchen table, with a casserole of wild boar, still gently plooping and bubbling like a geyser of hot mud in front of us. A large mound of potato and celeriac mash steamed slowly beside it, and a big glass of Brunello di Montalcino sat happily next to that.

'This is a treat.' I smiled, nodding towards the bottle, and lifted the glass to my lips.

'Well, I'm doing my best to educate myself to move from quantity to quality. Although there *is* another bottle of this, so don't get too alarmed.' She took a sip from her glass and held the wine momentarily in her mouth; she swallowed. 'Apparently one is supposed to hold one's mouth slightly open and draw air in to oxygenate the wine. However, I find that an almost impossible operation, and after dribbling copious amounts of fine wine down my chin I have given up on the practice.' She raised her glass and chinked it musically against mine. 'And moreover, tonight Alistair, I feel we have something to celebrate, don't we?'

'It's a whole new start, isn't it?'

'I'd like to think so.' She smiled, her eyes alive and glittering in the guttering candlelight, and then we both ate with some gusto.

Maggie suggested we had our dessert in front of the fire in the lounge. To be honest I had hardly noticed the fireplace before, apart from the dancing

Ganesh on the plinth and a slight recollection that there may have been some kind of floral display in the grate. But it was now revealed in its true glory: a magnificent open stone fireplace in which several over-sized logs lay flickering and glowing. I sank back onto the sofa, shutting my eyes to the memories that threatened to overwhelm me.

Maggie came bustling into the room carrying a chipped ceramic dish of what looked like hard russet brown tomatoes in one hand, a bowl of vanilla ice cream in the other.

'This is something very special,' she announced, proudly laying the dish before me. 'Do you know what they are Alistair?' I picked one up. It was obviously some kind of fruit, actually quite soft to the touch ... its skin giving easily to the pressure of my hand: its scent appley. I had to confess I had never encountered such a fruit before.

'Ah, but you have Alistair. They're exceptionally rare in reality now, but you will have met it in its literary state on more than one occasion.' I thought hard for several moments, but tiredness and wine fogged my brain.

'Now will he sit under a - 'bleep' - tree, and wish his mistress were that kind of fruit, as maids call- 'bleeps' - when they laugh alone. Ring any bells?' My face broke into a knowing smile, 'Romeo and Juliet? Medlars?' I nodded, 'They are medlars.'

'Indeed, they are Alistair, 'Mespilus germanica' from my very own tree. It is a hobby of mine to preserve and promote this ancient and most noble fruit.' She took a sharp knife and removed both the stem and the flowery looking part, peeled back the skin and spooned the pulpy filling over a portion of ice cream. 'Do partake, Alistair. It's an acquired taste, but once you learn to love its ancient honeyed taste, sort of apple sauce laced with cinnamon, and its custardy texture, you will find as the autumn approaches your mind will turn to medlars, and a longing to savour them once again.' I copied the procedure and spooned the contents of several medlars over my ice cream, which was already softening in the radiating heat of the fire. Meanwhile, Maggie picked a particularly large specimen from the bowl and held it, calyx towards me, for my examination.

'Of course, unless one is particularly unfussy and unsqueamish about the appearance of one's food, it is necessary to overcome all that 'open-arse' fixation, fascinating though it is. No, really one must go beyond the surface and acknowledge that this is a fruit to be celebrated. A fruit whose fruition, whose ultimate moment in life comes as it rots, decays, accepts that life as we know it is almost over.'

She reached for another fruit having scraped all the 'sauce' from her portion of ice cream, into her mouth. 'This wonderful fruit can only be truly enjoyed once rotted, Alistair, or 'bletted' as the French so beautifully put it. Once it's been through the mill of life, endured a frost or two, and learnt something of what life is like. Then, and only then, is it as sweet as honey.'
I looked up from my ice cream listening intently.

'Alistair my dear, I have just dropped one awfully big symbolic metaphor there; do be careful you don't trip over it on your way to bed.'
A smile was already on my lips. 'Thank you, Maggie. I'll remember that.'

Later that evening, in spite of being desperately tired, we sat together in the glow of the dying log fire, with the joy of a kitten on each of our laps, and plotted and formulated our brilliant plans. And much later still, when too much wine and lassitude took effect, we ambled wearily up the stairs to bed. '*Let us go then you and I... To sleep: perchance to dream.*' A hot water bottle had been placed in my bed much earlier that evening, and a large faux fur throw ensured I was not the least bit cold throughout the night. When I had agreed to come here, it was only on the basis that Maggie would never talk about Anna and the events of that summer, unless I mentioned it first. So far, she had stuck to that agreement. But by the time I lay inside the warmth of my bed, my broken heart flooded anew with memories of the past. I realised that the past lived in every cell of my body, still ran through every vein; existed in every breath I took. I hadn't physically cried for a long time over Anna, but I did now.

Chapter Forty-eight: Shantih shantih shantih

November 1984

How long is it since I last wrote something? A good year or so at least. I have been extraordinarily busy, and I only find the time to write something now because it is November, a quiet month for us.

Nobody wants to come and study painting and English literature in Tuscany in November, although we are considering one-off Christmas weeks in the future.

Yes, this was Maggie's great scheme – to run painting and literary courses, mostly for the middle-aged and middle-class, the retired, the divorced, the widowed, the lonely, the searching, the unfulfilled...the thirsty. Sometimes I have thought our advertising slogan should be:

Come unto me all who are weary and burdened, I shall give you rest (Matt: 11:28)

But Maggie says that would be rather sacrilegious. However, we both know there's some truth in it. We're giving more than a week's worth of chucking some paint around and studying and penning a bit of verse and worse. No, were giving them a lot more than that – a lot more than that.

It's like a school for grown-ups, but you're allowed to choose your favourite subjects, in our pupils' case – English and Art.

Our guests are conveniently accommodated in the large villa opposite which came up for sale at just the right time. Maggie had some local builders, (no, not Sergio's lot) create little boudoirs with en suites and we can accommodate at least twelve guests a week. They choose to study Art or English literature, or a combination of both at various times throughout the week. It always amuses me that so many of them eulogise how wonderful it is that a couple such as Maggie and I should be living the dream together in this way. It seems a shame to disabuse them of this notion, particularly as I know it brings a glow to Maggie's burnished cheeks. 'We're just good friends, very good friends,' I say. And Maggie usually gives me a hug as if to affirm our platonic closeness to the slightly bemused onlookers. But what an opportunity, to paint, express one's creativity, and of course a chance for would-be poets to 'let rip' as well. Hopefully, I make it as liberating for them as possible. I say we have two rules here: One: '*Don't* play with your food,' and two: '*Do* play with your words'... which always causes a ripple of feeble laughter. But we stick to those rules (at least the second one) – words are tossed into the air and we see where they fall, we squash them into compressed squidgy balls and stretch them out into endless strings, kick them around, place them in new and never before seen combinations... and then look at the mess, and sometimes, just sometimes, we find something beautiful. From somewhere, I hear Marion's voice: 'Here's a new combination for you, Alec – Load pretentious bollocks of.'

Our clientele, as I have said, are mostly singletons: many retired, or looking towards that day, when a lifetime of servitude is under their belt, and at last they are doing the one thing they really wished they'd done in their lives: taking time to try and make sense of it all – taking time to look, to think, to discuss, to create. It would not be going too far to say that in the course of a week, they discover not only themselves and something of the world and their place in it, but they often discover each other too. I wonder how many will keep their promises to each other when they return to England.

The pleasure I experience from sharing the odd fragment of literature with them is enormous. All of my books were sent over several weeks after I arrived, and we now boast the finest library in the village. We can dip in and out of worlds (or words) as far apart as the Metaphysical and the Postmodern, and still be back in time for tea. Incidentally, Maggie's Christmas gift was a copy of *The Divine Comedy* in the original Tuscan dialect' ('Terribly pretentious, I know darling, but one should never stop challenging oneself, should one?') and slowly, very slowly, I am learning to appreciate what a masterpiece it truly is.

To see the world through a poet's eyes feeds the soul... opens the soul. The voices of a million mouths that past; what do they whisper through the lengthening shadows of the day? More than words can say, that's for sure.

I often think of Ruth in her role of counsellor, because to some extent that's what I've become. Many times, we all just sit and talk for hours; the literature which we've read prompting endless conversations. The things people tell me... I've discovered that life is quite a challenge for most people... yes, really, quite challenging.

And then the chance to create your own vision from within. To communicate the inner beating of your heart to others, in words or paint, or music, releases your spirit. If I had not seen it happen so often with my own eyes, I would not make such hyperbolic claims.

The power of language in every form - it's what makes us human – being able to share the experience.

(There are many moments when I now reflect on my own experience of life, remember my past. Not just the past with Anna, but everything. If I have learnt anything, I suppose it is, that it was in the ordinary moments of life, that it was most extraordinary; the simple exchanges in which one glimpsed something beyond. I know now I had loved and needed Marion more than I realised, and regret our wasted years. And I know that the few months, the inside of a year that I was privileged to spend with Anna, gave everything else in my life, before, and after, meaning. She will be my last thought when I take my dying breath ...that I might remember all she was, throughout that never-ending night of insomnia.)

As a finale to our week, Maggie's current little girl (oh, yes, she's never managed to overcome that one), will cook up a sumptuous last supper for us, when we all gather round Maggie's ancient and impossibly long dining-table like old friends, (except of course we're not) but the illusion is good enough for me these days.

Wine flows freely, laughter and conversation, slip amongst our company like a live eel and not infrequently, someone – usually a not-unattractive widow or divorcee makes one last desperate attempt to seduce me – but I never respond beyond a playful rebuke. I expect they all think I'm a closet gay. After all, what other explanation could there be for an aging, single man such as myself to turn down a night of 'no-strings attached' sexual romping? This conclusion was also arrived at by a rather charming retired dentist called Anthony, who, after one-too-many wines, playfully ran his fingers along my thigh under the table one evening, while whispering that his door was never locked...ground floor, room three. But there is a reason, and you and I both know what it is.

Maggie of course says I should let myself go, enjoy myself while I can, 'gather ye rosebuds' and all that (or in this case 'gather ye overblown hybrid teas') but she understands why I don't. You see, I never know if tomorrow may be the day that there's a phone call, or in my wildest dreams a knock on the door, and I open it, and find her standing there; and she knows at last, what I have known all my life - that she, belongs with me.

So, I wait. I wait - and watch the seasons turn. I wait, never giving up hope.

Six months ago, Tom rang to say he'd bumped into Anna at the National Gallery. For a moment I couldn't even speak. He said he'd hardly recognised her at first as her hair was short now. (I could not even create an image in my mind of her without her flowing long hair.) 'Which painting were you by?'

He laughed. 'Are you going to camp out by it, Alistair? Strangely enough, I do remember.... it was *An Experiment on a Bird in the Air Pump.*' Apparently, they'd chatted for a brief time, initially about the painting: its amazing use of light, the suspended drama of the poor trapped bird – never to be resolved. She had said how much she adored the face of the scientist, with his slightly wild hair, warm skin tones in the candlelight and his eyes... tired, almost impassive, and yet seeming to gaze outward, drawing the observer into the drama.

She had looked well, was between jobs, living in London. Tom had invited her to go for a coffee, but she had declined on the excuse of some spurious appointment.

I had to ask, didn't I? 'Did she mention me at all?'

He replied, 'Not in so many words,' (whatever that means) but said he had volunteered that I was 'living the dream in Tuscany with Maggie,' and she had smiled.

('Living the dream'...I wouldn't go that far...) But my heart soared like an exultant phoenix to know she knew where I was. That she may turn up out-of-the-blue one day was now a real possibility.... mine is a very open heart these days, so I wait. Patience is a virtue, and anticipation, hope, is everything. And yes, in spite of everything, now I am someone who dares to hope.

****

In the warmth of the Italian sun and the caring love of my dear friend Maggie, I held fast to the burning hope I would not let die. The fragments and the shards, which had haunted me throughout my life, began to warm to a melting softness; the dissolution of brokenness; every phrase, every broken image, began to merge and meld. My shattered dreams became a sea of constant iridescence: A beautiful sea of living swirling colour.

The man who had once stood on brimstone, who had once picked his way through a minefield of shattered dreams, now walked miraculously like Jesus, on this sea of molten life. He felt his feet burning, a brilliant fear rolling in his soul, and yet somehow, somehow, he continued to tread his path.

April 1991: These fragments I have shored against my ruins

There was a persistent ring at the doorbell. My heart jolted. I knew what was due to arrive today.

The postman held out a pen, so that I could sign the recorded delivery slip for the two packages: one, a large, rectangular brown package, and the other a long box, both rather heavy. Peter Harris and Associates (family firm, three generations of solicitors) had finally tracked me down.

It had taken them several months to trace me, eventually, finding a contact through the records at the university, then via my old family address, to the current residents, who had passed on my parents' forwarding address... who'd contacted me. Initially, I was to telephone the solicitors; a few days later a letter had arrived, confirming in black and white what I already knew.

'Ms Anna Martin, who being named as a beneficiary in the last Will and Testament...'

He had set his lands in order.

I can still feel the sensation so acutely: a cold hand gripping my heart with the intensity of a drowning man...the raw, jagged impossibility of death.

Alistair was dead.
He who was living is now dead.
He'd been dead since late October.

Outside, unseasonable early lilac and cherry blossom bounced cheerfully in the stark April sunshine. And he was dead. Six, seven months dead...and I had not known. Dead. Long dead. And yet, somehow, I had not instinctively felt a sense of loss... had not detected a sudden shift in the universe. How many seasons had come and gone since our parting, unobserved? Now, I was shocked to the core, by the hollow abyss that had opened up inside of me: a howling hollow in a dry desert.

In ten years, I had not laid my eyes upon him, and now he was gone from my sight forever. I would never see him again, could never see him again – ever. An open door was slammed shut with a resounding wooden thud – shut forever. There are no *maybe* possibilities here. No, *perhaps. What ifs,* just a certainty I cannot deny. And my heart is a handful of dust.

And today, the packages arrived. All I knew was that part of my 'inheritance', along with several thousand pounds, was a file of papers. I suppose they could have been anything, but I suspected they would be his poetry, or a selection of academic essays or articles he'd written in his youth, in which he thought I might be interested. I was flattered I suppose that he had thought of me in his will at all; who knows what his life had been in the intervening years; who he had known and possibly loved?

I realise now, as the years have passed, that I was probably quite hard on him. And in the light of the other people I have had relationships with, that apart from that desperate time in Italy, he was without doubt the most devoted ... loved me the best. I had often wondered if he thought of me, reflected on our time together. But I had concluded the significance of that time to me was no measure of its lifelong impact on someone else. After all, whenever he protested his undying love for me, I knew I was only one of many, who had been or possibly would be.

Imagine then how I felt, when I began to read what had been left to me, his voice talking to me from beyond the grave. What a mixture of emotions. Seeing for the first time. Our shared experience... through his eyes. In some ways, I was spellbound to see myself as a young woman. It was like finding a collection of old photographs, or film footage, which you had never been shown before, and seeing images of yourself, for the very first time, from decades ago. What a stranger I seem to myself... self-centred, immature, and so self-assured – quite an idiot really. And in all honesty, I was never that beautiful, ever. But he saw something different. And my God, did he love me.

When I came to the part about losing the baby, losing everything, my heart filled with tears. All these years later and it still hurts. I wish I hadn't been so bitter. Although I did actually say it, I would like to set the record straight, by stating now that all that I said about forgiveness wasn't true. I knew it deep down at the time of course, but anger, outrage, and grief, made me lose all sight of such virtues. Perhaps, I just wanted to punish him; perhaps, I just wanted to punish myself. How little I knew. If only I could tell him how forgiven he is now. If only I could forgive myself.

Forgive me – but I could not help but want you – to consume you. Perhaps you were never mine for the taking. Forgive me...

We never really know each other properly, do we? The inner workings of our minds are all so private, so closed. I felt privileged to know Alistair a little better now. C.S. Lewis's oft quoted 'We read to know we are not alone' comes to mind. The truth is we are alone, but words at least help us find a path to the outside world of others; to glimpse the interior space of someone else; to slip into their shoes and see the story from a different perspective. And I wondered, not for the first time, if back then, I had made a terrible mistake. And that chance meeting with Tom...why didn't I?

Some weeks later, I wrote to Maggie. It was probably the most difficult letter I have ever written, but I wanted to offer her my condolences and to explain to someone, who had been there, both all those years ago, and at the hour of his death, how much I regretted the way I had behaved, and how unexpectedly bereaved I felt now.

Her returning letter was obviously full of the sadness of one who had recently lost a dear friend and companion. She wrote: '...it was all so sudden, you see, really quite a drama. We were in the middle of finalizing the fine detail our Christmas-themed poetry and painting extravaganza: *"Were we led all that way for Birth or Death?"* A tremendous thunderstorm, which had been heralded by the most threatening of eerie silver-yellow skies, was now reverberating all around – when without warning – he gasped and slumped sideward. For one extraordinary moment, I thought he'd been struck by lightning, and at first I was just confused thinking that I had no idea one could be struck by lightning through a window, but of course it was his heart – always the heart...the ambulance came as quickly as it could through the torrential rain, but it was already too late. I remember the most alarming sound of the thunder booming, booming round the villa. It may be a comfort for you, my dear, to know he died cradled in my arms – it certainly was for me. Of course, they tried all manner of resurrections, but I knew it was futile; he had gone; gone for good, long before they even arrived... *I know when one is dead and when one lives*. I miss him so dreadfully...it was all so unexpected. At least he didn't suffer the agonising pain of knowing that one was going to have to say goodbye to this world, to life, to all we have loved...which I imagine is somewhat challenging. Ironically, he did go out with a bang and not a whimper...'

But in spite of the intense sorrow, there was also something so uplifting in the way she also described how happy Alistair had been in his life in Tuscany – and I knew she had loved him too...really loved him.

To my surprise, she also suggested I might like to visit her sometime. She had, she said, obviously ceased to run the holiday workshops, and had found one day, that quite unexpectedly– she had painted everything she had wanted to paint. 'As a consequence, my dear, my days are rather long – somewhat empty, even. I would welcome the chance to see you again.... I find it difficult to understand why you feel such a sense of remorse, Anna. You were, after all, so young my dear, so very young. It may be difficult for you to imagine, but we were all young once, and I understand, I really do. And Alistair was not without his faults, as indeed none of us are. He was always ...how shall I say this... looking to be rescued by someone, saved even, and you were far too young, and dare I say, inexperienced, to want to take on that commission! But whatever you may think, Anna, he loved you with all his heart, and he never stopped loving you – ever. I don't know if you would find it helpful at all, but Alistair's ashes were scattered at the foot of my garden, overlooking the valley. I fear it is probably illegal to cast the final remains willy-nilly, as it no doubt was when Henry found himself there, but who's to know? It's not something I broadcast. And Alistair did so love the view. I often sit there with the cats and look out at the distant mountains and feel their presence...my dear boys.'

I have a strange sense that I should go. To lay some ghosts to rest and bury that part of me that can no longer live; perhaps something will develop; something may at last grow. I have no ties here at present, beyond my job. Not even a cat. It's time for me to wake up – to stop sleepwalking through life. It would not be untrue to say that I should acknowledge that now some part of me had already slipped beyond the grave; the memory of me dwelling somewhere in the mind of the dead. So, I will go, and try to make my peace with my past in order to live. *'I was much too far out all my life/ And not waving but drowning'*. Perhaps there was still time to swim to shore...

In case you are wondering, the other package was a bottle of champagne. I was mystified at first, but after reading his love letter (for that is what I believed it really was) I knew immediately it was *the* bottle from Mary, and for some time I wondered why he'd never popped the cork to toast the completion of his task, but then it dawned on me: he didn't think he'd finished. Always believing there might be yet another chapter to our story. Waiting for completion, for a perfect ending that was never to be.

Meanwhile, what to do with 'the few thoughts strung together with a lot of words'? Part of me felt it should remain private, 'the door we never open...' but another part of me felt I should try to attempt to publish them for him. If neither of us could leave any children in this world, perhaps we could send out this 'life' in words. *'For what they record in colour and cast is – that we two passed.'* And besides, what purpose has a door we never open?

However, for many years the package rested patiently in the box at the back of the wardrobe in quiet repose, only occasionally being taken out and re-read. *That corpse you planted last year in your garden, "Has it begun to sprout? Will it bloom this year?*

Then last year, realising to my dismay that I was now older than Alistair had been when we first met, I finally decided to breathe life onto these papery embers, ignite these leaves of grass. I have to admit, that in spite of my best efforts, my life had been more ordinary than I could have ever imagined. And even in the face of all I should have learnt, I had allowed life to slip through my fingers with careless ease... A growing sense that one could not outrun the dawn into an everlasting day, nor retreat from an inevitable sunset, had settled uncomfortably in my soul. The time was now.

Although before letting go, I felt I had to rewrite quite a bit of it. All the names, any allusion to time and place, I changed, slightly altering descriptions of people and events, obscuring the truth. All of this, in spite of there being a good chance that many of them by now were already dead. I knew for a fact that Maggie was long gone, after a long-denied cancer rose up in victory and dragged her under. And even Marion would be in her eighties now. One should protect people's right to the privacy of their lives. I hope Alistair would understand. Here and there, I made a few additions, which I think are seamless, cut one or two of his moments which even I couldn't allow Alistair to give life to, but in the main I left it as his words – just as he'd written them. It was after all *his* story. But none of us live in total isolation, and what we think of as *our* lives, as *our* story, are in fact the fragmented images of a thousand lives and experiences which interact with us. So, I felt quite justified in my editing. This wasn't *just* Alistair's story alone, but mine, Marion's, Maggie's, Tom's, Ruth's, Mary's, Fay Morgan's, even Thaddeus's – just about everybody, I guess. No one person could lay claim to a single life; we were all just part of life, a life that was all-encompassing and one.

Some stories still remain untold. Forgive me. One action leads to another and lives are made or destroyed. Back then, I did not see the connectedness of everything.

These fragments I have shored against my ruins.

I have the original copy, still tucked away in the back of my wardrobe, holding its secrets... safe... hovering between two worlds: one possible, one impossible – and standing next to it is the bottle of champagne. Well, you never know what might happen next...nothing is ever really, truly finished. Everything echoes forever.... It isn't a going or a coming, but a circling.

There are no beginnings. There are no endings. There is only life falling endlessly through time and space. And that's just the way it is.

Cheers, Mary.

"We shall not cease from exploration and the end of all our exploring will be to arrive where we started... and know the place for the first time."

Little Gidding
The Four Quartets
T.S Eliot

Copyright Permissions

The author wants to express her gratitude to the following for permission to include copyright material in this book:

Faber and Faber Limited, Royalty Department, Harlow, Essex, CM20 2HX for the extracts and chapter titles from: *The Waste Land* and *Collected Poems 1909-1962* by T.S. Eliot

David Higham Associates, 7, 7–12 Noel St, Soho, London W1F 8GQ for the extract from the poem *'Do Not Go Gentle Into That Good Night'* by Dylan Thomas, published by New Directions. Copyright © 1952, 1953 Dylan Thomas

Every effort has been made to trace the owners of copyright material and the author hopes that no copyright has been infringed. Pardon is sought and apology made if the contrary to be the case and a correction will be made in future reprints of this book.

Acknowledgements of Literary Influence, Titles, and Quotations within Copyright and within the Public Domain

Page 11	'Not waving but Drowning' 'I was much too far out all my life/ And not waving but drowning'. Stevie Smith
Page 11	'I have spread my dreams under your feet; Tread softly because you tread on my dreams.' He Wishes for the Cloths of Heaven. W.B Yeats
Page 14	'Looking into the heart of the light...' The Waste Land., T S Eliot
Page 22	'At Castle Boterel' Thomas Hardy
Page 34	This is just to say. William Carlos Williams
Page 36	The Emperor of Ice Cream. Wallace Stephens
Page 48	Good night, ladies; good night sweet ladies. Hamlet Act 4 scene 5 Shakespeare
Page 52	Do not go gentle into that goodnight. Dylan Thomas
Page 53	'We have but a short time to live. Like a flower we blossom and then wither; like a shadow we flee and never stay. In the midst of life, we are in death.' Psalm 103
Page 72	'Had we but world enough, and time....' To His Coy Mistress. Andrew Marvell
Page 77	'You mightn't think it, but Sloppy is a beautiful reader of a newspaper. He do the Police in different voices.'' Our Mutual Friend. Dickens
Page 82	'This man has not yet seen his last evening; But, through his madness, was so close to it, That there was hardly time to turn about'. The Divine Comedy. Dante Alighieri
Page 91	'Her lips suck forth my soul: see where it flies?' Dr Faustus. Christopher Marlowe
Page 96	'Our eye-beams twisted, and did thread. Our eyes upon one double string;' The Ecstasy. John Donne
Page 128	The Prime of Miss Jean Brodie. Muriel Spark

Page 141	Is not short paine well borne, that brings long ease, And layes the soule to sleepe in quiet grave'?' The Faerie Queen. Edmund Spenser
Page 141	I do not find/ The Hanged Man / Fear death by water.' The Waste Land. T. S Eliot
Page 141	'Vex not his ghost: O! Let him pass; he hates him, That would upon the rack of this tough world Stretch him out longer.' King Lear. William Shakespeare
Page 143	'I was neither Living nor dead, and I knew nothing' The Waste Land. T.S. Eliot
Page 148	'O, beware, my lord, of jealousy; It is the green-ey'd monster, which doth mock the meat it feeds on' Othello. Act 3 Sc.3 William Shakespeare
Page 157	'the past is a foreign country: they do things differently there'? L. P. Hartley
Page 157	'The dung heap cover'd o'er with snow.' . Piers the Plowman. William Langland;also Martin Luther.
Page 174	; What rough beast, its hour come round at last, Slouches towards Bethlehem to be born?' The Second Coming. W.B. Yeats
Page 234	'Nessun maggior dolore Che ricordarsi del tempo felice Nella miseria.' The Divine Comedy. Dante Alighieri
Page 246	Questi non hanno speranza di morte These have no longer any hope of death; e la lor cieca vita è tanto bassa, And this blind life of theirs is so debased che 'nvidiosi son d'ogne altra sorte They envious are of every other fate' The Divine Comedy. Dante Alighieri
Page 265	'And some like sliding down slopes and cannot look at Michelangelo's 'Night' on the Medici Tombs without dying the little death, because the statue seems to be sliding. Antic Hay.Aldous Huxley'
Page 268	'For as a lamb is brought to slaughter, so she stands, this innocent, before the king.' Man of Law's Tale. Geoffrey Chaucer
Page 270	'She's all states, and all princes, I, Nothing else is.' The Sun Rising. John Donne
Page 290	'floundering like a man in fire or lime' Dulce et Decorum Est. Wilfred Owen

Page 295	'As Gegor Samsa awoke one morning from uneasy dreams he found himself transformed in his bed into a gigantic insect.' Metamorphosis. Franz Kafka
Page 309	The very stones prate of my whereabouts. Macbeth.(Act 2 Scene 1) Shakespeare
Page 310	Porto sventura a chi bene mi vuole! I bring misfortune to all who love me. Fu in quel lore It was then, in my misery, che a me venne l'amor! that love came to me! La Mama Morta. Andrea Chénier. Umberto Giordano
Page 315	'Those are pearls that were his eyes.' The Tempest. William Shakespeare
Page 315	'The centre cannot hold, Things fall apart.' The Second Coming. W.B. Yeats
Page 324.	'Oh, Death where is thy sting?' (1Corinthians 15.55-57. King James Version)
Page 325	'solamen miseris socios habuisse dolris' (Misery loves company) Doctor Faustus. Christopher Marlowe
Page 338	'Take into the air my quiet breath…it's a quick death, God help us all. It is not.' Dante and The Lobster. Samuel Beckett
Page 347	'Mother died today. Or maybe yesterday. I don't know. The Outsider. Albert Camus
Page 350	'How far that little candle throws his beam! So shines a good deed in a naughty world.' The Merchant of Venice. William Shakespeare
Page 355	'Now will he sit under a Medlar tree And wish his mistress were that kind of fruit As maids call Medlars when they laugh alone' Act 2 Scene 1 Romeo and Juliet. William Shakespeare
Page 356	'Let us go then you and I' The Love Song of J. Alfred Prufrock. T.S. Eliot
Page 356	'To sleep: perchance to dream.' Hamlet. William Shakespeare
Page 363	'We read to know we are not alone'. Shadowlands William Nicholson.
Page: 363	'Were we led all that way for birth or death?' The Journey of The Magi. T.S. Eliot
Page 363	'I know when one is dead and when one lives.' King Lear. William Shakespeare

Page 364	I was much too far out all my life/ And not waving but drowning'. Stevie Smith
Page 365	'For what they record in colour and cast is – that we two-passed.' Thomas Hardy, At Castle Boterel
Page 365	That corpse you planted last year in your garden, "Has it begun to sprout? Will it bloom this year? T.S. Eliot, The Waste Land
Page 366	'These fragments I have shored against my ruins. The Waste Land. T.S. Eliot'

Film, music and song titles

Page 80	Prelude in C major: J. S. Bach
Page 80	John Cage's 4'33
Page 109	'When the Boat Comes In.' Traditional English folksong
Page 134	Alright Mr Demille, I'm ready for my closeup' Sunset Boulevard (film)
Page 135	'They call me Mr Tibbs" In the Heat of the Night
Page 138	'You don't bring me flowers anymore' Barbara Streisand
Page 170	Messiah: George Frideric Handel
Page 178	'Day Trip to Bangor': Fiddler's Dram
Page 179	'Starting Over': John Lennon
Page 353	Ave María, grátia plena, Dóminus tecum. Benedícta tu in muliéribus, et benedíctus fructus ventris tui, Jesus. Sancta María, Mater Dei, ora pro nobis peccatóribus, nunc et in hora mortis nostræ. Amen. Franz Schubert

Acknowledgements

Many thanks to the early readers of this novel who gave me a great deal of help and encouragement. I am especially grateful for the enthusiasm and interest of Jane Myles who also assisted with proofreading. My thanks also to other readers for their perceptive thoughts and feedback including: Paul Taylor, Ruth Binney, Jackie Beale, and Paula Protherough. And a big thank you to my dear friend, Karen Thompson for always being there, as well as providing technical support.

I am also most grateful to Julian Fellowes, Richard Morrison, and Sophia Myles for their insightful reviews and endorsements.

Finally, I would like to thank T. S. Eliot for the inspiration that his poetry has given me. I would also like to say how grateful I am to all the other writers, musicians and lyrists from whose works I have referenced or quoted. T. S. Eliot's paraphrased comment, "good writers borrow; great writers steal." is probably true of most writers. Everything we have seen and heard is lodged somewhere in our memory, until it is sometimes impossible to separate our own thoughts from the sounds of the world around us and the millions of words we have heard over our lifetime. Life is a never-ending symphony of creativity. Hopefully, through writing and all other forms of imaginative and creative expression, we can each contribute something to this music during our lifetime.

Front cover image

The Latona fountain in Versailles is based on the myth of Latona (Book V1 Metamorphosis of Ovid). Latona bore the gods Apollo and Diana by Zeus, which infuriated Zeus's consort Juno. She forced Lataona to flee and wander the earth to escape her persecution, but forbade any mortals from giving them food or drink. Desperately thirsty, she tried to drink from a local pond, but the peasants (following Juno's command) would not let her and jumped in the pond, trampling up and down to muddy the water. Furious, she cursed the Lycians to live in the pond forever as frogs. Immediately, they metamorphosed into frogs.

With thanks to Rafael Garcin for the beautiful photograph (Unsplash)

Printed by Amazon Italia Logistica S.r.l.
Torrazza Piemonte (TO), Italy